Wicked Thing

Kim Cormack

Acknowledgements

To my two wonderful children, my parents and the rest of my loving family that I've been blessed with. You give me constant inspiration and support. XO

To my amazing beta reading savants and editing gurus, Haley McGee and Leanne Ruissen you two ladies seriously rock! P.S Lori Souther, XO

Letter To My Readers

I would like to thank all of you for your devotion to these characters. Writing this series has kept me going through the difficult times and I hope to keep you with me on this magical journey for many years to come. XO

The Children Of Ankh Series

Kayn's Series

Lexy's Series

Prologue

She's a certifiably insane feral hit-woman for a Clan of immortals. Her Handler has intimacy induced amnesia. What could go wrong?

A comical, dark fantasy romp through the afterlife with three Clans of naughty, certifiably insane antiheroes who battle while collecting human teenagers as they survive the exterminations of their family lines. If they've demonstrated an impressive level of bravery during their brutal demise, they shall be granted a second chance as sacrificial lambs for the greater good. They must join one of three Clans of immortals living on earth and can be stolen at random by another Clan until their eighteenth birthday. Plot twist... To prove their partially mortal brains are capable of grasping immortality, they will be dropped into an Immortal Testing, which is a simulation of their personal hells. Like rats in a maze made of nightmares and ghastly depraved thoughts best left locked behind mortal happy place filters, they must come out mentally intact after being murdered in thousands of increasingly creative ways.

Take a trip into the metaphysical, spiritual world with endearing paranormal antiheroes and wickedly titillating warriors. *This series will be unlike anything you've ever read.*

No matter how far she ventured from this farm, she would always be the monster created within its walls of timber and shame. They would see what she really was. She was a murderer, a psychopath and a victim. She was all three of those things.

Chapter 1

In Angst And Servitude

They were going to have to stay in the Crypt for the night so they wouldn't risk disrupting the three newbie Ankh's week of Inter-Clan bonding before their Testing. *She wouldn't be able to hide from Grey for long. She just had to find a way to stop the blush of her cheeks whenever thoughts of Tiberius crossed her mind. If she didn't want Grey to think it was a big deal, she'd have to learn to disguise her thoughts and act like it wasn't.*

They'd either be sharing a hotel room in town or staying at the campsite after sending the three unsuspecting Ankh into Testing. Then, they would wait for them to either come back out, or become lost in it, as all who'd come before had for the last four decades. Lexy thought of their faces. There was Melody, the girl who turned out to be Orin's daughter. Kayn was Freja's daughter and the girl Frost appeared to have real feelings for after eons of appearing to care for only himself. Last, but not least, there was Zach, the boy she'd spent a whole year pretending to despise. It was ironic that Frost, the notorious player, had fallen for someone who was as good as lost.

Muffled laughter from her fellow Ankh caused a grin to form on Lexy's face. A genuine smile, not an imitation as it so often was whenever she was at a loss for which emotion she was supposed to display while endeavouring to disguise the fact that she hadn't returned from the solitude of the void. It was usually Grey, she used as her lead to figure out which facial expression was appropriate for the moment.

They'd arrived back at the Ankh Crypt hidden beneath the forest no worse for wear after the Summit. She'd been the one chosen to battle in the coliseum during the immortal gathering. She'd given a spectacular performance, destroying everything in her path. The battle itself left her nothing to ponder. She had the soul of a Dragon, and this was her calling. She'd been created for battle, born out of devastation and agony, but Lexy had never been left with lingering emotions after a fight before. *It was confusion she felt over the events that had taken place during halftime at the Summit. This was an emotion she wasn't familiar with.* Dragons usually felt clarity over their decisions. Dragons didn't wander around confused by uncharacteristically naughty behaviour. She'd been epically naughty with her enemy. Lexy purposely wandered away from the group, knowing her Handler might be able to read her thoughts, and her mind was overflowing with steamy, sensual visions of what happened between her and Tiberius while locked in that room between battle rounds. *This was going to cause her drama and she despised drama. Yes, she'd fully intended to move on from the endless heart-breaking cycle she'd found herself in with Grey, but her intention had never been to succumb to the aftereffects of adrenaline-fuelled battle by having an intoxicatingly intimate moment with her darkly twisted nemesis. It would have remained a secret, but she'd accidentally let the cat out of the bag about her wicked misdeeds. Grey had teased her a little and she fully expected that, but she knew his easy-going demeanour would change once he'd had time to contemplate what she'd done and with whom.*

Before the Summit, he'd made his feelings on their flirtation more than clear. She paced back and forth in the room of stone. *This would have never happened if they were allowed to be together.* Lexy was a Dragon and Grey was her Handler. A physical relationship between them was against the rules. This, of course, had never stopped the act from happening. Logically, she understood why this had to be. He'd awaken with no recollection of being with her physically but she'd remember everything. Her mind would hold on to his declarations of love as though they were real until he innocently shared the details of his next conquest. Yet, even after all of the pain he'd caused her while unwittingly breaking her heart, she'd always known he would sooner gouge out his own than intentionally hurt her.

It would be simple if she could walk away, but each time she felt the urge to move on, fate would pull his emotions back to the surface. Grey would declare his love for her for the thousandth time and even though Lexy knew all would be forgotten as the sun's glowing rays moved across his sleeping form, she'd never been able to deny her love for him each time he gazed into her eyes and asked her for the truth about her feelings. To others it may appear that Grey was the one who had sacrificed his life for hers. In reality, her Handler was her cross to bear as much as she was his. This bond that gave him the ability to calm her in her darkest moments was also what tied her heart to him and only him.

It had taken a good thirty years for her to conclude that she had to stop hitting herself and she had, even though she'd chosen a ridiculously self-destructive direction. Lexy had always despised Tiberius with every breath of her being. She'd always thought him to be without a redeeming quality. After they fought together during the Summit, the hate she felt for all of these years turned into want. She'd discovered that Tiberius had a softer side. She found out what it was like to be in the arms of someone as dark as she was and it had left her lost in the need to finish what they'd started while locked in that room between rounds of the battle in that coliseum.

She stood there in the light of the torch that flickered against the stone wall a couple of feet away. *Tiberius had caused a flame to form inside of her; it was a smouldering blaze that could only be extinguished by him. Whether it was a spark of hope that she'd finally be capable of moving on or a flame that would do nothing but burn her in the end, she'd yet to discover, but she wanted to, and that was a start.* Lexy leaned against the wall and slid down it to the cold stone floor. Perhaps the drama she'd be forced to stroll through with Greydon in the aftermath of Tiberius would be a welcome distraction from the real issue at hand. *Had she managed to teach the three newest Ankh enough to survive the Testing?*

It wasn't the grudge that she felt now, it was regret. She'd grown rather attached to this group of endearing teens, even though she'd held a grudge for a long time over the fact that young Zach had the balls to try to kill her before they'd taken him from Triad. She felt regret that she'd never taken the opportunity to really get to know him. She was feeling way too much right now. Her instinct was to shut it down but couldn't because she felt like she owed these three the ability to say a proper heartfelt goodbye. Lexy heard footsteps on stone and glanced up. *There he was...the love of her life. The fantasy that could never be.*

Her Handler, with his always slightly dishevelled blonde hair and soft probing blue eyes wandered towards her and teased, "You're not avoiding me, are you?"

Yes...she definitely had been. Lexy suspected the questions would begin the second he managed to get her alone. They hadn't had the opportunity to have a private conversation, since her battle alongside Tiberius at the coliseum. A wave of guilt passed through her as he silently sat down beside her on the cool stone floor and laid his head against the wall. One of Greydon's most endearing qualities was the fact that he always wore his heart on his sleeve, but there was something detached in his mannerisms. *He wasn't touching her. Usually he'd be finding a way to make that connection by resting his hand on her leg or on top of hers. There was distance between them. He was undoubtedly looking for details on how far things had gone with Tiberius. Truth be told, she'd wanted to hurt him when they arrived at the Summit, and he'd known she was mad as they'd travelled there in the tombs. He'd kissed her and blamed it on the fact that he'd been drinking. To add insult to injury, he'd ended up with Lily at the end of the night. She knew it wasn't that simple because Lily had ability related glitches that needed to be dealt with and Frost had pressured him into doing it. The situation wasn't simple. Nothing in their afterlives had been easy. He probably thought the self-destructive part of her he'd been trying to tame for the last forty years had gone out and done the one thing that would hurt him.* She knew he couldn't remember his true feelings for her but the confusion reflected in his eyes suggested he was starting to, at least on some level. Jealousy was one of the ways she'd brought his emotions back to the surface in the past, but that wasn't what she was trying to do with Tiberius. Grey shifted around to face her.

He stared into her eyes, gently caressed her cheek and disclosed, "You have an eyelash on your cheek." He held up his finger with a lash balancing on the tip. Grinning, he urged, "Make a wish."

She smiled and whispered, "I'm good." He closed his eyes and with a gentle puff of air, he blew her lash off his finger. She'd made a conscious decision to let romantic notions go, but when he did these things, she knew she'd never be able to, not completely. *Grey was her kryptonite. Her Achilles heel had always been her feelings for the only person she'd ever truly loved. He was the one person she could never have. Well, at least not in the way that she wanted him.*

He put an arm around her, pulled her against him and they sat there in silence. He kissed her head and whispered, "You didn't actually sleep with that tool, did you?"

9

She knew that was coming. Lexy slipped out of his embrace and provoked, "Am I about to get a fine from the booty call police?" Lexy was fully aware she could have just told him it hadn't gone farther than a steamy make-out session and that would have ended the conversation, but she'd never been able to resist the urge to push his buttons. *Why was she still trying to hurt him? This was silly.*

Taking her joke as an admission, Grey smirked, shook his head, got up and walked away from her as he muttered, "Forget about it."

He was visibly upset. Why did she feel this guilty? With an exasperated sigh, she went after him, reaching for his arm as she caught up. He stopped walking away and turned to face her. She explained, "It was just a kiss, it didn't mean anything, we were caught up in the moment."

Relieved, he smiled and teased, "No worries, I'll just spray you down with Lysol when we get to the hotel room."

She playfully shoved him and sparred, "Funny Greydon, that's hilarious. What have you done in the last couple of days? Perhaps, you'll need to pick up your own bottle?"

Her charmingly pig-headed Handler chuckled, "Touché," as he placed one of his arms around her, and just like that, all was forgiven. She recalled Azariah's words...*Love and lust are temporary but friendship can last forever. She could have him forever but only if she ceased to love him this way.* They made their way back to the group of animated, chatting Ankh.

As they approached, Frost grinned at her and declared, "You two have obviously worked things out."

Now, she was a little lost?

Grey gave her shoulder a buddy-esque squeeze and sighed, "What can I do? She's turning into a brazen hussy but I still love her."

Taking comic offence to his statement, Lexy stepped away from him and quipped, "Seriously? I'm a hussy? I'm sure you spent last night playing checkers."

Grey glanced at Frost and chuckled, "I did absolutely nothing last night but dwell on your uncharacteristically naughty behaviour with our enemy and get shit-faced on pimped out ceremonial wine."

Frost raised his hand and piped in, "I can vouch for that."

"What was it that you did the night before again?" She taunted. *That shut him up.*

Grey grinned as he sheepishly responded, "Point taken, but in all fairness if you get to repeatedly refer to me as a man whore, then I get to call you a brazen hussy at least once."

Orin and Markus walked in lugging coolers and placed them on the ground. Orin announced, "There are buns with meat and cheese and a choice of either beer or cider. He opened one of the lids, grabbed something, and said, "Here you go Lexy. I imagine you're famished." He grinned and winked as he chucked it at her.

She caught it, smirked at him and replied, "Thanks." *Oh, wonderful. They were all going to mess with her.* She unwrapped what he'd tossed at her and it was black forest ham and cheese on a bun. She devoured the whole thing in a couple of bites. Another bun came sailing through the air without warning, she caught it and smiled.

Orin flirtatiously chuckled, "Damn, you're good."

Lexy glanced up. *How far did they all think she'd taken things with Tiberius?*

Orin had been hitting on her at the banquet. She recalled that part of the evening. He tossed a beer across the room without warning her, still trying to catch her off guard. She caught it in one hand and gave him a cocky smile. They all began eating and telling tales of the Summit as she listened with a mouthful of bun, unable to speak. Grey was sitting by Lily. He whispered something in her ear and she giggled. *That was going to be irritating.* So, she grinned and gave her

11

can of beer a few good shakes before popping the tab in his direction. It started to spray all over them both.

Grey started cursing, "What in the hell, Lex?"

She placed her hand over the now slowly spurting beer and sweetly apologized, "Oh, I'm so sorry."

Grey stripped off his soaking wet beer scented shirt, dropped it on the stone floor behind him and glared at her. *He knew she'd done it on purpose. He couldn't prove it though.*

Orin had her back as he took the blame by piping in, "Sorry kid. That must have happened when I tossed it to her."

She covered her mouth to stifle her response before a giggle escaped. Grey hated it when any of the older ones called him kid. Theoretically, they were both in their late fifty's in mortal years, but next to almost everyone else in the Ankh Crypt, they were nine and a half centuries younger. Arrianna had her lips pressed together to stop herself from laughing. She couldn't even look at her because she was still hungry and if Grey stormed off, she'd be obligated to follow him. She went to place her hand on his leg, he shifted and it accidentally landed on his lap.

Grey's eyes widened and he pretended to be shocked, "Not now Lexy we're eating dinner."

She rolled her eyes and playfully smacked his arm. *These jokes were going to get old fast.*

Orin grinned at her and jested, "Well, I certainly hope this isn't how you treat Tiberius."

Funny. She crushed her empty beer can in one hand and politely requested another.

Beaming, Orin provoked, "I don't know. I'm afraid to give you anything you can use as a weapon."

Meeting his gaze across the room lit by flickering torches, Lexy sweetly responded, "But, I don't need a weapon, Orin."

Frost broke the tension by standing up and taking off his shirt. "If Grey doesn't have to wear his, I'm not going to wear mine."

She should just stand up and tell the whole room she didn't sleep with Tiberius but something made her want to keep that to herself. When Orin took off his shirt too, she found herself staring at his chiselled abs and forced herself to look away. *What was wrong with her today? These guys were always shirtless. Was it an immortal thing or just a guy thing in general? What was wrong with her? She never thought about this stuff.*

Orin caught her looking. He raked a hand through his hair and smiled mischievously as he grabbed a beer out of the cooler. He got up, walked over, passed the can to her and said, "Just so there are no more accidents."

Lexy went to take the beer from his hand and he flirtatiously held on to it, before letting her have it. *She was pretty sure she wasn't imagining this. He was hitting on her.* She glanced at Jenna and she appeared to be oblivious. *Maybe, it was all in her head? She still wanted another bun with meat and cheese.*

Her Handler walked over to the cooler, opened it and started rifling around. Grey hollered, "Heads up!" as he tossed a bun at her. He ruffled Arrianna's hair and she swatted him away as he walked back across the room and took his seat beside Lexy. She took an enormous bite of her sandwich.

Grey leaned over and whispered in her ear, "Yes, most guys like to walk around with their shirts off, even the mortal ones. Nothing's wrong with you for noticing it or liking it, and yes, Orin's shamelessly flirting with you."

He'd been listening to her thoughts. She nonchalantly nodded to signal she understood what he meant as she continued devouring her bun.

Markus got up, raised his beer in the air and toasted, "To Lexy. You did us proud at the Summit."

She almost choked on her last bite of bun but managed to disguise it with a smile. *She'd taken that the wrong way for a second there.* Everyone raised their beers in salute and then carried on with their conversations.

Markus made his way across the room to her, took a seat next to her and enquired, "Did you have fun catching up with Prince Amadeus afterwards? He's the only member of that whole family that I like. He's actually a good guy."

Lexy nodded as she answered, "Yes, he's always been a good friend. Thank you for not making me sit through something public after that whole mass murder thing."

Her Clan's leader chuckled and quipped, "I've known you long enough to know that would have been a horrible idea."

That, it would have been.

"How are you doing with everything?" Markus asked.

She nodded and gave her token response, "I'm fine."

"Alright, I was just checking to see if you were good to go for tomorrow." He gave her leg a fatherly pat, winked at her and added, "I'm off to bed. You should try and get Grey to go to sleep early; your Handler there was one of the reasons I had to stay at the banquet until the bitter end last night. He was a wreck."

Lexy smiled at Markus and replied, "I'll make sure he does. Sweet Dreams." She turned to look at her party animal of a Handler. She'd thought he'd been upset about what had happened between her and Tiberius during the little intermission at the coliseum. She was seeing the big picture now. *She'd been taken to Amadeus's chambers but nobody had informed Grey. If Tiberius was also missing from the banquet, he probably would have assumed the worst. Oh, everything was starting to make sense.* She waited until Markus was out of earshot before whispering, "You thought I was with Tiberius all night, didn't you?"

Grey squeezed her knee and quietly responded, "I'm your Handler. When I don't know where you are, especially after a day like that, I'm bound to be slightly agitated."

Smiling at him, she took the beer from his hands and urged, "Let's get out of here." She stood up and motioned for him to follow. As she scaled the stairs to the forest she glanced back to see if he was following her. The Crypt slid open with the grinding of stone rubbing against stone to reveal a starry night sky.

He grabbed for her and whispered, "We're not allowed to go out there until tomorrow. This is their last night to do the whole Inter-Clan bonding thing before their Testing."

Lexy dodged out of the way and in a hushed voice, she responded, "Oh, nobody's going to see us, we won't go far. If we hear anyone coming, we'll hide." Grey hesitated but followed her out into the lush green foliage of the forest. Lexy paused to savour the first breath of fresh air. This world was so much more than the place the Third-Tiers had chosen to call home. Everything was alive and vibrant in comparison.

They took a starlight stroll to the symphony of the woods at night. Crickets chirped and toads croaked as they took in the sensory delight of being outside of the stone Crypt. They decided it would be for the best if they travelled in the opposite direction of the campground. They couldn't risk being seen, so they made sure to stay away from cleared trails and forced their way through the bushes. After a few minutes of bush bombing, they stepped out into an isolated open meadow. They made themselves comfortable, sprawling under the spectacular ceiling of stars. At this point in her afterlife few sights left her awestruck, but as she lay in the lush grass next to the person that mattered most to her, gazing at the glittering display from the heavens, she smiled as her heart recognized the beauty of the moment... *It was close to perfection. She'd known what her Handler needed.* Lexy whispered, "Do you feel better now?"

Grey smiled up at the night sky, turned to look at her and replied, "Much better." He reached for her hand and laced his fingers through hers.

Her heart gave her a gentle tug in his direction. She squeezed his hand and said, "With all of the drama from the Summit,

I never asked you how you were doing with the Melody thing?"

He chuckled as he answered, "Which thing? The fact that she's going into the Testing tomorrow or the revelation she had a thing with Thorne?"

"All of the above," she replied.

Without looking away from the miraculous display of twinkling stars, he requested, "Can we save this conversation for tomorrow?"

Gently squeezing his hand once more, she whispered, "Of course." They remained there together under the sparkling display of night sky with their hands connected and their hearts at peace, until they both drifted off to dream.

Someone was shaking her.

Grey's voice urged, "It's almost daylight. We have to get back before someone notices we snuck out."

Smiling as his face came into focus, Lexy stretched and groggily asked, "What time is it?" He smiled with his eyes crinkling in the corners so even without seeing his lips, she knew he was deliriously happy. *Every time she opened her eyes, his smile meant she was safe and it was morning. It was a truly beautiful way to awaken.*

He leaned over, kissed her forehead and pressed, "It's almost dawn. The sun is just beginning to peak over the mountain top. We should get back."

Grey helped her up with his legs a touch more stable after being awake a few minutes longer and the pair dashed back towards the bushes. With her hand in his racing through the grass, she felt like the child she'd never had the opportunity to be. They plunged into the overgrowth, shoving their way through until they found their way out into the open area by the Crypt. Grey slipped his hand under the stone and the Ankh Crypt slowly ground open. Their stealth descent of the stairs was only hindered by the sound of the heavy breathing of those still lost in dreamland. They'd beaten the morning's first rays. The opening above slid closed and the duo crept across the room, searching for a place to pretend they'd been sleeping. They heard footsteps, Lexy grabbed Grey's arm and urged, "Pick a spot, any spot." They dashed across the room and dove onto a pile of pillows in the darkened corner. Lexy closed her eyes as Grey snuggled up behind her and they both tried to pretend they'd been asleep all along. As the footsteps grew louder, it became difficult to keep a straight face. She was thankful they were in a shadowed corner. There was a glow of light behind her lids. Without opening her eyes, she knew someone was walking around methodically lighting up torches. *It was obviously time to get up. They'd made it back to the Crypt just in time.* She opened her eyes and shifted like she was going to get up.

Holding her tighter, he whispered, "Don't move. This is nice."

She shook her head and remained in his arms until the torch closest to them was lit and their shadowed corner was no longer.

Chapter 2

In Solidarity They Stand

They all squinted as they scaled the steps of the Ankh Crypt deep in the wilderness and walked out into the glaring brilliance of the day. *It was gloriously warm outside. She could picture what they were doing. The newbies were probably lying on the dock, hanging out together having a grand time with no real comprehension of what sick torturously messed-up situations the Testing would hold. This was their last true escape from the reality of their new life and they didn't even know it.* They trudged through the greenery until they reached the path. Lexy squinted in the sun's rays and shielded her eyes with her hand as she looked over at Frost. *He was nervous. Kayn spent an entire week with Kevin and the unknown was killing him. The seemingly unbreakable guy was doing his best to make it seem like it was just a normal day, but it wasn't, not for him.* Knowing first-hand what it felt like to have feelings for someone still in love with somebody else, she could empathize. Judging by the group's solemn expressions, it wasn't a normal day for anyone. *Today was the day they delivered the lambs to the slaughter.*

As they came around a curve in the trail, approaching the campground, Kayn was standing there distraught. *Perhaps, it was instinct, the fantasy had come to an end.* Frost strode over. Even through obvious inner turmoil, her eyes lit up as she saw him coming. He smiled as they embraced. Lexy stepped out of view, observing their exchange. *They needed time alone.*

In Frost's arms, Kayn whispered, "I'm glad you guys are back." She blatantly put Frost back in the friend zone by giving his back a few sturdy pats before letting go.

Lexy winced…*Ouch, that had to sting.*

It didn't faze Frost as he teased, "You are, without a doubt, the strangest girl I've ever met."

Kayn was trying to be strong. Lexy knew what it felt like to shove emotions down and move on. Blinking away tears, Kayn mastered her deceased twin's fake smile and replied, "I try."

Frost didn't question her further as they continued their stroll towards the cabin to wake the others. Staying out of sight, Lexy had to stifle her laughter as Kayn tripped on the stairs while not so inconspicuously sneaking a peek at Triad's cabin across the way.

Frost grabbed Kayn before her knees hit the steps and whispered, "Chin up, or I'll start quoting country songs."

Kayn smiled warmly, nodded and excused her two left feet by saying, "I'm fine." *She felt the pain radiating from her young friend and wasn't usually this intuitive where other's feelings were concerned. I'm fine…that was her line.* Opting to stay hidden until they went into the cabin, she strolled over and sat on the slivery weather-worn wooden steps. Smiling, she listened to Frost telling animated tales of her bravery in the coliseum. Lexy gazed at the cabin across the way, recalling the naughty games she'd been playing with Tiberius before the banquet. She had a clear image of him teasing her by pretending to unzip his jeans, standing on the deck. She shifted the palm of her hand, felt a prick and knew she'd received a sliver from the wooden stairs. She raised her palm but not quickly enough to remove the shard of wood before her skin healed over top of it. Lexy wiped the speck of blood onto her thigh and looked at the sliver beneath the layer of skin. *In time, it would work its way out, but she wasn't squeamish about the logical solution.* She took a blade out of her pocket, sliced her skin, removed the sliver with her teeth, spat it on the stairs and wiped the blood on her leg. Her hand was healed to perfection in the blink of an eye. She glanced up at the deck of the cabin across the path and smiled. *It was best to not allow slivers or naughty men to take residence beneath the surface of her skin. She had too much going on right now to waste her energy thinking about inconsequential things.* The door opened. *She didn't need to look. She knew who it was.*

Grey sat beside her, slid his hand over her knee and probed, "There's blood on your leg and you're holding a knife. Do you need my help with something?"

She peered at her thigh and grinned. *She hadn't even thought to rub it in so the blood wouldn't be as noticeable.* She met Grey's concern with a matter of fact statement, "I got a sliver on the palm of my hand from the stairs. It healed too quickly so I cut it out."

Grey smiled, took her hand in his, unfolded her fingers and tenderly kissed her palm where her wound healed. "Was cutting yourself necessary or did you do it to take your mind off of things?"

She hadn't given it that much thought. Truth be told, her mind had added symbolism to the action after the fact.

Gazing across the way at the cabin she was staring at, Grey questioned, "What happened between the two of you at the Summit is messing with your head, isn't it?"

He knew her so well. There would be no point in lying, but she'd give him the choice. She disclosed, "Do you want the truth or a lie?" He released her hand, squeezed her knee and got up, giving her his response with an action.

Her Handler skillfully changed the subject, "Let's go inside and save this conversation for later. We have too much going on today to worry about something stupid. It doesn't even matter, I'm sure it will never happen again. You're too intelligent for that."

She had to save fantasies for when she was alone. Lexy blocked her mind from thinking up a saucy response. With their connection, she knew he'd be listening for it. Grey opened the door for her and they went in, just as Kayn came out of the bathroom. They embraced. *Damn it, she really liked her.* Lexy held on for longer than she should. *Please, come back.*

They helped the trio pack up their belongings and began their trek down the brush lined trail they'd used less than an hour earlier. Lexy took a deep breath of cedar scented campground air. *It was a gorgeous day.* Warm rays of sunshine filtered through the trees creating a strange effect, lighting up the path at regular intervals before them. Lexy watched for Grey's reaction, knowing he felt the beauty of these moments most. *For four decades she'd played witness to his beautiful joy searching soul. Her heart swelled with adoration every time she saw him like this. He was lost in a magical moment and she was in awe of him.* Grey raised his hand into the ray of sun on the trail, watching particles of dust flit around him like millions of tiny planets in a galaxy. The others kept walking but she remained with him. His wheat-coloured hair was just a touch too long and it was obscuring his view. He took his hand out of the ray of sunlight and raked his fingers through his hair to get it out of his eyes.

He noticed her watching and said, "Come over here and feel how warm this spot is."

Lexy wandered over and stood in his ray of light, smiling as particles of dust danced around her and sunlight caressed her skin. She felt his eyes on her and met his gaze of devotion.

He inched closer, tucked her crimson-hair behind her ear, tenderly kissed her forehead and whispered, "You don't have any idea how beautiful you are, do you? Listen, I'm not sure what came over me yesterday. It was ridiculous, I don't have any right to judge you."

She felt like an enormous asshole. He'd sooner die than intentionally hurt her but she would intentionally hurt him. Vengeance was a part of being a Dragon. She'd have to try harder to keep him in the friend zone. Friends were forever. They embraced, and as always, it felt so right. *This was where the line became crossed in her mind.* She took another deep breath. The scent of his skin always made her feel like there was nowhere else in the universe she was supposed to be.

He whispered in her ear, "There's nothing you could ever do that would make me love you less." He jokingly cringed and provoked, "Even Tiberius."

She stepped away, smiling as she playfully sparred, "I'm sure I could find something." She took off, jogging ahead of him to catch up to the others.

Laughing, her Handler chased her down, tripped over an enormous tree root in the path and accidentally tackled her from behind. He landed on top of her on the dirt path, with their lips so intimately close, she had to fight the urge to kiss him. Grey ruffled her hair like she was a sibling and scrambled to his feet. *It was like fate expected her to be able to shift her heart to wherever he needed it to be on that day. Today, it was taking her through all of the emotions.*

Holding out his hand, Grey chivalrously announced, "Madam."

Lexy couldn't help rolling her eyes as he helped her up and they continued their peaceful stroll to the RV. As they scaled the steps, it felt like coming home. *What was that smell?* She opened the fridge and cursed, "Shit." *This was one of her biggest pet peeves.* As the nasty scent wafted out, she complained, "You guys didn't touch the fridge, outdated milk stinks up the place."

Grey shoved past her, snatched the carton out of the fridge and chuckled, "I'll get rid of it. It's not a big deal, Lex."

To her, it was. Lexy gave Zach the stink-eye until he gave her a response.

Grinning, Zach replied, "I know, I didn't come back to the campground. I'm pretty sure none of us did. We had everything we needed at the cabin."

Mel walked past and piped in, "None of us came back here. I think we were all just enjoying the mental vacation too much to remind ourselves that's all it was."

Lexy glanced at the third culprit and watched as Kayn slid her backpack under the bunks in the hall and sat on the bunk she usually slept on, looking like she just lost her best friend. *Heartbreak sucks.* Frost sat beside her. Lexy decided to stop the interrogation and chill herself out. *She was amped up today for many reasons. One of them being the visions of Tiberius' deviously sexy smile, poised above her as she laid on the table like a naughty smorgasbord entree.* It kept popping into her mind, and each time it did, her pulse raced. *She needed a cold shower. She'd have to submerge her entire body in a bathtub full of ice for a measly five-minute break from the naughty images flooding her mind.* Zach cleared his throat, snapping her out of her seductive daydreams.

"I'm not sure I've ever seen that expression on your face. You look a little..." Zach started to say something but hesitated.

She knew what he wanted to say. "A little what?" Lexy not so innocently prodded. Grinning, Zach blushed, nervously tapping the kitchen table avoiding eye contact. Lexy smiled and said, "Spit it out, Zach."

He held his hands in surrender and chuckled, "Promise me you won't kick my ass if I say it."

Before Zach had a chance to respond, Grey filled in the blanks, "Yes, Zach. Lexy was a naughty girl at the Summit. Do you want to tell him or do you just want to wait until the dirty details trickle back through the rumour mill?" He snagged a beer out of the fridge and an extra one for Zach. Grey opened both and handed one to Zach as he slid onto the bench seat beside him.

Lexy recalled wishing she'd taken the time to get to know Zach. *What the hell, why not?* She grabbed a beer out of the minifridge and chugged some before responding, "I fought alongside Tiberius at the Summit, during halftime we were locked in a room together and we had to recharge our abilities to fight Abaddon. Afterwards, the lines became a little blurred."

Zach's jaw dropped. He grinned and responded to her confession with one of his own, "Let's just say, I've also done things this week I'm a little confused about."

She was impressed. Smiling at her unexpected partner in Inter-Clan debauchery, Lexy raised her beer.

Zach shrugged, lifted his and saluted, "Shit happens."

Grey joined in and chuckled, "To shit happening."

In an instant they'd bonded and Lexy had one more person she was about to lose. She looked at Zach and whispered, "What happened this week with Kayn and Kevin?"

Zach checked to see if Kayn was out of earshot and quietly responded, "They had a great week together and last night they said goodbye. I really wanted him to be an asshole but he's not a bad guy. None of them were. I think we all came to the same conclusion."

"I'd better go break up whatever is going on behind that curtain," Grey remarked as he shimmied off the bench and left. They heard Grey boisterously announce, "Okay, you two. Break it up," as he pulled the curtain back and disappeared behind it.

Lexy whispered, "Want to talk about it? I'm like a vault if you want something to be a secret, it will never go any further with me."

He looked into her eyes and quietly responded, "Have you ever been really drunk and ended up in a situation that felt both wrong and right at the same time?" *Boy had she ever.* Smiling, Lexy placed her drink on the table and sighed, "I don't even have alcohol as an excuse for what I did with Tiberius at the Summit."

With an understanding grin, Zach teased, "That was bound to happen. The sexual tension between the two of you at the banquet was even turning me on."

Lexy bit her bottom lip as she pondered his words. She looked at Zach and decided to give him truly intimate details about who she was as a person, "Honestly, sometimes I don't notice things like that. If we're being honest and this whole conversation is truly off the record, I felt it by the end of the banquet. All of that hatred was doing something for me. I remember thinking it was like foreplay between Dragons."

Zach choked on the last gulp and snickered. He met her gaze and disclosed, "We should have gotten to know each better, I think we would have been friends."

He knew the Testing was here, Zach was saying goodbye. Lexy got up, walked around and slid onto the bench seat beside the boy she hadn't given the time of day to in a year. *She wasn't allowed to give him any details about the Testing.* She placed her hand gently on top of his and summoned her inner Grey by saying, "Believing you can do something is more than half of the battle. If you go into a fight believing you'll lose, you will. I've seen what you've been through. You've already shown you're capable of surviving the unthinkable. Believe in yourself as much as I believe in you and nothing can stop you." She squeezed his hand and Zach smiled peacefully back. Lexy excused herself from the table, "I'd better get back there before the positive fortune cookie quotes those boys are spouting off to your friend become unbearable." *She'd just given him a couple of good ones in lieu of telling him what was really about to happen. There was no point in knowing the details, it wouldn't matter anyway.* Lexy paused to look back at Zach. *He was smiling.* She yanked the curtain open. Kayn was sitting on her bunk with both Frost's and Grey's arms around her. She laughed and taunted, "I'm not saying a word." Kayn grinned and sat up as straight as she could without smoking her head on the bunk above her. *It was time to change the subject.* Lexy jumped on the bunk, wrestled Grey to the mattress, and provoked, "While we're speaking of boneheaded moves born of necessity, you didn't get a chance to tell me all about your naughty deeds the night before we left, but I heard it through the grapevine in about five minutes flat."

"Seriously Frost, what did you do broadcast it?" Grey stammered.

Shaking her head, Lexy sighed, "I didn't hear it from Frost. You had relations in public, making a list of who didn't see you would be a hell of a lot shorter."

Frost chuckled, "Why would you automatically assume it was me?"

"Well, it wasn't my idea," Grey rebutted, avoiding eye contact with her.

"My friend, I only have one thing to say." Lexy placed her arm around Grey, hugged him and whispered in his ear, "Quit hitting yourself."

"Point taken," Grey answered. "It won't happen again." He gave Lexy a tight squeeze back and winked at Kayn.

"I heard something intriguing about your extracurricular activities that same night, involving a certain young Triad." Grey baited.

Funny, random men didn't bother him, just Tiberius. Lexy replied, "I don't really remember the details, but I'm pretty sure it didn't happen, for reasons I'm not at liberty to discuss."

Grey groaned, "Okay, you know what? Every time I try to use the excuse, I don't remember, you give me shit.

What was the speech again? I don't remember doesn't mean it didn't happen."

"Touché, but there are some situations where you know there's no interest from the other party involved," Lexy sparred. She met Kayn's eyes and could tell she was intuitive enough to know exactly what she meant.

Kayn changed the subject with brilliant timing, "So, I heard you were chosen to fight for Ankh and you fought everyone all by yourself."

Kayn hadn't heard about her extracurricular activities. Grey and Frost comically cleared their throats.

Giving her a strange look, Kayn questioned, "What was that about?"

Lexy smacked Frost before he had a chance to open his mouth and give her dirty details. She smiled back at Kayn and declared, "What happens at the Summit stays at the Summit."

Melody came out of the bathroom and praised, "Good job, Lexy."

Still lost in the comedy of what had been left unsaid, Grey and Frost burst into a fit of raucous laughter. Lexy glared at them and hopped up to follow Melody. *She wanted a moment alone with her.* Before pulling back the curtain to leave, Lexy cautioned, "You two saw what I did at the Summit. Just try me."

Frost teased, "To be honest, I'm tempted."

Lexy dove back onto the bed and wrestled Frost until she had him in a chokehold.

Ignoring Lexy strangling Frost, Kayn casually enquired, "Where's everyone else?"

This wasn't the time or place for this. Lexy's expression altered as she released her annoying Clan member and replied, "They're at the Ankh Crypt waiting for us."

Kayn turned back to look at Frost. A hint of concern flashed in his eyes. He turned away from Kayn and stared directly at Lexy. *He needed to use her emotionless response as a focal point.* Taking in his internal turmoil, she stared into his eyes as her inner Dragon began constructing the wall that dulled her emotions. She'd planned to fight against it for a while longer so she'd have a chance to say goodbye to Melody, but she could tell that time had passed. Kayn kept attempting to make eye contact with the boys and neither one was able to look her in the eye. *They'd all become far too attached this time and they were about to send the lambs they adored to the slaughter.*

With a solemn expression, Kayn announced, "I'm going to find Melody and Zach."

She knew it was time. Lexy nodded at Kayn and instead of hiding the truth in her eyes, she gave her a look of strength much like the one given to her before she was ordered to jump off a cliff and repeatedly die during her training in the in-between. Kayn nodded and Lexy did the same. *She wasn't allowed to explain until the three were standing on the top of the Testing ready to drop into the bowels of hell.*

"Don't be too long, we have to leave soon," Frost cautioned, grasping her arm, staring into her eyes as though it might be the last time, trying to warn her.

They were all way to emotionally invested. Lexy opened the curtain. *Zach was no longer at the table. He must have taken off with Melody.* Kayn left, the door slammed behind her. Lexy opened it and watched her departure, following her with her eyes as she walked briskly down the path towards the water. They followed, making sure to remain out of sight as Brighton marched down the rickety old dock to the others. *That endearingly goofy girl was walking to the end of a symbolic plank and there was nothing they could do to stop it. This was the next level of their evolution and in order to remain with them as a Second-Tier on earth, the Immortal Testing had to be completed.* Frost sat on a bench with a clear view of the trio. Zach and Melody were sitting on the edge of the dock with their legs dangling in the lake. Kayn sat down by them and dangled hers in the water. Zach put his arm around Kayn. They were all in a deep conversation for a few minutes and then, they started joking around.

Frost remarked, "I wonder why they're laughing?"

Grinning as he took a seat beside him, Grey commented, "That is why they are all going to survive."

They heard Kayn's high-pitched shriek. She yanked her feet out of the water. Frost smiled and explained, "A fish probably touched her foot."

The others lifted their feet out of the water, hysterically laughing. *Damn it, that girl was a sitting duck. Hell, they'd all become far too squirmy over a fish that had no interest in nibbling toes. This meant they'd be eaten by one in the Testing.* When it felt like they'd given the trio enough time to have a 'we can do it' pep talk. Lexy interjected, "Who wants to go collect our badass subjects for the Testing that are still squealing over a fish touching someone's toe in a lake?" Frost volunteered and with an optimistic skip in his step, he walked down the trail to the dock. *Grey was good. He'd given him a tiny amount of hope to cling to.*

"It's time to go," Frost loudly announced,

The trio helped each other stand and followed Frost up the dock. As they started up the trail, Lexy grabbed Grey and urged, "Let's go. We can beat them there."

Chapter 3

Lambs To The Slaughter

The light flowed in single rays through the trees, creating a heavenly looking pathway as it usually did, but this time, Grey didn't stop to experience the moment. They had a silent agreement to get ahead of the drama in the process of unfolding. Even the musical chirping of the birds did nothing to lure her Handler's beautiful heart into taking its time. They glanced at each other as they heard the voices coming closer. Neither one wanted to be a party to an awkward guilt-ridden stroll, so they sprinted through the trails towards the Ankh Crypt. *Perhaps, they'd even have enough time to take a beat and compose themselves.* Arriving slightly out of breath but neither worse for wear, Lily was the only one waiting.

Lily strolled over and explained, "Markus thought it would be best if those closest to the three accompanied them to the Testing."

Dragons don't do pep talks.

Walking towards Lily, Grey asked, "Are you alright?"

Looking at her feet, Lily kicked at the dirt, causing dust to rise and responded, "I'm okay."

Giving Lily's shoulder a knowing squeeze, her soft-hearted Handler called her bluff, "You don't look okay." She raised her eyes to meet his and gave him an answer they could all relate to, "I just wish I'd kept my distance." They heard the muffled voices of the Testing's sacrifices approaching. Grey looked back at the trails and mumbled, "I'm with you there."

A gentle breeze whispered through the trees rustling the branches above her and stirring up the forest floor beneath her feet. Lexy glanced at the ground in front of her and the sun had filtered through the trees on the pathway in the pattern of a number. *It was eleven...that was the number of the stall she'd spent five years held captive in. It was a coincidence, that's all it was...*The number eleven remained on the ground until it successfully sunk into her soul and gave her the reaction intended. *Her heart began to solidify against her will. She needed more time, a few more minutes to remain in the land of the sane. Grey was busy chatting with Lily. She needed him to keep her with him for a few moments longer.* Lexy felt herself sinking into the background. In the cricket's chirping, she heard a name repeated over and over. *Charlotte... Charlotte. This was the name of the child she'd failed to protect. The most painful goodbye of her life. Charlotte...Charlotte. Someone was messing with her mind. She didn't have time for her own drama right now. Charlotte. The Dragon dulled her reaction. Logic played no part when the beast within began to take hold. The Dragon was a necessary evil, it had come to save her as a sixteen-year-old girl after she'd been murdered and tossed to the bottom of a well with all the other forgotten children. The Dragon had given her the strength to heal and climb out of the waterlogged, rotting corpses to seek revenge upon the demons that enslaved her.* As visions caused her mind to drown in horrific images, Grey noticed her plight as he'd been destined to.

He cupped her cheeks in his hands and gazed into her eyes, giving her a gentle tug back to the here and now. He vowed, "I'll bring you back after they're in the Testing. If you need to go, you can go."

She wasn't gone, not completely. She couldn't vanish, she had to see one of them off. She shook her head to let him know she was still there and stated, "I can't." Distracted by whirling wings, she turned away. *Hummingbirds had always fascinated her. They always appeared to be working so hard and getting nowhere. Their plight was relatable.* She observed the lone hummingbird buzzing around the lower branches of the towering tree she was standing beside. *His fight for survival mimicked her struggle to stay in the here and now. They were almost here.* Their muffled speech was growing closer, there was a flicker in her heart, followed by an image of their faces. *She couldn't blink them away, she'd found a happy medium, her emotions were dulled not off. She heard Lily and Grey talking but couldn't allow herself to be involved in their conversation. She had to stay where she was, somewhere in the middle of lost and found. As long as she kept periodically looking at Grey with his endearing mannerisms and allowing herself to feel the pull to him, a part of her would always remain by his side. They were a strange pair. She was the girl meant to feel nothing and he was the boy who felt everything.* Lexy quietly observed the conversation between Lily and Grey.

"All we can do is drop them into the Testing and pray they find their way back out," Lily affirmed.

Grey responded, "I've always felt like these three might actually make it out. Maybe, it's because there's three of them just like when I went into the Testing with Lexy and Arrianna."

Smiling, Lily assured, "I don't want to get your hopes up, but I have it on good authority that if events play out as they're supposed to in there, they will." She paused and started to laugh.

He gave her a weird look and questioned, "What's so funny?"

"When does anything go according to plan?" Lily grinned and ribbed, "If you can tell me one instance, I'll stop laughing."

Nonchalantly leaning against a tree, he gave her a dirty look and sighed, "I was feeling all warm and fuzzy for a second there and then, I got smacked down by reality."

"That's the afterlife in a nutshell," Lily countered as their Clan's unsuspecting sacrifices appeared on the trail in the distance.

It was everyone's life. It didn't matter if you were mortal or immortal, you still found yourself sitting there wondering why life kept testing your sanity. Their sacrificial lambs had arrived. They didn't venture to greet them nor did they do a group hug to say goodbye, they couldn't. *The guilt of where they were sending them was too much in this moment, even with her emotions in the stifled state she'd managed to attain. If she felt this way, she knew her Handler was dying inside. This is what kept a part of her with him. If only she could give him just a touch of her ability in these painful moments.*

The unspoken sadness in Grey's glistening eyes created a window into his tender soul. He'd lost too many people over the years and his heart was breaking as he placed his hand under the lip of the rock. The staircase into the darkness became visible. Grey went in first, so his tears would be hidden. He casually touched each torch and they lit up as he passed by. The light of dancing flames revealed a long stone corridor ahead. Lexy caught up to walk at the side of her distraught Handler. In an act of solidarity, she took his hand. As she intertwined her fingers with his, she willed his tender heart the ability to harden itself just a touch. This would not actually work because she had no ability to do so, but when he squeezed her hand, she knew he appreciated her presence. By the time the others caught up and began walking with them, Grey had reigned in his response to the goodbye. He squeezed her hand and Lexy felt it in her soul. *He wanted her to stay with him. She was trying to remain by his side, by their side until they'd been delivered to the Testing.*

The sounds of nature were now gone and all one could hear was the hollow click of footsteps on the stone beneath their feet. Frost stopped the group and announced, "It's time for you three to see how we operate the Crypts. This is how we move to different countries around this world undetected. This is also how we travel to different realms." He pointed at the stone wall ahead of them and explained, "You must move quickly through each of these doors. If they close on you, you'll be trapped there." Frost placed his fingers in the ridges in the stone, pushing the heel of his hand down in the centre of the door.

The wall slid open. They all dove through and found themselves in another stone room with Egyptian carvings on the walls. Wall after wall shifted away until they found themselves standing in the dark.

Frost's voice spoke in the darkness, "Azariah, bring us light."

The room brightened. It was made of gold. The walls, the ceiling, everything was glittering gold. Sparkling jewels were strewn across the ground, rubies, diamonds and emeralds. In awe of its splendour, the three gasped in unison. In her slightly detached state, Lexy didn't see what they were seeing. She did observe their joy and found it about as entertaining as that hummingbird had been. Frost asked Lily to place her hands next to his. They laid their palms against the handprints on the gleaming wall of gold. The wall slid away, they all dove through and it slid shut behind them. The three followed suit and attempted to remain calm, standing in a room of white. They were all standing on nothing surrounded by nothing.

"Hold hands," Frost commanded. He shut his eyes and Lily also closed hers.

Lexy knew what came next, she just didn't need to close her eyes. The room of white began to swirl with colours and a vomitus display of a stomach-churning excess of visual information. There was a blinding flash of white light and they were standing on the infamous Crypt that spanned the horizon. The stone beneath their feet shifted ever so slightly and the trio looked nervous. Lexy felt her pulse race and smiled. *She missed it in there, the excitement of it all. Inside the Testing, she'd been able to embrace the Dragon within her for an extended amount of time. If she could go in willingly and take someone's place, she would...in a heartbeat.*

Frost announced, "We're here. This is, The Testing."

"We are fighting the other Clans on a giant floating slab of stone?" Zach blurted out.

Lily replied, "No, you three are fighting inside it. Under our feet is a floating Crypt the size of New York City."

Zach knelt and placed his hand on the stone under his feet as he questioned, "Is there a coliseum inside of this?"

"After a thousand years, do you not think the Third-Tiers would get pretty bored of watching that same old scenario?" Lily recanted sweetly.

Mel questioned, "So, it's a giant Crypt like what we just went through?"

Grey replied, "Sort of like a mix of that and a giant maze with walls that move and lead to anything that's ever crossed your mind. There will be randomly available weapons and powers. Remember, this place is magic. There could be anything or anyone in there. There is nothing I can say that's going to prepare you for this. You three can do this together."

Zach furrowed his brow and questioned, "So, it's like a giant video game?"

Frost solemnly said, "A bit... I guess."

"You need to keep your wits about you," Lily asserted. "They want to see how well you've been trained. They want to see what you understand; what you comprehend about who you are now. Every five years the Clans get a chance to acquire the tombs they need and this is how it's done. Only new Clan members can play for them. When you're finished, you will have earned your own tomb. You have to finish, no matter how many times you're killed. You must stand back up. You won't be fighting on even terms with everyone. Some Clan have been Enlightened, and some have not. You three are smart, you're fast. Remember, brains will defeat brawn every time. The Amber room is the end of the Testing. You'll know it, when you see it. You three have to make it there together in order to be released. One more thing...Kill everyone and everything you see. You are no longer friends. They have been told the same."

Her heart flickered again, this time she decided to let it be. *It was goodbye. They would only have a moment.* Lexy harnessed the instructor that had groomed the three for this challenge and said, "You're not allowed to enter the game in the same place. Find each other as fast as you can." She walked away and signalled for Zach to follow. Grey walked away with Melody. They all seemed to be having little private pep talks. Frost stayed with Kayn.

Standing there, Lexy looked into Zach's eyes and told him all she could, "This is going to be horrible. Pain is your friend it means you haven't lost your mind. Use the sleep chambers. Where there is water, there are sure to be predators. You're about to be killed a crazy amount of times, but you won't stay dead. I've trained you for this. You have an unlimited amount of lives in this game. Stay focused on finding that Amber room and no matter what happens, you stand back up each time you fall. Stand back up and always keep the others with you. If you lose them, there is nothing more important than finding them. You have to be together in order to get out. I've seen the end of your mortal life and you even managed to kill me. Whole Clans have tried to do what you did and failed. Your instinct for survival is strong. You can do this Zach. I'll be seeing you soon."

Zach stared into her eyes as the stone shifted beneath his feet and as an expression of panic flashed across his face, he dropped through the stone floor into the Testing. He looked up at her with terror in his eyes as the stone slab closed above him. Lexy stood there frozen in place as her Ankh symbol lit up and her pulse raced. *That was fast.* They all looked at each other, held their hands up in the air then placed them on them hearts as a silent salute to the warriors that had each been dropped into their own personal purgatory.

Distraught, Frost knelt and placed one of his hands on the Crypt. Lily made her way over, knelt by him and whispered, "I know you really care about her."

Without even looking at her, Frost got up and walked away, muttering under his breath, "It doesn't matter anyway. She was never really mine."

Remaining there, Lily closed her eyes with the palm of her hand flat on the Crypt. Grey crouched, placed his arm around her, gave her a brotherly squeeze and urged, "We should go." Frost turned back with his eyes brimming with tears.

Trying to console Frost, Lily disclosed, "You know we've taken measures to make sure they survive this."

Lexy wasn't sure what she meant by that. Extra measures? The guilty expression on Frost's face made her even more curious.

Grey knit his brow and questioned, "What exactly do you mean by, you've taken measures?"

Lily and Frost continued silently looking at each other.

Glaring at the guilty looking duo, her Handler demanded an answer, "What did you do?"

Looking into his co-conspirator's eyes, Frost confessed, "We're destroying one, to save them all."

Lexy grinned. *How exciting. They were trying to make a Dragon. Yes, they would need a Dragon in the group to ensure their survival but who would it be?*

Always the protector and restorer of emotions, Grey repeated his question, "What have you done?"

Turning to face Grey, Lily touched his cheek and whispered, "We did what we had to do. You know most of the time they don't come out of the Testing. Let's just say we're running a little experiment. If they survive, it worked. The plan's already been set in motion, all we can do now is just wait and see."

He didn't shrug away from her touch. Grey remained there, staring into her eyes like he was trying to read between the lines.

"You don't want to know the details," Lily cautioned. "Trust me on this one." She kissed his cheek and smiled.

Grey had been enraptured by Lily before. He'd fallen hard for her and it had ended rather badly. It irritated the hell out of her that Frost threw Grey under the bus to stifle Lily's ability after the banquet right before they left the trio alone and went to the Summit. If they rekindled their romance it was going to be annoying. Contemplating the wording of her rant, she looked at the teary-eyed immortal. *Her need to punish Frost shifted to a desire to point out the facts.* When Frost met her gaze, she stated, "They've been granted the tools to save themselves. If they follow their instincts, they will find their way out, it's as simple as that."

Frost's lips curved into a grin as he nodded and replied, "You're right, there's nothing else for us to do here. We should leave." He wandered over to the others.

Did she believe they had a chance? The Testing shifted beneath her feet. Her mind replayed Zach's terrified expression as the Testing closed above him. *She'd ceased to feel fear so long ago. She didn't want to think about this anymore. She didn't want to think about anything. It was time.* She closed her eyes and willed all thoughts to cease as she allowed herself to succumb to the emotionless void. Her mind became a blank slate and her heart a solid mass that no longer cared if she believed in anything at all. She felt her inner Dragon spread its powerful wings as it soared into the sky. *She was free of guilt and void of pain. Oh, the freedom that this ability gave her could not be explained with mere words.* Lexy peered down at the stone beneath her bare feet and noticed a second set of feet in her peripheral vision. She noted they were men's feet and they weren't Grey's.

Frost whispered, "That situation is my fault. I'll take care of it."

What situation? She no longer cared. Lexy kept staring at their feet. *Frost's feet had black hairs on them. Hers appeared to have none at all.* She saw another pair of feet and knew those ones belonged to Grey.

Her Handler whispered, "It's alright to care. Leave them on, Lexy. Let's all go spend time together. I'm sure we can find something fun to do to lift our spirits in the in-between. Our people will get through this, we did."

It was too late. The cracks in her emotional dam had filled themselves in and it wasn't losing water anymore. Only one emotion flickered to the surface in response to Grey's words...*Anger. Our people...They were all our people. All of the Second-Tiers, trapped within the walls of that game left behind to suffer in their own personal purgatory forever. They should fight back! These Third-Tier immortal pieces of shit had been controlling everything for so long and what were they to her? They were nothing.* It crossed her mind to run to the edge and leap from the edge of the Testing. She'd land in the desert of blood red sand, storm the castle and paint the walls with the blood of Third-Tier's. *She was the strongest of them all.* Looking at the stone beneath her feet, she had the overwhelming urge to pry it open like a can of magical sardines and take her people back. With no filter to tell her she couldn't do whatever insanity passed through her mind, the wild thing that fought impossible battles and ran head on into walls took control of her actions. Lexy's eyes darkened, she dropped to her knees and began savagely clawing at the stone of the Testing, snapping and splitting her nails into bloody ragged shards. An image of other's nails embedded into the well as she climbed up the stone towards the light of vengeance flickered through her mind. She heard Grey's soothing voice in the distance and felt the warmth of his palm on her skin. He accepted the torment weighing down her soul in a touch and it travelled away from her into him. The solid mass of ice encasing her heart began to thaw with each loving, gentle word that escaped his lips. If it had been anyone else that touched her, she might have grabbed them by the legs and smashed them against the stone Crypt as recklessly as a toddler throwing a temper tantrum. The adoration she felt controlled her actions, even now. His soothing tone lulled her inner beast into complacency.

Lexy heard her Handler clearly now as he whispered, "I know of the most beautiful place. We can relax and just lay in the sun together. It'll be fun, I promise..."

Her bloody finger nubs froze in place mid claw. *She needed to fight someone or kill something. She didn't need to sit in the frigging sun.* Against her will her pulse slowed and her mind left the past behind and returned to the here and now. *What had she been doing?* She lifted her hands and looked at her bloody fingertips, suspecting they were already healed she licked the blood off a tip to make certain.

Frost's voice whispered, "Well, that's not disturbing at all."

Grey playfully scolded, "The Third-Tiers might be watching, we can't have you trying to dig holes in the top of the Testing we're supposed to be behaving ourselves and pretending to be easily tamed. Although, I'm certain they understand you can't be domesticated after what you did during the Summit." He held out his hand and gently prodded, "Let's get out of here."

A light breeze tossed his wheat-coloured hair into his eyes. He squinted and crinkled up his nose as he gave her an adorable grin. Lexy wiped the blood on her sarong and scowled as she took his hand. *He understood a part of her would always regress to the wild thing he'd found in the woods if her emotions were turned off.* Lexy took her hand away as soon as she was on her feet. Staring Grey down, she coolly sparred, "I'm sure your job as my Handler would be far less complicated if I just wanted to watch sunbeams through trees while you pick flowers and listen to birds, but that's not what you signed up for. It'll be a cold day in hell before you'll find me sitting next to you singing uplifting songs while you strum on your guitar. I'm a Dragon. My job is to take that guitar from your hands, bust it into a million unsalvageable slivers of wood and kill something with it."

Grey smiled at her overly hostile response and sweetly replied, "I wouldn't have it any other way...Do you need a hug?"

When in doubt, annoy the hell out of her. Those were his go too emotional anchors. He was doing it on purpose. He was a smart one. She'd give him that. Lexy turned back to look at her Handler. He was whispering in Lily's ear. She tossed her glistening silken midnight hair and animatedly laughed. *With no filter in place this pissed her off.*

Grey noticed she was watching him and left Lily's side, wandered towards her and stated, "I love you just as you are, Lex."

Right, just as I am. Until morning when you wake up and forget we're in love. Lexy looked at her Handler and sighed, "Spare me the inspirational fortune cookie quotes and grab your balls out of Lily's back pocket so we can leave."

They all grinned at her well-timed jest as they linked hands. *For her, this was always the best part.* The scenery flashed with brilliant white light, and in an instant, the four of were rapidly descending through the in-between's sky of blue towards the endless clean slate of the white sand desert. They slowed just before making contact and landed on their feet. Travel to the in-between was only surpassed by the womb like feeling of being wrapped in safety and warmth as they landed in the clean slate of the desert. She met Frost's solemn expression with one of her own.

Grey grabbed his manly bits and teased, "Still have my balls. I'm good to go."

Lexy scowled as she gave him a gentle shove into the sand. He landed with a humorous thud, followed by a puff of dust that filled the air around him. He coughed a couple of times and laughed even harder. When the cloud of sand cleared, her Handler was sprawled flat on his back in the sand. He started making sand angels to prove her hostility hadn't managed to tick him off. *When she was in this state, his endless supply of optimism annoyed the hell out of her. Grey was a sneaky one. He was making her feel annoyed, 'feel' being the operative word. She knew what he was doing.*

Grey stopped making sand angels. He sat up, tossed a handful of sand in her direction and taunted, "Come on, Lex. You know you want to make one."

Before Lexy could wrap her mind around the merits of making sand angels, Lily sat down beside him and started drawing pictures in the sand with her finger.

Grabbing her hand, Grey ribbed, "That's not how you make sand angels."

Lily pointed at her drawing of a stick figure with wings and started laughing, "Fine." She laid on her back and moved her limbs up and down a few times. She was smiling when she sat up and looked at the impression she'd made in the sand. "That is pretty cool."

As Lexy observed the two, she realised she was being ridiculous. *He wasn't flirting with her he was just being himself.*

Frost smiled at Lexy as he brought up Grey's newly discovered extracurricular activities, "I'm curious, when did the thing with Melody start and how did you get away with it for that long without anyone knowing about it?"

Grinning, Grey responded, "You know, I usually keep the details of my secret dalliances to myself. It was a little uncomfortable when Orin found out, but I was just the relief pitcher, I always knew her feelings were elsewhere."

Lily looked up from her sand creation, smiled and exclaimed, "It was a surprise to find out she had a thing with Thorne. I definitely didn't see that one coming."

Unable to help himself, Frost provoked, "I'm curious, were your feelings elsewhere too?"

Without a moment's hesitation, Grey looked at Lexy winked and sweetly replied, "Always."

He meant platonic love. Best friend love.

Grey changed the subject, "I have an unrelated question. In forty years, I've yet to figure out why sometimes we need the tombs to travel and other times we just walk through the Crypt?"

Lily smiled at him and replied, "We need help from our Clan's Guardian to move back and forth between the realms via Crypt. The white room is the equivalent of one of our personal tombs, but it's operated by our Guardian Azariah. The only difference being, that we can operate the tombs all by ourselves using one of our own Healers. We can go to the in-between without permission. It's like travelling on earth, sometimes you need a passport and sometimes you don't."

That made perfect sense. She watched Grey as he intently listened to Lily's answer to his question. He was a truly beautiful person with his welcoming smile, sun-kissed, chiselled golden chest and arms. There was such character in his flaws. The true beauty was in his ice-blue eyes and the way they glistened in the sunshine that reflected off the white sand. She found herself lost in them. *Damn him. How was she supposed to move on from the one person she'd been born to love?* Grey reached up for Lexy's hand and his eyes crinkled in the corners. She took it and helped him up. He kept a laughably firm grip on her hand instead of letting it go once he was standing. She peered down as he loosened his grasp and laced his fingers through hers. *Frost had probably been trying to deter another Lily and Grey hookup by talking about the Melody one. He was trying to help but all he'd done was remind her.* She kept holding his hand even though the thought that crossed her mind had stung a little.

Grey smiled at her and urged, "I say we go and find something fun to do." He glanced at Frost and asked, "How long do we have?"

"Take as long as you need. Come find us when you're ready," Frost answered with a knowing grin.

"Come on, gorgeous. Let's find one of those hot springs and decompress," Grey playfully announced as he towed her away from the others. She went willingly, knowing they needed time alone. *It felt like their rhythm was off.* As they wandered through the endless white sand desert of the in-between under the brilliant sky of multi-hued blue, their laced hands swung back and forth to the soft repetitive rustling of their footsteps in the sand.

Chapter 4

Handlers And Dragons

She couldn't remain angry at him; she'd never been able too. As she held his hand, everything within her became peaceful and warm. As her eyes met his, she knew Grey was just happy to be with her. Her Handler was both the cause of her turmoil and the only way to find inner peace. Their relationship was complicated, to say the least.

Smiling warmly, Grey asked, "Do you ever think about the day we met?"

All of the time. Lexy smiled as she thought about him being snared in one of her hunting traps, cursing up a storm. *She'd been alone for a long time. A wild thing living in the woods with a pack of stray dogs. Eventually, they'd left her too.* Squeezing his hand, Lexy thought of how she'd felt when he followed her home and showed up at her cabin. *She'd been annoyed by his presence at first, but after a few minutes of companionship, she was sold. When he'd asked her to come with him, she'd gone willingly. Well, planned to go before uninvited guests attacked her sanctuary in the woods.*

Looking at her, he asked, "Do you remember the first time we danced together?"

She did. It had been all three of them, Arrianna, Grey and her. They'd been here in the in-between. She had never danced before she met him, it had been years since she'd heard laughter. *He brought those things with him into her life.* Lexy gazed into his eyes and assured, "I'm already back, Grey. There's no need to keep trying."

He laughed as he playfully tugged her to him and they started dancing. Her heart couldn't help but join her undeniably lovable soulmate as he smoothly spun her and dipped her.

"There's no music, Greydon," she laughed, dangling. As she finished the sentence, a song she'd always adored began to play. Pulling her close, they swayed together to the romantic song as he started goofily singing in her ear. *It wasn't remotely sexy but it filled her with joy.* She closed her eyes, rested her head on his shoulder and melted into his embrace. *It was in these moments she wished with all of her heart that they were allowed to be together. The fact that they weren't had never stopped it from happening.* The sensation of her toes in the warmth of the sand as they danced, along with the tenderness of his hand on her back deterred her from stopping the moment they were in the middle of. *Being with him like this, made her feel happiness worth every second of pain she'd be feeling in the aftermath. This was how she continued to break her own heart.*

The scenery flashed and they were deposited at the strangely placed little tidal pool that contained mystically seductive powers. *This destination had always intrigued her. It was a perfect swimming hole in the middle of a meadow, beside a lone apple tree in the in-between. Sometimes it was more like a miniature lake and you couldn't tell what lay beneath the surface. Other times, it was all white sand scattered with brightly coloured starfish. Today, it was the ocean version. Why had he brought her here?*

With a funny look, she questioned, "Why are we here?"

"I didn't mean to bring you here. I'm sorry, I guess all of that talk about Melody made this place cross my mind," he disclosed, as they strolled towards it. *Ouch. Yes… his unknowing insensitivity knew no bounds. She reminded herself once again that he didn't remember.* "We can't stay here. You know what this place does," she taunted. Lexy glanced at the tree full of ripe apples and remarked, "I'm just going to grab an apple. I'll only be a second." She wandered over to the apple tree. The orchard from her childhood flashed through her mind as she plucked an apple from a low hanging branch and tossed it to him. Grey caught it in mid-air. She tried to yank another one off for herself and couldn't. *Not a damn one would budge.* She grabbed for another, allowed her legs to go out from under her and dangled rather humorously from the apple with the full weight of her body. *Oh, Come on!*

Grey tossed his head back and howled laughing. He strolled over to stand beside her, as she dropped from her chuckle-worthy position and landed on her feet. He handed her his apple and chuckled, "Take a bite of this one and let me try." He leapt up, grabbed the branch, and dangled from it. Eventually, he lost his patience and started to comically swing up and down on the branch like an immortal yoyo. Not a one of the apples dropped to the ground. "Seriously, what in the hell is with this damn tree?" Grey laughed as he jumped up and tried again.

Lexy took a bite of the scrumptiously delicious perfect apple and savoured it as she watched him rather ineptly endeavouring to remove another from the branch. *Grey was a stubborn guy. If she didn't stop him, they'd be doing this for hours.* She felt a warm shiver and glanced back at the naughty thought inducing pool. *It was time to leave, with every second that passed her best friend slash Handler was looking more appetizing than the apples on the tree.* She grinned at him as her eyes travelled from his rippling tanned abs to his sexy toned chest. From this vantage point that loincloth he was wearing wasn't concealing much. *The pool was working its seductive magic on him as well. They needed to go. Tiberius had left her feeling rather unsatisfied at the Summit. It would be wrong, so wrong to be with Grey for the sake of a physical release. But you're in love with him. He loves you too he just doesn't remember. She had to snap out of it and now.* Lexy looked at the love of her life and asserted, "We need to leave. Right now!"

He dropped to the grass and started to chuckle, "Is that pool over there making me too sexy for you to handle?"

Yes, it was. She rolled her eyes.

Chuckling, he spun in a circle slowly and teased, "Well, take it all in."

Her increasingly sexy Handler glared at the tree, leapt up and dangled from the branch and started comically shaking it. *Come on, Greydon. She knew they'd be here for a while. He wasn't about to allow himself to be beaten by a tree.* She'd seen that pig-headed expression on countless occasions. That was the, 'I will continue trying to do this until hell freezes over look.' He growled and reefed on the branch then pulled himself up and straddled it. He was using every bit of strength he had to tug apples off the tree and they wouldn't budge. He started huffing and puffing, having a seriously comical testosterone-fuelled hissy fit. *In all of these years, she hadn't ever been able to stop herself from giving him a little push over the edge when he was like this.* Lexy grinned and taunted, "I thought I told you to grab your balls before we left the Testing?" She reached up, easily plucked an apple from one of the branches and then doubled over laughing. *It had randomly come off like it was nothing.* Lexy hollered, "Get down, or I'll knock you down."

Scowling at her from his perch in the tree, he provoked, "You wouldn't dare."

She'd never been able to resist a dare. She wound up and launched it at Grey as he jumped off and landed on his feet in the grass. *It missed him by a hair.*

He chased her around the tree, animatedly mocking her, "You think you're pretty funny, don't you? I'm so tough. I'm a Dragon." His face broke into a grin as she darted out of his way.

Giggling, she backed up and warned, "I'll throw another one if you come any closer."

He took a step towards her and cockily mocked, "Give it your best shot, cupcake."

Fully expecting him to step out of the way, she whipped the apple. There was a loud cracking noise behind him, the branch he'd been hanging from a moment earlier thudded to the ground, diverting his attention for a split second and that's all it took for her apple to smoke him on the back of the head.

Bent over, rubbing his wounded skull, he complained, "Shit Lex, you weren't supposed to actually do it."

She strolled over, smiled sweetly and baited, "Sorry, I thought you'd move out of the way." *He was faking her out. She knew it but took another step closer anyway.* He grabbed for her as she darted out of the way. He caught up and gave her a good shove into the pool of pheromone enhancing water. She grabbed for him as she toppled over and yanked him in with her. They both surfaced, still laughing as they splashed each other like children. They looked at each other and raced for the edge, knowing the first one out of the water would have the upper hand. Lexy scrambled up the embankment and was almost out, when he grabbed hold of one of her legs and towed her back in. He had her trapped against the sandy edge as something changed in his expression, she'd seen that look enough times to know what happened next. Lexy placed her hands against his chest to keep him from closing the space between them and whispered, "We should get out of the water and go somewhere else."

"Not just yet," Grey baited. Tucking her dripping hair behind her ears, he whispered, "I wish you could see how beautiful you are with the sun shining behind you. You've taken my breath away, twice in one day."

"Grey," she whispered. *Damn it, he was smooth. Her resolve was going to last all of five seconds if he didn't stop doing that sexy smile and eye thing.*

With his hypnotizing gaze, he confessed, "I acted like I didn't remember kissing you but that wasn't the truth. Tiberius was all over you and I didn't know what to do. I don't know. I guess I was trying to give you an option if you were needing that from someone. I know it's been a long time. I mean how long ago were you with Tomas?"

He actually thought she'd gone without since Tomas. The only person she'd been with since then was him.

He continued his speech, "I was only gone for a few minutes and when I came back, you were talking to Orin. I held back because being with him made more sense than risking complications in our situation. At the end of the night, I was put in the position where it had to be me or Frost who took Lily out of the equation and we both know Frost can't be the one to do that for ability control reasons."

Every inch of her being wanted to embrace this confession and take the beautiful experience that came with it, but she knew how this would play out.

"I know you were upset about the Lily thing in the morning but you have to know it wasn't what I wanted. I'm past her. You know I'm over her," he disclosed.

She stood her ground even though her heart kept saying, *fold, damn it! You know you want to.* "Grey, I think we should just get out of this pool."

Cupping her cheek tenderly, he admitted, "I was so jealous at the Summit. I was just wrecked when I didn't know where you were and I thought you might be with him. I spent all night telling anyone that would listen that I was in love with you."

Her heart swelled with a devotion that would always be undeniable. Lexy bit her bottom lip and shook her head.

What? She couldn't keep doing this to herself. She was breaking her own heart. She'd never been able to turn him away when he was in the process of laying his heart out on the line.

His voice cracked with emotion as he boldly declared, "I can't have you be anything but mine." His lips began moving towards hers.

Her resolve to stay away from him was growing foggier by the second. With her hand against his chest, she gave reason a last shot, "If we go somewhere else and you still feel this way then..."

His magnetic eyes, searched her soul for the truth as he pressed, "Tell me you don't love me back and I'll get out of this pool and never mention this again."

Lexy couldn't do that. She loved him more than anything. She always had...

With his heart on his sleeve, he whispered, "You want me too, don't you?"

Shit...this was going to happen. Lexy slowly nodded and whispered, "I always have."

Grey's eyes softened as he smiled and whispered, "Why didn't you just tell me how you felt?"

She'd told him countless times. His gaze radiated such adoration, her heart couldn't hold back even though it knew it should. He tenderly kissed her and it was like striking a match as his tongue darted between her parted lips. Undeniable, as always, she couldn't bring herself to stop the scenario from playing out. They made out with breathless abandon until she was shivering with desire. *At this point it didn't matter if it was wrong or right. She needed this.* Her pulse raced as Grey groaned her name. *Oh, hell...One last time.*

He slipped his hand beneath the soaking wet, nearly see-through material clinging to her chest. She gasped as his hand caressed the aching hardened peak of her breast as he nibbled on her neck and earlobes, it tickled. Giggling, she slipped off her sarong and tossed it onto the shore. He chucked his bottoms over his shoulder, laughing. *Why did she have to love him this much?*

"There is nothing I wouldn't give you," Grey pledged as he took her in his arms and nuzzled her neck as his fingers slipped between her thighs underwater. She gasped as he pleasured her until she ached for a more substantial appendage. He whispered in her ear, "Tell me what you want."

Knowing precisely what pushed him over the edge, she seductively darted her tongue between his parted lips as she reached for him and provoked, "You." His pained expression gave her reckless satisfaction. *For once he'd been the one driven mad by jealousy.* She brazenly wrapped her legs around his waist, arched her back and took the rigid length of him, consummating their smouldering submergence of souls. Grey groaned as he clutched her buttocks, roughly pinned her against the sandy ledge of the tidal pool and gave it to her with reckless abandon. His savage thrusting quickly brought them both to a mind-blowing crescendo, as water lapped against the shore. The surge of ecstasy rose until she cried out as a euphoric tidal wave of pleasure released within her. Every nerve ending was humming as she whimpered and slumped against him with his length still in her. *He was nowhere near done. She knew every move he made by heart.* She noticed that a half dozen apples had randomly fallen from the tree onto the ground. It was as though they'd secured themselves to the tree to keep them here until they gave in and did what they needed to do.

He gasped in her ear, "Why haven't we been doing this, every night?"

They'd been doing this for thirty years. God, she loved him. They couldn't be together. It was easy to pretend while spent in his embrace that it could be like this …always.

"This is going to be complicated," he whispered in her ear.

She smiled but kept her mouth shut. *No, it wasn't. He was going to forget.*

"We should get out of the water and lay in the sun for a while?" she suggested. They both struggled their way up the embankment and sprawled on their backs in the grass. She rolled onto her stomach on the luxurious cushion of greenery and grabbed for one of the stray apples that dropped from the tree. *It felt like a reward for allowing him to have his way with her. To say no, would have hurt him and he wasn't as emotionally durable as she was. Sometimes this tree reminded her of the apple tree from the story of Adam and Eve. Theoretically, they were in the in-between. It might be the actual tree. That made sense. The tree with the sinner's fruit right beside a pool of water that induced naughty behaviour. Nobody had ever warned them to stay away from the apples.*

He flirtatiously grinned and asked, "Can I have a bite?"

She dangled it over his lips and smiled as he took an over-ambitious bite of the fruit. He chewed his enormous mouthful smiling at her in that way that always softened her heart and made mush of her resolve. There was this satisfied, adorable crinkle in the corner of his eyes that wasn't present with every smile. Lexy leaned over and kissed him square on his apple juicy lips. Then she licked her lips tasting the fruity flavour of his as she stretched out in the grass and closed her eyes ever so briefly as the warmth of the sun's rays caressed her nude form. When she opened them, he was staring at her appreciatively. She grinned and taunted, "Why don't you take a picture it'll last longer?"

"Now, there's a thought," he lovingly teased as he traced a slow seductive path down her arm with one of his fingers. He whispered, "I feel like I should be worried about what we just did for fifty different reasons right now but all I can think about is how soft your skin is and how much I want to do it again."

She took his hand, placed it on her breast and tempted, "We'll worry about it tomorrow." *Meaning, she would worry about it tomorrow and he would be blissfully oblivious.*

Positioned above her, he began naughtily toying with her. He gave her a deviously naughty grin as he trailed kisses down her stomach to her abdomen. She gasped and grabbed a handful of the silken fragrant grass as he pleasured her until another explosion of ecstasy rocked her to her core. He didn't wait for her to finish shivering before confessing his love for her as he took her once again. Her heart soared as he drove her to the edge with his knowledge of what movements would pleasure her until he left her gasping and pleading as the aching within her became a swirling explosion of euphoria. In the end they lay wrapped in each other's arms, with their limbs still intertwined, completely spent. *She loved him too much. Why had she done this to herself again?* Her eyes grew heavy and she knew by the steady rhythm of his breathing that he was probably already asleep. Lexy stayed there for a moment longer and as her eyes filled with tears, she blinked them away, knowing there was no point in shedding tears over something that would only matter to her. *It would be best to treat this as a dream. It was just a beautiful dream that had never actually taken place.* She'd endeavour to move on with her life as she planned to do before slipping up and giving in to a desire that held no promise of evolving. *She needed to get dressed. She couldn't dress him. Grey was dead to the world and his limbs were as unmalleable as bags of cement. She'd tell him he went skinny dipping and fell asleep in the grass.* Lexy smiled as she thought of how many times the poor guy had woken up naked somewhere and never bothered to search for an explanation. She wandered far enough from the naughty pool to be certain they wouldn't end up having round three. *Next time she'd say no... Next time.* Lexy sprawled in the lush grass and closed her eyes, inhaling the fragrance with each breath until she drifted off to sleep.

After a luxurious nap, she awoke to find her Handler clothed, sitting beside her watching a caterpillar crawling in the palm of his hand.

Grey showed her his new friend and exclaimed, "Look at how fluffy he is."

The Friend zone version of her Handler had returned. Lexy smiled, as she sat up so she could get a better look at her Handler's fluffy orange and black companion. She nodded and exclaimed, "He's pretty cute."

Watching his palm, he remarked, "I woke up naked over by that pool."

If she told him something feasible, he wouldn't bother searching any further for answers. She got comfortable by folding her arms in front of her like a pillow and rested her head. Closing her eyes so she wouldn't have to look into his, she lied, "I wanted to have a nap and you weren't ready to go to sleep. I didn't want to hang out with you by that pool for obvious reasons."

He shook his head like she'd said something ridiculous, messed-up her hair in a brotherly way, and teased, "I don't think you ever have to worry about that happening."

Ouch, that unknowing barb stung a little. Swallowing it down, she suggested, "Let's go find Frost and Lily."

Grey kept rotating his palm around so the fluffy little caterpillar was walking in an endless circle. He sighed, "Do you really want to leave? It's so peaceful here and we don't have to think about everything that's going on. I could stay here for a while longer."

He was blissfully enjoying his moment with the furry distraction in his hand. In awe of his ability to find joy in the simple things, Lexy smiled and replied, "I guess, we can stay for a while." Grey beamed as he allowed the tiny caterpillar to meander up his arm. Lexy placed her hand in front of it and their tiny distraction strolled onto her palm and switched directions; the tiny feet tickled and she smiled. When Grey noticed she was enjoying herself his smile widened, and once again, his ability to find joy in everything made her feel more than she would have been capable of by herself. *This was how they were meant to be. Perhaps, he had the right idea. She needed a distraction to get her through the next few days of hurt as he obliviously moved on from what they'd shared. That's what she'd do. She'd find a distraction as soon as they got back to the land of the living.* They didn't have search for Lily and Frost because they appeared in the field just as she decided to put an end to Grey's special 'me time' and suggest they go and find the others.

"Azariah has something she needs us to do," Frost announced as they strolled over. "Come on you two, enough relaxation, it's time to get down and dirty."

Lexy muzzled her inner dialogue.

Grey grimaced as Lily knelt beside him to get a closer look at what he had in his hand. She placed her hand out and Grey let the fuzzy caterpillar crawl onto it. Lily smiled as she watched it crawl across the length of it. She placed her palm in the grass and it disappeared into the fragrant carpet of green. Lily rose to stand and held out her hand to Grey. He took it and she gave him a tug to his feet.

"Thanks, beautiful," Grey said with a wink. He inhaled the potent fragrance in the air and enquired, "Don't you love the smell of this grass?"

Grinning, Lily replied, "It does seem to be extra potent today, doesn't it? I wonder why that is?"

Frost placed his arm around Lexy as they started to walk away and whispered in her ear, "The pool…really? That doesn't seem proactive."

Lexy quietly responded, "It wasn't my idea."

Frost nodded and kept the rest of his observations silent as the scenery flashed around them and they found themselves standing at the bottom of what appeared to be the same sandstone multihued ringed canyon where she'd trained the three to die like champions. She smiled and wondered if they were going to be fighting enormous scorpions. *That would be a lovely way to spend the afternoon. She could burn off a little bit of energy and deal with some of that pent up rage.*

Grey shook his head at his Dragon's overly exuberant response to standing at the bottom of the ravine and sighed, "The vacation's over isn't it?"

Chapter 5

Dragon "Me" Time

A sword appeared in Lily's hands, she chuckled, gripped it firmly and gave it a skilled practice swing, "Yes, I'd say it is."

As a sword appeared in her hands, Lexy grinned and commented, "I guess it depends on what you see as a vacation."

Thunderous clicking of gigantic scorpions shook the ravine beneath their feet. *This is amazing, just what she wanted to do today.*

Grey cleared his throat and nervously piped in, "Hey, you guys. I still don't have a sword. I keep thinking about one, it hasn't appeared."

Frost swung around his spiked ball on a chain and suggested, "I couldn't think up a sword either. Think of something else."

A spiked club appeared in Grey's grasp, he groaned, "I hate these things. They get stuck and then you have to pull them out. It takes away valuable time."

Lexy grinned widely as a child on Christmas morning, her pulse raced in preparation for the battle ahead as she mocked, "Oh, quit whining Greydon and get ready to fight. This is going to be fun."

They all started to laugh. Well, everyone but Greydon who was still feeling pissy because he was a lover not a fighter. *Each scorpion was usually the size of a truck. Some were the size of a big rig...Why were they not visible?*

"Where in the hell are they?" Grey stammered. He had his weapon raised, ready to fight the impossible.

The ground trembled beneath her feet. Lexy grinned as it crumbled beneath her and she fell through the canyon floor into darkness. There was not a hint of light, not even a sliver, just isolating darkness and thunderous clicks of what sounded like dozens of gigantic scorpions. Lexy wasn't sure if the others were here but knew better than to call out. *That would only tell the predators where she was.* Lexy tightened her grip on the sword she was wielding and listened as she gingerly crept through the pitch-black feeling in front of her for solid ground with each foot before taking a step. *This was great!* Light flashed, she was surrounded. Deducing there was no visible cliff or drop off, Lexy dove forward and slid across the smooth stone floor maneuvering her way through clicking feet. Driven forward by nothing but instinct, she swung her sword and slid again, knowing if she took off a leg, the enormous scorpion would probably teeter over and squish her underneath its enormous frame. Lexy remained in one spot just a second too long and felt the excruciating sting of being impaled as something large and sharp pierced her stomach. Her body was raised into the air and lurched around. She choked on her own warm blood as it spurted from between her lips. Whatever she'd been impaled on, broke off and she dropped with a thud to the ground. With sight not one of her options, all she had to guide her was instinct and the exhilaration of battle. Lexy was fed a welcome shot of adrenaline. She shivered with pleasure as her healing ability tried to kick in. *There was something inside of her blocking her ability to heal.* She felt her stomach and yanked the object out of her midriff, causing a euphoric primitive response. *Round one was almost over. She was going to bleed out.* Lexy zigzagged away from her invisible assailant, knowing she had little to no time left in this round of her macabre pastime. The Dragon swung her sword as lights flashed. Aiming for coordinated movement, she teetered over as she maneuvered between clicking legs. Her senses were working overtime to compensate for her lack of sight; she could hear everything from her blood pulsating through her veins to the whooshing of the scorpion's tails as they gathered to finish her off. Something pierced her shoulder and speared her abdomen, tugging in either direction. *She was about to be torn in two.* She sliced the appendage off one of her assailants. Her body was tossed into the air. She landed on her back, knocking the wind out of her. *At least one of the objects must have been a stinger. Burning venom was seeping into her system. It was like she'd been stung by a thousand wasps. It felt like someone doused her in gasoline, struck a match and tossed it at her.* Lexy's mind screamed as her entire body went up in flames. The carnal heat of her ability kicked in as blood spurted from between her lips. That last wound had been the kill shot, but still always the Dragon, she endeavoured to crawl forward. The lights flickered once more, and this time, her vision was too blurry to make sense of anything. *She'd lost too much blood.* Flung by one of the abominations, she slid across the ground like it was an ice rink. Endeavouring to rise once she'd stopped moving, she felt woozy. A final rush of adrenaline urged her on. *How am I still alive?* Lexy struggled to her feet. Forgetting to check to see if there was in fact ground in front of her, she stepped forward. Sure enough, there was no ground beneath her feet, and Lexy plummeted into the unknown. She raised her arms to either side, closed her eyes and smiled as the wind rippled behind her. *Well, she'd been wrong about there being no drop-off.* Unfortunately, her entertaining otherworldly mind game did not reset before she made contact with a hard surface. *There was one final excruciatingly painful surge of agony and then nothing.* This scenario repeated itself countless times until she could feel no pain at all when she made contact at the end.

After the final illusion of her demise, Lexy awoke and before she ventured to open her eyes, she knew she was no longer lost in the darkness. *The game had ended.* The sunshine behind her eyelids gave her world a pinkish hue. Lexy clutched the ground. By the scent and texture, she was sure it was soil beneath her fingertips. She remained there without opening her eyes, basking in the warmth of the sun's welcoming rays, listening to the music of tropical birds. *Were those chimpanzees?* Out of sheer curiosity, Lexy opened her eyes. *It had only been the lack of sun that made her think it was shining directly on her.* She squinted in the sunlight filtering through tropical trees. *There was a sweet, invigorating scent in the air. Where was she now? Where was Grey?* He was always her first thought when she snapped out of her Dragon state. Lexy was struck on the head by something hard, it rolled across the ground in front of her. *What in the hell?* She picked it up. *It was a coconut, not a small one.* She glanced up and there was a mischievous chimpanzee, poised to throw another. She smiled and thought about the apple she'd thrown at Grey. *Karma was such a bitch.* She glared at the monkey. *You little asshole.* It gave her an enormous open-mouthed grin as it launched another coconut in her direction.

Lexy stepped out of the way and hissed, "Now listen, you little shit, I'm not in the mood to play games with you right now!"

It cackled boisterously and tossed another one at her as she dodged it and chuckled. The monkey vanished. She took note of her surroundings as she knelt to pick a flower and smelled it. It was the flower that made the incredible fragrance. She tucked it behind her ear and decided it was time to go find her absentee Handler. She'd thought she was in the clear when she was struck in the head from behind. *You little shit!* She spun around and there were at least twenty grinning chimpanzees poised in the branches ready to launch a coconut assault. *Shit, seriously.* Unless she was planning on wasting time climbing trees to ring each of their mischievous necks, she'd better get out of firing range. She sprinted away just as they pummelled her mercilessly with coconuts. When she was certain she'd lost the obnoxious monkey mob, she slowed her pace to a stroll. Lexy had never seen a monkey before. She decided monkeys were assholes and she didn't need to ever see one again. *Where was Greydon? She was a little surprised he hadn't found her already. It was his damn job, after all.* She scrolled through the mental checklist of reasons he hadn't found her yet, and only one thought came to mind, he was having too much fun with Lily. Lexy kept walking. *She was not going to allow herself to behave like a jealous shrew…anymore.* She heard monkey's laughter and it sounded too close for comfort. Lexy picked up her pace and darted through the jungle avoiding roots as stealthily as a jungle cat. She heard rushing water and decided that was the direction she should go. A thought popped into her mind and Lexy started giggling. *She'd been thinking about needing a distraction and that's precisely what Azariah had given her.* She wasn't sure how long she'd been away from Grey because time was a strange beast when they were in the in-between, but she knew her detour on the road to being done with her Handler physically had taken away the sting of his absence. *Good work, Azariah.* She continued her trek through vibrant colours, musical birds and exhilarating fragrance towards the rushing water. As Lexy stepped out of the brush and arrived at the waterfall, the scenery flashed and she found herself standing on a picturesque cliff bluff overlooking the place where the ravine's floor had crumbled beneath her feet. Lexy was standing alone beneath the backdrop of a crimson and tangerine hued sunset. *This was where she'd lost the others. Surely, they wouldn't still be hanging out at the bottom of the ravine.* Lexy sensed him behind her before she made a move to turn around and didn't flinch as he touched her shoulder.

Grey spoke, "I was told to leave you alone and allow you some time to find your balance. Did you manage to find it?"

She turned to face her Handler and replied, "I think so. What have you guys been up to?" They casually strolled away from the ledge.

He took her hand and said, "I'll take you there."

The scenery flashed, and in an instant, they were walking on a tropical beach towards Lily and Frost. Lexy released her grasp on Grey's hand and spun around so she could take in her surroundings. They were on a tiny island the size of a few city blocks with nothing but water in every direction. There was jungle in the center and a white silky sand beach that appeared to circumference the lush greenery. The water was a brilliant teal. She'd never been to this place before. *It was lovely.* The sky was now various tones of blue splattered across the ever-changing backdrop of in-between. *This was why time was impossible to keep track of.*

Their fellow Ankh were sprawled on their stomachs in the sand chatting, drinking Pina Coladas. There was a plate of fruit on the beach in front of them.

Grey smiled and stated, "It's pretty cool isn't it? I guess this is one of Lily and Frost's special places."

Frost noticed her towering above him and said, "Grab a drink and relax."

Grab a drink?

She glanced at Grey and he was already seated in the sand with a slushy drink in his hand. *His icy drink was red.* She took a seat beside him, thought of a drink and it appeared in her hand. *Well, this was a new thing for them to do. She'd never had the urge to eat or drink while in the in-between.*

Well, besides apples but she wasn't going to allow herself to think of that right now. Lexy took a sip of the icy beverage and it was glorious. The frozen treat danced around her taste buds as she noted it was warmer on this beach and that intoxicating scent from the jungle was still in the air. She assumed it must be the tropical flowers skirting the beach area. She remembered she'd tucked the flower behind her ear. *That'd be why she still smelt it.* Lexy grabbed it and smiled at herself. *She'd never claimed to be a brain surgeon.* She looked up at the shades of blue in the sky and then over at her Handler who was lapping this experience up.

She nudged Grey and questioned, "How come we've never done this before?"

Frost was the one to respond, "You'll find you become rather creative as time goes on."

Lexy placed the flower on the beach and scooped a handful of the white sand into the palm of her hand, allowing the delicate silky grains to trickle through her slightly spread fingertips. *She felt calm. She'd really needed to let off some steam.*

Lily raised her glass and added, "Isn't this a great way to spend your time, though."

Lexy glanced up and smiled at her. *It was.*

Lily's onyx hair was glimmering in the sunlight. It trailed like a waterfall down her back. Her olive skin always had her looking tanned to perfection. Frost's skin tone and colouring were the same as hers. *They would have made a stunningly gorgeous couple back in the day. They were just friends now and somehow managed to keep those lines clearly drawn, unlike her and Grey. Perhaps, that was why Frost was always keeping himself occupied with a sea of women. Well, that was until the Brighton twins had come into his life. His situation had become decidedly more complicated after that happened. She recalled the sight of the twins together. They had been truly identical on the outside. On the inside, Kayn's moral compass had been operating, while Chloe's had always appeared to be missing its needle. When the twin's souls had joined, Kayn Brighton had been the dominant one. Chloe had just sort of faded into the background.* Well, that's what she'd thought at first, but as the year progressed, Kayn had come into her own and gradually became a well-rounded person. *They were all innately flawed for different reasons. Kayn's flaws had always been incredibly endearing. She would miss her the most if they didn't find their way out of the Testing.* Lexy took a sip of her Pina Colada and closed her eyes as the warmth of the sun's rays belted down on her. She opened them and Frost was sitting beside her, lost in thought. *It felt like this would be an appropriate time to say or do something to console him. Would anything she had to say right now really mean anything at all if she didn't make it? Probably not.* She opted out of a pep talk. *If he wasn't speaking about it, he might be trying to stop himself from thinking about it. She knew what that felt like.* She glanced at Grey. His blonde sun-bleached hair kept falling into his eyes, he repeatedly brushed it away. *Her Handler needed a haircut. He'd always been slack as far as his hair was concerned. Between that, and his golden-hued tan, he looked like he should be surfing on a beach somewhere. Greydon looked like one of a million guys. Frost and Lily were obvious immortals but Grey wasn't. She wasn't an apparent one either with long crimson hair and skin that freckled at the first hint of sunlight.* Grey and Lily were having an intimate conversation and she wondered if that mixture would be as difficult to endure now that she'd decided to try to stop their intimate cycle. *He was a loyal guy. If he had feelings for Lily it might give her enough time to get over their situation and move on.* She shook her head and brought herself back to reality. *That was a horrible thing to even think. He'd fallen for Lily but his feelings weren't reciprocated and that had left him heartbroken. Maybe, if Melody made it out of the Testing something more serious could happen between them, now that she understood a relationship with Thorne wasn't possible?*

Touching her leg to get her attention, Frost whispered, "You know if you're thinking about another person for him, it means you're ready to move on."

"I don't have a choice, do I?" she whispered her honest response.

Frost glanced at Lexy and said, "You know, I've been where you are. If you ever want to talk about it, my ears are all yours."

She smiled at him, nodded and stated, "I may take you up on that someday."

Lexy watched Frost stare into his drink for a minute or two before deciding that maybe she should say something about Kayn. She picked up another handful of sand and ordered, "Hold out the palm of your hand." He humoured her by doing as he was told and she allowed the delicate grains to trickle from her hand into his. He knit his brow, wondering where she was going with this. She grinned and began her not so well thought out explanation, "These are the obstacles they have to get past in the Testing in the beginning and I'd imagine it seems like an insurmountable thing for anyone who is normal. If I'm right about my interpretation of your earlier conversation, you've set it up so Kevin will kill Kayn in the Testing. If he does kill her, this might work. She wouldn't have been my choice for the Dragon after seeing their Corrections, but I understand how the opportunity presented itself with Kevin."

Frost stared into her eyes and asked, "Can I drop this handful of sand yet?"

Grinning, she teased, "Be patient." Lexy brushed the sand off his palm and remarked, "Do you see your empty hand."

Frost shrugged as he replied, "Yes, of course."

She smiled and assured, "Once she's a Dragon, there will be no obstacles for her. She won't see them anymore. If Kevin does his part and Kayn becomes a Dragon, she is going to be seriously pissed at you when she finds out, but they are coming home."

He smiled at her and confessed, "She may hate me for a while but I guess I've got an eternity to make it up to her, don't I?"

"That, you do," Lexy responded as she took another drink of her Pina Colada, noticing that the ice hadn't melted a touch. *It was a truly magical place.*

Frost stood up and suggested, "We should get going. We can't stay in the fantasy forever."

Lexy took his hand and he helped her up. *Don't I know it.*

Frost grinned like he'd heard her witty inner dialogue and whispered, "Ditto."

The four were standing side by side ready to go as Grey asserted, "One second." He downed the rest of his red slushy drink, staining his upper lip.

"One more second," Lexy laughed as she tried cleaning it off with her finger.

Grey swatted her away like an unruly child, saying, "Thanks mom but it won't be on my face after we leave."

Mom…That's awesome. She shook her head. They joined hands, and in the time it took to blink, they were strolling through the warm silky sand of the blank slated desert towards their glowing Guardian Azariah. She greeted them with a welcoming smile. Lily walked towards her and they embraced.

She gently stroked Lily's glistening midnight mane and lovingly said, "It's nice to see you too, my child."

Something about Azariah's voice instantly put you at ease. It was like hearing a sedating lullaby. It had taken many years to not feel the urge to bow in her presence with that glowing light attaching her to the sky of blue above.

Lily stepped away from the divine being and enquired, "How are they doing in there?"

With a maternal smile, Azariah replied, "As well as can be expected. It's been brutal and savage. They are still fighting against it, trying to avoid different demises. They have yet to figure out the purpose of the Testing. They haven't risen to the occasion as I'd hoped they would by this point."

Frost silently nodded and made a valiant attempt to appear unaffected by the news. Lexy knew his thousand years of immortality had left him realistic in the face of adversity such as this, even though his heart wanted to see past it.

Frost turned away, looked directly at Azariah and said, "Has it happened yet?"

Azariah met his steady gaze with a response, "No, the boy hasn't been able to bring himself to do it."

Frost nodded again and confessed, "I'm not sure I could do it either."

With her hand on his shoulder, Azariah gave him a loving squeeze and assured, "I'll keep you updated through your Oracle. Right now, all you need to have is faith. Winnie is certain her grandson will do what is right when the time comes."

Lexy could tell their Guardian's speech had done little to sooth Frost's aching heart for he'd already stated aloud that he wasn't sure he'd be able to do the deed if the duty had fallen on him.

Azariah's eyes softened as she noticed Frost's stricken expression. She advised, "My child, it is pointless to spend your time worrying about something you have no control over."

Lexy couldn't make eye contact with her soft-hearted Handler. *Their plot was seriously harsh and that was coming from her. She understood creating a Dragon was a necessary evil for that described her duties in their Clan to a tee. They were sending Kevin after Kayn and her love for him ran as deep as her love for Grey. She'd seen it in her eyes. The logical warrior within her saw the genius in their savagely brutal plot. If Kevin went after Kayn it would be an emotionally crippling event. Would he be able to bring himself to do it? Well, that remained to be seen...*

Kicking sand, Grey mumbled, "You're going to destroy her. She is a kind loving person. This is wrong. Any way you look at it. It's just wrong."

Smiling maternally at her pouting temperamental child, Azariah gave him the explanation he needed to hear, "Our Clan's Oracle has assured us, there is only one way this group survives. Your trio would have been lost in that Testing if it weren't for Lexy, deep down you see this to be the truth."

This time when Grey glanced at her, she didn't look away. Lexy stared directly into his eyes and acknowledged him in a way she never had, "I wouldn't be anywhere at all without you."

Azariah grinned and declared, "This is why all Dragon's must have a Handler. An attachment so powerful, that even in their darkest hour their love for that one person can lead them home. Kayn's obvious choice for a Handler was altered and we've been forced to improvise. I believe this will work. Have faith that this trio will be victorious. They may be a little slow in the catching on department, but if everything goes as planned, our Oracle assures us they will survive this."

For Lexy, Jenna's premonitions had always rung true. After a few more minutes of conversation, Azariah asked them to join hands. As the sun set once again with symbolic timing, the sky above exploded with crimson light. The four did as ordered. Their bodies violently lurched with necks and spines bent backwards as they were launched into oblivion. This only caused momentary discomfort. They squeezed their eyes shut in the blinding strobing lights, followed by the sensation of being confined within their rose quartz healing tombs. They spiraled the all too familiar stomach-churning descent back to the land of the living. When the strobing lights ceased so did the spinning and for a moment everything was still....

Chapter 6

Shameless

This was the moment where Lexy always took a deep breath and awaited the sound of grinding stone on stone as the tombs opened. Her tomb shifted to the side and she smiled. The second the scrapping started Lexy began to guess who would be waiting on the other side. *Would it be Orin or Arrianna?* When Arrianna's head popped into view, she smiled at her and climbed out of her rose quartz healing tomb. Arrianna appeared to be the only other member of their Clan present to welcome them back to the land of the living.

Grey's voice piped in, "Well, hello there gorgeous. Aren't you an enchanting breath of fresh air."

And her shamelessly flirtatious Handler was also back. There was a time when talk like this directed at Arrianna would have upset her but she knew her best friend was more than happy in her relationship with Markus.

Arrianna directed her question at her, "All three Clans are waiting out the Testing at the same motel downtown. It's relaxing as long as you stay away from the pub downstairs. Triad's been there for the last couple of nights."

Lexy smiled at Arrianna. *She was warning her without directing the statement towards her. Tiberius would be a horrible idea with any serious intentions involved, but an extremely effective distraction.* She glanced back to make sure her Handler hadn't read her thoughts. *He wasn't even paying attention.* Lexy smiled as she strolled ahead in the dimly lit Crypt they'd returned to after delivering the three to their dark destinies.

The group rather nonchalantly left the Crypt and wandered out into fresh air. Grey continued to chat with Arrianna as they made their way down the trail. Lexy watched and couldn't help but smile at the sight of them strolling side by side. *The three of them had been inseparable before they went into the Testing and for many years after, but that was so long ago now. Time had changed them all, it altered the way she looked at everything and everyone, but not the two of them. They had come into this new world and proven themselves to be survivors in the Testing together. Perhaps, the three that went into the Testing would feel the same way about each other forty years down the road?*

Arrianna's voice sounded like music to her ears as she announced, "Your bags are in the back of the truck. I bet you're all dying for a hot shower and room service."

Right now, room service and a nice long rest in a bed with a mattress sounded glorious. Then perhaps, she'd go and check out that pub downstairs. Lexy exhaled as she climbed into the truck beside Grey and tried to stifle thoughts of the person her Handler didn't want to hear any inner commentary about. Lexy glanced at Grey and smiled innocently when he looked back at her. She sat in silence, listening to the conversation the others were having. A fly on the wall to their conversation as she battled intrusive naughty thoughts of her evil nemesis each time they slipped into her mind. They pulled into the parking lot at the hotel. Grey climbed into the back of the truck and started chucking bags out to each person. Arrianna asked them to come to her room. They all followed her into the elevator. *Markus probably had their room keys.* The elevator opened, they strolled down the hall until Arrianna stopped, knocked on a door and it opened to their makeshift leader's smiling face.

Arrianna strolled into the room, stood at the side of her boyfriend and said, "Will we see you at dinner? If you guys are feeling up to it, text me and I'll tell you where we are."

"I'm sure you guys are all dying to get some rest." Markus announced as he chucked a room key directly at Grey and added, "Here's the key to your room. There isn't a copy. I was only given one. You two will have to work that out if you split up later on and end up doing separate things. See you at dinner." Before he shut the door, he added, "Frost, if you're ordering lunch, the beef dip is all fatty and it kind of sucks but the burgers are amazing."

Frost strolled back towards the room carrying on a conversation with Markus as they walked away.

Lily paused in front of a door a couple of rooms down and called after them, "See you guys at dinner," and she went inside.

Lexy and Grey got into the elevator. Their room was one floor down. It always went without saying that they'd be sharing a room.

As they waited for the elevator," Grey commented, "They brought up beef dip. Now, I want one."

She smiled at him as they stepped into the elevator and suggested, "We can just order one from somewhere else."

Just as the elevator started to slide shut, Frost's voice called out, "Hold the door!"

Lexy held the doors open until he made it there. The doors slid closed in silence. They stepped out one floor down. Frost stayed behind.

He spoke just as the doors started to close, "See you later. Get some rest."

They strolled down the hall until they found the number on their key. Grey unlocked the door and held it open for her. Lexy strolled in and tossed her bag on the bed. Grey crawled under the covers, grabbed the remote and started listing off the pay per view movies. *It was the middle of the afternoon on a beautiful day, but he had the right idea. A long stay in the in-between always left them feeling drained.* Her stomach grumbled. Lexy suggested, "Let's order lunch, I'm starving."

Grey smiled and sighed, "I could eat a beef dip. I don't usually order those but it sounded good. Well, not from this hotel's restaurant after Markus' review, of course."

Lexy grabbed the pile of takeout menus, slipped under the covers beside him and teased, "It sounded good to me too. It's the power of suggestion."

They bickered over where they should order from and once the feat was accomplished, they bartered over which movie they were going to watch. He won by saying he'd massage her back until their order arrived. *Grey wanted to watch a romantic movie. She preferred horror. They were a different pair.* Lexy moved her hair aside and taunted, "Start on the left side my minion." Grey chuckled, obediently kneading her weary muscles with his magical hands. *He was stoked to watch the Notebook for the tenth time and didn't care if he had to win the argument with bribery. She didn't care if he won. He was going to fall asleep as soon as he finished his lunch and she'd be able to watch whatever she wanted. They would be in G-rated territory now for at least a couple of weeks with his memory freshly wiped.* She sighed as he kneaded her shoulders and scolded herself as the urge to take his hands and put them elsewhere popped into her mind. There was a perfectly timed knock on the door as their meal arrived. They ate watching a sentimental movie and once their garbage was cleaned up, they snuggled under the covers together to watch the ending.

He inhaled the scent of her hair and whispered, "Your hair still smells like the flowers from that bath." He cuddled up to her and mumbled, "I just think you can do way better than him."

Unable to help herself, she softly baited, "Who do you think I should be with?"

Snuggling her, he chuckled, "It can't be me that would be creepy, wouldn't it? Could you imagine the drama that would cause?"

He could hear her thoughts but couldn't see the eye roll that comment caused. Lexy turned around to give him the stink eye and he was out cold. *Of course, he was...*

She remained in his arms, unable to sleep after that last comment. Once again, he hadn't meant to hurt her, but he'd given her the equivalent of a gut punch. *He'd just made up her mind for her. It was time to find that distraction. First things, first.* She snuck out of bed and tiptoed across the beige industrial carpet into the bathroom to brush her teeth and fix herself up. Lexy applied her red lipstick, stared at her reflection for a moment and then glanced back at her Handler's peacefully sleeping form. *She couldn't allow herself to feel guilty. He wouldn't. No, she couldn't keep doing this with him. She had to get on with her life. Forty years loving someone that forgot each time they slept together was more than enough.* She crept past her sleeping Handler, snatched the keys off the counter and winced as they jingled and he stirred. Lexy remained frozen in place until she was sure she hadn't woken him up, and then grabbed for the bag she'd kicked off the bed. She always packed a pair of sexy heels because kickass shoes were her only girly obsession. Lexy snuck out the door barefoot with her heels in one of her hands without making a sound. She darted down the hall to the elevator, slipping on her heels before pressing the button. *The door opened immediately like it had been sitting there waiting for her to make naughty choices.* She stepped into the mirrored elevator with the sound of clicking heels and glanced at her reflection as she pressed the button for the lobby. *She was having a good everything day.* Her perfectly waved crimson locks were just a little longer than she usually allowed it to grow. Her lips a brilliant shade of red against her ivory ever so slightly freckled face. She wore jeans and a fitted black tank top, dressed up by red heels. Lexy usually didn't care about these things but she was on a mission this evening. *She was looking for trouble.* She arrived at the empty lobby and strolled out of the sliding doors with her heels clicking on the pavement as she descended cement stairs to the pub. As she entered, she noticed the brightly painted parrot on the window divider. *Now, the name of the pub made sense.* All eyes turned to her and her breath caught in her chest as her eyes met with her diabolically naughty companion from the Summit. Tiberius, otherwise referred to as Trouble with a capitol T, appeared to be equally affected by her presence as their eyes locked. He smiled at her. Frost called her name and signalled her over to their table. *Shit.* Lexy walked over to Ankh's table and sat down.

Frost slid his beer towards her and said, "I'll go and get another one." He grinned at her, leaned over and added, "I'm surprised Grey let you out of his sight. After you took off at the Summit and didn't know where you were, he was a hot mess. Did I already tell you this? I honestly can't remember now."

Frost was already drunk. She took a sip of the beer and innocently glanced up and replied, "He's having a nap. I decided to let him sleep."

Just then, the waitress magically appeared with another drink and passed it to Frost. He beamed and chuckled, "I've compelled her to bring me a refill, whenever she notices my hand is empty." Frost grinned, raised his glass in the air and toasted, "To the badass of the Summit." They clinked their glasses.

He leaned in again and whispered, "Why don't you just go over there? I know you want to. I won't tell."

She took another sip from her glass and felt out the situation, "Where is everyone else?"

Frost smiled at her and replied, "They went out for something to eat. I wasn't in the mood for a crowd."

Lexy knew who he was thinking about. "She's stronger than you think."

Staring into his glass, Frost responded, "I know. I still plan to drown my sorrows until she makes it back out of there."

Drinking her beer, Lexy glanced across the room towards Tiberius and their gaze locked. *He'd be a seriously messed up distraction, but it would be fun.* Her pulse raced as visions of their twisted time together at the Summit flickered through her mind. *The fact that they'd always despised each other made the situation even more titillating.* She licked her bottom lip and bit it without thinking about the visual cues she was giving him. *It was going to be difficult to act like she didn't want him every time the two Clans ran into each other. Maybe, if she just did this, the sense of urgency would go away.* Lexy turned away as Frost cleared his throat. *He was grinning at her.*

Frost shook his head and teased, "You know, all of this sexual tension makes it painfully obvious. You can talk about it with me. I promise it won't go any further."

She knew it wouldn't. She also knew he was the one to talk to about these things. Lexy gazed into the glass of amber liquid as she replied, "Sometimes, fighting turns me on and there was this pull between us afterwards that made me feel like doing something reckless. It was like he understood that about me. I don't know, I can't really explain it."

Frost whispered, "Believe it or not I understand. That's how I felt around Chloe. That's why I moved so fast. Well, one of the reasons. There was also she who will not be named."

Lexy chuckled and ribbed, "You know Harry Potter references will get you everywhere with Kayn." She felt his presence before looking up. *Sure enough, Tiberius was standing beside the table.*

He held out his hand, looked into her eyes and asserted, "Come talk to me for a minute? I promise I'll behave."

Everything about him turned her on, from the way he carried himself, to his devious, penetrating, chocolate brown eyes. *She didn't want him to behave.* Lexy glanced at Frost and enquired, "Are you going to be alright?"

He grinned and chuckled, "Get out of here, Lex. If anyone deserves sixty seconds of gratuitous fun, it's you."

Tiberius laughed and provoked, "That's you not me brother, I can do better than sixty seconds. Tonight, I'm just looking to finish a conversation."

Lexy knit her brow at his extended hand and stated, "I'm not holding your hand, but I'll speak to you."

Tiberius started to laugh. Raising his hands to signal his surrender, he backed out of her way as she got up. Grinning, Tiberius sparred, "Always the Dragon," as he walked away. She followed him through the pub, they passed the growing herd of patrons. *Where was he taking her?* He shoved open a side door with an exit sign and held it open for her as she stepped out into the cement stairwell of what was obviously the fire escape. He closed the door behind her and they were alone. Tiberius didn't wait for her to speak nor did he make an awkward attempt at conversation. *They both knew why they were here.* He took a couple of steps towards her and she stepped back, finding herself flush against the cement wall behind her.

He whispered seductively, "I'm surprised you came out here with me. Where's your Handler?"

"He's having a nap," she replied.

Tiberius grinned at her, bit his lip and questioned, "And you came to find me, with those incredibly sexy heels, and that red lipstick, didn't you?"

She parted her lips with the perfect denial prepared, but instead, she opted for the truth, "Maybe, I did."

Grinning, he placed his hand against the wall behind her, leaned in and whispered in her ear, "All I can think about is what you looked like stretched out on that table. The way that you gasped when I cut you and the expression on your face while you were healing. It's messing with a mind a little bit." *Heaven help her, she wanted him in a crazy way.* She'd blocked his advances out of instinct, her hands were against his chest. She boldly slid them down to the button of his jeans, calling his bluff by undoing it.

Surprised by her forward behaviour, Tiberius pulled away and looked into her eyes. He groaned, leaned back in and chuckled, "You're a naughty girl, Lexy Abrelle. Are you trying to get us arrested? You know I want you bad enough to take you right here."

Where she would have frozen and bolted at the mere mention of her birth name before the Summit, she let it slide, knowing he knew everything about her now. Her blood rushed through her veins as she huskily provoked, "Then do it." His expression darkened as he closed the space between them. Her lips parted as their mouths met and his tongue darted against hers, causing her pulse to race uncontrollably. Naughty to his core, he changed the game on Lexy by unzipping her jeans and slipping his hand underneath the lacy material of her underwear. She gasped as he began caressing her. *Well, this escalated quickly. She was so turned on, she didn't care where they were, or who might catch them.* Nibbling on her neck, he bit her hard to trigger her healing ability intensifying the gratification as he sped up his rhythmic strokes. He muffled her whimpers of pleasure with his hand. *This turned her on even more.* She cried out as an explosion of blinding hedonistic bliss overcame her. He held her against the wall to keep her from falling as her knees buckled.

Tiberius seductively whispered, "Good girl," into her ear and she shivered again. She cupped her hand over his rigid manhood, undid his zipper and slid her hand under the waist band of his underwear. Her eyes widened as she discovered his size. *He was ready for her and enormous.*

He placed his hand over hers and said, "We're not doing this here. I want to take my time with you. I've been waiting too long for this. I don't want to half ass it in a stairwell."

He'd waited too long for this? Was it possible that he'd really been wanting her for all of these years?

Tiberius grinned at her inner commentary, adjusted his painfully erect package and scolded, "Don't pretend you didn't know. I've been hot for you since you were that Wild Thing that tied me up and teased me mercilessly in the woods." Looking into her eyes for a minute, taking in her confusion, he probed, "You really didn't know, did you?"

Her senses were still humming from what he'd done to her as she responded, "You've always acted like you hated me."

Grinning at her, Tiberius confessed, "Well, a certain amount of it was wounded ego. You chose Grey over me. Don't you remember doing that?"

All of that animosity had been to hide the fact that she'd hurt his feelings? Lexy looked into his eyes and disclosed, "I wasn't capable of making choices based on things like who I wanted more back then. I didn't think like that. I chose Grey because something about him made me feel safe."

"I understand the situation a little more after what I saw during the Summit. I didn't know. I just couldn't explain this thing I've always had for you. I know logically we can't ever be together, but I've always wanted you. I honestly thought you knew."

His ridiculous behaviour for all of these years actually made sense now. She was about to speak when the door opened.

Frost stuck his head out and declared, "Grey just texted me, asking if you were with me and I said you were. He's probably on his way down here. So, unless you want to explain this moment you're having, you might want to dash into the bathroom and fix yourself up before he gets down here."

Lexy nodded at him, grateful for the warning and said, "Thanks, I'll do that." Frost grinned as he closed the door without saying anything else.

With a roguish smile, Tiberius teased, "I feel like the other man, Handlers can be such a pain in the ass. I'll sneak away up these stairs. If he sees me in this condition, it's going to cause you a shitload of drama." He took off, stopped halfway and baited, "You know I'm not done with you right?"

She wasn't done with him either. She smiled as Tiberius grinned, turned and dashed up the rest of the stairs. Lexy watched him until he vanished at the top and straightened herself up without a mirror just in case Grey was already there. *That was so hot, it was crazy.* She wiped away the blood on her neck with her black top. *He'd bit her so hard she'd bled.* Both shocked and impressed with herself, Lexy covered her mouth with her hand. *There was probably lipstick all over her face and her underwear were uncomfortably damp. For good reason. He knew how to mix pleasure with pain and take a Healer to the brink of euphoria. They hadn't gone all the way but she wasn't sure she was going to be able to walk in these heels after that. Her darkly twisted nemesis had blown her mind with that experience.*

Taking a deep breath, Lexy removed her heels and composed herself as she walked back into the pub. *He wasn't there yet.* She made her way through the packed pub and darted into the washroom. Smiling, she looked at her flushed face and rosy cheeks in the mirror. *She'd done a half-decent job of tidying herself up outside without a mirror.* There was still a smudge of blood on her neck. Lexy wet down a piece of paper towel and wiped it off. She washed her hands. The thought of what he'd just done to her made her legs tremble. *Pull yourself together.* She put on a fresh coat of lipstick and decided it'd be best if she went commando.

Lexy slipped into a stall, removed the evidence of her tryst and tossed them into the trash. *It felt like she was cheating.* She leaned against the sink and calmed herself down. *She was only cheating on herself. Grey had no idea that their relationship had ever gone further than just friends.* Looking at her reflection, she affirmed, "You're moving on and this is what you need to do for yourself." She took another deep breath and left the bathroom. *He wasn't at the table yet. This was good she'd just be sitting here with Frost when he arrived.* She sat in the chair directly across from Frost. He pointed at the full drink in front of her. *It wasn't beer.* She knit her brow, picked it up and smelled it. *It was whisky.*

Frost grinned and teased, "I thought you might be in the mood for a stiff one."

She smirked, raised her glass into the air in a mock salute and sparred, "That's right, get it all out of your system before Grey gets back."

"Well, you were gone for longer than sixty seconds. So, maybe it was worth it." He chuckled and took a drink from his glass.

Lexy grinned and sighed, "Anything else? I'm sure you can do better than that."

"I bet there were cameras out there," he casually stated.

That one hit its mark. She glanced up and nonchalantly remarked, "If someone posts anything about any of us the Aries Group will make it disappear, won't they?" *Now, she was going to have to go and check for cameras.* "I didn't have sex with him." *That was the truth...sort of. I guess it would depend on your definition of the word. Frost was managing to keep a straight face. That was good.*

He assured her, "You never have to explain yourself to me, Lexy. If anyone understands your situation with Grey, it's me."

With monumentally perfect timing, her Handler strolled in and waved at them as Frost chuckled and commented, "Don't worry about it. He's not going to be worrying about how he's making you feel while he's bedding some random girl."

This was true.

Grey slid into the seat next to her and questioned, "Where is everybody? I thought this place would be packed." A chesty waitress with a low-cut top came and took his drink order. He watched her stroll away from their table, not so inconspicuously leering. He mouthed the words, "She's adorable."

Her guilt instantly evaporated. She shook her head and took a swig from her glass of whisky.

Grey chuckled, "Whisky Lexy…Really? Are we having one of those go hard or go home nights?"

Frost choked on his gulp of whisky and was forced to cover his mouth so he didn't spit it all over the table.

That was funny. Lexy pressed her lips together to stop herself from joining in but watching Frost's attempt to reign in his laughter forced her to look away as she started to laugh. She quickly regained control over her innuendo induced case of the giggles and pulled herself together. She turned around and far too casually responded, "Yes, I guess it is."

Frost was practically tearing up as Grey scolded, "Alright, either I'm totally missing something here or you two are already bombed."

Lifting his glass into the air, Frost saved the day by saying, "Guilty as charged."

Their scantily clad waitress appeared with Grey's beer and a bottle of what they were drinking. She offered them another and they agreed.

Grey piped in, "Let me down this beer. I'll have what they're having. I won't be able to understand what they're talking about if I'm the only sober one." She started to walk away and he accidentally spilled his full beer. She rushed to get a dry cloth for the mess and leaned across the table to clean it up as Grey apologized profusely. *Oh, he'd totally spilled that on purpose.* Lexy took a good look at her flirtatious Handler and smiled. *You can always trust people to be exactly who they are.*

Before the pretty waitress left the table, Grey playfully enquired, "Can I ask you for one more thing?"

She paused, smiled at him and replied, "Yes?"

He seductively asked, "Do you have a pen I can borrow for a second? I promise I won't walk away with it."

The pretty, impressively busty waitress smiled at him and said, "Sure, I'll be right back."

Oh, she'd watched him pull this one at least a dozen times. Lexy took another giant gulp of whisky. *To hell with savouring it, she just needed her mind numb.*

The waitress returned with the pen and handed it to Grey. He asked her to wait for a second and she could have it right back. Lexy watched him jot down his number on a coaster along with an impressively ballsy little note, 'I'm in town for a few days, text me if you want to hook up.' He passed her the coaster along with the pen and gave her a charming smile as she shook her head, grinned and walked away.

They'd been sitting there for all of ten minutes when Grey's phone vibrated. Grinning, he took it out of his pocket to read the text. He shot their room key across the table and announced, "Don't bother to wait up, Lex." Grey stood up and waved as he wandered up to the bar, told them his drinks were on Frost's tab and strolled out of the pub.

It stung less than it usually did because she'd found her own distraction that evening. She'd honestly thought there was no way Tiberius could top the depravity of that moment they'd shared during halftime at the Summit, but now she knew what he was capable of. She tingled every time she thought about it. She glanced up at Frost. *He probably thought she was upset about Grey.* Lexy stared into her empty glass and brought the conversation back to normal as she questioned, "How in the hell does that pickup line always work?"

Frost placed his glass on the table and complained, "I just want to know why everyone thinks I'm worse than he is?"

"He's usually stealth about it. I guess he figured it was all good because it was only us in here," Lexy responded. *He wasn't coming back tonight.*

"I bet it wouldn't be difficult to figure out which room Tiberius is in?" Frost provoked as he signalled the new server over to order another drink.

He didn't really want her to go anywhere. She knew what he was doing. He was distracting himself too. Lexy ordered another one for herself and declared, "I think I'll stick around if you don't mind?"

Frost smiled at her and replied, "Not at all."

This was where it was handy to be a Dragon. She was content to sit in silence and not discuss the mushy things like love and loss. He didn't really want to talk about it. Frost just needed somebody to be there and truth be told, so did she. If she drank enough maybe, she wouldn't spend the whole night obsessing over what she'd just done with Tiberius. The new server placed their drinks on the table. Lexy grabbed hers, clutched it in both hands and looked at Frost. *Was she supposed to say something to make him feel better? Sometimes, she still missed social cues.*

He laughed and responded to her thoughts, "I appreciate the sentiment but what are you supposed to say? Gee Frost, I sure hope Kevin finds the balls to brutally murder Kayn in the Testing. I hope she doesn't find out you set it all up and hate your guts forever."

Yes. That was a little dark. Grinning, she pointed out her messed up circumstances, "Well, you could just have a laugh over my situation. I slept with my Handler and he forgot about it as always. So, I tried to make myself feel better by messing around with your diabolically evil brother. I was forced to cut an undeniably hot situation short because Grey was coming. As you well know, the whole subject of Tiberius is like poking a bear with a stick. He drives my option away, stays all of half an hour and takes off with our waitress."

Frost giggled as he recalled, "I almost peed myself when he said go hard or go home."

Lexy raised her glass in mock salute from one messed up situation to another and suggested, "After this one, we should try to get some sleep and try to forget this whole month ever happened."

Frost impishly grinned as he took another drink and agreed, "Now, that sounds like a plan."

After about five more drinks and another hour or two of Frost losing his filter and professing his love for Kayn eighty times in a row Lexy finally convinced him to leave. Frost attempted to stand. *He'd passed his ability to walk, long ago.* Lexy questioned, "Did you come straight here after we arrived?"

"Yes, as a matter of fact, I did," he proudly slurred.

"You just sat across the room from your brother and gave him dirty looks all day, didn't you?" Lexy ribbed as she steadied him and they attempted to make their way out of the bar together. *She was far to inebriated to help him. They were going to wake up in a gutter somewhere.*

He incoherently mumbled, "Thank you, Sexy Lexy. You are a wonderful person. I like your hair."

Oh, lovely. I guess if she had to get stuck with a drunk nickname, he could have come up with something a hell of a lot worse than, Sexy Lexy. She chuckled, "You're welcome, Frost. You have nice hair too." As Lexy struggled to get him up the stairs, she questioned, "What's your room number?"

He playfully pinched her side and murmured, "I don't know. What is it?"

Shit. Lexy checked his jacket pockets. He had nothing but his cell and wallet. She sighed, "Well, I guess you're coming to my room."

His head bopped up as he questioned, "Really?"

Now, that was funny. Laughing as she struggled to keep him moving, she clarified, "As my friend, you goof."

She leaned him against the door, as she unlocked it, and then led him inside. Lexy walked him over to the bed and he passed out cold the second his head hit the pillow. She stumbled into the bathroom, drank a bunch of water because she wasn't a complete idiot and wobbled her way back to the bed. Lexy yarded the covers out from under Frost's body because he was dead to the world. *Not being able to move as she slept, drove her nuts.* She tucked him in and slid under the covers beside him. Something poked her in the stomach. *It was her heels. She'd tucked them into her jeans.* Lexy tossed them across the room and dropped into a deep thoughtless sleep.

Chapter 7

Awkward Awakenings

Lexy stirred to the comforting sensation of being cuddled. Without opening her eyes, she smiled lethargically and snuggled against the person, she assumed was Grey. *What time was it?* She opened her eyes and they focused in on the arm draped around her. *It had black hair on it. Oh Shit. What had she done?* Lexy was afraid to move because she didn't want to awaken her bedmate. *She was drawing a blank on the night before. Well, most of it. The naughty events in the stairwell sprung to mind. Holy Shit! Had she slept with Tiberius? Oh, crap! Grey would be looking for her. He'd probably be freaking out by now. She had to get her shit together and think.* She looked around. *It appeared to be the room she'd been sharing with Grey. Maybe, the rooms all looked the same?* She tried shimmying her way out from underneath what she thought was Tiberius' arm, he hugged her tighter. *Shit, she was just going to have to talk to him.* Lexy winced, cleared her throat and whispered, "We should wake up before Grey catches us." Frost's voice mumbled her name and told her to go back to sleep. *What in the hell? How was she with Frost?* She struggled her way out of his arms as he clicked into where he was and leapt away from her. They stared at each other with alarmed expressions on their faces.

He looked around and stammered, "Did we? Are you in my room or am I in yours?"

Lexy pressed her lips together, exhaled and admitted, "I have no idea." *He still had his shirt on.* She looked down at her chest and felt her jeans under the covers and released a sigh of relief. *Oh, thank God.* She pointed at him and ordered, "Look under the covers, are you wearing pants?"

He did, exhaled deeply and replied, "Yes, I'm wearing pants. We must have just passed out here together."

That made sense because they both reeked of whisky.

Frost got out of bed, wandered to the bathroom and announced, "This is your room, my stuff isn't in here."

She heard the shower turn on and her drinking partner from the night before had the fastest shower ever. *That scared the crap out of her and she wasn't afraid of much.*

He came out with a towel around his waist and asked, "Where's Grey? I'm starving, we should go for breakfast."

Lexy was still sitting there trying to chill herself out. *How had they ended up in the same bed? Where in the hell was Grey?* She disclosed, "You're going to have to give me a minute to regain my faculties. When I saw the black hair on your arm, I had a moment there."

Frost leapt back onto the bed beside her and chuckled, "You thought you were waking up next to Tiberius, didn't you?"

"Until you spoke, yes, I did," she confessed, giggling quietly to herself. *Oh, the relief.* She covered her forehead with her hands, sighed and laughed, "That scared the shit out of me."

Grinning, he wittily bantered, "Now, what does that tell you? Glad I could provide you with a dry run for how you'd feel the morning after doing that."

Doing that. Lexy got up and stated, "Yes, it doesn't seem like the greatest idea anymore. I'll be right back." She escaped into the bathroom, closed the door behind her and just stood there for a second, staring at the painting in front of her on the wall. It was of two wolves standing side by side in the backdrop of a snow-covered mountain. She recalled the day she met Grey. *He'd been taken by Triad, she saved him from what he'd referred to as a fate worse than death. She'd spoken to Tiberius for the first time that day in the forest while she was still a Wild Thing and when she thought about what she did to him, it made her smile. She hadn't been in the frame of mind to even notice he was flirting with her. He'd held onto that moment for all these years and she'd barely given it a second thought.* Drawing her eyes from the painting of wolves that caused her thoughts to drift to Tiberius, Lexy stepped into the shower. She quickly soaped herself down, rinsed off and towel-dried her hair, choosing to leave it damp. After a quick makeup job, she carefully applied her favourite crimson lipstick and stared at her reflection. *She was probably going to opt out of following through with that tryst with Tiberius after her reaction that morning, but that didn't mean she didn't want to look gorgeous the next time they bumped into each other. The chances of that would be pretty damn high over the next couple of days.*

Frost bellowed, "I used some of your toothpaste. Don't worry, I didn't touch your toothbrush."

Someone knocked on the door and Lexy hurried in the bathroom. She leaned out and said, "Can you get that? It's probably Grey." Frost leapt up and got the door.

Grey's voice remarked, "You guys, it smells absolutely disgusting in here."

"We're going for breakfast," she called out. "I'll just be a second." Lexy paused before opening the bathroom door, hoping Frost had the sense to quickly put his clothes back on. She walked out to the sight of Grey opening windows, cursing about the scent of the whisky.

Grey passed Frost keys and asked, "Are these yours?"

"Well, at least we know how I ended up sleeping here now," Frost laughed, shaking his head.

Grey knit his brow and clarified, "You slept here?"

Lexy questioned, "Where did you end up?"

Her Handler smiled and changed the subject, "How long did you guys stay there after I left?"

She shrugged and replied, "I honestly have no idea. All I know is we woke up in bed together, fully clothed."

Ruffling her hair, Grey chuckled, "Don't worry, honey, I know that would never happen. Frost would never do that to me."

Frost's eyes widened as he steered the conversation back and enquired, "Where were you again?"

He grinned and responded, "A gentleman never tells."

She was still stuck on his statement. *Frost would never do that to me.*

They left the room. Grey was walking ahead as Frost placed his arm around her and whispered, "If I wasn't all hung up on someone else, I would totally do that to him." He gave her a playful squeeze and she laughed.

Grey turned and chuckled, "You're such a jackass. I heard that."

She wasn't about to knit pick about Grey's choice of nighttime activities while having hot and steamy flashbacks of her own. They descended the stairs hungover and uncoordinated. As they entered the diner, there was a table of well-behaved Ankh in the corner. Lexy's eyes didn't narrow in on that table. Her eyes noticed the booth full of Triad she'd have to pass along the way. *The table of Triad, with an absent Tiberius.* From their blank expressions, she knew Tiberius hadn't uttered a word about what happened. She touched Grey's arm and asked, "Order for me, I need to use the washroom."

He smiled at her and replied, "I know what you want."

She knew he didn't mean it the way she'd taken it. As Lexy walked away, she glanced back and Grey was seated at the table conversing with their friends. *Sometimes, it was difficult to adjust her mindset. For heaven's sake Lexy, you were with Tiberius and Grey seduced and slept with a random waitress last night. Get a hold of yourself.* She gave the bathroom door a good shove. *It was locked.* She tried the family bathroom and it opened. *She felt someone's presence.*

Tiberius shoved her in, closed the door and explained, "I have to leave. I just wanted to make sure we had an opportunity for a proper goodbye."

Smiling at her naughty frenemy, Lexy whispered, "Both of our Clans are out there."

"I'm aware," Tiberius whispered, without making a move. He remained in front of the exit, blocking her escape as his eyes travelled up the length of her legs to the zipper of her jeans that he'd undone the evening before. Trouble bit his lip and flirted, "I was disappointed you didn't come looking for me last night."

She'd wanted too. His flirtations were flattering now, they never had been before. Remaining across the room, versus closing the space only made her long for more of what he'd given her last night. Her eyes were drawn to the bulge in his jeans. Smiling, she exhaled and quietly cautioned, "They'll come looking for us and find us in here together."

Tiberius locked the door and tempted, "Is that better?"

Lexy wanted him in a crazy way, but she couldn't take that step after her reaction that morning. She looked into his eyes and stated, "We can't."

Grinning at her, he teased, "What happened between last night and this morning that changed your mind?"

Meeting his intense gaze, she gave him a version of the truth, "I woke up with a change of heart."

"It's not your heart I'm interested in, change it all you want," he sparred, with a flirtatious grin.

"I'll never love you," she asserted.

He grinned, stepped closer, intimately tucked a wild strand of crimson hair behind her ear and teased, "I'll never love you either."

Why had he tucked her hair behind her ear? That was Grey's move. Had he stolen that from her memories thinking it would draw her closer? Instead, it made her think of Grey. She loved Grey but this wasn't about love. They were playing a titillating game that would only lead to one thing. The undeniably dark union of two Dragons.

Tracing a path with his finger on her throat to where he'd drawn blood the night before, he provoked, "It's not fair to deny me after I've given you what you needed."

Her pulse raced as she smiled and taunted, "Who said the afterlife was fair?"

Tiberius chuckled as he rather abruptly turned around, opened the door and said, "Triad's out of the Testing. I'll see you at their banquet if Ankh makes it out. Save a dance for me."

"I'm never going to dance with you," Lexy called after him.

Tiberius confidently stated, "Yes, you will." As the door shut behind him.

She leaned against the dated, mint green linoleum counter, knowing he was right. *The counter was wet. Shit, of course.* She wanted to just walk out there and tell her Clan Triad made it out but needed to wait until he was gone. *Triad was out.* Lexy smiled. *She'd liked Kevin, she was glad he'd made it, but she also knew only two Clans could make it out. If Ankh wasn't fast, Trinity might beat them and then it wouldn't matter who was a Dragon. They would be lost in there…forever. Grey was probably going to come in there looking for her soon.* She pulled herself together and walked out. As she strolled to their table, all eyes were on her.

Lily looked directly at her and grilled, "Triad just left. Do you know why?"

Shit. By the expressions on everyone's faces, they'd seen Tiberius come out of the bathroom she'd gone into. Opting to rip the band-aid off, Lexy answered, "Tiberius just told me Triad made it out of the Testing." Frost's face sunk, he started picking at his meal with his fork. *The odds of Ankh's survival had been altered.* She sat down in front of the plate without an owner, and when she went to thank Grey, he wouldn't look at her. She attempted to touch his arm and he yanked it away. *Oh, she was sick to death of these double standards.* Lexy left her meal, without taking a bite, stood up and blurted, "You know what Greydon, this jealousy crap is getting old. You get to sleep with any random girl but I have a conversation with someone and you blow a gasket."

Looking at her, he scoffed, "Tiberius isn't just some random guy. The thought of him touching you and you climbing into the same bed as me, makes my skin crawl."

They'd beaten this subject to death. She hissed, "Do you think a random girl hurts me any less than the bloody thought of Tiberius touching me hurts you?" *She was either going to punch him or throw something at him.* Lexy picked up a full glass of orange juice and tossed it directly into his face, stormed away and left him sitting there shocked with sticky juice dripping down his face.

Fuming, he got up and marched after her. Frost glanced at Lily and remarked, "It's time you got with the program. You go get Lexy and I'll talk to Grey." They dashed away from the table leaving Arrianna and Orin sitting alone.

Orin whispered, "Does this mean we get to eat their bacon?"

Arrianna snagged a piece from Grey's plate, shrugged and replied, "We might as well, they won't be back." She popped it into her mouth. They both giggled and continued eating.

Frost caught up with Grey before he reached Lexy, snagged his arm, aggressively held him in place and stated, "We need to have a chat."

Scowling, Grey responded, "She threw a glass of juice at me."

"You deserved it," Frost coldly countered.

"How's that?" Grey questioned.

Keeping a grip on his stubborn friend's arm, Frost whispered, "You don't even know why you're this angry, do you? Come with me." They walked into the centre of the parking lot. Once they were out of earshot, Frost accused, "I'm tired of watching this bullshit. So, I'm going to break the rules and let you in on what's really going on. You're going to feel like the most epic piece of shit in the damn universe, my friend."

Greydon's gaze softened a touch as he spoke, "I thought we'd already talked this out. He's your brother and even you despise him. He held me captive and tortured me for bloody days. She's supposed to be on my side. I'm her damn Handler. My whole afterlife has been dedicated to her. You'd think if she knew something bothered me that much, she'd make a different choice."

Frost shook his head, clutched his friend's shoulders and asserted, "He probably accosted her while she was in the bathroom with the sole purpose of messing with her by telling her Triad made it out. What do you think they were doing in a public bathroom for ten minutes? Will you get a hold of yourself and think rationally?"

A lightbulb lit above Grey's head, he whispered, "What in the hell is wrong with me?"

"Would you like me to tell you?" Frost questioned, squeezing his friend's shoulders. Grey nodded and Frost stipulated, "You have to promise you won't tell her I told you."

Grey took a deep breath and sighed, "Just tell me. It can't be worse than where my thoughts have been taking me."

Smiling at Grey's irritating one-track mind, Frost began his explanation, "When a Handler sleeps with a Dragon all memories of the event are erased as he sleeps." Grey shrugged like he had no idea how that sentence would apply to him and Frost continued, "You're in love with Lexy. You've been sleeping together for a long time. I have

a feeling it's been going on for twenty or thirty years. Every morning you forget and most of the time, you hook up with someone before she's even had a chance to breathe. You've been gutting this girl that worships the ground you walk on for decades. I'm not sure how you keep remembering how you feel about her, but you do. You remember you're in love with her and judging by the fact that you don't know you're in love with her right now, she gives in to whatever you want. I've been in her shoes. I know how she feels. So, I'm asking you to be the one who consciously makes the decision to stop yourself from hurting her."

Soaking it all in, Grey replied, "But, I don't love her that way? What you're saying doesn't make sense?"

"My point is that in a few days, a week or even a month, you'll remember how you feel about her. I'm asking you to consciously allow her get on with her afterlife. You be the one who watches her with someone else and hurts. It's your turn. You owe her this. If she wants to get her freak on with my idiot brother so she can get on with her life, you owe her that. Think about how many times you've been with someone else and used her for an emotional crutch. How many times have you slept with someone else, slid into bed next to her and snuggled up with her? Do you think she didn't know? Do you think she wasn't dying inside?"

Sick to his stomach as he took in Frost's harsh but real words, Grey met Frost's eyes and confessed, "Sometimes I wake up in strange places or have no clothes on and I've always thought I was just partying too hard. Did it just happen while we were in the in-between?"

"Yes, I'm pretty sure it did. That's why she's drawn to Tiberius. She's probably willing to do anything she has to do to stop wanting you in that way. I know that's why I've always acted like I do with women." Frost admitted as someone unlocked their car and the beep startled them

both. They strolled out of the parking lot in silence and sat on a bench by the entrance to the motel.

"Well, congratulations, I feel like a piece of shit," Grey muttered. "Was she hurt last night when I took off with that waitress?"

Frost gave him a strategically worded response, "She was a little reckless last night, but I don't remember much. She obviously stuck around at the bar with me after you left and managed to get herself wasted enough to wake up in bed next to me. That speaks volumes about her mental state."

Searching Frost's eyes, Grey asked, "Are you sure you two didn't...?"

Frost grinned and assured, "We were fully clothed but that didn't stop either of us from having a complete jammer when we woke up in bed together." He reached over, gave Grey's shoulder a brotherly squeeze and said, "From this moment on, you have all of the information. You have to stand by her and allow her to make mistakes, she's allowed you to make plenty. She should be hooking up with people. Lexy has needs too."

Grey smirked, shook his head and divulged, "I thought she never dated anyone after Tomas."

Grinning, Frost questioned, "Does that seem rational when you say it out loud? I have a feeling it was only you. She's been in a one-sided relationship with you for longer than the span of most marriages. Don't you think she deserves to have fun? Lexy's an immortal. Gratuitous fun is the only upside to our situation."

"But Tiberius?" Grey sighed. "Why does it have to be him?"

"I'm sure she felt the same way about Arrianna, Lily, and Melody," Frost countered. "Think about that for a second. She had to bunk beside them and everything. Who gives a shit about Tiberius, honestly? That's never going to go anywhere. Now, Orin...if she ever gives in to his

tedious flirtations and you suddenly remember you're in love with her, that one is going to hurt. He's a great guy and it will be happening right in front of you."

"I'd rather it be Orin," Grey whispered under his breath.

"No, you don't," Frost chuckled. "Lily could sleep with as many damn strangers as she wanted but even after eight hundred years, you stung a bit. It was because as painfully stubborn as you are, you're a good guy. I'm asking you to go make up with Lexy and tell her you don't care who she is with as long as she's happy."

Grey was silent for a moment before saying, "If I ever start having those feelings for her again, I'll keep them to myself."

Grinning, Frost probed, "You're going to keep this conversation to yourself?"

"Of course," Grey replied with a nod.

"Good, let's go and find them," Frost remarked as they wandered back.

Huffing, puffing and seething with rage, Lexy stormed away from the diner. She made it all of way to the dog park on the far side of the parking lot before Lily caught up with her. *She'd never intended to share the heartbreaking details of their relationship with anyone but she'd already told Frost and she was livid so she spilled her guts.* They'd been sitting against a tree chatting for a long time, watching dogs and their owners playing fetch with balls and sticks when Frost and Grey found them.

Lily got up and announced, "Well, that's my cue. We'll leave the two of you alone to talk. I'll see you later, Hun."

Lexy peered up and found herself gazing directly into Grey's eyes. *He had an expression she couldn't place and she knew each one by heart.*

Frost raised his voice, "Heads up!" Lily dodged out of the way as an exuberant canine leapt directly at her chasing a ball. Frost's face split into a thoroughly entertained grin. *That was funny. The golden retriever's owner pitched the ball at Lily on purpose.* Lexy grinned and covered her mouth to stop herself from giggling. *It was a rather ingenious way to pick up a girl.*

"I thought you were going to end up on your back in the grass being slobbered on by that retriever," Frost laughed, not bothering to hide his reaction at all.

Scowling, Lily shoved him and accused, "You could have caught the ball and thrown it elsewhere."

As he maneuvered away, Frost chuckled, "And wreck that guy's game...never."

Clicking into what happened, Lily shook her head at the guy in his mid-twenties as the dog sprinted back to him with a tennis ball proudly gripped in his teeth. She playfully shoved Frost again as they wandered off.

After watching it all play out, Grey came over and asked, "Mind if I sit down?"

Her anger had been defused by her conversation with Lily and the young guy's rather inept dog park pick up attempt. Lexy patted the grass beside her and could tell by his expression, he was about to apologize. *She'd never been able to stay mad at him longer than five seconds.*

Grey sat down, leaned against the tree and started his apology tour, "I'm sorry, Lex. I was a complete shithead earlier."

Yes, you were. She smiled and replied, "I'm not sorry I threw a glass of juice at you."

He chuckled at her lack of apology and admitted, "I deserved it." She extended her hand. He comically warned, "I'm still sticky."

Lexy's eyes softened as she stated, "I don't care." *She didn't anymore.*

Lacing his fingers through hers, he confessed, "I really am sorry about what I said. I didn't mean it."

His eyes were full of questions as she yanked her hand away and laughed, "You are super sticky. Let's go back to the room and get you cleaned up."

As they started walking back, the tennis ball came sailing at her face. Lexy caught it in one hand and rifled it into the bushes like a damn superhero. Grey chuckled as the pick-up artist and his canine friend dashed towards the woods.

Grey's stomach grumbled loudly and he sighed, "I'm starving. We just left our breakfast there."

Lexy grinned and sparred, "Well, at least you got your orange juice."

He chuckled, placed his arm around her and pulled her in for a partial hug without breaking pace, teasing, "Funny, Lex."

"I try," she sparred as they made their way back to the room. *For a second she'd wondered if Frost told him everything, but he was acting normally again.*

Chapter 8

The Aries Intervention

They were about to cross the road when a black sedan cut them off. The passenger side window rolled down, there was a lady in a suit. Lexy recognized her. *She was with the Aries Group.* The lady smiled and said, "Hello, Lexy and Grey. My name is Agent Gingham. We have a few tests we'd like to run, while we're here cleaning up. Has Markus contacted you?" *Miss Gingham had her teeth whitened professionally. They were magnificent. Perhaps, it was the contrast with her gorgeous dark skin? She was seriously beautiful.* Lexy's eyes flitted to her own freckled arm and she crinkled up her face. She snapped back to the situation at hand when she realised everyone was patiently waiting for her to check her messages. She felt around in her pockets for her phone. *She'd felt it vibrating a while ago but assumed it was Grey and hadn't bothered to answer.* Lexy removed her cell from her pocket, and sure enough, the message light was flashing. She read it, glanced at Grey and replied, "I guess so." *It was the last thing she felt like doing right now, but she knew they were supposed to play nice with the Aries Group.* They both slid into the back of the obvious looking vehicle with tinted windows. *You'd think they'd at least use a variety of muted colours when every government vehicle on every show she'd ever seen was a black sedan with tinted windows just like this one?* Lexy sighed, "Isn't this vehicle a bit of a cliché?" Her comment was answered by laughter from the occupants of the front seat.

The driver, a middle-aged man with brown hair and sunglasses answered, "It is, isn't it?"

Yes, it totally was. Pedestrians on the sidewalk were noticing it and staring at the vehicle as it passed by.

Randomly, Grey questioned, "Does anyone have hand sanitizer? My hands are sticky."

The lovely Agent Gingham smiled and asked, "Tree sap from the park?"

"No, orange juice. It's a long story," Grey responded.

Agent Gingham flashed him another disarmingly kind smile as she passed a bottle back to him and replied, "Someday you'll have to tell it to me."

Grey washed his hands, handed it back and changed the subject, "So, what kind of tests are we doing this time?"

The agent with deep chocolate brown eyes peered into the backseat and disclosed, "We just need to update some data about how fast you heal and the strength of your abilities. We have a small mobile unit back at the campsite. The rest of Ankh will meet us there."

They drove past the college campus, scattered with students. *They were almost back at the campground.* Lexy had never been thrilled about guinea pig day. *At least they'd had the opportunity to make up before being ambushed by the Aries Group. She should have seen it coming though... they'd helped finance the banquet and usually stuck around afterwards to check in with each of the Clans. It was never a big deal.* Lexy gazed out the window as they turned down the gravel road to the campground. They continued travelling for a few minutes before turning down an alternate route with a sign in the shape of an arrow directing them to the rodeo grounds.

The Aries Group had to clean up for the Clans on a regular basis. In return, all that was required of them was the opportunity to document their abilities. Well, and a few supernatural policing jobs, but those were few and far between. They pulled up to the familiar rodeo grounds. *This place had always been special to her. She'd carved Kayn's name on the bleachers before they left for the Summit next to Tomas' on the bleachers. He'd been her first attempt at a relationship. She rarely allowed herself to think about him. Since then, it had only been Grey.* Lexy glanced at her Handler and wondered how much he remembered from the days preceding the Summit. *Their last trip to the bleachers had been erased by morning.* Lexy recalled her Handler's confessions of undying love and the night they'd spent wrapped in each other's arms, by the large tree at the edge of the grassy meadow that spanned the rustic stadium. She stared out of the window at the enclosed bleachers. *If Kayn was lost to the Testing, in less than five years, she would find herself back at this place, etching someone else's name into the bleachers.*

The doors to the entrance were partially blocked by a rig with scratched blue paint on the hood. *That must be the mobile unit. This made more sense to her than the pimped out black sedans they drove around in. Nobody would look twice at someone driving this.* The group got out of the vehicle and Agent Gingham opened the back of the rig, revealing a fully operational lab. *These guys were kind of awesome. It was like one of those top-secret government labs from a movie. Only this secret lab was not full of complete morons that endeavoured to control what they could not explain.* Lexy recognized almost all of the half dozen staff that equipped the unit from random jobs over the years where they'd crossed paths when it came time to clean up the evidence. Knowing the drill, they wandered in and took a seat in the beige pleather chairs, prepared to have their blood drawn.

Agent Gingham took a seat in a chair opposite them, crossed her legs, smiled widely and pointed at a guy who looked to be in his mid-twenties as she announced, "This is Agent McNeil. It's his first day. Fun fact, he has no idea what we're doing here or what you are."

This promised to be entertaining. Lexy grinned at McNeil.

McNeil gave her the fakest smile she'd ever received and sparred, "I was top of my class. I assure you, there is no situation I'm not fully prepared for and absolutely nothing you could show me that I haven't already seen or heard about."

Yes, he was an ass. Mc Anus face should be his new nickname.

Trying not to smile, Grey mumbled, "Shhh, Lex. We're supposed to be taking this seriously.

Well, that might be difficult with Mc Douchetastic here. She glanced at Grey. He had his lips pressed together to stifle laughter.

Crinkling her nose, Lexy critically gave their recruit the stink eye. He appeared to be in his early twenties with dark features and a wry smile. *This guy thought he was the most intelligent person in the room. It was that attitude that made him ugly. Her attitude probably made her downright hideous on occasion.* Her own thoughts struck her as funny and she smiled. *She'd just pulled a Kayn.* She heard an annoying repetitive squealing sound. *Her Handler was spinning his chair.* Lexy grabbed his armrest, shot invisible daggers with her eyes and slowly shook her head. Grey grinned back at her and stopped moving.

"Do you mind if we weigh you?" A lady politely asked as she gestured towards the scale in the corner of the room.

Lexy shrugged, rose to her feet and only had to take a couple of steps before stepping on the scale. She didn't bother looking at her weight.

From behind her, Agent Mc. Doucheface ignorantly commented, "She's heavier than she looks."

What an ass. Lexy directed her attention to the mortal and with a sugary sweet voice, she sparred, "Muscle weighs more than fat. By the looks of you, you're not familiar with the weight of muscle."

The youthful tool scowled at her, untucked his shirt and lifted it up to show her his chiselled abs. How's that for muscle?" he jousted.

Seriously?

Unimpressed, Grey looked at Gingham and commented, "Is this guy for real? I don't remember you show me yours and I'll show you mine being part of our regularly scheduled testing?"

She sighed, "It's not." Gingham scrutinized her idiotic recruit and reprimanded, "Clever people don't claim to know everything. The intelligent see multiple sides to each situation and understand there is always something new to learn. The truly wise embrace each new experience life gives them and understand there is a lesson attached to every situation they find themselves in."

Grey's eyes softened as he listened to Agent Gingham. *Her Handler had the sweetest soul.* The obnoxious young guy appeared to be gathering his thoughts before attempting to respond to his superior. *This ought to be good.*

Agent McNeil cleared his throat and spoke, "I apologize. I know girls don't like it when you bring up their weight. That was ignorant, and of course, I don't claim to know everything. I just meant I know more than most people."

This guy was a piece of work. It was entertaining. You could see the headache he was going to be for Agent Gingham. Gingham exhaled and didn't bother responding to his ignorance. *It reminded Lexy of what it was like when they acquired a new Ankh. It was surprisingly similar. Zach had run her down with a damn truck before they'd taken him from Triad and he'd grown on her. Perhaps, this kid would grow on Agent Gingham? She felt the recruit's eyes observing her mannerisms.* Lexy grinned and cocked her head. *He was probably trying to psychologically evaluate her. Good luck with that.* Grey sputtered out a burst of laughter from between his pursed lips from the chair beside her.

Agent Gingham introduced them, "This is Lexy, she's a Healer. The other handsome devil over there is Grey; he's a Fire Starter and Lexy's Handler."

Lexy grinned, the new guy thought this was all a prank. He didn't appear to be buying anything Agent Gingham was selling.

The recruit strolled over to Lexy, touched her on the tip of the nose and chuckled, "I want to play too. Can I be Batman?"

Oh, she was going to have to kill this guy. She clenched the beige padded arms of the chair on either side of her and shot daggers at him with her eyes. Grey placed one of his hands on her arm. A sense of calm washed over her as her Handler did his best to handle the situation before it escalated.

Meeting the new agent's eyes, Grey ominously advised, "Do not touch the Dragon. Trust me on this; you do not want to see her upset."

"Why not? Is your friend an assassin? Dragon is her call sign, isn't it? I know, she's a martial arts expert," the unknowing fool mocked.

Massaging her arm, Grey whispered, "Remember, he's just a First-Tier. We're supposed to protect even the fools."

Reigning in the urge to smash McNeil's smug face into the metal countertop, Lexy impatiently scowled at Agent Gingham.

Reading her immortal guest's annoyance, Gingham rapped with her knuckles on the stainless-steel countertop and one of the staff passed her a scalpel. Commanding the moron's attention, Agent Gingham announced, "Let me show you what you're dealing with here before you keep speaking and get your ass kicked by an immortal." She placed a large bucket beneath Lexy's arm, handed her the scalpel and suggested, "Why don't you go ahead and give me a blood sample. We'll kill two birds with one stone and show him how your healing ability works?"

Whatever. Lexy took the blade, pressed it against her skin, glanced over at the new employee and grinned.

The new guy held up his hand and spoke, "Wait a minute. This joke has gone far enough. Who put you up to this? Was it Stevens?"

Smirking, Lexy far too casually sliced open her arm, without flinching. Her blood poured in a thick stream of burgundy into the bucket. The superficial flesh wound closed up almost immediately.

The colour drained from McNeil's face. He whispered, "What is she?"

Agent Gingham smiled as she explained, "I told you she has a healing ability. Superficial injuries like that heal quickly. Deeper wounds take more time to heal. Do you mind coming out to the rodeo grounds where we'll have more space to show him what you're capable of? Bullets bounce off the metal interior of this unit."

Gingham was a badass. Grinning, Lexy ribbed, "It sounds like you're speaking from experience."

Gingham winked at Lexy as she unlatched the door and opened it, revealing the abandoned rodeo grounds. Agent Gingham directed an order at McNeil, "Come with us. You need to watch this."

He followed her, whispering under his breath, "I didn't sign up for this. It isn't what I trained for."

Agent Gingham grinned and asserted, "Your aptitude testing suggests otherwise. Also, I'm afraid leaving once you've seen what you've just seen isn't one of your options. I'd just suck it up and get with the program."

She'd always wondered how they recruited for the Aries Group. Lexy stood up and followed the mortals down the ramp, through the entrance into the dry, dusty rodeo grounds.

Taking a gun out of her holster, Gingham looked directly at Lexy and offhandedly enquired, "Do you mind if I shoot you a couple of times?" She opened the chamber, and spun it around, as she strolled away, with each footstep stirring up dust.

She was putting on a rather impressive show for the nervous recruit. Lexy shrugged as she followed her to the center of the grounds.

Agent Gingham aimed and the Aries Group's recruit realised his superior really intended to shoot an unarmed girl. He panicked, "I refuse to be a party to this madness."

"Follow along, McNeil, she'll be healed before you pick your jaw up off the ground," the saucy female agent teased.

It was a little funny. Lexy waved at Gingham and asserted, "Let me take my shirt off and hand me a towel before you shoot me. Bloodstains tend to make things awkward at the laundromat."

"Understandable. I'd imagine they would," Agent Gingham politely replied, as she lowered her weapon.

Once Lexy had taken off her shirt and been handed a towel to hold over her pants, she suggested, "Make sure the bullet goes straight through, it takes longer to heal if it's left inside, it has to slowly work its way out." Much to the new guy's mortification, Lexy stood in front of Agent Gingham and urged, "Alright, I'm ready. Go for it."

Agent Gingham aimed and fired two rounds into her stomach. It didn't even knock Lexy off her feet. Blood flowed graphically from the bullet wounds and soaked into the towel. She felt the warmth of her healing energy doing its job as the wounds closed. Lexy wiped the excess blood off her abdomen and asked, "Are we almost finished?" She glanced over at Mc Douchetastic and he was frozen in place with his mouth wide open.

Grey strolled over and scolded, "You've got blood sprayed all over your pants, it's my week to do laundry."

"I'll come along," Lexy countered. "Can't you see I'm topless? I grabbed a towel and removed my shirt."

Grey knelt, picked up a stone, rifled it over the top of the rodeo grounds and it disappeared into the sky.

Show off.

Grey mischievously grinned at her and sparred, "Why didn't you just take an extra second to remove your pants? I'm sure they'd survive the sight of you in your underwear." *She was wearing a G-string.* Lexy wasn't about to take off her pants and stand there with her butt in the breeze. She'd given Grey a look that was supposed to shut him up and he hadn't taken the hint, so she hooked one of her fingers over the thin lacy material on her hip and showed him.

Her Handler raised a brow and flirtatiously teased, "Those are nice, you wouldn't want to wreck those ones."

Rolling her eyes, Lexy glanced over at the new guy having a panic attack, pacing back and forth, incoherently muttering to himself. *Oh, no! They'd broken McAssface?*

Grey chuckled from beside her, "You're quite the inner commentary comedian today."

Agent Gingham impassively removed a tiny concealed weapon that looked like a gun and stated, "Agent McNeil just needs to chill out." Without explanation, she fired and it made a whooshing sound as it soared through the air.

A dart hit his thigh. Agent Mc Douchetastic teetered over and crumpled. A cloud of dust rose around him as he dropped to the rodeo ground floor.

Unfazed, Lexy looked at Grey and disclosed, "I'm going to need some of your energy if she's going to keep shooting me before I've had a chance to have something to eat."

Gingham holstered her tranquillizer gun and loudly announced, "Well, we might as well take a break. He'll be out for at least twenty minutes. Hopefully, he'll be relaxed enough to take it all in stride when he wakes up. Sometimes those ultra-realistic stick in the mud people are harder nuts to crack. Your Clan will be showing up here and staying in the campground until you know what's going on with the others. They're bringing your things. I'll send someone into town to pick us up an early lunch though. Any special requests?"

They gave her their lunch orders, closed the rig and they all sat in the grass chatting about news, sports and random things anyone would be talking about at any given time. Lexy and Grey were ravenous by the time their meals arrived, having blown off breakfast for a silly spat. Just as they'd began devouring their lunches, the new guy woke up in the grass by the mixed group of casually chatting companions.

Agent Gingham passed the groggy agent a styrofoam container and said, "I wasn't sure what you wanted, we don't know each other well enough yet, hope this will do?"

They spent the afternoon messing with the new guy until nothing phased him anymore. It didn't take them long to figure out this was the reason they'd been asked to join the Aries Group that day. They were breaking in a new employee. By the time the rest of their Clan arrived, stodgy Agent McNeil had come to terms with the fact that there were some things in life that couldn't be explained. Lexy shook his hand before they left and it was obvious, he no longer feared the unknown. They watched the Aries Group pull away, waved and made their way back to the cabin they'd stayed in before the Summit.

As they strolled through the woods, Lexy announced, "That was kind of fun."

Grabbing a stick, Grey smiled as he answered, "It was, wasn't it?" He found another and added it to his growing collection.

He was already preparing for the bonfire they'd be having that evening, finding sticks for roasting marshmallows. She saw a good one and snagged it off the ground as she suggested, "If we travel off the beaten path, maybe we can find enough sticks for everyone?"

"Sounds like a plan," Grey replied, beaming. He swung back like he was preparing for a homerun in a batting cage with his stick as he proposed, "We should play baseball one of these days when we're looking for something to do."

Lexy grimaced as she answered, "I guess we could." They wandered towards a tree with a rather enormous wasps nest, hanging from a lower branch.

Grey glared at her and warned, "Don't even think about it."

And her shenanigans had been foiled by his logic once again. Lexy smiled at her Handler and opted out. *He knew her so well. She had totally planned to smoke the nest with the stick in her hand as she walked under it.* As they strolled away Lexy fought the urge to run back and give it a good swat just to liven up their evening.

They scoured the brush for sticks of the appropriate shape and size and once they'd found enough, the two walked back towards the path. Finding the camp easy enough, Lexy took a seat on the log in front of the firepit as Grey ran into the RV to grab knives so they could whittle the tips of their sticks into sharp hotdog piercing daggers. They sharpened the piles of sticks in silence. *Well, verbal silence. The woods were far from silent.* In the background toads croaked and crickets chirped, with the oddly timed hooting of an owl. It was the otherworldly serenade of creatures that took over during the night in the forest. They were always there, but in the daytime, it was less noticeable. *For her anyway, Grey probably noticed everything.* She finished whittling her sticks in record time and asked Grey if he'd made coffee while he was in the RV, knowing full well, he hadn't.

Grinning at her, he baited, "Would you like me to make some coffee, Lex?"

"That would be amazing," she replied, with a wink.

Grey had only been gone for a couple of minutes when the door creaked, his head popped out and he sweetly asked, "Would you mind taking a stroll over to one of those cabins? We're out of toilet paper."

In forty years, she swore he'd never looked before sitting down. Lexy smiled to herself as she got up and sighed, "I'll be right back." She wandered away from the RV and began her jaunt down the pathway towards the rustic log cabins they'd been staying in before the Summit. A part of her expected to hear voices as she approached the front stairs. *Leftover memories from days gone by.* Lexy smiled as she glanced across the way at the cabin Triad had been staying in, recalling Tiberius' flirtatious escapades as she opened the door and wandered across the wooden floor to the bathroom. She grabbed the roll off of the holder and the one from behind the toilet. *They'd get more later.* She paused by the dresser, recalling the notes they'd hidden many years ago. Lexy haphazardly tossed the rolls on the bed and one unwound and rolled off the bed on the other side. *Shit. She'd get that later too.* She crouched and carefully removed the notes. She'd always wondered what Grey had written, and because she was in a breaking rules frame of mind, she cautiously opened his letter, without tearing the four-decade old envelope. *She was good.* Lexy made herself comfortable on the floor so she could sneak a peek at it. *It was probably all about Arrianna. That had been his frame of mind back then.*

It read… **I know we survived the Testing because we had Lexy in there with us and I'm certain we're all still friends. I hope we've all found happiness and love. Arrianna, tell me you've given me a chance by now. Lexy, I hope someday you get to know what it feels like to kiss someone and mean it. I pray you'll find out what true love feels like and have a chance to feel safe in someone's arms.**

Well, that was sappy and predictable. She wouldn't want him any other way. Lexy smiled. *Ironically, it was him she'd kissed and him that had made her feel safe.* She carefully placed the note back in the envelope and secured it under the dresser like it had never been disturbed. She stood there allowing her heart to ache for only a moment about the love that could never be, before collecting the toilet paper rolls and leaving the cabin. As she reached for the door, one of the floorboards creaked. She paused briefly and gazed back at the room. The complaint in the aged flooring hadn't been there five years ago. *Perhaps, it happened today to remind her there would always be a creak in her heart for her Handler. It wasn't news to her but the timing was strange after reading his note. Even if she endeavoured to get over Grey, her soul would always have a weakness for him, just as the wooden flooring now appeared to have a weakness for her.* She stared at the dresser one final time before closing the door behind her and descending the stairs. This time she didn't glance up at the cabin with thoughts of Tiberius. Lexy kept her eyes directed at her footing as she made her way back to the RV where Greydon was already sitting outside on the log waiting for her with a steaming coffee in one of his hands. She thought of his written words and swallowed the lump in her throat. The love she felt for him swelled in her heart as she watched him, watching her. The door opened and Frost stepped out of the motorhome carrying the condiments for the hotdogs. Lily followed with a package of wieners in one hand and a coffee in the other. *Their alone time was over.*

Grey placed his coffee on the ground by his feet, glanced up and said, "They brought toilet paper with the groceries."

Of course, they did.

Her Handler was about to start the fire with his ability when Markus' voice came from behind her, "Hold that thought, Grey. We've been summoned back to the in-between. The last Clan made it out. Before you start questioning me, I have no idea which one."

The colour instantly drained out of Frost's face, he appeared to be frozen in place. Lily skillfully pried the condiments out of his clenched hands and stated, "I'll put these away for you, Hun." *She wanted to be hopeful. She truly wanted to believe it was their people that made it out but she'd been let down too many times. She couldn't allow herself the luxury of hope.*

The group left everything. They dashed through the woods into the Ankh Crypt hidden beneath the forest. None of them spoke about it, but as they met up with the others Lexy tried to read the expressions on their faces. *If any of them knew the outcome it was impossible to tell. She knew better than to ask.* They all climbed into their tombs and the lids unceremoniously slid shut with the grinding of stone against stone. Lexy closed her eyes as the rose quartz that encased her body began to strobe with blinding light. *Please, let it be Ankh.* Her stomach lurched as her tomb was shot into the heavens, strobing with brilliant explosions of light. It paused as always before its swirling uncontrolled descent. As soon as she felt the wind rippling wildly against her flesh through her hair, Lexy knew she was descending into the in-between free of her tomb. The exhilaratingly euphoric sensation of her reckless descent came with the built-in instinct that told her it was time to use her energy against the impact. Lexy slowed her fall in those final moments as the endless desert of their clean slated arrival sight came into focus.

Chapter 9

Welcome Home

They all landed side by side once again in the white sand wearing only the sparse coverage of their god and goddess attire. Azariah was nowhere to be seen. Lexy caught Jenna's joyful expression and knew they'd made it out.

Their Oracle addressed the anxious group, "Our Clan made it out, they should be here any second!"

They'd actually made it out. Frost's eyes were glistening with tears of happiness. She felt moisture forming in her own and blinked it away.

Grey beamed as he flung his arms around Frost, embraced him, excitedly announcing, "I knew it! I knew they were going to make it out, I could feel it! You got the girl, buddy."

Frost's expression changed. *Lexy knew why. She'd survived, but Kayn wasn't going to be the same girl, and she was going to be pissed at everyone who knew about the plan. They were going to have another Dragon.* Lexy allowed the thought to sink in for a second while watching celebratory hugs and laughter. *There was going to be a new Dragon.* She followed the group on their stroll through the warmth of the welcoming sand as they awaited the return of the three. Grey glanced back at her and raised both arms into the air, silently cheering. *He was deliriously happy.* Lexy returned his smile. *She was going to have a murder buddy for those cutthroat jobs. That might be fun.*

It was then that she saw them approaching. *Five? How was there five of them?* They were walking towards them in the distance against the backdrop of a breathtaking sunset. They were still too far away to make out the faces of the five people coming in their direction. Some of the group broke free from the pack and began to sprint towards the three that went in and the two mystery Ankh. She squinted and focused. *Holy crap, it was Astrid and Haley. How in the hell?* Kayn remained behind the others as the four dashed towards the group. The new Dragon simply observed as the others laughed and embraced. Zach noticed Kayn's absence, grabbed her hand and towed her towards the rest.

Jenna strolled over, hugged them both at the same time and whispered, "Dragons need a Handler. Zach, you are now Kayn's Handler." Jenna walked away and embraced Haley without further explanation.

Really…Zach was Kayn's Handler?

Kayn released a burst of laughter and said, "I don't think so."

Zach hollered at Jenna, "She's not going to listen to me! This is a bad idea!" He shook his head and grimaced at Kayn. "I know you're not going to listen to me."

Kayn grinned, shook her head and responded, "Probably not." Zach took off, chasing after Jenna.

I guess they didn't have many people to choose from? This was going to be seriously entertaining. She noticed Frost hugging Astrid. *He'd gotten his friend back even if it was going to take Kayn a little bit of time to warm up to him again. She should probably go and greet the new Dragon.* At first glance, Kayn didn't appear to be changed but as she approached Lexy saw the tell-tale flicker of darkness in Kayn's eyes. She took the final steps towards Kayn, embraced her and said, "I'm glad you made it." As Kayn stepped back, there were so many questions in her eyes. She probably could use a private chat with the only other person capable of understanding what she was going through. Smiling at the fledgling Dragon, Lexy steered her away from the group, listening to her thoughts. *'Kayn understood the expectations that came with the Dragon ability. It made her nervous. She was supposed to be a hurricane, a plague, an apocalypse. She was a method of destruction. It was an intimidating job description.'* Lexy whispered as they wandered away, "From one Dragon to another, you don't have to listen to anyone. They won't expect you to." Lexy tuned in to Kayn's thoughts once more, *'She had to lose one version of herself, in order to find another. Tiberius had been wrong. She wasn't a lion or a lamb. She was destined to become a Dragon.'*

They strolled with warm sand underfoot for what felt like hours into the backdrop of the glorious crimson sunset. Something changed and the warm, soothing sensation of her steps in the sand gave way to the rustling of grass underfoot. They were now standing in the center of an endless field. Lexy smiled for she knew she'd had no part in this destination. Kayn's soul had brought her to a familiar place. Brighton had always loved places like this but she appeared to be distressed. Lexy understood where she was in her soul. *The scenery that she'd adored was now a devastating symbol of her mortality.* The field was overflowing with delicate purple flowers. It was a vision to behold. Grey would be all over this but Kayn closed her eyes. Lexy closed hers for a second out of curiosity. She could hear the soothing hum of the bumblebees. *Well, that was boring.* Out of nowhere, Kayn ran at the bees, waving her arms wildly, and they took flight. She crawled around on her hands and knees, yanking the flowers from the soil. Lexy made no attempt to stop her. *It was rather entertaining. If her fellow Dragon wanted to destroy the whole damn in-between, she wasn't about to get in the way.* Lexy grinned as Kayn screamed, tearing handfuls of grass from the earth. She de-winged and squished unsuspecting bumblebees in a fit of rage. *She felt her. Sometimes she just needed to break things and nothing that was broken here would really be destroyed. This wasn't reality and it was the safest place to carry out a fit of rage.* Kayn randomly stopped murdering imaginary things and stayed there, kneeling in the grass.

Should she say something? Lexy broke the silence by saying, "I didn't know about the plot to make you a Dragon. I understand why it had to be done, but I didn't know beforehand."

Kayn looked into her eyes and said, "I knew we had to kill our enemies during the Testing, but when he slit my throat... I guess on some level, I never believed he'd be able to do it. When I woke up, I felt nothing, but all-encompassing rage. I killed everyone that crossed my path until I caught up with him. I'll never be able to forget the expression on his face or the feeling of embracing the hollow sensation inside of myself as I slit his throat. I was lost for a while after that and my memory of that time is sketchy, to say the least. All I can recall is the warmth of the blood as it sprayed on my skin, and how good it felt. I fought and repeatedly died until the pain didn't matter anymore. When Kevin coldly tossed me into a room full of demons, I was eaten alive, and that was the moment I understood we were both gone."

It had been worse than she thought. *Kevin must have lost it too while he was in there. The demon thing was a little bit excessive for someone that truly cared about her.* There was a drawn-out silence as Lexy carefully thought out her reply. When she'd found the words, she professed, "You're not gone. Your perception of everything has been altered. All you have to do is embrace the change and accept the new version of yourself."

"How do I do that? I used to imagine myself as a noble creature, a golden stallion, or perhaps a lion. I know better now. I'm a hurricane, a plague, I'm an apocalypse. I am a Dragon. I'm a method of destruction."

She was saying that like it was a bad thing. Well, I guess she wouldn't know how it felt to be anything else. Maybe, that had been a blessing in disguise? Lexy pointed to the lush landscape before them and said, "We can burn this field to ash if you want to. My instinct has always been to burn it. Even though you are meant to be a warrior, you will always have a choice. We choose to work with the Clan instead of against them. We choose right over wrong. We choose when to be a lion and when to be a Dragon. We choose to be warriors instead of methods of destruction. You're still the same person. You just need time to sort through what happened to you during the Testing. Some of the dark things you've done will stay with you always, but those acts are important. You now know that you can survive the darkest of times. You will always know you led your Clan through that dark place and came out on the other side. You found your way back to the light because you're a survivor. You can choose to be a lion. My attachment to Grey allows my Dragon to sleep. I know having Zach as your Handler might be complicated. It takes time and it's not always easy. You'll both make mistakes maneuvering through this situation you've found yourselves in."

Kayn glanced down at her foot and a tiny red ladybug was taking a casual stroll across her skin. She scowled but didn't do anything to stop it.

Lexy grinned and teased, "Is that big bad ladybug bothering you?" She smiled as she listened to Kayn's hamster wheel spinning inside her head. *Brighton's inner commentary had always been hilarious.*

Once again, Kayn appeared to be fighting the urge to stomp on the tiny insect. It remained there, taunting her as it continued its ticklish stroll across her foot. Lexy couldn't help herself. Her fellow Dragon was teetering on the edge so she playfully shoved her and the ladybug spread its tiny wings and flew away. *Kayn wanted to kick her ass. She'd heard that part of her inner commentary loud and clear. This Dragon version of her was seriously cocky.* Lexy winked and teased, "I wouldn't try it. You can't take me, Brighton." She grinned at Kayn and shook her head as they continued their stroll into the scenic backdrop of the in-between.

They wandered aimlessly for quite a while in silence before Lexy continued her, it's good to be a Dragon speech, "Being a Dragon isn't a bad thing. The good and the light need Dragons to do what they can't. They don't want to step into the dark. Not even to do what's right. It's not always light outside when it's time to make a stand. Dragons can be beautiful things when properly attended to. I love my Dragon and every once in a while, I let it out to play. My Dragon enjoys the kill. My Dragon's a warrior and that's what warriors do." She heard the rustling of footsteps in the grass. Lexy knew it was Grey without even looking.

Grey began his apology, "We didn't know about what Kevin had been asked to do, until after the three of you were already in the Testing. They were right not to tell us." Grey cautiously inched closer. Kayn scowled at him, her furrowed brow, a silent suggestion that she still required personal space. He paused, gave her one of his overly charming grins, and said, "Kevin was ordered to kill you. It was a means to an end and you know I liked the kid. In destroying you, he more than likely destroyed himself. He was asked to do this to help you evolve into what you needed to become to survive. Your survival outweighs the trauma you went through, in the long run. You don't see it now, but someday you will. The plan was set in motion so the three of you could make it back home. People tend to lose their marbles in the Testing. It could be that Kevin lost his while trying to do what was best for you."

That had been her take on things too. He'd lost it in the in-between. She'd seen the love between them.

Kayn wiggled her toes in the luxurious grassy carpet of brilliant green underfoot and frowned. *To be quite honest, the hostile version of Kayn intrigued her.* They walked away as a trio, their footsteps rustling in the grass. Kayn stopped moving and just stood there staring at the grass. Lexy grabbed Grey's arm and towed him along with her, giving her well-meaning Handler a silent hint that their new Dragon needed some space. Lexy glanced back as Kayn began stomping on bees again. They stopped to watch as Kayn placed her hands on her cheeks, confused by her reaction to the pain of their stingers. Lexy's lips slowly turned up into a knowing smile. *She knew how the pain had made her feel.* Raising a finger to her lips, Lexy signalled for her to keep that a secret between Dragons. Kayn glanced at her injured foot. *There wasn't going to be a stinger. The in-between was a magical place, a place where you could feel the pain, but not suffer permanent physical repercussions because your body was elsewhere.* Kayn met Lexy's eyes and pressed her lips together. *It wasn't necessary to say the words aloud. She wanted to know if Kevin made it out.* Lexy nodded and answered the question she'd only asked in her mind, "Kevin made it out."

"Triad was the first Clan out of the Testing," Grey cautiously disclosed.

Kayn responded with a question, "That means Trinity didn't make it out?"

Grey sweetly cupped Kayn's chin in his hands and said, "It's okay to be happy he survived. The Testing is meant to destroy what's left of your mortal emotions. Don't let them do it. That's why we fight to keep them. Your spirit can only be broken if you choose to allow something to break you. You are truly immortal now, in every way. You fought your demons and survived in the Testing. Now fight like hell to get the Kayn we all know and love back. You have to try to find the joy in everything again. If you spend time looking for it each day, you'll find it. If you consider yourself ruined, you will be. It's quite simple, cause and effect. They can't destroy you physically once you are claimed by a Clan, but they can and will continue to try to destroy you emotionally." Grey pulled her into his brotherly embrace, but Kayn's body remained as stiff as a rail. He stroked her hair gently and whispered, "Let it go. That is the secret to a happy life. When somebody hurts you… Let it go. Take it as a learning experience and move on."

Lexy joined into the sappy conversation Grey was having with her and this was a peculiar thing for her to do, "I know where you are inside of your head right now. You don't want to feel anything and until you do, you won't. Just take all the time you need." Lexy joined their embrace and whispered, "I wish I could heal you emotionally, but that's the one thing I can't heal."

When they freed her from the group hug, Kayn took a deep breath and sat in the grass. She plucked a handful of grass from the ground, motioned like she was going to toss it behind her, but stopped herself. She allowed it to slip through her fingers and settle on the bare skin of her legs instead. Kayn brushed it off herself, laid down and rested her head in the lush greenery. Kayn inhaled the fresh scent of the grass as she quietly observed the clouds drifting across the sky above her. They found a spot in the grass by her. Mel and Zach had joined them. Kayn's absentee Handler maneuvered himself between Grey and Kayn. He sat beside her and Kayn glanced his way.

Zach spoke, "I'm sorry I reacted unfavourably regarding my new job."

Kayn nodded and replied, "I'm sorry you have to be my keeper, Handler, whatever it means. I don't think I'm going to need one. It's going to be easy. I wouldn't worry about it."

Grey started to chuckle and Lexy socked him in the stomach. Zach squeezed her knee tenderly, and Kayn didn't punch him in the face. *It was a good start.*

Zach grinned and continued, "I just wanted to say that I'm sorry, and I'm in." He pointed at the clouds as he observed the sky above and said, "I see something in that cloud to the left. Can you guys see it?"

Melody brushed her auburn hair away from her eyes, stretched out in the grass, stared at the clouds above them and answered, "I'll bite. What do you see?"

"Can't you guys see that Moose? It's completely obvious. The antlers... and wait... there's Frost driving the motorhome in the next cloud." Giggles erupted within the group of immortals lying in the grass.

Kayn randomly added to their conversation, "One of you will have to teach me how to drive."

Grey playfully chucked a handful of grass at her face as he volunteered his services, "I will. We can start after the banquet."

Kayn shook her head and asked, "What banquet?"

Grey sat up, plucked a flower from the earth and tried to tuck it behind her ear. Lexy started swatting him away as he replied, "There's one for the survivors of the Testing and their Clans. We have some time here to unwind before we have to go back there."

She had once again deciphered Kayn's thoughts. Lexy leaned over and whispered, "Don't worry, you'll sit beside me. I'll remind you that you are badass and strong until you feel that way again. That's what friends are for."

Haley and Astrid were standing above them smiling. Astrid smiled and asked, "Mind if we join you?"

Grey nonchalantly tossed a handful of grass up into the air and it came back down and landed on his face, he spit it out of his mouth and replied, "Feel free. Come lie down and guess what the clouds look like."

Beaming, Haley got comfy and confessed, "I can't even tell you how much I've missed this place. I never thought we'd see it again. It feels like coming home."

*She might as well join in…*Lexy pointed to the sky above her and said, "I see a Dragon."

Grey winked, looked into her eyes and whispered, "Isn't it magnificent."

Lexy glanced at her Handler and smiled.

Kayn sighed, "Yes...yes. I guess it is." Zach threw a giant handful of fragrant grass directly at Kayn's face and she blew it out of her mouth with a gust of air.

Zach shifted around in the grass and muttered, "I must be a strange anomaly. I made it out of Testing, became Enlightened and I still don't know what I am."

"Worry about your position as Brighton's Handler. Your abilities will come," Lexy commented.

Grey shifted, sat up again, averted his gaze to Melody and asked, "How are you doing with the whole Testing thing, Mel?"

Melody didn't meet his eyes. Continuing to stare at the clouds, she replied, "I'm healed on the outside."

They all understood what she meant.

Grey plucked another handful of grass and tossed it behind him. Kayn was staring at him with a look on her face Lexy couldn't quite place.

Astrid looked directly at Kayn and chuckled, "Isn't that the story of our life?" She nudged her and Kayn nodded mechanically, giving her a response without laughing.

Zach shuffled closer to Kayn in the grass and whispered, "Frost knows you know about the getting Kevin to kill you deal they made with Tiberius. I have to be honest, it's messed up, but it was the means to an end. Even I can see that, and I'm not the deepest guy around."

With an enormous grin, Kayn whispered, "Whatever do you mean? You are super deep?" She nodded and said, "I'll go talk to him. I think I just need a few more minutes of this."

Sprawled on his back beside Kayn with his arms behind his head, Zach teased, "Oh, look at how emotionally evolved you are. I'm impressed."

Kayn sighed, sat up and started to brush the grass Grey had tossed into the air off of her sparse white attire.

Sitting up, Zach said, "Wait a second." He plucked grass out of her hair and chuckled, "Now, you're all good. Go get him tiger."

Kayn rolled her eyes and shook her head slowly from side to side as she stood up and wandered away from the group.

They sprawled in the luscious grass awaiting Kayn's return. There were lots of places to go in the in-between, and so many miraculous sights to see, but right now, all they wanted was each other's company, knowing times of madness always seemed to follow the calm. With her head in the cradle of Grey's crossed legs, Lexy peered up at him. The glow from the sun had created an otherworldly halo of light behind him. He'd commented on how beautiful she'd appeared while seeing her from a similar vantage point, twice in the last couple of days but she couldn't imagine herself appearing more angelic than her Handler did in this moment, with his blonde hair and crystal blue eyes. Grey was lovingly playing with her hair. It tickled, causing her to smile as she met his gaze of adoration. He was her tether to everything of beauty and when she thought about what it meant to truly love someone, Lexy knew she'd never be capable of loving anyone more than she loved Grey. *I will always love you most.*

As he lovingly ran his fingers through her hair, he smiled and whispered, "Me too."

Lexy's eyelids grew heavy so she closed them to the hum of the steady stream of voices and she must have fallen asleep...

Lexy opened her eyes with her head still resting on Grey's lap.

He leaned forward, kissed her tenderly on the forehead and whispered, "You dozed off there for a while."

Lexy groggily struggled to sit upright. *That was rather odd timing for a nap?* She questioned, "How long have I been asleep?" Before Grey could answer, the group was waving someone over. Lexy turned around to see who it was. *It was Kayn and Frost.* Kayn strolled up and scooted back into the spot she'd been sitting in before she'd gone to find Frost. *Well, they'd obviously worked things out.* Lexy gave Frost an ominous look and teased, "You'd better be nice to her."

Frost winked and flirtatiously countered, "Whatever do you mean? I'm always nice."

They all ganged up on him and began throwing grass. Frost ducked, shielding his face from their playful attack. The glare of the sun dimmed as the backdrop of the in-between changed. The group of immortals sprawled in the lush silken carpet of green to watch the fading expression of the day. This spurt of time appeared to be run by their emotions as the final two made peace, they were given the reward of an exquisitely breathtaking sunset. The crimson hues appeared in circular patterns across the sky, and it was as though someone swirled an invisible paintbrush across the heavens, creating the masterpiece of an awe-inspiring sunset on the canvas above. As always Lexy turned to watch the awestruck expression on Grey's face. *For her, the sight of Grey's joy was more wondrous than the crimson hues that had been artistically painted across the sky.* Lexy smiled as she watched him. *This never-ending devotion for her Handler was the one thing she'd always felt the full strength of. He was undeniably the most beautiful soul she'd ever seen.*

Haley randomly piped in, "After 20 years in Astrid's happy place. I keep expecting there to be clowns."

Well, that was random. Lexy grinned as she glanced at Haley. *She'd missed the girl with the fluorescent pink hair and wit that sparked up conversations as quickly as matches left on the ground in a brush fire.*

Intrigued, Grey rolled onto one elbow, knit his brow and chuckled, "There were clowns?"

Haley grinned as she replied, "There were always clowns."

Zach exclaimed, "I can vouch for that. Her happy place was getting more than a little bit warped."

Frost's eyes lit up as he dared, "For old times' sake, I say we all go and check out this happy place right now."

Grey gave an immediate response, "No, thank you. I think I'm good."

"Oh, come on. Don't be a wuss," Lexy baited, tossing grass at her prissy Handler.

Kayn came to his defence by saying, "The last time I was in her happy place. The balloons were really chainsaws and the clowns tickled us when they caught us."

Grey stammered, "Like hell!"

Well, this promised to be more entertaining than staring at clouds and mocking each other. She was in. Lexy leaned in and kissed Astrid square on the lips.

Grey leapt to his feet and sprinted away from her, shouting as he ran, "Don't you bloody dare!"

Don't you dare was just like saying, I dare you to her. Lexy grinned, launched herself up and caught him in no time. She tackled him into the grass, pinned him down as he squirmed and planted a far sexier than intended kiss on his lips. *He kissed her back.* In the moments before the hallucinogenic took hold, there was confusion on his face. Lexy couldn't think about that now. There were dozens of clowns wearing colourful costumes, towing bouquets of swaying balloons. The seriously creepy hallucinations were skipping through a field of floating bubbles towards her. In the background, there was the tinkling music of an ice-cream truck. *She'd seen some epically messed up shit over the years but this was kind of awesome.* Lexy staggered around, clutching her head in the palms of her hands, giggling, "This is so messed up." The group scattered in terror. Lexy glanced towards the laughter she heard through the insanity. *It was Kayn laughing hysterically.*

The sound of her laughter snapped her out of it and the image began to flicker on and off. The entire group joined in on the twisted clown game, just as the hallucinations lost their effect on her. *She could tell the difference between reality and the fantasy Astrid's remarkable ability had created.* Lexy could still see the clowns but they were an obvious hologram, having lost their hold on her conscious mind. She glanced at Kayn, who also appeared to be able to tell the difference. *Did she have a healing ability too?* There was an explosion of light as the rest of the Clan appeared. A group of freaked out Ankh sprinted past the others squealing.

Markus hollered after them, "What in the hell are you guys doing?"

Lexy recalled how entertaining Astrid's ability had been to experiment with back in the day. Out of nowhere, Kayn dropped to her knees. She couldn't breathe. Lexy snapped out of it and rushed to her side.

Markus had beat her there, he whispered, "It's going to be okay, Kayn. The Enlightening... it's not one moment. Sometimes it's a process that can take days or even weeks. The Testing was only the beginning."

Kayn laughed through her agony as Grey sprinted past with a frightened expression on his face.

Lexy grinned at her terrified Handler as he fled from the imaginary clowns.

Markus crouched beside Kayn and whispered, "What are they running from?"

Kayn glanced up, smirked and said, "Clowns...they are running away from the clowns."

Markus chuckled as held out his hand and helped her up. Melody wandered over to Lexy already healed and the two laughed as Grey bolted past them again.

Watching Grey sprint away from imaginary assailants, Markus laughed, "I guess we can let Grey do a few more laps before we go."

Jenna appeared and joined the group as they stood together watching Grey running comical laps. He was the only one left under the influence. Jenna repeated, "What is he running from?"

Kayn grinned as she replied, "Imaginary clowns."

Jenna watched Greydon and giggled, "I always miss all the good stuff while I'm off having Oracle conversations with Azariah." Jenna left Kayn's side and walked over to Markus. She whispered something his ear. He glanced at Kayn with concern in his eyes.

Wonder what that look was about?

Kayn took a deep breath and asked, "What is this banquet?"

Lexy looked at the fledgling Dragon and gave a blunt response, "They'll bathe you and dress you up. There will be some form of entertainment. Oh, yes, there will also be food and dancing."

Kayn knit her brow and replied, "Refresh my memory as to why would I allow a stranger to bathe me? I'm not a toddler."

She could empathize with that feeling. Lexy grimaced and sparred, "If I had to allow strangers to bathe me, then you do too. It's a respect thing. Trust me; we take any tiny bit of respect that we can get from the Third-Tiers."

Markus announced, "Is everybody ready to go?"

They all began to disintegrate into the air. Lexy watched Kayn, there was no panic in her eyes. She held her palm in front of her face and observed as it turned to sand and the delicate grains of her essence floated away on a gentle breeze.

Chapter 10

Once Upon A Banquet

They solidified twenty feet in the air in the center of the deserted colosseum and abruptly dropped with no time to stop themselves. Ankh landed on their feet in perfect unison as an explosion of red dust rose around them. Somebody cleared their throat, Lexy turned. Silas was strolling towards the group flirtatiously eyeing her up and down. *This was getting weird. For so many years, it had felt like she was the last girl in the group that anyone would make eyes at and now, it was happening often.* He signalled for them to follow. Lexy caught up in a few strides and kept pace with him.

Without missing a beat, the scantily clad muscular Adonis leaned in and whispered in her ear, "You look gorgeous."

Lexy smiled back and teased, "Even without the fancy dress and jewels?"

He grinned and flirted, "Especially, without the fancy dress and jewels. Save a dance for me later?"

She wasn't a fan of dancing unless it was with Grey. Lexy glanced back at her Handler. *He wasn't amused by Silas' flirtations.*

Her undeniably buffed suitor whispered, "As much as I'd like to ignore everyone but you. I should go and greet your newest Clan members."

"You probably should," Lexy agreed, shooing him away with a hand. He chuckled as he left to go meet the newbies. *She wasn't going to worry about how Grey felt tonight. They'd talked everything out. She'd more than likely be spending the evening after the banquet with her friend, Prince Amadeus.*

Lexy walked towards the large intricately engraved arches that led out of the colosseum into the adjoining network of stone and marble corridors, attaching the colosseum to the castle. Lexy glanced back at the rest of her Clan and smiled. *She felt powerful here after proving herself at the Summit.* The breeze picked up and blew Lexy's scarlet hair around, giving it the appearance of fire. Her crimson flames flickered in the wind like a victory flag as the survivors of the Testing were led past her, away from the group. *Kayn was a Dragon too. It was ironic that the girl who'd always thought of herself as a drunken moose in her internal dialogue was now a Dragon. She still wasn't sure how she felt about that little tidbit of information. A part of her was going to miss the carefree girl that had been left behind within the horror-filled walls of the Testing. Maybe, parts of that girl would return, in time? Their situations prior to the Testing had been different. Lexy had become a Dragon long before the Testing. Sometimes, she wondered if she'd been born one. It had just taken her a while to hatch.* Kayn vanished from sight. *She understood where Kayn was in her mind at this moment. She was a lit match, and eventually, anyone that attempted to hold her down would have their fingers burned. In this fledgling Dragon state Kayn wouldn't be capable of playing well with others, nor would she be able to filter reactions. These things would be required of her during the banquet. Perhaps, Prince Amadeus would endeavour to save her too?* The thought of Prince Amadeus' kindness made her smile. *The Prince had aged but was still an attractive man. He was a decent man, that was the operative word.* Frost was silently walking beside her. *He'd talked things out with Kayn but still seemed to have a lot of stuff floating around in his head. He was walking beside the right person.* *She wasn't about to question him about what he was thinking, even though she was curious.* Grey was lagging behind, chatting with Lily. *Where this would have irritated her not long ago, it now made her glad he was occupied so he wouldn't be eavesdropping in on her thoughts.* She glanced at the marble beneath her bare feet as she strolled down the corridor. *Tiberius had also told her to save him a dance.* *She had no desire to dance with him…in public.* The large wooden doors opened as they approached. *Were they automated?* She noticed a man on either side holding them open as they strolled into the curtained bathing area. *It felt like she'd just been forced to do this.* The ladies were ushered to one area and the men to another. It seemed like they were being rushed through the motions this time. Lexy looked at Lily and complained, "It feels like we just had to do this."

Lily stood proudly, allowing the servants to disrobe her. Unashamed of her glorious nude form, she responded, "I quite like the princess treatment."

She would. Watching the breathtakingly beautiful Lilarah of Ankh royally descend into the pool of scented petals, Lexy's attention was elsewhere as they removed her clothes. *That was a first.* She stepped into the warm pool of water, it felt glorious for a second. An overzealous flock of immortals began washing her. Lexy scrunched up her nose as she tried to inch away. *It felt like she was being deloused this time, with how quickly it was done.* *They were probably viewed as savage earth dwellers.* *Lord knows what kind of diseases they have.* Lexy grinned as she was directed out of the bath and dried off without a moment to relax and enjoy the water. The girls were led to intriguing people dressing cubicles. *This was weird, even for her.* *What a strange thing to use technology for?* She stepped into the tiny room and stood there, waiting in the dark as someone chose what she was going to wear this evening on a screen by the entrance. *Oh, they'd taken another wacky step forward with their odd technology.* She was wondering if they could see her perplexed expression as the room began humming and grew uncomfortably warm. A strong wind blew over her entire body. The door opened, Lexy stepped out and glanced down at the slinky form-fitting teal strapless stretchy lace and silk gown she was wearing. *Impressive. It didn't even need to be adjusted. They were good.* She stepped into the next booth. There was a less aggressive humming and the sensation of a breeze caressing her skin. They were spraying her makeup on, it was like a temporary tattoo. She recalled being told each application would last for days. *That had been peculiar information to share, knowing she wouldn't be around for it to matter. It always made her giggle when she thought of this planet's relevant technology. Nobody wore shoes but they found it necessary to have rooms that dressed and spray-painted perfect make-up on your face. It was a strange place, indeed.* They weren't brought to the room full of jewels next. This time, their jewelry had been preselected. Lily was stunning as always in chiffon and Jenna was wearing an amazing tangerine coloured dress that hugged her curves. Lexy glanced down at her teal gown, knowing the colour always looked good on her. They were led towards the banquet area where they met up with the guys.

Grey smiled as he strolled towards her, took her arm and whispered, "You look…"

"Hideous?" Lexy teased. *He hadn't bothered to finish his sentence, rendered speechless by Lily. Hell, even she was. Lilarah was in her element.*

Her Handler tightened his grasp on her arm, stared into her eyes and finished his sentence, "Breathtakingly beautiful."

For a second, she wondered if he was slipping out of their platonic zone, and then, he leaned over and kissed her hair. *Awesome, she felt super sexy now.* The doors opened as they arrived. Without the ceremony of the Summit, they coupled up and strolled in, following other guests into the dimly lit colosseum style banquet room with dining on all levels, and made their way to the long table reserved for Ankh. The royal family was sitting with a bunch of famous actors from earth. *Were they clones or the real thing? It was impossible to tell. They usually took the real thing for a couple of days, cloned them and then dropped them off back on earth in a hotel room somewhere with a room full of booze and a missing patch of time.* Prince Amadeus was watching her entrance, smiling to show his admiration. Knowing he'd probably summon her to be his companion by the end of the evening, she returned the intimate gesture with a genuine smile. All they had was friendship and a single kiss that happened long ago, but he'd proven himself worthy of her respect.

Leaning over, Grey quietly sang, "Someday my prince will come."

Lexy glared and shook her head, knowing stomping on his foot right now would only make her appear more the, Wild Thing they'd always known her to be. She'd never had true romantic feelings for Prince Amadeus, but he'd always had her back and protected her in a way no one else could in this realm. She looked forward to the time they'd spend together later this evening. Against her will, her eyes strayed to the table where Tiberius would be seated. *Always caught in the past whenever she tried to do something stealthy, this was no exception.* Tiberius saw her, grinned, and winked as he raised his goblet of wine in her direction. The reckless moment they'd shared in that stairwell flashed through her mind, she miscalculated her footsteps timing with Grey's. Her Handler caught her before she went down, snickering. *Grey wasn't stupid. He knew why she hadn't been paying attention to the timing of her feet. No longer embarrassed by her naughty behaviour, she was fighting against the urge to ignore ration and do it again. This was not the time or place for that. She didn't want to offend Prince Amadeus.* She felt Tiberius' mischievous stare, glanced back at her dark nemesis and he laughed as she purposely looked away.

Squeezing her arm as they reached the table, Grey loudly preened, "Doesn't my girl look gorgeous in this dress?"

Arrianna grinned at her and replied, "She's absolutely gorgeous."

My girl. Cringing on the inside, Lexy left his side and strolled around to the back of the table, so she could sit directly across from Grey. It was more than just that one thought that attributed to her opposite side of the table decision. From that vantage point, she wouldn't be able to see Tiberius unless she cranked her neck and made her interest obvious. *It would be a cold day in hell before she did that.* Frost gallantly pulled her seat out, leaving a space between them. She smiled knowing he was saving it for Kayn. Lexy took a sip from the goblet in front of her and stealthily glanced towards Triad's section. *He wouldn't be able to see her either. Good, this was good.* She peered into her enormous goblet of red Third-Tier wine, dunked her finger in and licked the droplet off. *Don't you dare lead me into temptation.*

She heard Frost say her name and snapped back to reality, "Yes?"

He chuckled, "You're off in la-la land, aren't you? Are you looking forward to the after-party with your Prince?"

She pressed her lips together, nodded and baited, "Yes, there's nothing like our G-rated parties."

Frost grinned back at her and replied, "You look lovely tonight. I'm sure he'd rather it didn't have a G-rating, but I understand… It's complicated."

With an enormous grin, Lexy laughed, "You look lovely too and he's married."

Frost leaned closer and whispered, "He's royalty. It's probably little more than a business agreement."

Lexy smiled, opting out of a response because she knew way more than she was letting on. *It hadn't been a business agreement. He'd loved her until his wife started spending her nights bedding his brother.*

"Clan Triad," a man's voice announced.

Her eyes darted upwards only long enough to catch a quick glimpse of Kevin's face. *She wasn't sure why she couldn't bring herself to look at him. Possibly it was because she didn't want to see the monster they'd created, by forcing a boy to murder the girl he'd loved his whole life.* She peered up at Frost. *He wasn't looking either.* Grey turned around in his seat and stared at her, she gave him an understanding smile and now wished she'd chosen to sit beside him instead of across the table. *Her Handler was a softer soul, guilt ate at him.*

In a well-timed subject change, Frost casually asked, "So, how are things with your other half?"

She'd just popped a grape into her mouth from a tray on the spread. Smiling, Lexy quickly swallowed it. "Back in the friend zone," she answered, reaching for a branch.

"I'm curious, is that really what you want?" Frost enquired with knowing eyes as he took another sip of wine.

She glanced his way as she responded, "That's a trick question, isn't it?" Drinking wine before adding to their conversation, she admitted, "It's not what I want, but it's how it has to be." She placed her almost empty goblet on the table and knit her brow. *She'd better slow down. How had that happened?*

A man wearing a ridiculous outfit strode into the center of the banquet hall. The muffled talking subsided until you could hear a pin drop. Their Clan's name was announced. The doors opened and the five newest members of Ankh walked into the hall as somebody played a trumpet. *She still couldn't get over the fact that they had five new Ankh. It was going to be a tight fit in the RV.* The trumpeter began to play a well-known pop song. Once the newest of the Ankh had taken their seats, silken ropes dropped from the ceiling. At least twenty women walked in a procession through the main arched doorway dressed in white, bound the ropes around their wrists and began to dance. They wrapped and entwined themselves up higher and tighter until they were suspended in the air performing. It was as though they were dancing in mid-air.

Frost leaned over and whispered in Kayn's ear, "You look absolutely breathtaking. Don't spill wine on your dress love."

Kayn glanced up at Frost under a veil of eyelashes and replied, "Thank you, I'll do my best."

Lexy grinned. *Wonderful, she was going to be listening to the sexual innuendo Olympics all night. Heaven help her.*

Kayn crossed her legs and whispered, "Is something wrong?"

Frost's gaze travelled the slit in Kayn's golden gown, he teased, "You're not wearing any underwear."

Kayn replied, "I hadn't thought about it, but I guess I'm not. With the whole no shoes thing, I just assumed everyone wasn't wearing any."

Frost took a drink from his goblet, and as he lowered it, he chuckled, "Now, there's a thought."

This was getting painful.

"Am I really the only one who isn't wearing underwear?" Kayn whispered back to Frost.

It was time to put a stop to his teasing. Lexy leaned over and whispered, "None of us are, just ignore him. He's messing with you."

Kayn smacked Frost's knee under the table. Chuckling, he looked at Lexy and complained, "Party pooper."

Lexy grabbed meat and a tortilla off the table. She had no idea what they were called here but they resembled tortillas enough to use that word as her point of reference. There were also tiny baguettes and fruit.

Frost put some on Kayn's plate and urged, "If you don't eat anything, it's an insult. Just eat it. You don't want to know what it is."

Grinning, Lexy ate her tortilla wrapped meat. *It wasn't great by earth standards but she'd once eaten mutant lizard meat while in this realm. She wasn't going to complain about cooked anything. It was probably dinosaur meat. The Third-Tiers were feeding the dinosaurs, stolen cattle and celebrity clones. Maybe, when she had a moment alone with Amadeus, she'd suggest cloning the cattle and eating it instead? Beef tasted way better than this oddly stringy mystery meat. Something occurred to her, and she winced as she attempted to inconspicuously sniff the meat in her tortilla. They could be eating cloned mortal meat. It didn't smell like human meat though...*

Always the attentive big brother figure to Kayn, Grey tossed a thick rough-edged tortilla across the table at Kayn and advised, "Make sure you eat lots of these if you're drinking tonight." He pointed at her empty wine glass. Kayn took a giant bite of the bread and smiled.

As her wine was refilled, Lexy found herself staring at Kayn. *When she was dressed up like this, the resemblance to her mother Freja was uncanny. It might be a bad thing here.* Recalling the ominous look between Markus and Jenna in the in-between, Lexy glanced at the head table nervously. *It wasn't that she didn't believe Kayn could defend herself if she ended up in a precarious situation tonight. It was that she wasn't allowed too.* Lexy downed her wine and placed it on the table. *She couldn't think about it. This was the one situation where defending yourself or anyone else was never an option.* They brought around bowls of orange soup. Some people picked up the whole bowl and drank from it, while others were dipping their tortillas in it. The whole table of Ankh began to lighten up and joke around as the wine took hold. Her eyes were drawn to the head table once more, and this time, Lexy noticed the King was watching Kayn. *There was something about his intense unwavering gaze that was triggering the protective instinct within her.* Kayn noticed the King staring, smiled pleasantly and looked away. Kayn smiled at the boy who brought pastries and politely thanked him, he smiled back, confused. *This evening was about to take a messed-up turn. She could feel it in her bones.*

Nudging Kayn, Frost explained, "They aren't supposed to speak to us. Let me rephrase that, they aren't allowed to speak to us."

"That's pretty stupid," Kayn remarked as she picked up a pastry and stared at it critically.

Frost's eyes softened as he responded, "Yes. It is."

Kayn sniffed the pastry and whispered, "What's in this one?"

Frost took it from her and placed it on his plate. He found her another one and whispered, "Open your mouth."

Lexy glanced over. *Frost was feeding her pastries. He was coming on strong and the Dragon version of Kayn would be feeling the urge to be more than a little reckless.* Lexy decided to keep her mouth shut and let her have fun. *Why shouldn't she be reckless? She'd just survived a simulation of hell.* Frost naughtily licked cream from the treat he'd fed her off his finger and Lexy soundlessly giggled. *She couldn't help it, she had to watch. The Frost trying to seduce Kayn show was quite entertaining.*

Grinning, Kayn whispered, "What was in that one?"

Making a face as he chewed the pastry, he'd taken from her, he winked and disclosed, "Nothing good." Frost smiled at Kayn and motioned like she had something on her face. Her eyes widened and she unsuccessfully attempted to lick it off. He chuckled as he deviously suggested, "Let me get that for you." Frost used his finger to wipe the cream off Kayn's face, showed her his finger and asked her if she wanted to lick it off.

Alright, she'd better stop this before it went too far in public. Lexy rolled her eyes and piped in from the other side of her, "Lick that cream off your own finger, Romeo."

Music began, and from the wall on the far side of the room something resembling a rock-climbing surface slid up from the inside of the floor. It kept going until it was flush with the ceiling and spikes slid out. The set up was white, it appeared to be made of sculptured ice. A young man had come to stand on a circular platform about ten feet away from the sculpture. It rose until he was a good forty feet in the air. *This promised to be messed up.* Six young people appeared and walked slowly to the base of the structure. They began to climb to different positions. If they slipped, they'd either fall to their death or become impaled on the frozen spikes. They extended themselves with athletic majesty from the structure and began a slow climbing dance routine. This went on for the remainder of the meal. *The muscle tone it would take to move lengthwise was nothing short of miraculous.* They all watched in awe as the climbing dancers began to lose hold of the rigid surface and dropped. *Here we go.* The dancer was bleeding to death to raucous applause as a pool of blood formed beneath him on the marble floor. A showy man in a red gown with intricate gold threading around his neck and waist strolled over and pointed something that looked like a flashlight at him. The wounded man turned grey and solidified. The immortal in the flashy gown kicked the statue, it turned to dust and he flounced away. A woman in white swept up the dust with an oddly enormous golden broom and walked the pile of what had once been a Second-Tier under the elaborate archway and out of the double doors. When they swung closed everybody applauded once again.

Kayn whispered, "What in the hell was that? Why are we applauding?"

Quietly, Frost explained, "They are prisoners. Don't worry, they're all Second-Tier, they can't really die. I'd imagine they were offered a chance at freedom if they were willing to play along and play a part of this evening's festivities. The ones who survive will be released. We're applauding, because we don't have a choice. Play along, Brighton."

Kayn asked, "How many usually survive?"

Laughing, Frost disclosed, "Nobody, they have to keep going until the King says dinner is finished. Nobody has the endurance to continue doing that bullshit for hours. One by one they'll all die."

Kayn questioned, "So, in this realm you have to win the Summit to be treated with respect and other than that the only Second-Tiers that remain here are being held captive?"

She was catching on. Lexy smiled as she sipped her wine. *She hadn't noticed any Grande gestures of respect. Her goblet had been topped up and she hadn't even seen it happen. She'd been too busy watching, the Frost and Kayn show. I guess she could be watching Grey flirting up a storm with everyone that draws breath across the table show but that would be silly. She should be thinking about her own options.* Orin popped into her head as she glanced down the table at Jenna. *A thousand years. Now that was a long-term relationship.* Mel spoke and Lexy remembered why they weren't together. *He did deserve a high five in the vengeance and revenge on your ex category.* She grinned as she drank. *Orin impregnated his ex-girlfriend's mortal look alike. That should be on the first page of every epic ex revenge handbook.* Lexy tuned back into the conversation beside her as Frost started giving Kayn the, we have no rights while we're here speech. *This would be her cue to go to the ladies' room. This whole speech just pissed her off.*

Smiling politely as she rose, Lexy excused herself from the table. Grey glanced up at her and gave her a look that he'd given on countless occasions. *It didn't need to be spoken aloud. He wanted her to behave.* Lexy winked at him, turned around and shimmied past her Clan on her side of the table. *She had no firm plans to misbehave. It was more of an avoidance strategy. Stay away from Tiberius, don't react to Grey's shenanigans and behave until her friend Amadeus summoned her to join him. At least the naughty dynamics between Frost and Kayn had kept her mind occupied for a while.* Everyone gasped, Lexy paused to watch another acrobat slip and impale themselves on the spikes. The man with the strange flashlight gadget strolled over and turned it on the girl. She solidified, turned to dust and disintegrated into a pile on the floor. A lady with a broom swept up what was left of her and walked her out of the sculptured archway past the doors. She winced. *This ridiculous public display was meant to impress the victorious Clans and make them fear the royal family. She was pretty sure she could take this whole room if she wanted too.* Lexy felt someone's eyes on her. Her Handler was staring at her slowly shaking his head. She could read his expression from here and in her mind, she heard him say, *'Don't even think about it.'* She smiled in his direction and blew him a kiss. *Frost was wrong, Grey was the party pooper.*

Her attention was diverted back to the performance as the final three exhausted acrobats plummeted to the marble floor with a splat. The man in red swooped in and turned them into piles of dust. This time more than one lady in white swept up what was left and walked their remains through the majestic archway and out of the double doors. With the blaring of trumpets, the spiked wall slid down into the floor with no evidence it had ever been there. With rather odd timing music began to play. Good music, easily comparable to what would be playing on the radio back home. Everyone stood up, paired up and made their way towards the dance floor. With her escape plans foiled, Lexy knew she'd have no choice but to dance. *Everyone would be watching. She had no partner. This was awkward. She'd need to find someone before it was noticed.* Lexy spun around and there he was, as always, ready to bail her out of an awkward situation at a moment's notice.

Grey scooped her up in his arms and chuckled in her ear, "What are you up too?"

"I was just trying to escape the crowd," Lexy innocently replied. *Crowds had never been her thing.*

Dipping her without warning, her Handler sparred, "Are you telling me the truth?"

As she dangled in a comically precarious position, Lexy laughed, "Yes. Yes, of course."

Grey kept her there, teetering on one foot with her body leaning all the way back as he offered, "I'll dance you towards an escape route but then, you're on your own." He righted her position, skillfully waltzed her over and spun her towards the double doors. He released her and in the next movement, he'd stolen Kayn from Frost. Lexy grinned as she snuck out of the hall and walked right into Silas.

Stopping her, he flirtatiously scolded, "Where do you think you're going?"

It occurred to her that she'd never used the washroom while she was here and didn't even know where it was and that's where one would usually go to escape a crowd. Lexy smiled and confessed, "To the bathroom, if I can figure out where it is?"

The sparsely clothed Adonis answered her question with a grin, "You my dear, are not allowed out here. There are washrooms right behind your table at the end of the hall."

She hadn't noticed a hallway or seen any bathroom signs.

Silas responded to her confused look with, "They don't mark bathroom doors here because they're all unisex."

"How come you're out here and not in there enjoying the party?" She countered with a grin.

Smiling, Silas provoked, "I'm here to make sure the partially immortal riff raff, aren't roaming the halls getting themselves into trouble."

"Theoretically, you're partially immortal riff raff too," Lexy baited.

He grinned and sighed, "I'm housebroken well-trained riff raff." Silas glanced at the other guard and declared, "If you've got this for a few minutes, I'll escort this gorgeous troublemaker to the bathroom."

"Take your time," the other guard chuckled.

Silas opened the doors and led her through the dancing slightly inebriated crowd towards the back of the room, where he directed her to a long hallway. He ushered her down it. When they reached the end, there was a doorway that led to another hall. Silas grabbed her arm to pause her escape and said, "I wish we had more time to get to know each other."

Flattered by his interest, Lexy allowed him to detain her as she toyed, "Staying here is voluntary, isn't it? You could always choose to come back with us and live out your warped life of servitude without the luxury or flower petal baths?"

"I'm afraid, it's a little bit more complicated than that, gorgeous," Silas sparred as he released her arm and set her free.

She could tell he wanted her to stick around and ask him why he couldn't leave but decided against it. Attachments always came with complications and this guy had, 'it's complicated' written on his forehead. Lexy was curious but not enough to add his drama to her pile. The last week of her life had been filled with an unusually large amount of it. "Well, it was nice to meet you. I'm sure our paths will cross again someday," she remarked with a smile as she turned and walked away. *Maybe, she'd ask Markus about Silas once she was back in her world.*

Chapter 11

Otherworldly Bathrooms And Other Shit.

The door opened by sliding into the wall before she had an opportunity to reach out her hand. *They really did choose the strangest things to automate in this world.* Lexy strolled into the largest bathroom she'd ever laid eyes on. There were dozens of stalls down each row, a half a dozen rows deep. Everything was spotlessly clean, white and black marble. There was no space at the bottom to see anyone's feet like home. Ignoring the urge to count the stalls, Lexy started laughing. *She must be drunk.* Unsure of what she'd find behind it, she pushed on a door. *It looked normal. This place was so weird.* She closed the door, it locked and the hum of the music was gone. *A soundproof, unisex bathroom with automated stalls; that was a brilliant idea. At least she wouldn't have to spend ten minutes diving from stall to stall trying to find a bathroom door that locked.* Lexy smiled, thinking of her usual public bathroom experience. *She always seemed to choose the one stall with a lock that wasn't close to level.* Lexy sat on the toilet. When she finished, she noticed there was no toilet paper dispenser. *Oh crap. She was trapped on the toilet in a unisex bathroom. Normally, she'd just ask the person next to her and they'd pass her some. If nobody else was in the bathroom, she'd dash to another stall with her pants around her ankles.* She looked behind her for something to use. *There was nothing. Shit! What was she supposed to do?* She looked up and noticed she was in a fully sealed box. *That made sense, it was soundproof. She had to be missing something here? It would have been nice if Silas filled her in on the complicated bathroom situation.* There were primary coloured handprints on the back of the door. *She'd assumed it was art. Problem-solving skills, this had to be easier than it appeared. The handprints were red, green, blue, and yellow. So, stop, go and caution? Was she supposed to put her hand on one of the prints? Why did it feel like this could go horribly wrong? Were the instructions written on something?* Lexy leaned over and saw a button on the rim of the toilet. *Maybe she was overthinking this?* She pressed it. A bubble-like substance pressed against her bottom, the door slid closer and stopped uncomfortably close to her knees.

A deep voice said, "Choose your desired temperature and place your hand on the wall."

Alright, now we're talking. There are instructions. Red could be hot. Blue might be cold? What in the hell did yellow and green mean? The voice kept repeating the command. *Quit pressuring me, damn it! Yellow or green. Yellow or green. She winced and placed her hand on green.*

The voice announced, "You cannot choose the option for go until you have chosen your desired temperature."

Well, Shit! If green meant go, did red mean stop? What if it meant hot? She could do without a hot water doused Yoo-Hoo. So, blue or yellow? She pressed yellow because it was her favourite colour. *Nothing happened.* She remembered she had to press, go. There was a spray of warmth down below followed by a warm breeze. *This might very well be the most awkward moment of her afterlife.* She was sitting with a warm breeze blowing, wondering how to stop it.

"Press stop," The booth instructed.

She was way too drunk for complicated toilets. Laughing at her predicament, she pressed red.

The booth spoke in a monotone voice, "Repeat."

Lexy hissed, "Shit, no! Don't repeat! Stop, I want to stop!"

The air stopped blowing. A voice spoke again, "Do you want to use the voice control option?"

Oh, good. "Yes?" She declared.

The voice said, "What is your command?"

Exhaling to calm her frustration, Lexy firmly stated, "Stop!"

A gust of air sucked the bubble film into the toilet and politely said, "Have a productive evening."

Lexy leapt up, shoved the door open and escaped as the chamber filled with lovely scented mist. She closed the door so she wasn't doused with air freshener and muttered, "What in the hell was that shit?" She heard laughter and spun around.

Grinning from ear to ear, Tiberius chuckled, "You just used that bathroom for the first time, didn't you?"

Shit. She'd had way too much to drink. She needed to avoid him. Unable to help it, her serious demeanour crumbled as she laughed, "What in the hell was that madness?"

Keeping his distance, he teased, "It is madness, isn't it? It doesn't need to be that complicated."

Smiling, she countered, "It definitely doesn't." Their eyes locked as she caught the hidden meaning. *She needed to make good choices. This wasn't the place to do this.* She hesitated, "I should get back before someone comes looking for me."

Her undeniably sexy nemesis blocked her escape and asserted, "That's why I'm standing here. I came looking for you."

"Tiberius," she whispered his name as he came closer.

He seduced, "Tell me there isn't a part of you that wants me as much as I want you and I swear I won't bother you for the rest of the evening."

For the rest of the evening. That was the fine print in his naughty verbal contract. Grinning, Lexy maneuvered past and escaped.

Tiberius hollered after her, "I knew you couldn't say it."

She really couldn't, he had her there. She walked through the sliding doors into the hallway, directly into Grey.

He slowly shook his head, grinning and light-heartedly scolded, "You're such a naughty fibber. You promised you'd behave."

She'd promised no such thing. Lexy wasn't in the habit of making promises she had no intention of keeping. She smiled at her Handler and clarified, "I got stuck in the bathroom, it had nothing to do with him."

Greydon winked as he placed his arm around her in a brotherly fashion and confessed, "I was going to say something about that. Last time we were here, I ran in there, tossed my cookies in the toilet and tried to flush it with that little button. Well, you can guess what happened next."

With a hilariously clear mental picture of how it went down, she started to giggle. In a few steps, they were both howling, thinking about the slapstick comedy of drunken suffocation that would have followed an unknowing flush. Much to her surprise, Grey didn't continue harping about Tiberius as they strolled back into the banquet hand in hand. Instead, he towed her out onto the dance floor with the rest of their Clan, where they danced until they were breathless. The repetitive words were easy to pick up and the song had a dance music vibe. Ankh began to sing along. Occasionally, she found herself looking at Kayn. *Maybe, she'd been seeing danger that wasn't there?* She appeared to be having a good time, but every so often, Lexy caught her a sneaking peek at Kevin. *That was going to be a difficult habit to break. Frost was doing his best to keep her occupied, she understood the feeling. It was difficult to let go of the fantasy of what might have been.* Lexy's eyes locked with her dance partner as Grey spun her around, tugged her back to him and comically sung any goofy words he wanted to the tune of the music in her ear. She was laughing as the song changed to a slow one and Grey held her captive in his arms with his body against hers as they slowly swayed to the music. The seductive combination of his breath in her ear and the scent of his skin had always aroused her. Lexy closed her eyes and allowed her heart to envision the incredible night they could have together if she pushed him just a touch farther. He'd caressed her back as they moved together. Her eyes met with Frost's, she snapped out of it. *The wine-induced euphoria was messing with her, that's all this was.* With perfect timing the song ended and a fast one began.

Grey abruptly pulled away, cupped her cheeks, planted a kiss on the tip of her nose and said, "One second." He left her standing there.

Lexy was about to leave when Kayn danced her way over and asked, "Have you seen that Patrick kid?"

She'd seen him. He wasn't difficult to miss. Grey grabbed her from behind, kissed her neck and started swaying her back and forth. Lexy laughed, "Stop it, Grey! I can't even think!" Laughing as she struggled out of Grey's clutches, she gave Kayn a hint, "Picture him without the extra weight and take another look around." *Her sexuality confused friend from the banquet before their Testing was now the hottest guy in the room, next to Frost.*

Releasing her, Grey pouted and complained, "I take offence to that."

Lexy turned to face her pouty Handler and recreated his last move cupping his cheeks with the palms of her hands as she stared deeply into his eyes and whispered, "You'll always be the hottest guy in the room to me."

She saw it register in Grey's eyes as he placed his hands over hers and made sure she read his intentions loud and clear as he, friend-zoned her with his words, "We're best friends, you have to say that."

She had to stop reaching in trying to retrieve his feelings. She'd become quite the hypocrite. Lexy grinned and sighed, "Go have fun. I'm all good tonight. I promise." He kissed her cheek, smiled at her, messed her hair and goofy danced away, leaving her standing there with no partner. She scanned the room to see if Kayn had figured it out and saw Zach take a page out of the Grey handbook as he grabbed Kayn from behind and startled her. Kayn laughed as she spun around to face him. Kayn's new Handler took her hand, twirled her and whispered something in her ear. It made Lexy feel better to see Zach doing his job, instead of leaving the fledgling Dragon to fend for herself. She made her way through the crowd back to the table.

Frost snagged her around the waist and taunted, "If I have to stay out here dancing, so do you."

Their Clan danced until they were so exhausted and giddy, someone started up the joke dance moves. They did the lawn mower and the sprinkler. They began to make up new ones like the race car and the teacher. Kayn added the tiger lizard and spider rat. Grey added Frost driving. *Frost didn't find that one funny.* It turned into a giant game of dance charades. They kept making up new ones until they were all doubled over laughing. Lexy noticed Kayn sneaking another peek at Kevin. Another slow song came on and everyone partnered up. Frost had disappeared so Grey grabbed Kayn and her lack of partner was the perfect excuse to sneak back to the table. Almost in the clear, Lexy felt someone's gaze and paused, her eyes were drawn to Triad's seating. Kevin's eyes locked with hers. *He was upset. Kayn wasn't even dancing with Frost? Where was Frost?* She scanned the room and saw him in a deep conversation with Jenna. *He had the same expression on his face. Something was happening that she wasn't privy too. There was always Clan drama.* Lexy made her way back to her seat. She picked up her wine and took a sip, watching the ominous exchange of looks between Jenna, Frost and Markus. *What now?* It was then that she noticed the squished yellow flower on Kayn's napkin and her heart solidified in her chest. *No... Not her.*

Lexy calmly got up and made her way to the washroom. Before going down the hall, Lexy caught the leader of Triad's attention, signalled for him to follow her and started down the hallway towards the privacy of the washrooms. *Kayn looked too much like Freja. From the moment she walked in, this one fact, kept slipping into her mind each time she saw the King staring at Kayn. It was easy to read between the lines in this scenario. The King wanted to spend the night with Kayn. The King was a violent beast of a man and she was using the term man loosely. She knew no one in her Clan would disobey the rules to stop it. This scenario hit a nerve. Her first time had not been by choice and all first times should be. Tiberius had front row seats to the depravity of her childhood and Triad was known for their flexible interpretation of the rules. How far would he be willing to go for what he desired? Now, that was the question.*

The doors slid open. Tiberius entered the bathroom, Lexy walked into his embrace and whispered in his ear, "Help me stop this and I'll do anything you want."

He stiffened and whispered, "Let's take this conversation somewhere private."

Allowing him to guide her into one of the stalls, Lexy turned and said, "We don't have time for this now."

Closing the door behind them, Tiberius questioned, "I want to trust you. Can I trust you? I need you to give me your word as a Dragon."

She nodded and whispered her reply, "You can trust me. I give you my word."

"Are you capable of keeping a secret from your Clan, even your Handler?" Tiberius asked.

If she had to, she could. Meeting his concern, with a steady gaze, Lexy professed, "I gave you my word. You've seen inside of my mind. You know what that's worth."

Tiberius' eyes softened as he whispered his response, "I'm guessing you've heard about the virgin sacrifice?"

He'd said the words she'd been thinking aloud. She nodded her reply, and as their gaze held, she disclosed, "You know why I can't let this happen."

Tiberius' expression softened as he replied, "We already have a plan to stop it. You need to understand, if you're a part of this and we're caught, we'll all be entombed?"

Lexy whispered, "You already have a plan?"

Touching her hair, he explained, "Kevin came to me with several versions of a vision. At first, I thought I could keep you out of it, but the only version of this plan that works includes you. I was going to tell you about this earlier but you took off before I had a chance to say anything. We need a member of the royal family on board to pull it off and you happen to have a personal relationship with one. If there's a chance he'll turn you in, just forget I mentioned this."

"No, he won't turn me in," she replied, with certainty. *She'd never been able to explain her connection to Prince Amadeus or why he'd helped her with no gain on his behalf but she knew he'd never hurt her.* Curious, Lexy looked into Tiberius' eyes and probed, "I understand why Kevin's doing this, but why would you?"

Emotion flickered in her enemy's eyes as he responded, "I saw what they did to you at that farm when you shared your memories with me at the Summit. It's taken you forty years to come through it. How could I claim to have feelings for you and then stand by and watch while someone you care about is violated that way?"

"You can't love me," Lexy whispered.

Smiling, Tiberius whispered, "I don't." Playing with her crimson curls, he tenderly kissed her lips.

Stunned by how she felt as their lips parted, the inner voice that denied what she wanted was silenced. Her lips were still tingling as he began his explanation, "I know you recall the drama that ensued after I erased my grandson's memories. Well, an unfortunate side effect of my ability is that I get to know the people they know and feel their emotions. I was already going to do this before you tried to lure me into your web of debauchery by promising me naughty things you have no intention of following through with."

He'd planned to do it anyway. A wave of real emotion washed over her. Lexy's lips remained parted. She could still feel the warmth of his mouth against hers. *Her enemy was willing to chance the immortal equivalent of death for the right reasons.* She didn't want to look into Tiberius' eyes. *He was acting like the man she'd had a brief opportunity to spend time with during the halftime of the Summit. It confused things for her.*

"They should be here by now," Tiberius placed his hands on the handprints and opened the stall with ease. Kevin and Patrick were waiting outside of the door. He signalled them in and the group squeezed into the stall together.

Kevin smiled at her and asserted, "Don't accidentally lean against that button on the toilet seat. The stall will shrink."

She imagined that they'd all had a similar messed up experience the first time they'd used the bathroom in this place. "I only figured that out earlier this evening," Lexy replied to the boy who'd briefly been in their Clan. *He'd just done the unthinkable to the girl he loved for the greater good, and now, here he was, about to sacrifice himself for Kayn once again and she'd never be able to know.*

Kevin caught Lexy up with their plan, "Silas will be slipping Kayn something to keep the Dragon at bay. We'll also be drugging the wine in the King's suite. With any luck it will temporarily knock out the King and he'll think he blacked out. There's more to it, but long story short, we'll need to use the room next door, and it belongs to Prince Amadeus. Can you get us all in there?"

If the King drank the wine from his bedroom and if Kayn took Silas's advice, this might work. There were a lot of ifs involved in this plan's success. Lexy answered, "I think I can get us in the room next door."

Kevin nodded at her and said, "Let's do this. We'll need to get back to our seats and act appropriately shocked when they take her."

Tiberius opened the door for the two boys, gestured them out and added, "Get back to your seats, we'll wait a minute and follow." He shut the stall, once again leaving the two of them all alone. Tiberius whispered, "Just in case everything goes wrong tonight, can I kiss you goodbye?"

She nodded as their parted lips met. Her pulse raced as she thought of *Tiberius' words, Just in case everything goes wrong.* As their lips parted, she stared into her enemy's entrancing ocular pools of seduction. *Oh, hell, they were probably going to end up entombed for a hundred years for this. What did she have to lose?* Becoming the aggressor, she passionately kissed him, erotically tormenting him with her tongue until he stepped away and groaned, "Oh, sweetheart, I know I'm going to kick myself for stopping this, but you have a Prince to speak to, and we have a virgin sacrifice to stop."

He was right. What was she doing?

Enemies once again, they left the bathroom and walked down the long hall in silence. Without even looking at each other, they parted ways and strolled out. Lexy made her way to her seat. The music had ceased to play and no more began. The announcer came on and asked the stragglers on the dance floor to take their seats. Everyone wandered to the tables. Grey pulled out Kayn's chair before and Lexy smiled at her Handler as they passed each other.

Grey grabbed hold of her arm and whispered in her ear, "If I disappear for the rest of the evening are you going to be okay with that?"

Lexy squeezed his shoulder, smiled and whispered back, "Do whatever makes you happy." She paused and teased, "Just don't drink too much and puke in that bathroom again." *She wasn't going to be around to peel anything off of his face.*

Grey chuckled as he walked away. Lexy grinned as she made her way back to her chair and sat down beside an unsuspecting Kayn. The fledgling Dragon smiled at her as she took a drink from her goblet of wine.

Giving her a rather comic giant grin, Kayn asked, "Do I have purple teeth?"

Her teeth were fine. Lexy replied, "No, you don't, and this makeup stays on for days. It's like a temporary tattoo. Kind of cool isn't it?"

"I wish it was a permanent tattoo," Kayn sighed. "I'll never be able to copy this masterpiece. I had no idea I could look like this. What's going to happen now?"

Do not react. Don't think about it. Lexy kept her mind blank as she responded, "It's probably another sick and twisted show."

Frost took his seat and Lexy didn't dare look his way. She glanced across the table at her lifeline to humanity and he was grinning at her. *Grey was obliviously happy that they were all together again. He probably thought nothing could rain on his parade but a shit storm was about to hit.* She looked back as a concerned expression flashed across Kayn's face. *She wasn't stupid. Everyone was avoiding looking at her, it couldn't be more obvious. The fledgling Dragon sensed the darkness coming.*

Sidetracking Kayn's thoughts by touching her arm, Lexy smiled, looked directly at Grey and whispered, "I love seeing him like this."

Grinning back at her, Kayn replied, "Me too."

Lexy looked into her goblet and there were a couple of yellow flowers bobbing around in the deep burgundy liquid. *Oh, this is bullshit. They were trying to calm her Dragon down too. Now, she was pissed.* She glanced up as she sensed her Handler watching her.

Grey mouthed the words, "What's going on?"

It was her Handler's job to sense her anger and attempt to rectify the problem before it got out of hand but there was little he could do in this situation. Lexy mouthed the words, "Trust me." She casually disposed of her tainted wine by dumping it into Kayn's when she wasn't looking. *It couldn't hurt.* Someone passed by and refilled her wine. Trying to keep Kayn occupied so she wouldn't notice the sedating flowers in her drink, Lexy praised, "I'm proud of you guys. You were amazing in there."

Knitting her brow, Kayn peered into her goblet, fished out the flowers and wiped her hand on a napkin as she answered, "Could you see us in the Testing?"

She was a smart girl. Lexy replied, "No, but Winnie told Jenna how you were all doing every once in a while. Each Clan's Guardian and Oracles were able to witness parts of the Testing." Lexy glanced at Frost. He was pensively staring into his goblet of wine, tracing the rim with his finger. *He knew and couldn't say anything.* As Kayn turned to look at Frost, Lexy placed the yellow flowers from Kayn's napkin back into her wine. *It would be easier for her if she were sedated, upfront.* Before Kayn had a chance to drink from the goblet, the trumpet played to get everyone's attention. *Here we go.* Bracing herself, Lexy did her best to maintain an emotionless expression. *This would be a true testament to her inner Dragon. She couldn't shut her emotions down. She had to be cunning not reckless. Nobody in her Clan could know what they had planned, not when the penalty was entombment. The four of them would be the only ones compromised if the whole plan went south.* She glanced up at her Handler and checked herself. *If he heard her thoughts, he would never allow her to go through with it. This one time, even Grey couldn't know.*

A man dressed in flamboyant clothing marched to the center of the room. He cleared his throat and announced, "As decreed by pureblood immortal law. The unbroken Dragons shall surrender themselves to the King."

Kayn glanced at Frost. His voice caught with emotion as he whispered, "Stand up and walk over there. You have to go. It's not a choice."

Kayn spun around to look at Lexy and whispered, "This isn't seriously happening?"

They weren't going to do this. She wasn't going to let them do this... Lexy squeezed her hand under the table. She looked into her eyes, and said, "If you don't go willingly, they'll take you by force. Do you trust me?"

Kayn responded, "Of course, I do."

Squeezing her hand again, Lexy prompted, "Then stand up with all of the grace and dignity you can muster and walk to the center of the room."

As Kayn rose to her feet, their entire table was furious but no one more than Lexy. *She didn't care what happened to her. She was going to stop this.*

Markus mouthed the words, "You have to go."

Kayn walked around the table with her head held high. When she reached the center of the room, she glanced back at the table of friends and sworn enemies, and in true Dragon form, she mouthed the words, "I'll be okay."

Lexy was so proud of her. The frilly man summoned Kayn to follow and they walked out through the archway.

Chapter 12

Virgin Sacrifices

There was a long, intensely volatile silence as Clan Ankh fought to reign in their reaction to the virgin sacrifice. *It was more than that, it was everyone in the room.* You could hear a pin drop. Lexy's heart thudded in her chest with nervous energy and lack of faith in her acting ability. *She was lying by omission to everyone. She had to appear to be just as shocked and mortified as the others were. This was not a rule or a law. The King had created one to suit the situation and unfortunately, there was no Guardian present to veto the King's twisted demands. Second-Tier had no rights. Her Handler was suspicious. She'd remained far too composed for it to be believable. Grey wasn't stupid, he knew she was up to something. She'd seen that look of disapproval on far too many occasions to misread what he was saying with his eyes, don't you dare do anything stupid, Lexy.* Meeting Grey's unimpressed gaze, Lexy mouthed the words, "Go help Zach deal with this. I'm fine." *Perhaps, she should have reworded that last sentence. I'm fine rarely meant she was.* With a skeptical look, Grey calmly rose and made his way over to Zach. *She was a fledgling Dragon. Zach was new at the Handler thing, he needed to understand this was a situation he couldn't fix.*

Grey had been in Zach's shoes at one time. He'd been the Handler of the girl that was taken by a Prince. The only difference being, she'd been taken by the good brother, Amadeus hadn't touched her. This situation was different. The King wouldn't be feeding Kayn pastries and chatting about life. He'd be unleashing unresolved feelings for her mother in an alcoholic fit of rage. Lexy watched Grey reasoning with Kayn's agitated Handler. Before Lexy had the opportunity to even think about what her next move would be, a voice behind her announced, "Prince Amadeus requests the pleasure of your company."

Lexy glanced at the head table. Amadeus made eye contact with her but didn't attempt to leave. He would stay until she'd been escorted to his quarters. She exchanged a look with Grey. *He knew she was safe with this royal. He'd stay by Zach's side for the remainder of the evening and make sure he behaved himself.* Lexy stood up and turned back to look at the table of worried Ankh she adored. *These were her people.* Her gaze lingered on Grey. She fought the urge to confess everything she had planned with Triad. *He'd never let her do it without him, and if this scheme backfired, they'd all end up entombed. She could roll the dice on her own freedom but not on his.* The urge passed as she briskly followed the guard across the empty dance floor and out of the banquet hall without looking back at the keeper of her heart. Lexy exchanged a look with Silas as they passed by each other and knew he'd given Kayn the flower. *She didn't like to think about those flowers but they were a much-needed means to an end in this scenario. The flowers would calm down Kayn's Dragon as they'd once calmed hers.* A memory of the pile of yellow flowers the lady had left buried in the corner of stall eleven, under the hay flashed through her mind. She blinked the horrors of her adolescence away, but her mind wouldn't allow her to blink away the truth. *The flowers in Kayn's wine earlier that evening had been to sedate her so she wouldn't fight back as the King violated her. If she fought back, he would have her entombed as he'd done to many of the Ankh that resided in this realm as slaves.* She checked out the palms of the man directing her to the Prince's quarters as his arms swung back and forth. His chest was covered by golden half-top length armour. She couldn't tell if he was Triad because she couldn't see the brand on the flesh above his heart. If he was Trinity or Ankh, his brand would be on the palm of his hand. After paying attention for a few dozen swings, she was pretty sure his hands were free of marks. *This is probably why the Third-Tiers had this guard wearing armour. It was to hide his identifying mark. Was that a keyhole on the back of his armour?* Lexy balled the fist of her hand branded with the symbol of Ankh. *This symbol was a part of who she was now. To have their mark of Clan hidden away would mess with a Second-Tier's mind. They disguised their brands under fingerless gloves back home. They could get away with the marks as body art on earth, but if one of them was seriously injured, their symbols would glow, and a group of people with glowing hands tends to freak mortals out.* She wandered barefoot on marble behind the guard, taking in the colourful woven tapestries adorning the walls, wondering if they told a story. *She didn't have the time to stand and stare for an hour to decipher the plot. She'd ask the Prince someday. There would always be a someday, even if at the end of this day, she found herself entombed. She was immortal and this was a worthy cause. It was time to stand against the dictatorship, even if it was a mini stand that nobody would ever know about if everything went according to plan.*

Lexy was led past where Kayn was into the room that belonged to Prince Amadeus. She was ushered inside and the door was closed behind her. Lexy couldn't help but smile as she thought of the first night she'd been ushered into his room. *She'd assumed he was going to try to defile her, but instead, he'd befriended her. Prince Amadeus was a truly miraculous being. He'd been young and handsome when they met, but he'd allowed himself to age. Probably, so he'd continue to appear older than his children. He was a good man and she was about to drag him into this plan of theirs.* Lexy sat down on his bed and touched the silken sheets beneath her fingertips. *This had to work.* She got up, wandered over and stood by the door joining the rooms. Lexy placed her Ankh branded palm against the door and willed Kayn to feel her presence. *Kayn wouldn't be afraid of what the King was going to do to her, she'd just survived a simulation of hell. There was no dignity in this situation and even though Kayn was like her in so many ways, she didn't have to be like her in this one. The beginning of her afterlife didn't have to be tainted by defilement as her own had been. Lexy was a Healer, that was her ability. She'd healed from many things over the last forty years with Ankh but had never been able to fully repair the damage from being a victim of this heinous form of abuse.* Lexy turned to look as the door opened, relieved to see it wasn't three Triad. *She wanted to warn Amadeus, she didn't want to just spring it on him.*

Her royal companion strolled in, closed the door and strolled across the room. As Prince Amadeus approached, he apologized, "I'm sorry. I had no idea my brother was going to do that. I wish there was something I could do to stop it but she looks so much like Freja."

Opting out of beating around the bush, Lexy ripped off the band-aid, "If there was something you could do to help me, would you?" Prince Amadeus stopped himself from saying whatever was on the tip of his tongue. He winced and nodded, yes. *She was putting him in an impossible situation.* With faith in their friendship, she confided, "All you have to do is dismiss the Guards. We have a plan to stop this, but it can only work with your help. No harm will come to your brother."

Prince Amadeus exhaled and scolded, "All I have to do is dismiss the guards?" He paced back and forth, paused and questioned, "Do you know what you're asking me to do?"

"The right thing," Lexy abruptly responded.

His expression softened, and she knew he was in, as he shook his head slowly and quietly countered, "You know what will happen if we get caught?"

"I do," she curtly replied.

Without saying another word, Prince Amadeus briskly marched over to the door and loudly dismissed the guards. He closed it, turned around and addressed her, "You'd better have one hell of a plan."

She met his eyes with her own as she apologized, "We do. I'm sorry we're dragging you into this. If there's ever anything I can do for you…" *There was no point in promising him anything when their future was this uncertain.* He opened his arms and they embraced.

The Prince whispered in her ear, "Let's just say true friendship is a rather difficult thing to acquire with my social standing and if ever I need anything, I'll let you know."

Lexy pulled away from him and smiled as she looked around. A half dozen, four-foot-tall transparent crystals were positioned around the room. She knew what they were for, but thought it prudent to be certain, "Those are for privacy, aren't they?"

"What goes on in the royal suites cannot be monitored by even the most powerful Oracles. Let's just say they've been placed there to disguise my brother's sick, depraved habits with the ladies. There's nothing us royals fear more than humiliation."

Now, the success of their plan seemed even more plausible. Lexy smiled, nodded and disclosed, "That's what we're counting on."

There was a quiet knock on the door. The Prince strolled over and opened it, revealing her co-conspirators. Prince Amadeus grinned as he stepped aside, ushered them in and announced, "Come in…Triad? This ought to be good." He turned to Lexy, chuckled and teased, "Aren't you full of surprises today. Look at you all in bed with the enemy."

She had to smile, that comment hit close to home. Lexy bit her lip and glanced at Tiberius as her comic inner dialogue whispered, *Not yet. They were about to do something utterly insane, but to be honest, for Lexy, finding herself in insane situations was a common occurrence.* Kevin, Patrick and Tiberius of Triad cautiously entered, unsure as to whether they could trust the Prince. She directed her statement to the group, "You can trust him, he's a friend." She smiled at the Prince.

He responded to her declaration of friendship by taking her hand, looking at Tiberius and saying, "I know he deserves it but I've been assured no physical harm will come to my brother. Setting him up in an embarrassing situation to save the girl, sounds like a fun-filled evening I'd like to be a part of. Let's just say I owe him one for a few things."

Grinning at the Prince, Tiberius extended his hand and exclaimed, "I always knew you were the good brother."

Giving the leader of Triad's hand a firm shake, Prince Amadeus sparred, "To be honest, I've always heard Thorne was the good brother, out of you three heads of Clan."

"He's definitely the vanilla ice-cream of the three, I'd like to consider myself more of a butter pecan man, just as sweet but a little nutty," Tiberius joked.

Sprawling provocatively on the Prince's silk bedding, Patrick flirtatiously sighed, "These sheets are incredible, I could get used to sleeping on these."

Kevin grinned, gave his friend a look and chuckled, "I'll buy you some if you can promise you'll stay focused."

Patrick launched himself off the bed and wandered over to stand by Lexy as Tiberius filled Amadeus in on their plan.

Tiberius could be personable when he wanted to be. Lexy didn't want to be impressed but she found herself wondering what it would have been like if they'd met under normal circumstances. *What was she even thinking? They'd never been normal. Neither of them had.* The rest of the group shook hands with their royal co-conspirator like they were long lost friends as they adjusted their plot to the circumstances. They even managed to devise a plan for if everything went wrong.

Kevin took the lead of the conversation, "We've been trying to drug Kayn all evening. We don't know if she took the flower from Silas and understood why she needed to ingest it. He wouldn't have been able to explain anything. He probably had just long enough to pass it to her."

Curious, Prince Amadeus questioned, "What are the odds of her eating a flower someone passed to her with no explanation?"

Visibly stricken, Kevin confessed, "She'd not the same person anymore, I don't know. I do know if she objects to anything the King does, she'll be entombed. If she hasn't been sedated, fighting back is in a Dragon's nature. We've created a second opportunity to drug both the King and Kayn. The carafe of wine in the King's room has also been drugged. If that doesn't work, we'll make sure our party disturbs his..."

It might work. In no time at all, the group devised the perfect cover story. Amadeus invited them up to his suite and they heard a commotion in the King's adjoining room while they were out on the balcony. With that, they went outside to listen for the start of trouble. Lexy glanced at Tiberius and caught him watching. He immediately looked away.

Prince Amadeus flirtatiously whispered in her ear, "I'm probably not supposed to act jealous because I'm married to someone else and nothing has ever happened between us, but I am."

Tiberius had turned away a second too late. Flattered, Lexy sparred, "After watching me fight at the Summit, your family would never allow you to be with me."

"Nonsense," Amadeus teased. "You'd be an amazing princess. Nobody would dare mess with me, they'd all be afraid my wife was going to kick their ass."

Wife... that was funny. She had Grey, so marriage wasn't really an option. This is my Handler. He needs to sleep with us, it's important we maintain our bond. If I go on a murderous rampage, he's the only one that can stop me. The Handler Dragon bond could be considered a marriage of souls and what was marriage, if not that? The courtyard overlooked a gorgeous botanical garden. As she inhaled the intoxicating fragrance, the visual sprung to mind. She heard something in the room. *It was starting.* The King's voice boomed and she fought the instinct to defend Kayn. They were all out there watching as the King began his verbal assault. *He thought Kayn was Freja.* Lexy's eyes darted to the disgusted Prince, standing beside her. *Drink the wine asshole. Drink it.* The easy version of their plan hinged on the King drinking from the goblet of wine on the table. They watched as the King drank straight from the carafe. *He'd be out cold in no time.* Relief spread across everyone's faces. *They would only have to allow the scenario to play out for a few more minutes.* The King brutally smoked Kayn's face with the heavy carafe. She covered her face with her hands, lost her footing and staggered backwards, the wall stopped her from going down.

Cursing under his breath, Prince Amadeus hissed, "That's enough for me." He walked into his brother's room, grabbed a large ceramic vase off a pedestal as he passed, wound up and his brother passed out cold before he had the opportunity to clock him with it. Prince Amadeus took a well-timed step back against the curtained velvet wall as Kayn removed her hands from her injury and wobbled around, fighting against the effects. She closed her eyes and Amadeus stealthily slipped back into the room next door.

"We'd better get in there," Lexy whispered.

Tiberius winked and said, "I've got this." He left her side and strolled into the room. Kayn opened her eyes again to find Tiberius standing in front of her. Tiberius winked at her and teased, "He tagged me in. The King was far too drunk to keep going."

Barely coherent, Kayn gasped, "What?"

"I'm only joking, don't get your panties in a twist," Tiberius laughed.

She quietly slurred, "Did you drug me?"

Gently touching her face where she'd been injured, Tiberius provoked, "You drugged yourself."

Kayn staggered sideways towards a tapestry on the wall and grabbed it to stop herself from falling. She crumpled to the floor, tugged it down and the material landed on top of her.

Shaking her head, Lexy walked over to Kayn's crumpled body, socked Tiberius' arm and scolded, "He tagged me in, what's wrong with you?"

"Oh, come on. You know that was hilarious," Tiberius chuckled as he dodged Lexy's fist, grinned and deviously flirted, "Hold that thought. I'll let you smack me around later."

He was incorrigible. Lexy no longer felt the need to deny her growing attraction to her alluringly suggestive adversary because today they were allies. As were Kevin and Kayn. She watched as Kevin knelt next to the girl he'd loved enough to destroy during the Testing. He tenderly caressed her bruised cheek, glared at the King's crumpled form and commented, "It's probably for the best if one of you guys moves the King's body into his bed."

The Triad with the beautiful soul named Patrick offered, "I'll do it."

Amadeus wandered back in with stellar timing and announced, "The hall is still clear. I'm guessing everyone is out cold?" Prince Amadeus grabbed his brother's legs and helped Patrick lug his deplorable excuse for a sibling on to his bed.

Lexy watched for a second and suggested, "Strip him down, it needs to be believable. Kevin, can you bring Kayn into the other room?" Kevin answered by lifting Kayn's body and cradling her in his arms as he carried her limp form into the next room, where they'd covered the floor with one of the King's sheets so they could soak up the mess they were about to make. Amadeus and Patrick stripped the King down.

As Patrick tugged off his final article of clothing, he comically exclaimed, "Well, at least we know why he's such a dick. He doesn't have one so he's got to throw his whole being into it."

She really liked this kid. The Prince and Patrick went into the other room to make sure Kayn didn't wake up alone. Unsure of her abilities strength, they needed her to play along. Kevin wandered outside with Tiberius to make sure their story was believable, being obnoxiously loud as they drank from goblets. Lexy strolled back into the King's suite, kind of looking forward to setting up a horrifying struggle scene as she plotted where the blood would go. Kayn had already done a wonderful job of tugging the curtains from the wall. *This had to be messier. It needed a gruesome amount of blood. If there was blood everywhere this whole virgin sacrifice scenario would be buried and never repeated. She was going to set this up to be a humiliation unlike anything the Royal family had ever seen.* Lexy glared at the King's unconscious nude form sprawled on the bed. She looked at her pinky. *Her pinky finger was larger than his manhood. Well, now she just felt kind of sorry for the abusive psycho. It was sad really.*

Kevin stuck his head into the room and whispered, "She's awake. I'm going to keep out of sight. It's better if she doesn't know I'm involved."

Lexy nodded at her co-conspirator, understanding why he couldn't take credit for saving her. Kevin couldn't risk the possibility that any act of bravery or love on his behalf would draw Kayn's heart back to him when she needed to be able to move on with her life. She walked out onto the balcony to sneak a peek but left Prince Amadeus and Patrick to deal with her. *Kayn was confused and groggy but she was awake. That was fast.*

Patrick, the gentlest most beautiful Triad, wandered over to where Ankh's fledgling Dragon lay and assured, "We're not going to hurt you. You've been drugged to subdue the Dragon. You probably don't recognize me, do you? It's Patrick and this is Prince Amadeus. You'll have to stay hidden in here with us for a little while."

Kayn felt her face and winced as she questioned, "Am I remembering this right? Did Tiberius just help me?"

Patrick grinned and replied, "It was Lexy and Tiberius. Oddly enough they were in on it together. Shocking, I know, but none of us were down with the new sacrificing a virgin policy."

Kayn stared at the Prince with distrust in her eyes. Prince Amadeus disclosed, "I'm friends with Lexy, I was also close friends with your mother, Freja. I helped her escape. My brother won't know what happened. He usually blacks out when he's been on a bender, he never remembers a damn thing. We'll need to make it look convincing though..." Amadeus came over and placed large chamber pots on the floor. The good Prince handed Kayn a knife and instructed, "We're going to need a lot of your blood. Enough blood to cause embarrassment to the royal family. That way, none of this will be questioned." Kayn sliced her arm and blood slowly dripped into the pot in a thin line of red.

Grinning, Patrick prompted, "There's no time, Kayn. We don't even have time for you to use blood from both wrists. You do it, or I'll do it for you. We're all involved now."

He wanted her to slit her own throat and drain it into the pot. Lexy recalled Kayn's story about the event that made her a Dragon during the Testing. *The boy she'd loved more than anything had slit her throat. This was probably part of the reason Kevin wanted to leave. A normal person would have hit pause during this moment but not a Dragon. Kayn Brighton was a Dragon now. She wouldn't back down from this request.* She wasn't the least bit surprised when Kayn grabbed the knife out of his hand, leaned over the bowl and ran the blade across her own throat. Blood gushed an oozing crimson river of victory from the fatal wound. Kayn's body slumped. Patrick rushed to her side and held her over the bowl, making sure they didn't lose the precious evidence of the violence she'd been forced to inflict upon herself. Her eyelids flickered and closed as the first chamber pot filled. Patrick moved her over to the next one as Lexy grabbed the full one and rushed into the King's chambers. *This was going to be fun!* She sprinkled the covers in red and painted the walls with blood, leaving brilliantly placed bloody handprints smudged down the white marble bed posts and on the edges of the sheets, giving the appearance of a brutal struggle. The bloody handprints added a particularly gruesome effect to the morbid display. She was impressed with herself as Tiberius appeared with the second pot of blood.

"You my dear, are having way too much fun," he chuckled.

Lexy grinned at her diabolical counterpart as they made sure to paint the deplorable King's palms and clothing. It was quite relaxing. She finger-painted a whimsical crimson happy face on the white marble headboard and stared at it.

Tiberius chuckled and provoked, "Seriously, are we drawing happy faces at murder scenes with people's blood now? You really need to find a new hobby and I mean something other than murder."

With a swipe of Lexy's hand her creation disappeared. The diabolically creative duo left a tell-tale trail of blood and gave Amadeus' door a few bloody handprints for shock and awe. *The scene had been set and it was just about perfect. She rather enjoyed painting. Perhaps, she'd try using a brush and water-colours rather than chamber pots full of blood next time. Kayn's blood really was a delightful shade of red.* Lexy pouted as she left her artistic ventures behind to join the others and plan for the next stage of their nasty little plot against the King. *Amadeus's room was spotless. The others had done a wonderful job of covering their tracks, leaving no hint Kayn had been anywhere but in the King's room being brutally murdered.* Peering back into the King's suite, Lexy glanced at Tiberius and whispered, "We need to get out of here before he wakes up."

Tiberius grinned and replied, "He'll be out for hours. Don't worry about that part."

Smiling at her co-conspirator, Lexy spoke, "You guys deal with her body. I'll go with Prince Amadeus. Story adjustment, we were on the deck drinking, the party went inside. We heard a struggle and smelled blood from the open balcony. Amadeus was concerned for his brother's safety." Kayn gasped as she awoke, clutching her throat. *That was fast. She wasn't a Healer, was she? How did her Conduit ability work?* Lexy stepped back into the other room so she could remain out of sight and still hear their conversation. Tiberius gave Kayn a brief rundown of the plan and convinced her to eat yellow flowers, explaining they were used to sedate immortals, even Healers and she had to be unconscious. Surprisingly enough, Kayn ate the flowers without a fuss and in less than a minute, Ankh's fledgling Dragon was dead to the world.

Tiberius lifted one of Kayn's arms and let it go. It flopped and he announced, "We're good to go. She'll be out cold long enough to pass for dead."

They placed her in her own blood by the King on his bed and tore her dress off her lifeless body. Her throat was slit again, and the knife was left in the sleeping King's hand. Amadeus and Lexy stood in the doorway as the others made sure not a speck of evidence remained. Hoping Kayn was down for the count, they went to alert his family to the King's debauchery.

Amadeus whispered something to the first guard they came across. In a couple of minutes royals Lexy recognized from the head table appeared and followed them back to the King's suite in refined silence. She wasn't sure what Prince Amadeus told the guard, but the royals appeared prepared for the worst. Prince Amadeus opened the door and ushered the others in. *There really were no words for what they had walked into.* Lexy felt a surge of pride in her work as a solemn looking lady's lips parted in shock. Visibly appalled by the insanity, a woman in a golden gown spun around to look at the others, who wore comically matching expressions. *She had to be a close relative of Prince Amadeus's with her matching dark features, perhaps a sibling.*

Scowling at Amadeus, the woman in gold accused, "You were right next-door partying with this group of Second-Tiers the entire time. Surely, you must have sensed things had gotten out of hand long before it came to this."

That hit a nerve. Lexy had never seen the gentle Prince furious but his relative's comment caused fire to flicker in his usually kind eyes.

He flippantly countered, "Shall I bust in here every night? Things are always out of hand with our dear sibling. His abusive habits have always been an issue, but you allow him to do whatever he wants, including my wife by the way. I'm sure you've known about that one for a while. If I can't stop him from doing that, I sure as hell can't stop him from doing this, now can I? He was your choice for King. You deal with the consequences. You fix this with the Clans and Guardians. I'd imagine a virgin sacrifice and a brutal massacre of this magnitude would be frowned upon."

The woman Lexy now understood was the Princess appeared defeated. She directed her gaze at Kevin, Lexy, Tiberius and Patrick as she vowed, "I shall never disclose the identity of the Second-Tiers involved in the discovery of the body. I'll say I came to Amadeus' chambers to discuss a personal matter and thought perhaps my other brother would like to join us. We saw the bloody display and I suggested we rectify this humiliating situation by removing the girl's body. The King would never harm me, but he may harm Amadeus, especially since he covets something he has. One of you may quickly enter to collect the girl's body. We'll leave our brother here to awaken to the horror of what he has done."

They were all doing well in the acting department but Kevin's face as he walked in and scooped Kayn's blood-drenched body in his arms was Oscar-worthy. Her limbs dangled limply as he carried her out with a heartbroken expression that almost made her forget they were the ones that set up the bloodbath. *He was good.* The solemn group was escorted to a room Lexy had never seen before. It was a room of pristine grey and black marble with an enormous sandstone tomb that lay dead center. This lavish tomb was much fancier than the ones they used to travel around in, with its ornate engravings and rich-toned gems embedded into the stone. Lexy was drawn to touch it as though she were nothing but a newbie Ankh who didn't know better. All three Clan's symbols were intricately etched into the stone. It slid open. *The gemstone interior was green.* Lexy felt panicked as they placed Kayn's Ankh body on the bed of what appeared to be emerald. *It had to be rose quartz. This looked like one of Triad's tombs.*

The graceful Princess with elegantly pinned up black hair explained, "This tomb can be used for all Clan as an escape hatch from this realm. We're just transporting her soul back to the in-between before our brother wakes up." Prince Amadeus stood regally by his sister as she vowed,

"You have my word, this will never be allowed to happen again. I know you understand this incident must never be spoken of to protect all parties involved, including your companion, little brother."

Little brother. She must be next in line for the throne. The four nodded in agreement as the lid to the Crypt ground closed and they followed the royals out of the room.

Prince Amadeus paused in the hall and spoke to the group, "You should go now. Quickly gather your Clans and leave." He started walking away, stopped and said, "Hey, Lexy… Be happy."

Lexy gave her Prince a grateful smile. Unable to speak the words that lingered on the tip of her tongue, she stored the gratitude she felt for his selfless actions in her heart. *She would save it there and in his name, she would choose to do something good.* As he walked away with the other royals, her heart caught in her chest. *His brother was bedding his wife. What if the King was just looking for an excuse to get him out of the way? If he found out about his part in this, she'd just handed it to him.*

Tiberius spoke, snapping her out of her fog, "Get the rest of your Clan out of here. The shit is going to hit the fan when the King wakes up."

She called out his name, "Tiberius!"

He turned back, winked and replied, "I know."

Lexy was laughing on the inside as she watched him walk away. *This had been a severely messed-up oddly enjoyable night.*

Chapter 13

Covenant Of Dragons

It had only been twenty-four hours since they'd arrived back in the land of the living. Everyone had made a silent agreement they wouldn't speak of the unfortunate virgin sacrifice situation and lumped that horror in with the Testing. The five newest members of Ankh were doing well, only Kayn appeared to be having ability related issues. *In all fairness, she had two somewhat volatile abilities at play and a Handler that had no idea what he was doing.* The first ability Kayn decided to absorb was Frost's. *It wasn't like she hadn't seen that coming.*

Their table in the diner was humming with the chatter of animated voices. It was always funny how many of these little places still had the same things. This one had painfully seventies mustard yellow pleather seating in the booths. They preferred to sit together, but on the rare occasion, they were all in one place and had far too many people to squeeze into a booth. Lexy smiled as Kayn's predictable order arrived and watched in awe as the fledgling Dragon dumped an insane amount of hot sauce on her food. *What in the hell was that about? It must be a Dragon thing. She was also obsessed with hot sauce.* She found herself intrigued yet knew there would be no point in asking Kayn why she was doing anything at this point. *She probably had no idea. The whole group sounded like they had one of those go hard or go home nights planned, but she already had plans to watch a movie with Orin. It was a friend thing, not a relationship thing, but she hadn't mentioned it to Grey and honestly wasn't sure why she hadn't.* She glanced up from her drink and accidentally met Frost's gaze. He smiled and she returned the gesture. *She'd confided in Frost that Kayn's virginity had been protected because she suspected it wasn't going to take him long to figure it out the old-fashioned way and didn't want him to blow the whole thing. She hadn't told him anyone else was involved. All she'd said was that it was stopped before anything happened and he'd read between the lines.* Kayn abruptly got up from the table and rushed to the bathroom. Jenna excused herself and followed their distressed friend. *There was drama going on and she'd missed it.* She watched Jenna knocking on the door until Kayn let her in. *It was probably just more ability related issues. She'd had Grey to help her through hers.* Lexy turned to look at her Handler. *She was always grateful for him even when he was being an idiot.*

Grey placed his arm around her and whispered in her ear, "Should I talk to Zach? He hasn't even noticed she's left the table."

"It couldn't hurt," Lexy quietly replied. *Zach was too busy flirting with Melody to notice anything.*

The waitress came around to refill their water glasses and the whole table ceased all conversations mid-sentence. As soon as the mortal wandered away, the steady hum of chatter began again.

Grey leaned in, lovingly kissed her cheek. As he pulled away, he whispered, "Jenna's dealing with it. I bet you a back massage we're eventually going to have to split Zach and Melody up, so he'll be able to concentrate on his job."

Just like they'd done to Arrianna and Grey so he could concentrate on her. They'd probably have to separate Kayn and Frost

174

too. She met his eyes with her own and in a hushed voice, she sparred, "I bet they'll separate Kayn and Frost first."

Grey sipped his honey ale and nonchalantly popped a ketchup covered fry into his mouth as he contemplated her bet adjustment. He swallowed his mouthful and whispered, "Alright, if they separate Zach and Melody first, I win. If it's Kayn and Frost, you win."

"Deal," Lexy decreed and they shook on it. Kayn sat back down at the table much calmer than she'd been before she'd left. Jenna strolled over and whispered something in Zach's ear. He glanced over at Kayn with a guilty look in his eyes. *He didn't want to be Kayn's Handler. If it was painfully obvious to the entire table, it would be just as evident to Kayn.* Once again, Lexy turned to Grey thankful he'd never acted like this when his job as her Handler had been thrust upon her. She took a sip of her drink and recalled the day they met and how he'd followed her back to her cabin deep in the woods. *Had it been anyone else, she may have killed them first and asked questions later. There was something about Grey that made her certain she could trust him, and she was the girl who trusted no one.* Lexy glanced over at Kayn and observed her flirtation with Frost. *A part of her wanted to take her aside and tell her about the role Kevin played in her rescue. Perhaps, that would slow this thing with Frost down?*

She heard her Handler's raspy whisper in her ear, "It's too late. She's fed from his ability. You know what Lily and Frost are like when their abilities have been triggered."

Had Grey just heard that whole thought, or had he guessed what she was thinking because of the concerned expression on her face? She peered over at Grey. *He was intently observing the flirtatious exchange between Frost and Kayn. He hadn't been tuned into her thoughts.* Two emotions washed over her, relief and guilt. *She was relieved he didn't know she'd left him out of the loop that night to keep him safe but felt guilty because she had a secret and it felt like she was lying by omission.* Lexy stuck the fork in her steak and savoured the mouthful. *Beef was so much better than that sketchy stringy meat they'd been eating at the banquet.*

Frost whispered, "You might want to pace yourself. Pick a drink and stick to it. If you mix beer and cider with those sweet drinks Lily likes your night will end badly."

Kayn reached across the table, stole one of his fries, dipped it in his ketchup and popped it into her mouth. She sparred, "This isn't my first time."

Frost slid her beer back across the table and teased, "I warned you."

Kayn licked the ketchup off her finger, picked up her glass and took a sip. *Oh, boy. This wasn't going to take him long at all.* Lexy gave Frost a disapproving look. He winked at her and shrugged. Lexy had to smile, she couldn't help it. *Kayn couldn't be with Kevin. She had to let that go and Frost was a beautiful distraction.* Lexy slid her hand onto Grey's bare leg without thinking about her actions. He slid his over hers and they laced their fingers together, keeping her from pulling it away when she realised what she was doing. *She hadn't done that on purpose. She had to stop luring Grey back to her with intimate actions, especially when she was actively trying to move on.* He loosened his grasp and Lexy casually slipped her hand off his thigh. Using her hands to shield her mouth, she pretended to cough. *Markus got up. They were calling it a night.* They said their goodbyes and left the diner with the jingling of the bells on the door. *The entire group was preparing to leave.*

"I'm out of here," Frost announced. "Are you guys still coming with me?"

Grey looked at her and asked, "Are you sure you don't want to come with us?"

Lexy smiled and answered, "I'm all good. I told Orin I'd watch a movie with him. Have fun. Don't do anything I wouldn't do."

About to walk away, Grey paused and provoked, "After your shenanigans at the Summit, I guess that leaves me pretty open."

Lexy glared at him and ominously threatened, "You like to live dangerously, don't you?"

Grey yelped, "Shit!" As Lexy leapt out of her seat and chased him out of the jingling door into the parking lot.

She pursued him all the way to their room, pinned him up against the door.

He raised both of his hands, grinned and laughed, "I surrender. I surrender!"

She started tickling him. He managed to unlock the door while swatting her away, dashed to the bed and leapt onto it. He burrowed under the covers as she straddled the lump in the blankets created by his body and questioned, "You just can't let that go, can you?"

Her Handler popped his head out from under the nonexistent safety of the layer of mauve blankets, smiled at her and exclaimed, "For the record, I think Orin would be a wonderful option. I'm all for you and Orin. I'll even get team Lexor T-shirts made."

Giving him a dirty look, she sighed, "It's a friend thing, Grey. Orin is my friend. We're watching movies not auditioning for a role in Caligula."

He looked into her eyes and taunted, "Maybe you should be?"

She slowly shook her head. *He'd probably be happy to practice for a starring role in a remake of that movie with damn near anyone this evening.* Rolling her eyes as she got up, Lexy wandered to the bathroom, baiting, "I'm using the bathroom first. I guess I'll put some effort into it, you never know what might happen. After all, Orin was around back then." *She'd only been teasing him. She didn't really think anything would happen between them but knew if an ounce of jealousy remained that comment hit its target.* She found something to wear in her bag and changed into a comfortable silky navy dress with give to the material. Looking into the mirror, she applied her fire engine red lipstick, ran her fingers through her wavy crimson locks and grinned at the result. *She looked alright.*

Appearing in her reflection, Grey playfully kissed her cheek and announced, "Well, I'm off then."

As he walked away, she sang after him, "Have fun."

"Always," he called back, with a skip in his step.

Lexy stared at herself for a second longer and exhaled, imagining a different scenario where he'd chosen to stay. She sat on the edge of the tub and took another deep breath. *You're moving on. You are not going to do this anymore. You have to move on...* After a moment of forward thinking, Lexy stood up, briskly strutted across the room, grabbed her purse off the nightstand and left. Taking her time on the stroll to Orin's room, she paused and leaned over the balcony to gaze at the stars that lit up the night sky. *Grey would have stopped to look at these stars. This whole moving on to get over him plan was useless. No matter who she tried to move on with, she would always love him most. Anyone else could never be more than a pleasurable distraction.* Smiling as she shook her head, Lexy figuratively and factually stepped away from the ledge. *Her heart had a good argument, but her head kept fighting for her to take that step away from Grey so she could find something that could be more. Orin could be more if she let him. As pleasurable a distraction as Tiberius was, that could never be more than a fleeting affair.* She paused outside of Orin's door. *Perhaps, this wasn't the right timing for a new entanglement? She wasn't finished with Tiberius. That didn't matter. She was being ridiculous. She was overthinking everything.* Lexy knocked on his door,

After making her wait for longer than it would have taken him to make it there from anywhere in the room, Orin opened the door. *Maybe he was having the same thoughts? Well, minus the desire to sleep with Tiberius of course.* Smiling, he held the door open for her as she stepped over the threshold into a room that was a mirror image of hers with everything on the opposite side.

He leapt onto the bed, grinned and announced, "Do you have anything you've been dying to see?"

It took her a second to respond as she filtered his question through her now dirty mind. *Tiberius had done this to her with their continuous naughty exchanges.* She answered his possible naughty question with her own, "Do you have anything you want to see?"

With a twinkle in his eye, he took a chance with his response, "Come sit next to me on the bed and we can scroll through the options."

She slipped off her shoes and climbed onto the bed with her long-time friend. *She'd always thought he was attractive but he'd always been Jenna's. This felt wrong. There was no way Jenna could be alright with the thought of them being together as more than friends.* Knitting her brow, Lexy confessed, "It feels like Jenna couldn't possibly be okay with us being out on a date."

"Technically, we're staying in and it was her idea," he countered as he passed her a beer.

She took it from him and said, "You still love her though."

He grinned as he sparred, "You still love him."

Yes, they were in equally screwed up situations, weren't they?

Orin raised his beer can, "To moving on."

Lexy knocked her drink against his, noticing his five o'clock shadow was gone. *Orin was cleanly shaven and he'd obviously just had a haircut. His aftershave smelled incredible.* Smiling, she admitted, "You smell amazing. I love that aftershave."

"Frost is responsible for this date night makeover," he admitted.

This was probably Frost's way of saying thank you for what she'd done for Kayn. He'd spruced up her date. It was a little bit funny. Grinning, she suggested, "Well, let's pick out a movie."

They settled on an action movie and snuggled under the covers fully clothed. They drank a few beers and consumed a bag of chips but remained painfully in the friend zone. *Why wasn't he trying anything?* Lexy smiled as she clicked to what it was… *She'd spent forty years programming everyone to stay away from her. Orin wasn't going to make the first move. She didn't know how to make the first move with a guy other than Grey either. Tomas popped into her head. She'd made the first move once, with him.* Lexy shifted closer to Orin on the bed and realised she'd just devoured an entire bag of sour cream and onion chips. *She should have eaten the Salt and Vinegar chips. Her breath was probably nasty.* She excused herself. Orin paused the movie as she went to the washroom. *Where was his toothpaste?* Lexy found it and ate some, rubbing it on her tongue. She unwrapped one of the glasses and drank a full glass of water. *Now, at least she didn't smell horrible.* Lexy wandered back in and climbed onto the bed next to him. He started to laugh. She beamed and questioned, "What?"

He inched closer, looked into her eyes and teased, "Now, I have to go brush my teeth too."

She grinned and sparred, "I was eating sour cream and onion chips."

He nervously took her hand and assured, "It wouldn't have mattered to me, but it's become painfully obvious that we need to loosen up a bit." He jumped up, walked across the room to the minifridge and returned with an armload of tiny bottles. "I'm sure the Aries group won't mind the charge after shooting you multiple times for a new trainee."

Dropping the booze on the bed, he playfully provoked, "Pick your poison."

She took a tiny bottle of vodka and he did the same. Lexy twisted off the lid and cheered, "Bottoms up."

They both downed their first shot glass sized bottle as Orin said, "I have an idea.

Feeling the pleasurable numbing sensation, she grinned and replied, "Do tell?"

"How about a game of truth or dare?" Orin baited as he took the lid off another vodka bottle and passed it to her. She held hers up. They clinked bottles as she toasted, "To loosening up an awkward situation."

Laughing mid drink, he kept it together, swallowed and volunteered, "I'll go first."

Grinning, she enquired, "Truth or dare?"

"Truth," he replied, meeting her gaze.

She gave him an obvious question she already knew the answer too, "Are you over, Jenna?"

"Not yet," Orin admitted, without looking away. He drank another bottle, even though he didn't have to and urged, "Your turn."

Meeting his steady gaze, she stated, "Truth."

Orin passed her a bottle as he asked, "Are you over, Grey?"

Lexy downed the tiny bottle and made eye contact with Orin as she used his exact wording, "Not yet." She wasn't sure if it was the alcohol or the brutal honesty that was making her want to see how far the boundaries of their friendship could stretch, but she kept the game going as she whispered, "Truth or dare?"

He chuckled, looked into her eyes and said, "Truth."

She asked him the question she'd been curious about, "Are you sure you and Jenna won't get back together?"

Orin answered, "At first I thought Jenna was just punishing me for the whole impregnating her mortal look-alike revenge scenario, but we've had a chance to talk and she's adamant that we have different life paths to explore. Things are supposed to happen that our relationship has been keeping us from. You know the whole I love you but…conversation."

With the rules no longer a thing, Lexy passed him another bottle and whispered, "Truth."

Orin mischievously grinned as he shot her an intensely personal question, "How far did it go between you and Tiberius. Full disclosure no cheating."

She'd known this question was coming. Biting her lip, Lexy grabbed a bottle of amber liquid and downed it. She looked into his eyes and tried to explain what happened, "I promised him the ability to see into my past during the battle at the Summit. After he did, it created this connection between us. He showed me kindness and it confused me."

Grinning, Orin scolded, "The truth, Lexy. Remember, I'm a Healer too."

It occurred to her that he might also prefer things a little darker. He'd never seemed like the type. Lexy gave him the unfiltered version, "Let's just say we played extremely naughty healing games involving knives at the Summit. After that, we met up once in a stairwell. We've messed around but he's never had me. Not yet…"

Intrigued by her naughty confession, Orin provoked, "But you want to and if you had the opportunity to go through with it, you would?"

"Yes," was her unwavering response.

He stared into her eyes and whispered, "Truth."

Inching closer, she enticed, "This whole conversation turns you on, doesn't it?"

He took her hand, placed it on the painfully erect bulge, straining against his jeans and tempted, "You tell me?"

She'd always been curious as to why Jenna stayed with him for a thousand years. She'd guessed he had mad skills in the bedroom. Lexy straddled him, revealing her sexy black lace G-string underwear. He gasped as she rocked back and forth a little, leaned in and whispered in his ear, "That's not an answer."

He roughly clutched her hips and bucked as he groaned, "God, yes."

She kept slowly rocking her hips, grinding against him as she whispered in his ear, "Dare."

"Take off your dress," Orin commanded.

She seductively slipped off the thin layer of material and tossed it aside, revealing the overflowing cups of her black lace bra and barely there matching G-string panties. Orin responded to the sexy visual with one word, "Dare."

Lexy ordered him to take off his shirt and it was the fastest shirt removal, she'd ever witnessed. A giggle escaped as she took in his chiselled abs. *This was crazy but she was having far too much fun to stop.* Her fellow Healer's eyes darkened as she trailed a finger across the ridged peak of his nipple. He'd started to rhythmically move beneath her. She gasped as the friction made her shiver and ache for more. *Her panties were soaked. She wanted more.* Lexy gasped, "Dare."

Orin gripped her hips and deviously grinned as he ordered, "Take off your bra."

She continued moving with him while trying to unclasp her bra and this proved to be impossible. She ended up slipping her arms out and sliding it down to her waist. He skillfully undid the clasps and tossed it aside. Lexy shivered as his lips met with her tingling peaks. *She was so close.*

He groaned the word, "Dare," as he continued to grind his strained manhood against her. She gave him the one order that would push this little game they were playing to the edge, "Undo your pants."

Orin obediently undid his top button and unzipped his jeans. His impressively rigid manhood sprung out of his pants. *Of course, he'd be going commando.* She didn't even allow him the time to struggle the rest of the way out of his jeans before shifting her panties to one side and slipping down onto the length of him. *Oh God, she'd needed this so badly.* She could tell by Orin's expression of surprise that he hadn't expected it to go this far… *neither had she.* Lexy abandoned all doubt as she wildly rode him, taking what she needed until the aching within her became unbearable. His hands began to heat up where they were gripping the pliable silky flesh of her hips. Lexy gasped as his palms created a titillating current of sensual energy that flowed into her. As soon as the first wave reached the pit of her stomach, her own hands heated up in response. *What was happening? They were doing something to each other with their healing abilities. Something in their union was causing this heightened euphoric response, unlike anything she'd ever experienced. Her nerve endings could feel nothing but bliss.* With every thrust upon the member joining their beings, she felt the towering walls around her inhibitions crumble, like the petals of a sun-dried rose between two fingers. She watched his face as he fought to remain in control, he appeared to be losing the battle. Lexy wanted to kiss his lips and slow down a little to keep him going but she couldn't bring herself to stop the steady rhythmic movements bringing her such pleasure and joy.

His voice rasped, "Oh, shit. Honey, it's too much, I can't hold it in."

He started bucking hedonistically beneath her as their explosive energy ignited and imploded from where their bodies were intimately joined. Without a care of being heard, they simultaneously recklessly cried out. That initial wave of intense pleasure was followed by a mind-altering euphoria as continued shivers of pleasure rushed from where they were joined, blissfully trailing down her limbs. Lexy collapsed on top of him, breathless and slick with perspiration. *How long had they been at this? Why were they sweating this much?* She couldn't even maintain her thought process as she fell asleep with Orin still deep inside of her.

"This definitely lands in my top ten best ways to wake up," Orin whispered.

Oh, that woke her up. He was still balls deep inside of her... Awkward.

Grinning, Orin began rhythmically moving beneath her as he whispered, "Don't overthink it, I'm not."

The rippling trails of pleasure had already begun as Lexy gave him her breathy response, "Good."

They spent the entire night exhausting each other until the sun crept across their nude forms. *She'd better get back to her room.* She quietly got up and slipped on her dress, deciding to carry the bra and underwear she'd discarded. After taking a last appreciative look at the unassuming sex god's sleeping form, she snuck out of his room. *She hadn't seen that coming. Orin would understand if he woke up alone.* She made it back to her room unseen and braced herself as she opened the door, hoping Grey spent the night elsewhere. *She heard him breathing but couldn't see him. Where in the hell was he?* Lexy snuck around to the other side of the bed. *He'd rolled onto the floor.* She sprinted to the bathroom and got into the shower. *No matter how hard she scrubbed, she wasn't going to be able to wash that naughty away.* She smiled as she thought about it. *They'd probably had sex five or six times and they'd never even kissed. She felt like a horrible person for sleeping with her friend's ex-boyfriend. That was against the friend rules in any book. Jenna was an Oracle. She probably already knew about it.* Cringing, Lexy towel-dried off and readied herself for the repercussions and merciless teasing that was sure to follow her choices. She thought about tossing out her underwear but stuffed them into her bag. *At this rate, she'd be going commando indefinitely. She'd had a spectacularly naughty slot of time. She'd gone from decades with the same person to this…She wasn't even sure how to describe her predicament. It was like she was thirty years late and going on a twenty-year old's sexually explicit journey of self-discovery.*

Chapter 14

Something Wicked This Way Comes

Lexy looked like she'd been innocently watching Netflix all night with Orin by the time Grey woke up. He didn't even ask about her night as he started to tell her about the drama she'd missed while opting out of going out with the group. Having a difficult time focusing, she only caught, *Kayn...Drunk...Vomiting. That's really all she needed to know. She'd had the pleasure of being granted the duty of drunken hair holder, while many a friend had been trapped praying to the porcelain god of the bathroom. It was to be expected.* They made their way down to grab something to eat. It went without saying that they were supposed to opt for the free continental breakfast if the motel provided one versus the restaurant. *Grey still hadn't attempted to question her. Not about anything. It was a little strange but still a relief.*

"By the way, if anyone asks if you were there, just agree," Grey continued. "I helped Zach give Kayn a bath because she'd puked all over herself and for some reason, he added your name to the list of bathers. It just sounds better if a girl's name is involved in the whole bathing while passed out scenario."

Lexy shrugged and replied, "No problem."

Grey held open the door for her and they wandered into the large room with enormous carafes of cereal, tea, coffee and a large tray of bagels.

He grabbed them each a bowl and announced, "Raisin Bran, Cornflakes or Bran Flakes?"

"Raisin Bran," Lexy answered. She grinned as she watched him pour way too much milk into each of their bowls. *They had little routines like most people who'd lived in close quarters for many years.* She grinned, grabbed two styrofoam cups and questioned him on his choice of beverage, "Tea or Coffee?"

"Coffee," Grey replied as he wandered over to one of the minimalistic metal-framed tables in the center of the room and found a seat, placing her cereal bowl directly across the table from where he was sitting. She filled the coffee to the rim of his styrofoam cup, just to be a pain in the ass and placed it in front of him without spilling a drop.

When she took her seat with her own coffee in hand, Grey beamed and chuckled, "You realise I had a long night helping with vomit duty and I'm hungover. Drinking this coffee without spilling it is going to be impossible."

Grinning, she traded coffees without spilling a drop and teased, "Is that better, sweetie?"

He took a sip of piping hot coffee, winked at her and sparred, "Much better."

Lexy's back was to the door as Grey's eyes lit up and he waved someone over to their table.

"I'll be there in a second," Orin's voice answered.

Being a redhead, her freckled skin came with the ability to blush ten shades darker at a moment's notice, but she'd never been much of a blusher. That wasn't what she was worried about. She'd snuck out of his bed telling herself he wouldn't mind, but what if he did? Preparing herself to see her naughty companion from the night before, she casually sipped her coffee. *It was a mind-blowing experience, and she wanted to repeat it, but they weren't in love and she'd never had a booty call before, so she had no idea what to say or do in the cold light of day.* Orin sat down beside her and Lexy politely greeted him, "Good morning."

He grinned as he took a drink of his coffee and replied, "It is, isn't it?"

What in the hell was she supposed to say back to that? She peered over, trying to gauge his temperament. *He didn't seem upset. He appeared amused by her confusion.*

Grey piped in, "Oh, yeah. How was your movie night? What did you guys end up watching? I forgot to ask Lexy with all of the drunken drama."

What was she supposed to say?

Orin answered for her, "We watched a movie and had a couple of beers, it was nice. I was exhausted and fell asleep. She was gone when I woke up."

Lexy smiled at Orin. *He hadn't said a word.* She explained, "I didn't want to wake you so I snuck out. I knew you wouldn't mind." She couldn't resist baiting, "Did you sleep well?"

"Like a baby," Orin answered, maintaining an innocent straight face.

Markus and Arrianna sat down across the table and Markus said, "Hey, what did you guys end up watching last night? We watched that new Comedy. It was hilarious." He glanced at Arrianna and asked, "What was it called again?"

Arrianna laughed, "It was the one with the brothers. You know what, I totally can't remember the name. It was funny. I'll probably remember in ten minutes when I'm not trying to think about it. I'll text it to you later."

Grey got up to get another coffee. He snagged Lexy's empty cup from in front of her so he could also refill hers. Markus repeated his earlier question, "What did you guys end up watching again?"

"It was one of those long-winded dramas," Orin casually responded. "It was funny and then got super dirty halfway through."

Lexy choked on her mouthful of soggy Raisin Bran.

Orin gave her a few friendly pats on her back, then addressed Arrianna and Markus and disclosed, "We'll have to watch it again, we fell asleep and missed the ending."

She could read between the lines on this one. Orin was telling her without having to say the words that he wanted to do it again. She glanced up, both Markus and Arrianna had that blank morning autopilot thing going on. *They had no idea.* Most of their Clan showed up looking seriously rough. Kayn and Zach were missing.

Grey came back, handed Lexy a fresh coffee with a travel lid on it and announced, "We should all take a coffee to go."

Markus stood up and announced, "Do me a favour Grey. Can you go ask that guy in the window over there if they have any apple pie?" Grey hopped up, strolled over to the window and started to speak to someone.

The door opened again. *There they were.* All eyes were on Kayn as she walked through the door, but they carried on eating and nobody said a word about it. *It was more than moderately entertaining watching Kayn try to choke down toast.* Once everyone finished eating, they wandered out and got into their RV, taking up multiple spots in the parking lot. *It was time to go.* Lexy scaled the steps.

"We're driving first," Grey announced as he took off up front.

Lexy quickly stowed her backpack and made her way past the group already seated at the table, rifling through cupboards searching for a board game. She smiled at the group as she passed by with her fourth coffee of the day in hand and got into the passenger seat. Grey was messing around with the radio station.

He glanced at her and whispered, "I think Frost is purposely reprogramming every station I like to something else and hiding all of my CDs."

Lexy grinned. *She could totally see Frost doing that just to piss Grey off every time it was his turn to drive but he didn't need help building conspiracy theories.* She took a sip of coffee and countered, "Maybe you left them in the other vehicle?"

"Maybe," he replied as he rifled around in search of his music, succumbing to the frustration.

Smiling, she suggested he plug in his cell and play the one playlist that couldn't be easily tampered with.

"Good thinking," Grey said as he plugged in his cell.

They pulled out of the parking lot and hit the highway, chatting about life. When a song came on that they both knew the words to, they started singing. The table behind them joined in. *It was beginning to feel normal again. The drama of the Testing and Summit had passed.* After a day of taking turns driving, Lexy was in the passenger seat. With heavy eyes caused by her extracurricular activities the night before, the endless humming of the tires easily lulled her to sleep.

She awoke to her Handler's voice, "I let you sleep, Hun. We've already set the site up and the campfire is going. We're roasting hot dogs."

Lexy stretched, let out an enormous yawn and made her way to the door of the motorhome. She asked, "Do I have to go find a stick and sharpen it or have you already done it for me because you're the best friend ever?"

He winked at her, draped his arm over her shoulder and preened, "I'm the best friend ever. Of course, I've already done one for you, but if you want a drink, you'll have to grab one out of the fridge. I didn't know how much you drank last night so I wasn't sure what you wanted."

She grabbed a beer. *If she was going to have to sit around a campfire in an awkward situation with Jenna and Orin both there with a straight face, she'd need something.* Grey opened the door for her. *It was already dark outside. How long had she been asleep?*

Wandering out, she inhaled the familiar campfire scent. The flickering flames beckoned her towards them. *It was just Zach and Lily outside sitting on a log. Where was everyone?*

Grey handed her a pre-sharpened stick and remarked, "Frost is out searching for more sticks."

Lexy offered hers to Lily because she'd been sitting there longer.

Lily smiled at her and said, "I'm not that hungry yet. Frost will bring one back for me too."

Lexy placed her wiener on the stick and held it over the fire. Grey picked up her beer, popped it open for her and passed it to her, she laughed, "Alright, what did you do? Why are you doing everything for me?"

He chuckled and confessed, "I can't put anything past you, can I? I lost the bet. Melody is off with the others doing a job. Do you want your massage now?"

While she was eating a hotdog? That might be a little too phallic for her present state of mind. She turned to Grey and teased, "Why do you ever bet against me? You never win."

Zach piped in, "So, let me get this straight. You two make bets for massages. Well, that's a win, win situation isn't it?"

She wasn't sure what he meant by that.

"It's not like that," Grey sparred, giving Zach a dirty look.

Yes, it was. She grinned as she shook her head and started to eat her wiener without a bun. The door squealed as it opened. Kayn walked down the steps to stand in the gravel.

Lily's voice ominously announced, "It lives."

Kayn shook her head. Lexy smiled at her. *She'd better get used to the jokes, at least until someone did something crazier.*

"If you'd like a beer there's a six-pack in the fridge," Grey playfully suggested. Her eyes widened, Kayn shook her head from side to side. He chuckled, "Didn't think so."

Kayn looked around for something to cook her wiener with. Lily motioned to the bushes. Lexy was mid-second wiener roast and wondered if she should offer this one to Kayn. She met Lily's eyes and she motioned no. *She had Frost's back. It was kind of cute.*

Kayn asked, "Where did everybody go?"

Grey chimed in, "They're on a job." Kayn nodded and took the hint as she ventured off into the overgrown brush by herself in search of a stick to roast a wiener with.

Lexy was watching Grey as he disappeared into the motorhome. He popped his head back out and said, "Do any of you need anything?"

"A bag of chips, pretty please with sugar on top," Lily called back.

The door slammed shut behind him. Grey disappeared for a couple of seconds, reappeared and yelled, "Heads up," as he tossed a giant bag of chips to Lily. It landed in the fire and the flames raged. She tried to snatch it out but it went up instantly. Grey was howling laughing as he disappeared again.

He may be a dork but he was her dork. Lexy stood up and sighed, "I'll go save the next bag of chips from his crappy aim."

He appeared in the doorway with two more bags and carried them down the stairs himself, dodging out of the way as Lexy laughed and tried to snatch one. Grey dashed over to where Lily was seated and exclaimed, "You can pick first. Sorry about that."

She smiled at him and chose salt and vinegar. Grey hollered to Lexy as he yanked the bag open and urged, "Come sit over here and share these ones with me."

Lexy strolled over feeling pouty she had to share for a second before noticing Lily and Zach were sharing. *What in the hell was taking Frost and Kayn so long? They must have bumped into each other while searching the swamp for sticks.* She plopped herself down next to Grey on the log and reached into his bag, smelling the scent of the chip between her fingers as she placed it into her mouth…It was sour cream and onion. The highlight reel of the intensely pleasurable self-satisfying night she'd spent with Orin flashed through her mind. *It was still difficult to believe how quickly that escalated from a harmless game of truth or dare to a full on hot steamy sensual romp. Not to mention the amazing thing that happened when two Healer's united physically. She should stop thinking about this.*

Grey shoved her and prodded, "What are you thinking about? I can't tell. Usually, I just know."

"Nothing important," she answered, snagging another chip.

He casually enquired, "Thinking about Tiberius?"

No, Greydon. I was thinking about the other guy, Orin. The friend I randomly slept with last night. Lexy winced as she snatched another chip from the bag and shoved it into her mouth to curb the urge to confess the details of the night before.

"You know you can tell me anything," he whispered as he fed her a chip like she was a carb consuming sultan and smiled at her, with his blonde hair shaded by the orange of the flames.

She felt guilty. It was irrational, she knew that, but everything about her feelings for her Handler were. In the sky above a trio of fireflies began to dance around the mystical backdrop of sparkling stars. She pointed towards the heavens and Grey gazed up at the lights pirouetting in the darkness. *Oh, how much simpler her life would be if she could just love him.* Her eyes swelled with tears, she blinked them away. *What in the hell was going on with her lately?*

"Hey," he whispered. "I know something's wrong."

Meeting his concern with a smile, she gave him a version of the truth, "I've just been stepping out of my comfort zone lately, you know I'm not the biggest fan of change."

He put an arm around her, pulled her against him and they watched the fireflies dance, enjoying the sights and sounds of night until they heard voices approaching. Kayn and Frost came over to the flickering flames of the campfire together. Frost handed one of his sharpened sticks to Lily. She grinned, thanked him and moved over to give him a place to sit beside her on the log.

They sat around the campfire, talking about the weeks ahead. The others were eating as Lexy's stomach muscles constricted and she glared at Grey. Her eyes narrowed suspiciously as she mouthed the words, "Is this a Test?" Waves of excruciating pain wracked her being. She doubled over in agony as her abdomen savagely cramped again. The symbols on all their palms lit up and flashed. Lexy leapt to her feet but didn't move, fighting to keep a piece of herself as her emotions began to dissolve. *It wasn't time yet. She knew the drill.*

"Not yet," Grey whispered, touching her arm.

She was being swallowed by the pit of rage engulfing her being. Her gaze was drawn to the fledgling Dragon also on her feet, ready to go on a rampage of destruction. The whooshing of everyone's hearts was distracting as the excitement of the hunt took hold. *Grey. All she had to do is look into Grey's eyes, his presence kept her lucid.*

Frost's voice faintly chuckled, "Hey killer, sit back down. There's no need for us to move a muscle unless they all go down. That just means somebody's been wounded. Six, are still standing."

Lexy's stomach muscles constricted as another wave of nausea washed over her. Their brand of Clan flashed once more in unison. Her head pulsated with excruciating pain. *Grey. This was the war-cry she couldn't ignore. The flashing symbol on her palm had always taken her from domesticated wild animal to savage beast in about four deaths.* She only heard muffled voices and couldn't make out what they were saying anymore as her symbol strobed. Looking at Grey as her chest heaved, he caressed her arm and the sensation of his flesh on hers anchored her as always to the here and now. Adrenaline shivered through her being as pain triggered her Healing ability and everyone was surrounded by vibrant swirling colours. Aware of the other Dragon's volatile energy as her palm flashed a fourth time, she felt herself sinking into the nothing.

Keeping their connection alive, Grey pulled her close and whispered, "It's not real. It's a test. We have to stay with her."

On the verge of succumbing, his undeniable pull lured her back. Lexy repeated Grey's words in her mind. *It's not real. It's a test. We have to stay with her.* Teetering on the edge of sanity, an earth-shattering shriek pierced her soul and crushed her ability for reason. Her head turned towards the battle cry and she saw Kayn clutching either side of her head, shrieking in agony. Their palms lit up once more and this time, everyone got up. Grey released his connection to her and nodded. Her headache ceased, and in the absence of his touch, she felt the hollow flow through her being, silencing any lingering ration, and now, there was nothing but the overwhelming drive to find the wounded Ankh and destroy those who hurt them. Lexy started running, vaguely aware of the other Dragon keeping pace. Their footsteps pounding a steady rhythm into the damp pliable swamp beneath their feet with tribal symbolism. Darting through the trails with the agility of predators in pursuit of prey, they came upon their Clan standing there unharmed. Fighting instinct, she froze. *Grey. Grey was calling her name.* The wild thing turned towards her Handler's soothing tone as he approached. Seeing only him as he held out his hand, Lexy took it as she knew, she always would. They embraced and she was sedated. With her chin resting on Grey's shoulder as he rubbed her back, her breathing calmed. *The swirling colourful hues in the darkness made her Clan as glorious as fireflies. It occurred to her that she may still be mentally unhinged.*

Gently towing her away from the rest of their Clan, Grey whispered, "Come on, Hun. Let's go somewhere to talk this out. It's best if we don't allow this wound to fester."

Her Handler had always been an intuitive guy. His lack of warning about the part she'd be playing in this night's Dragon response time festivities had hurt her feelings, but she'd also been keeping secrets from him. What right did she have to remain choked about something this silly? They strolled hand in hand through the woods. *It felt like there was emotional distance between them. Was it because she'd randomly slept with Orin? She hadn't had the opportunity to fully process what she'd done the night before, but that uncomplicated sexual experience with him made her feel freedom she'd never known. She'd needed that release and she'd taken it. It didn't feel wrong. Would she be able to sleep with Tiberius with the same lack of emotion? It felt like she was towing him.* Lexy realised, she was walking aggressively fast, he was struggling to keep up. Feeling the disconnect, she slowed herself down.

Chapter 15

Mending Fences

Grey started the small talk, "I'm sorry I didn't tell you what we were doing, they needed your reaction to be authentic so Kayn's would be. Zach did pretty well though."

Any residual guilt she felt over the virgin sacrifice thing with Triad immediately dissipated. She squeezed his hand and sparred, "So, I didn't really win that bet then?"

"No," he chuckled. "Theoretically, neither of us have… yet." Grey kept up the brisk pace beside her until they were far enough away from the others to have an unfiltered conversation. *The sounds of night that had always soothed her, now made her feel nothing but frustration.* They found a half decently dry place to sit.

He sat on a large rock and questioned, "Is it just me or does it feel like something's off between us?"

The shadows from the trees blocked out any residual light coming from the moon. *She could barely see him.* Sitting on a large rock close by, she looked in the direction of his voice and admitted, "It's not just you, I feel it too. I think I know what it is though."

Her Handler's voice travelled through the darkness, "What do you think it is?"

She knew he was smiling even though his face was hidden in the shadows. She'd feed him a few breadcrumbs of the truth and see how he dealt with it. She answered, "For many years I haven't been dealing with my wants and needs in an emotionally progressive way. I have them, and you need to understand that even though you've been my whole world for a long time, sometimes, I'm going to need to do something for myself." *Now, that speech had been a long time coming.*

There was a long, drawn-out silence where the only response was a few long croaks from a toad, before he replied, "I know."

She wasn't sure how to take those two words. Lexy called him out, "What do you know?"

"I know there are parts of our relationship I can't remember, and I also know how much I've hurt you over the years. Lets' just say somebody filled me in on what an asshole I've been. I thought I was going to be able to just keep it to myself, but I think that might be what's causing this odd vibe between us."

Maybe it wasn't all her. She wished she was still holding his hand. The distance between them was magnified by isolating darkness and lack of contact. *Frost had told him everything after the orange juice incident. She'd initially suspected he had, but then, he'd acted normal afterwards. She'd always fixed this situation by sleeping with him and erasing his memory, giving him a guilt-free slate. But for the first time, that didn't feel like the answer to anything. She could probably thank Orin for her enlightened point of view. He'd shown her sex could just be for recreational purposes. It didn't have to be complicated. It didn't always need to end with a broken heart.* Even though he couldn't see her, she smiled and probed, "What can we do to fix this?"

Grey laughed and said, "I have an idea, but we need to take off our shoes and socks, it's going to be muddy."

Why? Lexy didn't bother saying it aloud. She just took off her shoes and tucked a sock into the toe of each. *This ought to be good.*

Giggling as he squished his way through the muddy swamp towards her, he gallantly held out his hand. *What a weird thing to want to do?* She took his hand and scrunched up her face, knowing how much she hated the thought of what they were about to do.

Grey led her a couple of feet and exclaimed, "If we lose our balance, it's going to be messy."

"Do we really have to do this?" Lexy sighed, as she humoured him by going along with his little game.

"Live a little," Grey provoked. "I bet you haven't done anything new today. This will be something new for both of us. It's a bonding experience."

Well, actually... she had done something new today...Orin. She smiled to herself. *Oh, the things she had to do to placate her Handler.* Lexy became squeamish as her bare feet sunk ankle-deep into the muddy marshlands. *Ewww. It was the creepiest feeling.*

Laughing as he pulled her against him, he announced, "I think we should dance the stress off."

Now, Lexy didn't find many situations that gave her an unsettling feeling but this one was in the top five. She might even go as far as to say it was epically disturbing. She rested her head on Grey's shoulder and they tried to dance but it was probably not as easy at he'd imagined it would be. *She did not like this game at all.* The squishy mud slid between her toes and it felt like they were sinking each time they swayed together.

Grey kept the marsh dance going as they awkwardly waltzed to the tune of a toad's baritone croaks for a few minutes before he whispered in her ear, "Yeah, I was totally wrong. This is disgusting."

Laughter sputtered from her lip as she wholeheartedly agreed, they helped each other to solid ground. *Well, now what were they supposed to do?* They sat back to back on the stone she'd been sitting on before their swamp dancing experience.

"Well, I obviously didn't think this far ahead," Grey chuckled.

Laughing, Lexy jousted, "Are you're referring to the inability to put our shoes and socks on for the walk back to the campsite because we're covered in mud?"

"Oh, we're not covered in mud yet," was his response. *She could tell he was smiling without being able to see him.* Lexy asserted, "Don't you even think about it, Greydon." He jumped up and darted towards the swamp where he picked up a handful of goo and raised a hand ominously into the air.

The way Lexy saw it she had two choices. She could grab her shoes and sprint back to the campsite hoping she could outrun him and dodge his swamp bombs or just leap up, run over there and give him the face wash he deserved in the goopy marsh. She glared at him and threatened, "I wouldn't do it." Grey was poised with mud in hand oozing between his fingers and dripping down his arm as fireflies danced in the space between them. *He couldn't throw anything without hitting them.* Smiling, Lexy grabbed her sock filled shoes and left him standing ankle-deep in the swamp. As Lexy strolled away, she called out, "By the way, I saw glowing eyes behind you over there! Hope it's not anything looking to eat you!" Lexy started running because she knew he was coming after her now. She heard him pursuing her all the way back to the campsite but as always, she maneuvered through the woods in the dark using nothing but her senses. This had always been one of her strong suits. She was way ahead of him. The crackling fire through the brush ahead was beckoning her. Lexy stepped out into the cleared area by the fire and announced, "What did we miss?" Everyone's eyes travelled to her hilariously muddy feet.

Grinning widely Frost got up and walked over to her, commenting, "It's been a long time since I got muddy like that on purpose. Did you guys have fun?" He looked over her shoulder and slowly shook his head from side to side. Lexy sighed, "It's right behind me, isn't it?" Both Frost and Lexy ducked as a ball of well-formed squishy swamp mud soared through the air. With the most hilarious timing ever, Markus wandered over to stand by the fire and took it right on the back. It sprayed everyone sitting on either side of him. Grey froze as everyone began to howl.

Markus turned around, glared at Grey and growled, "Are you five years old?"

Grey started apologizing as Markus sighed, "Come on muddy people. Well, and you two. It's all over your backs and in your hair." He signalled Astrid and Orin over. "Let's go to the public bathroom. None of us are walking into either one of the motorhomes like this." Orin stood up and followed the muddy herd to the showers.

Jenna hollered, "Wait a second. You guys are going to need soap and shampoo." She darted into the other groups' RV and returned with a basket of hotel shampoo and soap. They all grabbed what they needed, except for Lexy. *She hadn't had the opportunity to speak to her friend alone since she'd broken girl code.* Jenna called her over as the group walked away and held out the basket. Lexy took the toiletries she needed. *This was a seriously awkward situation.*

"We should talk, I'll walk with you," Jenna whispered.

As soon as they were out of earshot, Lexy whispered, "I should have talked to you about watching a movie with Orin before I did it."

The Clan's Oracle grinned at her and replied, "Don't worry about it, Lex. Our relationship has been over for decades. We have to learn to be friends now."

She looked at their Clan's Oracle and asked, "You were together for almost a thousand years. It can't be easy for you to walk away."

Emotion flickered through Jenna's eyes as she answered, "It's not easy but I have front row seats to the big picture.

We don't end up together. I've known it for hundreds of years. At first, I tried to ignore the visions, but when I left to be Azariah's right hand, having decades apart allowed me the distance I needed to see clearly. I'll never regret our time together but it's centuries past when I should have allowed him to move on."

Lexy smiled and nodded. *Tempted to ask what she'd seen in the big picture, she didn't bother, knowing she'd never say a word for fear of affecting the future.* Jenna placed her arm around her as they strolled down the trail. They approached the others travelling in the opposite direction. *They must already be on their way back to the campsite. That was quick.*

Jenna whispered in her ear, "Do yourself a favour, don't stress about anything. It's high time you had some fun with your afterlife."

Lexy felt the weight lift off her shoulders. *Jenna appeared to be fine. She was relieved.*

Once they reached the bathrooms, Jenna turned back and waved goodbye. As Jenna wandered away, she called out, "We have to take off before dawn. We're sending the five out on a job alone. Thanks for playing along tonight, Lex. Make sure you grab your backpack and put it in our motorhome."

"How long do we have?" Lexy hollered back. *She didn't even know what time it was?*

Jenna paused as she yelled her response, "We're leaving in a couple of hours. Make sure you have a shower if you need one."

Lexy waved and tugged on the girl symbol door. It was locked and there was an out of order sign on it. *Of, course.* She gave the men's door a good shove and it opened. Lexy didn't need a shower, she'd had one this morning, all she needed to do was wash her muddy feet. It took her a while to wash the mud from beneath her toenails and it proved to be more difficult than anticipated, balancing on one foot with the other in the sink. The mirrors were all steamed up.

She wiped one of them with her hand and in her reflection, she noticed Orin shirtless standing behind her. She turned around and apologized, "Sorry, I thought I saw everyone leave. The girl's washroom is out of order."

Smiling, Orin gave her an explanation for why he was standing there partially clothed, "My shirt was dirty. I thought I'd just carry it back." He held up the recently washed shirt as proof.

Unsure of what she should say, Lexy shoved the unused bottles of shampoo in her pockets and reached for the door. Orin grinned as he silently opened the door for her. They started to walk back to the campsite in uncomfortable silence to the backdrop of randomly timed croaking toads.

Orin casually teased, "I'm so glad this isn't going to be awkward."

Lexy grinned, stopped walking and explained, "I've never done that before, I have no idea how I'm supposed to act."

He started to walk, smiled back at her and replied, "Just relax, there are no expectations here. If you ever feel like you want to do that again, you just let me know."

She watched him walk away. *His butt looked incredible in those jeans. Did he expect her to chase him down and say something more? She definitely wanted to do that again but was afraid he'd fall for her. She'd always viewed him as a relationship guy but if she was taking his words at face value and he was looking for more of a casual friend with benefits situation that thought was intriguing, to say the least...* Lexy wandered over to Grey, roasting marshmallows over the crackling campfire. He'd saved her a place to sit as per usual. He shimmied over to give her more room as she sat down.

He asked, "Are you still hungry?"

Lexy smiled at him as she took in a lung full of smoky air as the smoke switched directions and came at her. She remarked, "I could roast a marshmallow." Grey pulled his stick out, braced it between his knees, slid one of the perfectly golden marshmallows off the tip and brought it towards her lips. She opened her mouth. He fed it to her and licked the sticky sweet remnants off his finger. With her hand over her lips, Lexy mumbled with her mouth full, "That was smoking hot." Well, that's what she'd aimed for, it had come out sounding more like, "Mat wub moking ot."

Grey ate the other one. His body shook as he laughed with his hand over his own mouth. He finished chewing and stated, "So was that one."

Zach and Kayn emerged from the RV. *It looked like Kayn had fully regained her sanity and Zach was carrying a jar full of fireflies?* He released the fireflies into the night. Kayn wasn't watching the fireflies, she was staring at the group around the fire. Kayn walked over to Frost and kissed his cheek. A little shocked, he smiled. *It felt like she'd missed something big during her side trip to the bathroom.*

Grey whispered in her ear, "Frost caught her some fireflies to cheer her up."

Lexy smiled. *Damn, he was smooth.* She watched as Kayn grabbed a stick, placed a wiener on the end of it, and went to go sit down beside Zach, across the fire from Frost. The old version of Kayn had never wanted to burn her hotdog. The new version dangled her stick directly into the flames and watched it scorch until it was blackened in various places. *Lexy could appreciate that, it was also how she rolled.* Zach was sitting by Kayn, cooking his wiener over the embers as she took hers out, blew on it, and tried to remove it, but it was still far too hot to touch. Lily passed her a napkin and Kayn used it to shield her fingertips from the heat.

Orin laughed and said, "Heads up!" He tossed a bun in Kayn's direction and she caught it.

Grey had already finished roasting their seconds, but this time, he whispered, "Let these cool off for a second."

Lexy smiled as Orin tried to catch Kayn off guard by whipping a plastic mustard bottle at her.

Kayn caught it a second before it smoked her and sat there staring at the bottle in her hands. She held it up and enquired, "How did I catch this? I wasn't even looking." Markus chimed in, "It's heightened sensory awareness. You will find that your eyesight is better. Your sense of hearing is amazing, but it's about so much more than that. You guys already know we can sense danger coming. You'll have an upset stomach and know, it's something more. See, we're using a larger portion of our brains. Well, some of us use a larger portion." Markus winked at Frost. "You'll find it handy to be able to hear each other's thoughts, when you're on a job. Most of the time, it takes both parties being receptive to non-verbal communication. Only Oracles can hear your thoughts even when you don't want them to be heard. We'll teach you how to close your thoughts off when you want them to be private. Can you imagine the drama we'd have around here if everyone heard everything you thought?"

Kayn was easy to read. Lexy had given her a few witty responses to her inner commentary over the years. Kayn glanced up at Frost, her eyes widened. Frost began to choke on his hotdog.

Lily started smacking Frost's back, laughing, "Are you okay?"

"Thanks, I must have inhaled that last bite of hotdog," Frost mumbled, with a wry smile.

Orin was poised to throw something else at Kayn and Melody smacked his leg. He started to laugh as he sat down beside her and decided to behave.

"We should get some sleep," Markus announced. "There's a long drive ahead of us. He got up. Jenna, Orin, Arrianna and Lily followed him into the second RV.

Kayn stood up and declared, "Well, I'm going to bed. Goodnight guys. She climbed the steps.

Zach called after her, "Sweet Dreams." Kayn paused and everyone started to laugh. Kayn grinned as she shoved open the door and let it swing shut behind her.

Standing up, Mel said, "I could watch a movie. Who's with me?" All the newbies got up and went inside.

Grey and Lexy remained by the fire. Grey chuckled, "I guess it's up to me to put this out?"

Knowing they planned to take off on the newbies, Lexy got up, stretched and whispered, "Want me to sneak in and grab our bags?"

Grey wandered around to the back of the truck. He got in and disclosed, "Our bags are already in the cab. We're driving this. We're leaving before the others."

Strolling around to the cab, Lexy ribbed, "Don't you need keys?"

Grey gave the keys a few jingling shakes and countered, "I already have them." He grabbed the shovel out of the black plastic storage bin, leapt out of the back with catlike agility, walked over to the fire and smothered it with shovel loads of dirt.

She was thirsty. Lexy thought about going into their usual motorhome to grab a few cans of juice out of the fridge, but decided against it, knowing she'd be taking it from the newbies. She watched Grey work for a minute, before wandering over and saying, "I want to stop in town to get drinks and munchies, I can drive first. How long is the drive?"

Checking the pit for embers, he replied, "Around four hours depending on the traffic." He grabbed the keys out of his pocket and chucked them to her. Catching them with one hand, she strolled back to the truck. *It was the middle of the night. There wasn't going to be any traffic.* Lexy smiled as she got into the driver's seat and waited for Grey to finish up. She made herself comfortable and noticed two sealed cans of orange juice in the cup holders. *He had her back as always.* She popped open the can and downed the entire thing. She heard him, moving around in the back of the truck putting the shovel away. The passenger door opened. Grey slid into the seat. Knowing he'd be thirsty after putting out the fire, she opened his juice and passed it.

Downing the entire can in one go, he sighed, "I was really hoping to get some sleep tonight. I bet you're glad you got some last night. I didn't lock that box in the back, remind me later."

Sure, she got lots of sleep. Stifling a giggle, Lexy replied, "It's two am, I might not remember by the time we get there." She put the keys in the ignition. As the engine began to purr, the radio turned on and they drove away, leaving the five newest Ankh to fend for themselves. Lexy turned on the cold air and aimed the vents at her face. She found it helped keep her awake whenever they were forced to pull an all-nighter. *There was a slow sedating love song on the radio.*

Digging around for CDs, Grey commented, "Guess what I forgot?" Dramatically reclining his seat, he sighed, "I'm going to have a nap."

Lexy shoved him and hissed, "Like hell you are. You haven't even told me what we're doing. Put your seat up, pull up your panties and try to find something half-decent on the radio. I can't search through the stations while I'm driving."

Grey chuckled as he put his seat up and started clicking through stations, leaving it on one playing eighties rock. He looked at her, grinned and teased, "Better?"

"Much!" Lexy answered as she pulled into an all-night drive thru. They ordered food and continued their journey down the seemingly endless highway into darkness.

Chapter 16

Lampir Spittle

They'd just finished a lovely rendition of, "Don't stop believing," belting out the tune at the top of their lungs, barrelling down the highway with the windows rolled down, when Grey checked his text messages and announced, "We're supposed to pull off the highway at the turnoff to Smithsville. Once we're there, we need to find 3420 Dunbar St."

"And why would that be? You do realise you've been dodging my questions about this job all night?" Lexy sparred as she pulled off the highway and they travelled down the road into town. She took note of the sign as they passed by. The sign read, population 3100.

Grey grinned as he answered, "I don't have any details. The first text contained the address and the second says it's a Correction."

"This morning... Really? I'm exhausted," Lexy muttered.

He scolded, "What are you complaining about? You've only been up for twenty-four hours. I've been up for forty-eight."

A part of her wanted to turn around and snottily huff back, *Well, I'll have you know I was up all night having hot unexpected sex with Orin.* Instead of rocking the boat and saying something sure to take both of their minds off the task at hand, she opted for, "You didn't have to stay awake all night. Don't feed me that line. I'm not a fish. Zach could have figured out how to give a girl a bath all by himself."

"I was trying to be helpful," Grey replied and then he started laughing, "I can't even say that with a straight face."

They pulled up on the opposite side of the road. The address they were looking for was a small forest green rancher style, with pink and white rose bushes on either side of the door. The yard was fully fenced but the fence was run down and only about three feet high.

His phone vibrated, Grey grabbed his cell, looked at it and announced, "There's another message. Alright love, guess who we have to murder this morning?"

His wording made the job sound intriguing, but she was far too exhausted to pretend to be spry and play his games. Lexy yawned as she gave her reply, "Is it...a demon?"

Grey scowled at her and complained, "Stop yawning, you know what will happen...And no, it's not a demon. Guess again." He yawned and stretched in response to Lexy's yawning and pointed at her menacingly as she yawned again.

This could go on for hours. Lexy yawned again in response to his yawn, pointed laughably back at him and queried, "Is it a Lycanthropos issue?"

He yawned and asserted, "First things first. Look away or we won't stop yawning."

They'd been in close confines for forty years. They had set routines for all inconveniently timed bodily functions. If they yawned more than twice in a row, they both had to look away. Recalling an incident, she smiled. Many years ago, they kept yawning until they were exhausted, so they pulled over on the side of the road to nap. While they were asleep, a thief stole all four of the tires off the truck. *They were probably never going to live that down.* Lexy stared out the window. *The entire street had not a hint of life.* She looked at the flashing digital clock on the dash and remembered it wasn't that time zone anymore. *That clock was never right. How early was it?* Grey yawned, and even though she wasn't looking at him, she yawned again. *Damn it.*

Grey's cell vibrated and he stated, "Change of plans. I guess Frost will be joining us. We're supposed to wait in the vehicle."

There was a long comical pause as they looked away from each other long enough for the yawning spirts to pass. *Why was he being so secretive about this job? She might have to beat him up and take his phone.*

Grey kept looking the other way as he questioned, "Why would you guess that? You know a Lycanthropos would never choose to live in the suburbs."

Crickets in her brain. Oh, yeah. She was guessing what the job was. True, that was true. "Is there a serial murderer in that house?" Lexy guessed as she pulled down the mirror on the visor and looked at her reflection. *She usually didn't care about her appearance, but damn, she looked rough this morning.* Lexy felt around on the floor for her purse and retrieved her lipstick with gold rim and smiled. Lexy put on a fresh coat of crimson lipstick, awaiting Grey's response.

He replied, "Sort of?"

She glanced his way, knit her brow and guessed, "So, not mortal then…Which species?"

Reclining in his seat, Grey disclosed, "It's a Lampir Correction."

It had been a long time since they'd been ordered to interfere with anything Lampir related. They usually dealt with their issues privately. Most of the time it was either a Demon or a Mortal scheduled for Correction. Grey grabbed a cold French fry off the floor and popped it into his mouth. She grimaced and commented, "Gross, Grey."

He grinned and teased, "It's not my fault you're sitting here watching me eat cold French fries off the truck's floor instead of in there, kicking Lampir ass. It's Frost's fault. Text them and find out how long they're going to be. This truck looks a little obvious parked here."

Lexy sighed and stared at her phone. *She loved him, but right now she wanted to drive his head through the dash, he was getting on her nerves due to her lack of sleep.* Lexy found herself staring out the window entranced by the perfect lawns and gardens everyone had on this block. This was the picture-perfect suburb, not far from a big city that everyone strived to live in. *Why did they need three immortals to kill one Lampir?*

Lexy glanced at him and probed, "Why do you think the Lampir community hasn't dealt with him in house?" *The Lampir population hadn't had any issues with anyone in a good fifteen years.*

They heard the familiar hum of the RV's engine in the distance. *There they were.* It stopped in the middle of the street a block away. Frost jumped out and started walking towards them as the others drove away.

Frost got into the backseat and announced, "They're waiting for us a couple of blocks from here. We're supposed to text them when we're finished. I guess there are multiple jobs in this town. Man, do they ever have some shit going on here."

"Of course there are multiple jobs," Grey sighed. "I should have gotten some sleep. I know better."

Famous last words. She watched Frost as he stared at the tiny house. *There was way more going on here then they'd been privy to.* Lexy probed, "I thought Lucian had his population under control? It's been a long time since one of them went rogue."

Frost answered, "The Lampir have been holding down jobs and living successfully within the confines of the code of conduct for a long time. This is just one egomaniac of a man and a bunch of brand-new Lampir that probably don't even know a code of supernatural conduct exists."

Grey confirmed, "So, we're not being sent in to kill just one person?"

Grinning, Frost chuckled, "Nobody told you anything about this job, did they?"

"When do they ever?" Grey answered as he tried to drink from his empty can of juice.

Frost began to explain the details, "Lampir are only allowed to feed from mortals if it's voluntary."

"You know that rule has never been followed? They always use compulsion to gain consent," Grey sparred.

"Many of us feed off energy the same way the Lampir feed off blood, it's overlooked as long as there's no death toll. The odd accidental murder slips by, but fifty or sixty in a month in a town this size doesn't. This is a cold hard extermination," Frost revealed as he opened the door and stepped out onto the street. He leaned into the truck and instructed, "Chuck me the keys to the box."

Grey winced as he admitted, "I left it open."

He still hadn't told them the details of the job, but they knew it was a Correction. After hearing the words cold hard extermination, Lexy understood all she needed to. Stoked, she got out of the truck. Frost passed her wooden daggers, she discreetly hid them.

Frost took a small velvet pouch out of the storage box, leapt down out of the back and directed his next order at Grey, "We'll catch anyone that tries to get out. Grey, you hang out at the backdoor, I'll stay at the front. Kill everyone, even if they haven't fully turned, this is a hive situation, we're supposed to deal with it aggressively."

She was intrigued. How many could there possibly be in this one little house?

Getting out, Grey quietly closed the door, took a few wooden daggers from Frost, and asserted, "I've got it."

Looking at Lexy, Frost sternly decreed, "*No witnesses.*"

That was the polite way of saying, be as quiet as possible while you murder a house full of people or we'll have to kill innocent bystanders. Lexy reached into the truck, grabbed a bobby-pin out of her purse and strolled up to the door. *There was a tiny window covered with tinfoil. This place must only have one bedroom. The blinds would be drawn to shield the inhabitants from sunlight so it would be pointless to sneak around and peek through windows.* She stuck the bobby-pin into the lock, maneuvered it around, unlocking it easily. She tried the door. *It was still locked. Use logic Lexy. They could have ten locks on each door. Getting into the house the stealth way would take too long. The windows would lead to the kitchen, the living room, the bedroom and the bathroom. If the place was full of Lampir, entering through the bathroom would be her best bet.* She strolled around the exterior of the house. *The bathroom window was too small to fit through. If she broke a window to the other rooms, she'd wake them up long before she made it inside. She didn't see a version of this Correction that wouldn't come with mortal casualties. Brains before brawn. What should she do? She could try to slip one of the windows out of its frame. No, that wouldn't work, they'd start screaming and scatter as they burned and the neighbours would be outside in two seconds flat. She saw no other choice.* In a bold move, Lexy strolled up to the front door, looked into the mailbox, snagged a letter out and rapped her knuckle lightly on the door.

Grey booked it for the backyard. Frost stepped back into the bushes as she knocked a second time. The door opened, revealing a heavy-set elderly woman in a fabulous zebra print moo-moo. *Interesting.* Lexy smiled politely and said, "Hello, I just moved in about a block over. I think I've been delivered your mail. It's crazy, I know, I don't even live on the same block."

The sluggishly tired lady gave her a strange look as she questioned, "You do know it's five am in the morning?"

"Is it really that early? I apologize, sometimes I forget everyone isn't an early riser like I am," Lexy innocently replied with a well-acted smile. Lexy noticed the tell-tale puncture marks on the lady's neck. *There was an open bathroom door right behind her.* With another disarming smile, Lexy whispered, "I know it's a strange thing to ask but I think I ate something bad last night. I might not make it home without having an accident. Would it be terrible of me to ask if I could come in and use your washroom quickly? I'll be super-fast. I swear you won't even know I was here."

The lady in wild zebra print hesitated, before whispering, "Alright, but please be quiet. Trust me, you do not want to wake up the rest of the household."

Lexy grinned. *My, my, what a strange way to word that last sentence?* The presumed owner of the house stepped out of the way. Lexy maneuvered around her into the house with little more than the sound of quiet knocking. *She was almost impressed with herself.* As the lady in zebra print closed the door, Lexy grabbed her in a sleeper hold as she violently struggled for air until her body became limp and her knees buckled. She gently placed her on the floor without making a sound and took note of the two closed doors on either side of her. *Man, she was exhausted. The décor wasn't disarming, it was creepy as hell.* There were tiny porcelain figurines of children with cherub faces in lederhosen in various poses on shelves that lined the entrance. *It was weird and she'd seen some crazy shit.* With no coin to toss, Lexy used intuition and chose the door on the right, turning the knob, without the faintest noise, she stepped into the room. *Holy crap.* There were easily thirty people asleep on the floor. A few were lounged across a plastic protected couch. *On the bright side, the old lady's sofa wasn't going to be destroyed by the bloodbath this morning. Not that it would matter once they burned the house down to cover up the evidence.* Surveying the occupants whose auras were faint, she was relieved they hadn't asked her to sort them out. *It would be too difficult to tell the full Lampir from the partially mortal. She'd only know who was what, after killing them all. Full Lampir turned to dust and partially turned required disposal. Snuffing them out as they slept, seemed cold, but it would save noisy neighbours from adding themselves to the death toll. Stabbing them in the heart first wasn't an option. She'd have to snap their necks, rendering them silent to buy the time to stake them without screaming and drama.*

One by one Lexy snapped their necks, without waking a soul and proceeded to methodically stake every last one. Some solidified and turned to ash, but in the end, only three had mortal shells. Lexy wasn't upset about the loss of mortal life for she knew, she'd saved three mortal souls on this day. If they were more mortal than Lampir, they'd be sent back through the hall of souls to be reborn. Standing in front of the twenty-seven piles of ash and three soulless corpses, Lexy smiled. *Maybe, she'd have time for a quick nap before the next job? Wait a minute...this was far too easy.* With ironic timing, someone smoked the back of her head. The room wavered. *Shit. She should have checked the other room.* Everything went black.

Listening to the hum of conversation as she came to, Lexy remained silent and kept her eyes closed, knowing she'd have a beat to figure things out if she played dead. Without opening her eyes, she knew her wrists were restrained behind her back with tape. *It was usually duct tape. This was always a laughable moment. Using duct tape to detain an immortal was easily comparable to using toilet paper to restrain a mortal.* The being behind that decision wasn't the sharpest pencil in the drawer. There were multiple voices in the room, it went without saying, they were seriously pissed about her murder spree. She listened to the conversation for a minute longer and deduced, they thought she was involved in the mass murder of their fellow Lampir but didn't know, she'd done the deed by herself. *If they'd used tape to restrain her, they knew nothing about anything. She might as well open her eyes and see what she was dealing with.* Lexy opened her eyes and grinned. *Well, shit. There were at least twenty fumingly furious Lampir with onyx orbs as eyes. She knew that was far too easy.* They were ignorantly brawling, shoving, hissing and gnashing their teeth like wild animals infected with rabies. *They were all slightly deformed. Lampir were usually attractive and eloquently mannered, but not these ones. These monstrosities had spittle flying everywhere. What in hell? This wasn't how Lampir were supposed to act? She'd known plenty of Lampir over the years, they could easily pass for mortal, but these guys were obviously the missing links of the Lampir species. These things were not normal Lampir. These were something else. Once again, they'd sent her into a situation with only half of the story. Their behaviour was more than moderately amusing. They really weren't paying any attention to her at all. What kind of bad guy doesn't have at least one person out of what looks like twenty, watching the hostage?* Lexy was pretty sure she could just rip the tape off, stand up and stroll right out of the room without any of these infected looking creatures noticing. *She was supposed to kill them all. That was the job. Maybe, this is an infection within the Lampir species?*

A much darker looking version of the robust woman in zebra print appeared in the doorway with fangs, a distorted face and long-clawed nails. The beast spat everywhere as she growled, "That's enough!"

Lexy winced as an unusually large amount of spittle sprayed at her face. *So, gross.* The others were silenced. *The harmless looking woman who answered the door was the one in charge. She'd mistakenly assuming the woman was still mortal. She was far too tired to be doing this today.* Meeting the elderly woman's hostile expression, Lexy casually enquired, "Just out of morbid curiosity, what in the hell are these things?"

Deformed by transformation, zebra print lady had a leg twisted in the wrong direction as she creepily hobbled over and gazed into Lexy's eyes with hypnotizing onyx orbs. With eerie sweetness in her tone, she grilled "You will tell me where the rest of your army is."

She was trying to compel the truth out of her, how adorable. Lexy cockily confessed, "I've never needed an army." Zebra print lady jerked and spasmed as she paced back and forth. *Was this an attempt to intimidate her? Wearing a silky zebra print moo-moo made intimidation unlikely. The sight of her moo-moo flowing behind her as she writhed and twisted gave her a creepy animated Disney villain vibe.* Unable to help it, Lexy giggled. Robust Cruella with rabies paused in front of her and creepily reached out a deformed savaged gnarly fingertip and stroked her arm with one of her nails. More spittle sprayed directly at Lexy's face as she hissed, "I will make your death tolerable if you tell me the truth. Where are the rest of your men?"

Where are the rest of your men? Now, that was just offensive. Lexy glanced down at where the woman's razor-sharp nail sliced a trail down her arm. A thin stream of blood oozed from the wound before it closed. *There was a light film of sputum all over her and that was just nasty.* Lexy curtly replied, "I'm alone and you've found yourself in an unfortunate situation. You're obviously doing something sketchy with these backwoods looking Lampir. I'm honestly not even the slightest bit concerned for my safety here, but you should be." Lexy casually tore off the tape that bound her. The woman stepped away, intrigued by her strength. Lexy stood up and peeled the leftover tape from her wrists as effortlessly as tearing masking tape off a birthday present. Grinning because she'd been restrained by pink camo duct tape and it was kind of awesome, Lexy removed a wooden dagger from her pants. *They didn't even take away her weapons. Wooden daggers came with flames and high-pitched shrieking, crap it would be way too noisy. A fistfight might be fun.* Lexy cleared her throat and announced, "So, I'm going to have to kill you all now. I'd like to say it's not personal, but in truth, all of this saliva you guys have going on is just annoying the hell out of me."

Zebra print lady pointed a gnarly nail and commanded, "Kill her."

Fistfight time. A swarm of savage beings surged at her. All Lexy saw was a hoard of gnashing teeth and flying spittle as she commenced breaking backwoods Lampir necks, laughing. *She was ridiculously outnumbered. What in the hell were these things on? They were strong.* She lost count of how many times she'd been chomped on and tossed into walls a few minutes into the fight. The backwoods Lampir in zebra print rifled her over the plastic covered couch and Lexy landed with a thud on the floor behind it. *Shit, she was getting her ass kicked by these freaks. Well, she couldn't allow that to happen.* Lexy stood up, dusted herself off and flippantly provoked, "Is that all you've got?" *Hot damn, she was dizzy. She'd probably lost a lot of blood. It was more than that...It felt like the room was spinning. This wasn't blood loss. It was something else. Did these assholes have venom?* One chomped down on her arm. Lexy launched the screeching salivating wasteland looking being across the room as another tackled her and sunk its fangs into her throat from behind. *Shit.* She grabbed the salivating beast by its head, swung it over her shoulder and as she flipped it, the shocked creature released its jaws. *Oh, darn.* Lexy felt the warmth of her blood flowing from her throat. *If they'd hit an artery, she might bleed out before she had the opportunity to finish them off. Nothing was working out as it was supposed to today.* Within two minutes she had them all down and was staggering around valiantly staking them, as Frost strolled in dragging zebra print lady's body behind him.

He declared, "I caught this one trying to escape."

Stumbling, Lexy mumbled, "You're going to have to kill it," as she blacked out.

She heard humming tires and Grey's steady breathing. Lexy opened her eyes. She was on a bunk in Markus' RV. She closed her eyes and went back to sleep.

Chapter 17

Just A Little Bit Of Stalking

Lexy felt something land on top of the covers and opened an eye, forgetting where she was for a moment. *It was a bag with two wrapped subs and Grey wasn't lying beside her anymore.*

"Rise and shine, naptime is over my drugged-up friend," Jenna's voice announced. "We've already finished the next job. You and Grey have to head back to watch over and most likely bail out the five newbies while we travel up north for another job."

Of course, they did. She'd known they weren't ready. Lexy groggily sat up in bed. *It felt like someone had beaten her with a baseball bat while she was asleep.* She stretched, glared at Jenna and grilled, "What in the hell were those things? Those were some seriously messed up looking Lampir."

Grinning, Jenna disclosed, "Lampir infected with Stryk venom. A rebel Lampir captured a Stryk to use as a guard dog, after finding out Lucien knew of his assassination plot. Their venom is passed by saliva, and they have a slight spraying issue, as I'm sure you noticed. In my dream, it sprayed a partially turned mortal, a chemical reaction

219

happened and when the change was complete, there was a deformed Lampir with an extra dash of crazy that spit Stryk venom. I had that vision shortly after the five returned. I didn't realise it was a time-sensitive situation or that it had spread as far as it did. Markus mentioned you and Grey dealt with a nest a few years ago just outside of New Orleans."

Recalling the reptilian eggs in the nest they'd destroyed, Lexy replied, "We found a cave with a full-grown dead Stryk lying on the ground by dozens of eggs. Grey burned the cave and we left."

Jenna grinned as she explained, "They have remarkably potent venom in their saliva. It stunted your healing ability. I'm sorry, I didn't see that in my vision. We couldn't risk our Healers by staying in that town after Frost told us you weren't healing. That's never happened before, so we destroyed the other hive without entering the premises and were forced to put down infected mortals in the street. I thought we might be able to sneak into this town and get out without mortal casualties, but we were forced to call in the Aries Group. We're going to need a largescale accident to cover this up, we don't have the time in our schedule to stick around for a few weeks to be certain the situation has been contained. We have a ridiculous amount of jobs ahead of us, we'll be working steadily for the next five months. That town and what happens to it is out of our hands."

Lexy hated leaving anything partially finished. *It felt like they'd just done half of a job and walked away, leaving a mess behind for the mortals to clean up.* She quizzed, "Why did you guys wait this long to wake me up?"

Jenna answered, "I'm not going to lie, it was a shitshow. Everyone on your job had to be decontaminated, we couldn't risk taking out our remaining Healers. We burned everyone's clothes and left you asleep. It was a big job. By the way... How are you feeling?"

"Sore, my muscles are throbbing, that's not normal, I'm usually healed by now," Lexy answered as she unwrapped the sub and chomped into it. *This toxin could be used as a weapon on a Healer.* She swallowed her mouthful and asked, "You didn't mention what the venom did to me…did you?"

"Don't worry, I didn't say a thing. When I was a child, there was a morally stunted group called, The Legion of Aries. They took part in the first mass Correction of immortal children in Rome. You know the story. I was one of the seventeen original, Children of Ankh saved by the Guardian Azariah. Let's just say the name, The Aries Group doesn't make me feel all warm and fuzzy inside. We play along and they fund us. They've done a miraculous job covering up after us by protecting our identities but out of all of the names they could have come up with, why that one?"

Smiling, Lexy teased, "Wasn't Delores Aries the founder and original funder?"

"Point taken," Jenna laughed.

Lexy had already devoured a whole sub and begun the second. She swallowed her first bite and asked, "So, what's our next job?"

Jenna smiled as she answered her question, "We don't want to lose this Second-Tier, so you and Greydon will be inconspicuously watching the five as they try to complete their first job. Hang out in the background, and when things go south, you two make sure you grab the new girl."

Stalking was always fun. "Are they already messing up?" Lexy questioned and couldn't help but grin. *Their mission that morning had gone epically wrong. Discovering a new Healer power stifling repellant wrong.*

The RV pulled over. Grey pulled back the curtain to the sleep quarters, stuck his head inside and announced, "This is our stop sweetheart. Let's go see how our newbies are doing."

Lexy grabbed her backpack. Jenna passed her a credit card and said, "They used their credit card at the Comfort Inn. Trinity is already there, Triad is en route."

Lexy smiled as she realised they were leaving them by the side of the highway on the outskirts of town with miles of nothing in every direction. *Wonderful.*

Frost unrolled the passenger side window and shouted, "I've called you a cab, it'll be ten minutes! Good luck! Stay out of sight! We have another job so you might want to make sure they don't take off and leave you guys behind!"

"Thanks for the heads-up!" Grey yelled back as the motorhome drove away. They stood there watching it as it became nothing but a small speck as it disappeared into the horizon.

In less than ten minutes a cab arrived, they got into the backseat as Grey made small talk before instructing, "We have a room at the Comfort Inn."

They got out at the lobby. Their room had been paid for, all they had to do was get the keys. They were on the first floor in a suite with sexy mustard yellow shag carpeting and the bathroom fixtures were baby blue. They were beside the restaurant. They spent the remainder of their afternoon figuring out where Trinity was staying. They found out they were on the third floor directly above their newbies and had a good chuckle about it. They had the picture window cracked and a clear view of the cement alcove by the office from the bathroom window. This was the perfect room to keep tabs on the others. If they didn't leave the room until it was imperative, they wouldn't have to risk being seen. They recognized Trinity's voices. *Thorne, Jakob, Glory and Frey were here for sure.* They peeked through the curtains as they passed by and dashed to the bathroom to see if they were headed upstairs. Kayn and Zach were standing in the alcove by the office. *Oh, no.* With quick thinking, they started making out. It looked like they'd successfully pulled it off as Trinity continued talking and the group scaled the stairs. Lexy looked at Grey. There was a problem, they didn't stop their steamy make-out session after Trinity walked away. They switched positions and it looked like neither one was capable of rational thought. *Kayn must have inadvertently used Frost's ability.* Kayn began to fumble with Zach's zipper. *Oh, shit, should they stop them?* The pheromones Kayn siphoned were working overtime. Lexy looked at Grey, he shrugged. *Of course, he was fine with letting them go at it under the spell of Frost's ability. That dirty stinker. If the passion-filled, make-out session started as a distraction, it definitely wasn't anymore, there was pillow talk.*

"I want you so bad," Zach groaned against Kayn's hair.

A random passerby hissed, "Get a room."

They shoved away from each other. *That snapped them out of it. Oh, thank goodness. She was a second away from blowing her cover and dousing the horned-up teens with a hose.* Kayn covered her mouth. Against the wall, Zach slid down until he was sitting on the cement with his face in his hands. Kayn did the same, trying to calm herself.

With a weak smile, Zach confessed, "That's a powerful ability you've borrowed, Brighton. Five more seconds and I would have taken you right here in public. Without any ability for rational thought, I might add. Do you get to keep it, or does it go away?"

"I honestly have no idea," she admitted. They sat there staring at each other, confused over what almost happened.

Zach struggled to stand and chuckled, "My legs feel like they're made of Jell-O. For future reference, that's how you kiss a guy." With a roguish smile, he held out his hand to help her up.

She took his hand, he tugged her to her feet. Kayn grinned and taunted, "You didn't do so bad yourself. That must be what has Mel so hot and bothered." She brushed down her shirt and wiped her lipstick off his face. She attempted to fix his hair. He fixed the lipstick smeared around her lips with his thumb and patted down her hair.

Zach grinned and teased, "If you'd kissed me like that earlier, we'd still be in the bathroom." Their eyes locked and he started back-pedalling, "We were drugged by your ability. I was just kidding about the bathroom thing, we're friends. We are always going to be friends. Just friends. I know that. Just like I know in this life we've been given, sometimes we're going have to do things we normally wouldn't. This doesn't have to be a big deal if we don't make it one. We kissed and it was hot, but we did it so Trinity wouldn't see us. There was a method to our madness. On a happy note, you calmed yourself down faster this time. If they'd sensed the pheromones, they'd be down here already. We'll just go back upstairs, tell them what happened and figure out another way to get into the room." Kayn responded with a slow nod as they climbed the stairs.

Once they were out of earshot, Grey chuckled, "Consider me impressed, I didn't know Zackie boy had that in him."

Lexy perched on the edge of the tub as Grey stepped away from the window and put the toilet seat down to use it as a chair. He slipped off his t-shirt, revealing his cut abs and whispered, "It's seriously hot in here. I'm in dire need of a cold shower."

So was she... Lexy found her eyes drawn to the over-sized bulge in Grey's jeans, she quickly averted her gaze, but not before he caught her sneaking a peek. The arch of her foot ached, she massaged it.

Grey reached over and tempted, "Let me get that for you, I think I'm the one that ended up owing you a massage."

He began to knead her sore, heel wearing arches with the expertise of forty years of bets and losses. *She shouldn't be letting him do this right now. Kayn had dosed them both with pheromones.* She felt the aching need for him return as his hands worked their magic. *She didn't want him to stop. It was selfish, she knew that, but he also knew about everything now.* He started to massage her calf and inched his way up into the sensual area behind her knee. It forced her to shift closer.

She knew she should stop him, but the pheromones also affected her. She allowed him to gently tug her even closer as his fingers caressed her supple thighs with professional expertise. *They were far too close.* His thumb grazed the area that always made her squirm and she gasped. His eyes lit up as he gently teased her again by softy feathering another touch between her legs. Her lips parted as he moved towards her, lost in the spell of the sensual magic.

Their lips were almost touching when Grey abruptly pulled away from her and stated, "I need a cold shower, and you need to leave before we do something only you'll regret."

The reality of what they'd almost done smacked her in the face. He was right. He knew he wouldn't regret anything because he wouldn't remember. He was trying to be a stand-up guy. Lexy cleared her throat as she stood up, as she left, she whispered, "I'll have one after you're done."

She briskly walked over to the bed as the shower started in the other room, leapt onto the bouncy mattress, buried her face in the soft pillow and screamed. She laid still, thinking, *Trinity knew they were here. They had too. There was no way they missed those pheromones, and even if they did, Jakob was with them and he had heightened hearing. Trinity was staying in the three rooms directly above the five. They knew... There could only be one reason that Trinity hadn't already taken off with the girl. They must not know who she is. They're waiting for Ankh to figure it out, then they'd just take the new Second-Tier and it would be like taking candy from a baby. They had three rooms. They must have a large crew here against five new Ankh. Well, they were about to get a surprise. She could find the new Second-Tier in the time it took to have a cold shower.* Lexy grinned as she dug through the front zipper compartment of her backpack and removed the switchblade. Lexy slipped off her shorts so she wouldn't get blood on them, grabbed the black plastic bag that was always in her bag for situations like this and placed it beneath her as she sat on the bed on top of it in her G-string underwear. She was going to knife herself to freshen up her ability.

Grey strolled out of the washroom and said, "Don't do it unless you have the bracelet."

Smiling, she opened the palm with her Ankh brand. She was already holding the spelled bracelet she'd been given long ago.

He grinned and urged, "Fine then, go for it."

She knifed herself in the thigh, purposely missing the artery and yanked the blade back out. Blood gushed from the wound as her thigh heated. She began to heal as the blood pooled on the plastic bag beneath her.

Grey disappeared into the bathroom and returned with a box of Kleenex. He tossed it at her and teased, "You're going to have to throw out your underwear."

She knew that. It had been a conscious choice to leave them on. She smiled and countered, "I'm not sure taking them off would have been the greatest idea all things considered." She wiped off her thigh and soaked up the blood with the leftover Kleenex. She got up and padded barefoot across the mustard coloured shag carpet to the bathroom as she flippantly taunted, "And now it's my turn for a shower."

Grey called after her, "You know those blood smears on your ass from stabbing yourself almost suck the sexy right out of those, barely there, panties."

He was still flirting with her, this wasn't good. She grinned, glanced back and provoked, "Congratulations, your cold shower almost worked."

Just as she was about to step into the shower, Grey knocked on the door and disclosed, "I just got a text from Markus. Apparently, Trinity and Ankh are having dinner together at the diner. Shall we join them or just wait until the fighting starts?"

What in the hell were they doing? She put her hair up. *There would be no time to wash it now because the newbies had lost their damn minds.* She answered, "I'll be out in a second."

A minute or two later, she reappeared with a towel wrapped around her. Lexy could feel Grey's eyes on her as she wandered over to her bag. *They'd both been dosed with pheromones.* He might not be remembering his feelings for her. If he was, this time, it would be different because he knew about their history upfront and he'd just proven he could walk away because it was the right thing to do, even when his senses had been corrupted by the spell of an immortal's potent pheromones. *This would be alright. They'd be fine.* She announced, "Turn around unless you want an eye-full."

Grey turned as she dropped her towel, slipped into her black lace undergarments, and her jeans and t-shirt. *She was supposed to be inconspicuous, but she wasn't sure that was a realistic expectation.* When she glanced up, she knew Grey hadn't looked away. *He'd seen exactly what she was wearing.*

Grey probed, "Is that new underwear?"

"When would I have had the time to go shopping? You've been with me every second."

He smiled, tossed her shoes at her and sparred, "Not every second."

She cracked an enormous grin and teased, "It's not like we get to bring souvenirs back from the Summit or the banquet."

As he reached for the doorknob, they heard muffled familiar voices. Grey grinned as he took his hand away, spun around and whispered, "Triad's already here."

Lexy smiled and casually responded, "Good, I need to take a round out of someone." *She hadn't meant it to sound naughty. It had just been her mentioning that it would be lovely to kick someone's ass this afternoon.* A thought popped into her brain as she realised what that must have sounded like to Grey. *Triad's here and then, I need to take a round out of someone. Oh, she'd just accidentally opened that freshly sealed can of worms.* Lexy winced as she followed him out of the door. *It didn't look like Triad had entered the diner. They'd be coming in through the backdoor.* Lexy peeked through the window as two eyes behind the business flyers taped to the glass.

Grey whispered, "Can you tell who it is from here?"

She could see her. It was the waitress that was waiting on the table of the two Clans. It was funny. Poor Melody, she had no idea what she was looking for, and Thorne was probably holding his breath waiting for her to pick out the Second Tier. Why in the hell were they having dinner with the enemy? She was totally being played. They all were. Three girls from their Clan excused themselves and went to the washroom at the same time. *That was highly suspect.* Lexy whispered, "Let's go back to the room for a second, I left my knife on the bed."

Grey turned, looked at her and teased, "You really have to stop saying things like that when I'm trying this hard to behave."

She shook her head as he unlocked the door. They both stepped into the suite and quietly closed it. Lexy grabbed her blade as Grey went into the bathroom and exuberantly waved her over with a finger pressed against his lips. Lexy tip-toed to Grey. *There he was, in all his evil nemesis glory. Man... had they ever won the stalker's lottery by staying in this room.* Tiberius was directing Triad in the enclosed cement area by the office where Kayn and Zach had a magic-induced sexy moment in earlier. *Why hadn't he gone in the backdoor? Maybe, they'd all just walked around the building to scope out the situation?*

One of his men started to explain Triad's plan, "It's in the water carafe for the Second-Tiers table, it's also been sprayed in their food. I compelled a waitress to deliver that carafe of ice water to their table roughly ten minutes ago. We also set off gas in the air-conditioning system to knock out the mortals. In ten minutes, there will be nobody left awake in that restaurant, and it should be easy to go in and take the girl." Triad remained hidden in the alcove for a good ten minutes, in silence while one of them watched the clock on his cell.

Tiberius announced, "Alright contestants, it's time to play, snatch a Second-Tier waitress and dash. If you get caught just speak another language and make it convincing. It will take the police some time to find an interpreter and give us an in, to get you out." He started walking, then paused, and added, "Please, do your best to avoid killing the humans."

Lexy smiled, *Tiberius was actually quite funny when you were interested in what he had to say.*

Grey scowled and whispered, "If you start mooning over Tiberius this early in the fight I will march right into that diner and stab myself in the forehead with a fork."

He was jealous. She turned and whispered, "You had no problem when I was mooning you as I walked away earlier."

Looking into her eyes, Greydon confessed, "That's the problem."

Were his feelings for her coming back? There was silence outside the bathroom window. They'd been sidetracked by their own drama. They raced to the front door as they heard jingling bells. *Triad just entered the diner.* They silently opened the door. After making sure the coast was clear, they waited outside the entrance, allowing Triad to think they had their bases covered.

Peeking between posters, Grey whispered, "Everyone's out cold, even Thorne and Frey."

If the Second-Tier were out cold, the mortals could be damn near dead. That dumbass. Suddenly, his witty commentary wasn't that funny anymore. One of the Triad walked out of the diner with an unconscious waitress slung over his shoulder, directly into them. They all stared at each other for a heartbeat before Lexy ordered, "Catch her." She decked the Triad and Grey caught the girl. She peered through the window between the posters once again, turned back, smiled at her Handler and laughed, "It looks like Tiberius is on a strange trip but he's not down. His men are trying to restrain him. This is going to be fun. Go secure her in the RV and grab everyone's things. I've got these guys."

The bells jingled, signalling Lexy's arrival as she walked in. Tiberius was standing on the table fending off his men. *He was higher than a kite.*

He animatedly jumped up and down, hollering, "The lava is coming! Come with me if you want to live!" Five Triad turned to face her. Tiberius saw her. His demeanour changed, "Well, hello beautiful."

She'd deal with Tiberius later. Lexy cockily strutted towards the Triad with weapons raised and roundhouse kicked the first one. The second charged her, she stabbed him in the gut as she booted the third away, broke the neck of the fourth and then took off in pursuit of the one who booked it for the kitchen, leapt over three unconscious Ankh and caught up with the Triad, snapping his neck before he reached the kitchen. Lexy gave Astrid's body a shove with her foot. *She was out cold.* She turned back and casually maneuvered around the bodies towards Tiberius, who was still on the table panicking about invisible lava. *It was strange to see him this way.*

He was waving his arms in the air, yelling, "It's coming! You have to come with me!"

Why not play along for a minute?

Tiberius leapt from the table, and repeated his warning, "Come with me!" He darted towards the kitchen. Out of sheer curiosity, Lexy followed as he mowed over Triad's bodies like they weren't even there. He yarded open the large stainless-steel freezer door and whispered, "We'll be safe in here."

Intrigued by insanity, Lexy followed the leader of Triad into the freezer. Inside were stacked shelves full of meat and frozen goods. *Because why wouldn't you hide in a giant freezer to protect yourself from lava?* He started blocking the door with random things. *This drug-induced hallucination was getting good. Why not let it play out for a second longer before she killed him? Oh yes, she had a job to do. As entertaining as this was, she'd have to shut it down and get with the program.* It was time to send her lava fearing consort off to dreamland. Lexy tapped him on the shoulder and spoke in a soft sultry tone, "We only have five more seconds together. Do you really want to spend it blocking that door?"

He looked into her eyes and whispered, "Kiss me, and then kill me before it gets to us. This is the shittiest way to die."

Tiberius truly believed he was somehow in the middle of a volcanic eruption. She stepped towards him, gently kissed his lips and snapped his neck. His body slumped to the floor. She gave him a kick to make sure he was going to be down for the count before shoving the boxes aside and stepping out of the freezer. Lexy bumped right into her concerned Handler.

Grey peered into the freezer, saw Tiberius' body, with a tell-tale crimson lipstick smear on his lips. He chuckled, placed his arm around her and teased, "Having a moment in the freezer with lava boy?"

She changed the subject, "Is the RV parked out front?" Lexy closed the door on Tiberius and locked it, smiling as she walked away.

Grey had already moved all their Clan's bodies except for one. She saw what Grey was doing and smiled as she lugged the last body out of the diner to the RV. After gently placing Kayn on her bunk, she noticed he'd already gathered their belongings from the room. *He was good. He really had to quit messing around. They had to get some distance between them and the other Clans before this girl woke up.*

Lexy dashed back into the diner and asserted, "Come on, Grey. We need to get out of here."

Grey was busy posing sedated Trinity and Triad in inappropriate ways together. She loved that idiot. He really couldn't help himself. She took in the comic majesty he'd created. Wow. Lexy shook her head and sighed, "If anyone ever asks me who did this, I am so throwing you under the bus. Come on, Caligula. Let's get out of here before everyone starts waking up." She grabbed her side-tracked giggling Handler and ushered him out the door, prodding, "I'm serious! We have to get out of here!"

Chapter 18

Adventures In Babysitting

They got into the RV to the silence of their drugged youthful naïve companions. Grey turned the key, started it up and drove away as she took a tour around to see what he'd done with the waitress. *Where in the hell was she?* Lexy opened the closet. *No waitress?* There was a sign on the locked bathroom door that read, 'Waitress in bathroom.' Lexy sighed as she opened it. *The waitress's body was in the shower, slumped on one side. Come on, Greydon. Where were they supposed to pee?* Relocking the latch, she made her way back to Grey. As Lexy sat in the passenger seat, she complained, "Where are we supposed to pee?"

He grinned at her and provoked, "Go by the side of the road like a man. There's toilet paper in the closet."

Shaking her head, she sighed, "Just drive." Grey passed her an empty pop can from the cup holder in the dash and shrugged, she questioned, "Seriously?"

"I'll find us somewhere to go. Once we're safely off the highway we'll have options," Grey explained, messing with the radio. He turned to face her and whispered, "Why would you kiss that tool while he was under the influence of something?"

Oh, she'd known that was coming. Lexy smiled and explained, "He asked me to kiss him, then off him before the lava got to us. It seemed like a reasonable request."

Her partner in debauchery shot her an unimpressed look. Finding a station worth listening to, Grey cranked up the volume, signalling the end of their conversation. *Maybe he was going to try to let the knowledge of that kiss go?* They rode in silence, with nothing but music and the steady hum of spinning tires to pass the time. Eventually, Grey started serenading her with undeniably charming off-key falsetto. He turned off the highway and started their usual evasive maneuvers to lose the other Clans by taking the backroads. The bumpy, dusty un-cemented side roads weren't helping her need to use the washroom and it went from maybe I might need too, to urgent.

Sensing her predicament, he laughed, "It's probably safe to pull over for a minute, pee speedy my friend."

When she got back inside, Grey was reclined in the passenger seat, pretending to be asleep. *He wasn't really, she'd been gone for five minutes.* Ticked off, she started her driving stint early. *Guess it was her turn to evade the other Clans.* As Lexy pulled out, she jerked the steering wheel, he smoked his head on the window.

"Funny," he mumbled, closing his eyes again.

Lexy despised driving while Grey was asleep. *It was painfully boring when the scenery was bland and monotonous at night.* It was all dusty side roads, and darkness. Everything was muted shades. She decided to pass the time, thinking up a comical list of excuses for why the five went to dinner with Trinity. *That had been insane. What were they thinking?* She kept glancing over, wishing Grey was awake so she could share her witty one-liners, but he was dead to the world, drooling on the seat. *This was far from his sexiest moment. Real love wasn't about the big things it was about the little ones. She adored him, drool and all. He knew about everything now and she wasn't sure how that was going to play itself out. That kiss had bothered him.*

After hours of evasive driving, Lexy heard someone clunking around in the back. *Somebody was awake.* Kayn appeared, dishevelled and confused. She steadied herself by clutching the back of the seats. *She was dying to hear their excuses.* Shaking her head with a grin, Lexy enquired, "I'm curious. Why would you guys be in a diner having dinner with Trinity? What in the hell was that about?"

Surfing the bumps in the uneven gravel road, Kayn confessed, "I knew it was a bad idea. Thorne showed up at our room and told us they knew we were there. He said they'd heard everything we'd been talking about because we hadn't used salt."

Lexy knit her brow and questioned, "Used salt?" They drove over a large bump. Lexy smiled as Kayn almost lost her footing.

Steadying herself, Kayn continued explaining, "The salt circle and that chant. Silence inside or outside of the circle. You know what I mean."

Grinning, Lexy disclosed, "Jakob was with them. He's good. He can tune into anyone… anywhere." She scowled in Grey's direction. *It was time for him to wake up.* Lexy said, "Smack him for me, he's not supposed to be asleep."

Kayn smacked Grey and his eyes popped open. He looked at Lexy, wondering how she'd slapped him from way over there. Kayn giggled and Grey noticed she was standing behind him.

He smiled at her and ribbed, "Oh, she got you to do her dirty work."

Maneuvering the winding road, Lexy chuckled, "It's a good thing we were following you guys. Rule of thumb…if two of the Clans are at a job, the third is bound to show up." *The expression on Kayn's face was glorious. She was wondering how much they'd seen.*

Grey grinned at Kayn and teased, "Yes, I totally saw that. You're a glorious kisser. Anytime you want some more practice, feel free to call on me."

Glaring at her obnoxiously flirtatious Handler, Lexy stated, "Oh, just go ahead and smack him again." Kayn smacked Grey again. He chuckled, rubbing his head, pretending to be deeply wounded. They went over a bunch of potholes as the newbie surfed the thumps in the road like a champ. As the road levelled out, Kayn apologized, "Hey, I'm sorry we screwed up and lost the girl."

Lexy glanced at Grey and grinned. *She didn't know.*

Kayn's voice questioned, "What?"

Lexy maneuvered the steering wheel to avoid the next pothole as she replied, "We didn't lose anybody. The girls locked in the bathroom. We haven't had time to deal with her yet."

Kayn glanced back at the bathroom and said, "I almost went in there. What if someone else gets up and goes in?"

Grey shrugged and quipped, "She's out cold and there's a sign on the door."

"How did you get her from Triad?" Kayn questioned, surfing the road.

With a saucy look her way, Grey piped in, "Let's just say, Lexy's Summit shenanigans came in handy. Hey, did Astrid kiss Tiberius? He was higher than a kite. I doubt he'd be stupid enough to drug himself."

Kayn was grinning like the Cheshire cat from Alice in Wonderland. It was her turn to appear to have a secret. Lexy smiled and said, "Oh, just spit it out."

"It was me. He kissed me, right before I passed out and I'd taken some of Astrid's ability," Kayn confessed.

Why hadn't she been drugged when she kissed Tiberius? Lexy knit her brow as she heard Kayn's thoughts. *Kayn was wondering if she'd made her jealous.* Lexy responded to Kayn's private commentary, "Not jealousy, just confused. I kissed him, it had no effect on me."

Grey mumbled under his breath, "It didn't affect you because you're already crazy."

Lexy gave Grey a dirty look. Kayn smacked him without her having to ask and she smiled. *They needed to find somewhere to deal with the girl. Maybe, she didn't have to be the one to do it this time? There was another Dragon.* Lexy looked at Grey and explained, "The others are going to be up soon. Everyone will need to use the bathroom." She motioned to Grey. He opened the glove compartment and handed her a gold ring with the symbol of Ankh on it. Lexy gave it to Kayn and instructed, "This one is for you. You're going to wait until she wakes up, give her the speech, brand her and kill her."

Holding the ring between her fingers, Kayn slipped it on and flippantly responded, "Why not?"

Lexy's face exploded into a genuine smile. *Dragon Kayn was kind of awesome.* She winked and replied, "Now, that's how a Dragon responds to a challenge." She'd seen a sign for a campsite a few miles back and knew, they were close. *There it was, a wooden sign that could be easily missed.* They turned into the campground. When the RV came to a complete stop, the newbie Dragon casually turned and walked back towards the bathroom. *This was going to be good.*

Grey leaned in and whispered, "Are you sure Brighton's ready for this?"

If her suspicions were right, the Dragon part of her would be able to do what she'd asked without even flinching. Lexy glanced back as Brighton disappeared into the back, smiled and quietly replied, "I certainly hope so, but you should go put on your running shoes just in case."

With a funny look, Grey taunted, "You gave Kayn the job, you're the one that's running after the girl if she gets away."

Her Handler chuckled as he got up. She heard the door open and slam as he went outside to set up. *She should let the newbies figure it out.* She heard Grey's footsteps crunching in the gravel. Lexy sat there trying to trust they wouldn't screw it up. *She should go back there and do it herself.*

"It's hooked up. You're good to go!" Grey yelled from outside.

Her stomach grumbled. *She was hungry. Maybe, they should eat first?* Lexy hollered to her fellow Dragon, "Come have breakfast before you kill her. I'm sure there's plenty of time." *What was she hungry for?* Lexy sorted through the disappointing choices. *There was nothing but bland breakfast cereal in the cupboards. Lily must have done the last grocery run. She always bought a variety of grainy, nutty granola and healthy crap nobody else enjoyed.* Lexy stood there staring at the cupboard, pouting at her options. She poured cereal into a bowl, and took the milk out of the fridge, giving it a sniff before she poured it. *Yes, the milk was still good! In moments like these, her life felt almost normal. Well, except for the waitress they'd kidnapped and locked in their bathroom.* Grey was brewing a pot of coffee. She maneuvered around him in the small kitchen, as she opened the cutlery drawer to grab a spoon. He intimately cupped her waist with his hand as he reached above her. They were joined by a few of the others, and as they ate, the rest awoke from their Triad induced slumber. As they made their way to the table, they were informed about the girl in the bathroom. *Grey kept looking at Zach and Kayn with an enormous grin on his face. He wasn't going to be able to keep his mouth shut about their sexy, almost hookup. There was no way.* They'd all been sitting there, chatting and drinking coffee for an hour when Lexy began wondering if Kayn intended to go through with what she'd ordered her to do.

Zach stood up and complained, "I really need to go to the bathroom. We need to find another place to store the waitress."

Taking a drink from his mug, Grey urged, "Well, what are you waiting for? Go back there and see if she's up."

Lexy struggled to keep her emotions from registering. *It had been her experience that lessons learned the hard way always sunk in faster.*

Zach sighed dramatically and wandered back to the tiny locked bathroom, muttering under his breath about how this wasn't his job. Kayn took that as a hint, as she got up and went with him.

Giggling like a ten-year-old with a well-hidden whoopee cushion, Grey jumped up with his coffee in hand and waved for her to come, excited to watch the insanity unfold. Lexy casually got up and followed her astounding toddler Handler. *It was great. They'd underestimated this girl. Not only was she awake, but she was fighting back like a teeny badass with a plunger as her weapon.* Kayn captured her, gave her the perfect, 'sorry for your family's murder, but you've been given a second chance' speech and then, she asked the girl if she would like to be one of them.

Quietly doing his best Terminator impersonation, Grey commentated, "Come with us, if you want to live." Lexy scowled. *Come on, Greydon. At a time like this, he had to at least appear mature.*

Without hesitation, the brave girl extended her hand. Kayn branded her flesh with the symbol of Ankh. She only had time for a shriek, before Kayn snapped her neck and she crumpled to the floor. *It was done. Molly was Ankh.* Kayn twisted her ring around, walked down the hall towards the others and met Lexy's eyes. *She was so proud of her. It was like having a slightly sadistic child. Good job on that murder. Now came the actual work for the Healers. She'd help them out with this part.* They had two Healers but because Kayn's Conduit ability reared its head, she was able to act as a third. The trio healed the girl and Molly was now Ankh. *It felt like the beginning of a new chapter. Where usually nobody survived the Testing, five had come out and this had altered her perspective.* Lexy didn't feel foreboding as she looked at Molly, she felt hope.

For weeks they drove long stints and hid to conceal Molly's location from other Clans, stopping every couple of days in a campsite to sleep, shower and stretch their legs. It had stopped feeling like they were babysitting the newbies. It now felt like they were all protecting Molly as equals. They were sent word via text from Markus that the other half of their Clan also acquired a new member and his name was Dean. *This was good. Ankh had two new members and it had only been a short time since the last Testing. Would they be able to hold on to both, until they were eighteen... now, that was the question?*

Lexy awoke in the middle of the night to the crumbling noise of tires in gravel. *Had they been found?* She harshly shook Grey, slipped on her jeans and shoved her cell into her pocket. *Just in case they had to contact the others.* She tiptoed into the dark kitchen and grabbed a knife from the drawer, without making a sound. *She would need a weapon if it was Trinity or Triad. They wouldn't have the numbers, but they would have the most important thing, the element of surprise.* Lexy sensed Grey behind her.

He whispered, "Kayn's the only one in her bunk. The others must have fallen asleep in the backroom."

Lexy tossed him a steak knife without warning in the dark kitchen and could tell by his lack of swearwords that he'd caught it. She whispered, "Let them sleep, it might be nothing." Lexy carefully opened the door, wishing they'd taken time to oil the squeaky hinges. They simultaneously grinned as they saw their Clan's black truck.

The hum of the driver's window rolling down revealed Frost's face. He whispered, "I'll go inside and get Kayn and Zach. Get in. Lily wants to find somewhere to watch the sunrise before our next job."

Frost got out of the truck and strolled past with only a quick smile in their direction. They got into the backseat.

Lily glanced back to where they were sitting and said, "The whole sunrise thing wasn't my idea, he's trying to do something romantic for Kayn."

Shaking her head, Lexy sparred, "He didn't even text her once."

Lily shifted around in her seat so she could look at Lexy as she gave her response, "I know, I told him he was being an idiot."

The door opened. Zach jogged down the steps, walked around to the passenger side and waved. Lily opened the door and motioned for him to get in.

Zach yawned as he took his seat and they all got a, not so fresh, nose full of the Nacho chips he'd been eating earlier that evening. Lily crinkled up her nose, dug around in her purse and passed him a pack of gum.

Zach took a piece out and said, "Thanks."

Lily politely smiled and whispered, "Chew two, they're small."

He took another piece, unaware of his issue, he popped the second into his mouth and asked, "What time is it?"

Nobody had a chance to respond before Frost opened the driver's door, slid into the seat and announced, "She'll just be a second."

Lexy was excited about the idea of some action. She grinned at Grey.

He shoved her and playfully teased, "You don't even care what the job is, do you?"

Lexy was still smiling as Kayn climbed into the backseat with them and repeated Zach's question, "What time is it?"

Grey held up his wrist with no watch and ribbed, "It's the crack of frigging dawn. We're going to go somewhere cool though to watch the sunrise. I knew you wouldn't want to miss it."

"No breakfast then?" Kayn questioned.

Grey chucked her a granola bar and Kayn grimaced as she took it.

Lexy smiled as she recalled the fixation with food she'd had back in the beginning when she'd first joined Ankh. *It was a different situation. She'd been starving for years.* She turned to look out the window at the view of endless black. The only light came from their headlights as they barrelled down the backroads. Grey slipped his fingers through hers and gave her hand a squeeze. She recalled Grey's words the day he'd convinced her to come with him, *'Come with me to Clan Ankh and I will always be your friend.'* He'd stayed true to that promise even though he had gotten a lot more than he'd bargained for out of that deal when they'd made him her Handler. As always, holding Grey's hand felt right. *Would a piece of her always wish they could be more? They couldn't be together, and no passage of time would ever change that fact.* Grey released his hold on her hand. Free from the connection, she fantasized about what could be, *her thoughts travelled to Orin and the uncomplicated night they'd shared. He'd shown her what it was like to be with another Healer. It had been unexpected and simple.* She turned her thoughts to Tiberius and his wickedly naughty ways. *He understood the Dragon that slept beneath the surface of the woman she was pretending to be. She identified with the dark parts of him because those were the parts, she kept hidden away so other people would be comfortable.* Grey took her hand and squeezed it again, bringing her back to the here and now. *Neither was Grey.* She looked into her Handler's eyes as he raised her hand to his lips and pressed a tender kiss on the back of it. *Even though he knew the worst parts of her, it had never stopped him from falling back in love with her, time and time again.*

They'd been driving for what felt like hours when the sun began to rise. They parked at a lookout, perched over a small town. Everyone got out of the truck. They stood there as the sun peeked over the mountain top in the horizon and streetlights flickered out in the town below. Grey put his arm around Lexy and held her close, gently stroking her side with his thumb where his hand curved around her waist. Her heart began to thud. *This was his move. The thing that he did that caused her to fold like a cheap deck of cards.* While focused on trying to shut down her reaction to his touch, she heard the gist of the conversation the others were having. *They would be staying here for a couple of days, and they'd buy everything they needed in town.* Lexy looked at the population of 207 on the large green sign and her stomach cramped. *She knew what they were here for. This was her favourite kind of job. Her Dragon would have an opportunity to come out and play.* Lexy looked at Grey, gave him a knowing smile and cheekily taunted, "Awe, this is so sweet Greydon. You shouldn't have. My birthday isn't until next week."

Crinkling his nose, he smiled and countered, "Anything for you, Babe."

Frost motioned to the truck and suggested, "Come on, everyone. Let's go have breakfast."

As they pulled into a picturesque town with perfect sidewalks, and cobblestone planters full of flowers, Lily rolled down her window. *There was just a hint of fall in the air.* They slowly cruised down the main street. As they passed a man walking out to his vehicle, Lexy could tell he was mortal by his aura. Her stomach muscles kept clenching at regular intervals. *Her predatory instincts rarely led her astray. That man was probably just passing through. This town was full of dangerous things and they would meet their match in her.*

Kayn looked her way and stated, "Now, that's trippy."

Lexy chuckled, "You haven't seen anything yet, Hun."

Zach twisted around in the front and enquired, "What are you guys talking about?"

Kayn pointed at the man, now a speck in the distance, and explained, "I could see that guy's aura and it's been almost a month. I assumed it would be gone by now."

It had been closer to three weeks, but she wasn't about to correct her.

Lily squirmed in her seat and proclaimed, "There it is. That's the place. Jenna said it was named after a children's poem."

Humpty Dumpty's. That was irony at its best for she was going to make sure every demon in this town fell down hard. They parked and Ankh wandered in. *Only a few mortal patrons were dining in the restaurant. She wasn't wrong about this place. She knew she wasn't wrong.* Her instincts shifted into high gear as her stomach tied itself in knots. Her heightened senses put a species to the scent of the meat cooking in the kitchen. *Mental note... Warn others about the people meat. There was a time when it wouldn't have mattered what species she was ingesting as long as the aching desperation of starvation was quenched, but she wasn't desperate or starving anymore. These demons were cannibals. This was only one more reason why she was proud to be a part of their destruction. There was a seriously creepy amount of burgundy in this room. It was everywhere, from the pleather seating to the light fixtures, everything was burgundy.*

A waitress appeared from the kitchen, trailing an aura with misty hues of black and smoky grey. She froze as she saw them at the table. The demon-possessed shell of a waitress gave them an overly hospitable smile and darted back into the kitchen.

Kayn and Zach looked panicked. She hadn't made them. She was probably just checking the freezer to see if there was enough space. Lexy grinned at her comical inner commentary as she kicked Kayn under the table and whispered, "They can't tell we're anything other than normal people unless they see the symbol of Ankh on the palms of our hands. Just play it cool."

Her attention was brought back to Grey as he nudged her and quietly spoke, "Are they all good?"

Lexy was just about to say, yes, they're fine when Kayn abruptly stood up. Zach grabbed for her arm.

Kayn darted out of the way and chuckled, "I'm just going to go over there to get menus. They're sitting in plain sight on the counter. Our waitress appears to be missing in action."

The fledgling Dragon wandered over to the counter and snagged six menus just as their not so mortal waitress appeared from the backroom. The lady with the smoky aura apologized as Kayn assured her everything was fine, she thought she'd save her a trip by grabbing the menus.

"I'm sorry about the wait, we're a tad understaffed. Would you all like coffee?" the pleasant voiced lady asked.

Smiling sweetly, Kayn answered, "Yes, coffee would be wonderful. How come you guys are open so early?"

The waitress responded, "We get a lot of truck drivers passing through early in the morning. It tends to be our busiest time of day. This morning is obviously an exception. I'll be there in a second with your coffee." She nodded at Kayn and briskly marched back into the kitchen area.

Kayn strolled back to the table with menus in hand and a knowing smile, as she passed menus to everyone and slid back into her seat with a self-satisfied grin.

Lexy smiled to herself. *Miss Brighton had done well... Extremely well.*

Frost started to laugh, "You should have seen the look of sheer terror on Zach's face when that waitress came out of the back. It was amazing."

Kayn glared at Zach and said, "Mello yourself out, my friend. Have a beer or something."

"It's six o'clock in the morning. Who drinks at six am?" Zach mumbled as he opened his menu, pretending he was interested in ordering and not the least bit terrified at what Kayn might do next.

Grey started laughing. Lexy scowled and questioned, "Is something funny?"

"Nope, nothing at all," Grey chuckled as he opened the menu sitting in front of him.

Lily shook her head slowly and sighed, "You guys are so whipped."

Zach looked up from his menu and questioned, "How exactly am I whipped? She's not my girlfriend or anything."

Hiding behind her menu, Lily teased, "That's not what I heard."

Damn it, Greydon. Lexy had known he was going to tell someone but Lily…really?

"That was just a distraction to get out of a sticky situation with Trinity. It went a little further than it was supposed to because our Kayn has amped pheromones and I'm…" Zach stopped speaking because Frost looked stricken.

Frost looked at Zach and questioned, "No headaches or anything when you kissed her?"

Zach raised a brow, and gave him a strange look as he responded, "No, why would I get a headache?"

"Interesting," Frost replied and then stared back down at his menu.

Frost was seriously choked. Lexy peered up from her menu as the door to the kitchen opened with a squeal and a groan.

"They should grease the hinges on that door," Grey noted from behind his menu.

The waitress made her way back to the table, coffeepot in hand and they took turns passing her their mugs. When she was finished, she courteously added, "I'll be right back to take your orders."

Lexy looked directly at Kayn and mouthed the words, "I'd avoid ordering anything that has meat in it."

Kayn knit her brow and nodded.

Giving Frost's arm a squeeze when the waitress returned, Lexy whispered, "It's your turn."

Frost looked up, ordered oatmeal and handed his menu to the waitress. They all did the same as they ordered. Lexy's adrenaline raced as the door to the restaurant opened. *Calm, she had to be calm.* Grey took her hand under the table as half a dozen human shells with ominous smoky dark auras came into the establishment. Lexy sensed the anxiety from her fellow Dragon, kicked Kayn under the table and whispered, "Shut it down."

Kayn nodded at Lexy as her stomach growled loudly. Everyone at the table turned and looked at her. Lexy felt a slight jerk as Grey followed her example and kicked Zach under the table.

Moving closer to Kayn, Zach whispered, "Just breathe."

"I need to get out of here for a second," Kayn asserted as she tried to stand up, but couldn't because Zach had a death grip on her hand.

Frost questioned, "Where do you think you're going?"

Kayn looked directly into his eyes and explained, "I'm just going to the bathroom. I need a minute. I'll get it under control."

"Just think about something else," Lexy whispered.

The waitress arrived with Kayn's breakfast and placed an omelet in front of her. She politely thanked the waitress, grabbed the hot sauce, and dumped a disgustingly impressive amount of it on her omelet. *She was putting it on everything, now.*

The waitress placed Zach's order in front of him and Lexy grimaced. *He ordered the bacon. Oh, crap she'd just assumed Kayn would warn him.* He took a bite and she scrunched up her nose. Lexy turned to alert Grey, who was already watching Zach with morbid fascination as he devoured his first strip of human meat. *Shit.*

Making a strange face, Zach picked up his next piece and whispered to Kayn, "I think there might be something wrong with this bacon, it smells off. Should I tell the waitress?"

They both had to bite their tongues to stop themselves from laughing as Kayn's eyes widened. *She'd forgotten to warn her Handler about the meat.* Kayn picked up one of Zach's pieces of bacon and sniffed it. Lexy had to look away as Kayn realised what her Handler was eating. The scent of burnt human flesh always left an imprint on one's memory. Slowly moving her head from side to side, Lexy mouthed the words, "Don't tell him."

247

Kayn whispered in Zach's ear, "It's probably gone bad. Don't eat any more."

Zach grimaced and complained, "That was a waste of money." The waitress came back to refill their coffee and Zach addressed her, "Excuse me, I think there's something wrong with my bacon, it's gone bad."

The waitress gave her token response, "I apologize. We serve thin strips of moose meat as bacon. It's not pig. I keep telling them they should have it written on the menu somewhere."

That hadn't made sense but seemed to pacify Zach's need for an answer. Zach smelled a piece and took another bite, right in front of the waitress. He looked at Kayn and she had to look away. The waitress smiled as Zach chewed up his mouthful and swallowed it. She wandered to the next table to refill their coffee. The restaurant was full. Everyone's auras were an ominous dark cloud. *Lexy was trying hard to fight the urge to decapitate everyone in the diner. They were all demons hidden beneath a veil of mortal flesh. They needed to leave because she had a reasonable amount of control but Kayn did not.* Lexy squeezed her Handler's hand as tightly as she could, and Grey gave Frost a good shove.

"Let's go buy toiletries and clothes and find somewhere to stay for the night," Frost announced rather loudly, as the waitress walked by their table.

She paused and suggested, "There are some really great cabins with a lake view a few blocks away. You'll see the sign. It says, Eagle Perch. Those are reasonable."

Frost nodded, smiled at her and said, "Add an extra ten dollars for the tip." He handed her their card.

"I'll be back with your receipt," she replied, smiling.

After she brought it back to the table, they made their way outside, appearing to be nothing more than tourists. *They'd look like easy targets, a group of teenagers planning to spend the night partying in one of the cabins by the lake.*

Kayn caught up to Frost and whispered, "So, what's the plan here? Are we really spending the night in a town full of...?"

Frost lifted his finger and pressed it against his lips, to stop Kayn from saying what she was about to say.

Chapter 19

An Echo In The Calm

They got into the truck and started driving, scoping out the town as Frost explained the job, "We're going to go rent a cabin, then we'll stop by every business in town and make sure we tell them where we're staying, and that we'll only be here for one night. They'll come for us and when they do, we'll show them what two Dragons are capable of."

Fun. Lexy grinned as her eyes met with Kayn's and knew, the fledgling Dragon wasn't the slightest bit afraid of the evil that was coming.

Concerned, Zach questioned, "What are they? How many of them are there?"

"This is a demon infestation," Frost replied. "The sign as we arrived said the population was two hundred and seven."

Kayn couldn't stop smiling. Lexy understood how she was feeling. *This was going to be so much fun.*

Zach's lips were still parted. He was stunned. He stated, "There's no way we can kill two hundred demons, it's impossible."

Laughing, Frost sparred, "You just survived the Testing. Nothing is impossible."

They pulled down a long dirt road that led to the cabins the waitress told them about. The Dragons grinned at each other as Frost parked and everyone got out of the truck. *Her new murder buddy appeared to be equally down for the demonic mass murder they had planned for this evening.*

Wandering over to the office, Frost hollered, "Wait here you guys, I'll be right back" He darted into the inconspicuous rustic log cabin office.

There were gift shop items displayed in the window. It made her want to giggle. *They probably sold souvenirs to their guests and after they murdered them, they just placed them back in that window for the next sucker who came along.* Lexy inhaled the fragrant scent of the forest. *This town was the perfect place for a demon infestation, it was isolated. There was only one road into town and one way out.* She spun around, surveying the lay of the land. *Yes, this was going to be fun.* The branches of the trees fluttered as an icy breeze rippled its way through the branches. *Even the breeze was colder than it should be. This place was nothing more than a beautiful trap set for mortals.* Goosebumps prickled on her flesh, warning her of the evil sure to come as soon as the sun set and the forest became lost in the shadows of towering trees. There was always an uneasy stillness in the air before a tornado. She felt that now. It was coming and as the brutality of those volatile winds could savagely rage their way across the land, she was capable of the same destruction. She could weather any storm, no matter how volatile. This was her calling. She was meant to be a weapon, a method of retaliation, leaving nothing but utter devastation in her wake. She was a Dragon, the fire of vengeance raged within her being for the two hundred and seven mortals that had their souls displaced so these foul demonic entities could use their shells. When the fight was over, she would remain standing while those who defiled the mortal species, she'd vowed to protect were left scattered on the ground as no more than shards of metal in a class five's wake. The demons that had taken over this town would end up being nothing more in the end than an echo in this moment of calm.

Frost reappeared with keys dangling from his fingers. He grinned and explained, "I told them we needed privacy. So, they've put us in a cabin down by the water. Everyone get back into the truck. It's a bit of a drive."

They all got in and continued driving down the long narrow road. *There wasn't room for more than one vehicle. If they met someone coming in the opposite direction, they'd be screwed.* They drove for a while through the lush greenery of the woods before turning down a numbered driveway and parked in front of a rustic log cabin. Grey climbed into the back of the truck, unlocked the storage box and leapt out, lugging the case towards the door as Frost unlocked it. He lifted up the welcome mat and of course, there was another key under it.

Frost grinned, as he held up the key and chuckled, "So, this is how they planned on getting in." He strolled into the cabin. Grey followed him, hauling the heavy case.

Walking in behind Grey, Zach whispered, "Tell me this isn't going to be a bloodbath, our bloodbath."

Grey looked back, grinned at Zach and disclosed, "We probably won't even have to leave the cabin. Lexy and Kayn are going to enjoy this one. It'll be a cakewalk." He opened the case of ten-pound bags of salt, removed a smaller case and placed it on the bed by the larger one, suggesting, "Grab one the bags and start circling the room on the inside."

Lily grabbed a bag and did her part circling the room with salt. She piped in, "Don't worry about it, Zach. This is just a small town where demonic souls have possessed the entire population. There won't be any of those big scaly ones or any of that sedating mist involved. These are just strong shells. We're going to send them back to where they came from. The Aries group will clean up after us."

The cabin reeked of bleach. This must be the routine. Somebody comes into the diner and they suggest the cabins. They came out here and were murdered in their sleep and eaten by the patrons of the diner. She really had to give these demons two thumbs up and a finger snap for creativity. Lexy opened the smaller case, inside were a half dozen silver daggers with the symbol of Ankh etched into the blades. She noticed Kayn staring as she stroked the weapon appreciatively and explained, "These daggers send them to where they are supposed to go without having to mark them with our blood and say anything. We're only supposed to use them when the job is as big as this one."

Frost came out of the bathroom and announced, "Time to go get to know the town's residents. We'll drive in together and split up. We can cover more ground faster that way. I'd like to come back out here and relax, it's a beautiful lake. It's just a shame the whole damn town is full of cannibals."

Zach looked at Frost and said, "What did you just say?"

Lexy elbowed Frost and he dodged the question, "Nothing. Don't worry about it, let's go." He quickly strolled out the door.

As they drove into the town full of cannibalistic demons, only some were anxious, others were excited. Well, mainly the two Dragons in the backseat. Neither one could wipe the smiles off their faces. They pulled over down the street from the diner where they had a sketchy breakfast and got out. The girls took off in one direction and the boys in the other.

Taking an Aries Group card out of her pocket, Lily announced, "Let's go buy new clothes."

Both Dragons grimaced at the idea, but Lily appeared to be stoked. They entered a small trendy boutique. For Lexy, shopping was about as exciting as having her toenails removed with pliers, but Lily was a girl with a mission.

Their resident beauty queen moved around the store with the skill of someone that worked there. Lilly grabbed jeans for Lexy and Kayn to try on and sent them to the change rooms as Lilly loudly told the ladies who worked there about the cabin they were staying in for just tonight at the gorgeous picturesque lake. They left the store with a bag of clothes. *It wasn't nearly as painful as Lexy thought it would be.* They stopped into a florist and chatted with the people in the store about where they were staying, asked directions to the pharmacy and headed out to get toiletries and makeup. Everyone appeared to be a demon with an ominous cloud hovering.

It was almost three in the afternoon when one by one their stomachs started a lovely chorus of, feed me ladies or I'm going to make this awkward. Lilly texted the boys, told them they were ready to go and asked for their takeout order. They needed food and rest before this fight. By quarter after three, their order was done. The guys showed up with no bags explaining they were already in the truck and Zach was waiting there. They passed off a few of their bags to Frost and Grey to lighten the load. With food in hand, they followed them out to the vehicle loaded with the supplies. Zach beamed and over exuberantly waved through the window. *What in the hell? He was blitzed. Those Morons.*

Lilly sighed, "Really, you guys?"

Grey chuckled, "He's a little bit drunk. Not sick drunk, just happy drunk. Nobody is coming for us until after nightfall. It won't be dark outside for hours."

Lilly slid into the front beside Zach, he stared until she sighed, "What do you want, Zach?"

He preened, "You're so beautiful. I really want to touch your hair."

She glanced at the backseat and hissed, "Greydon, I'm going to smack you for this when we get out of this truck."

Grey flirtatiously provoked, "Alright, sounds good gorgeous, I'm willing to take one for the team…again." He glanced at Frost.

He wouldn't go from mooning over her to flirting with Lily in the same day. They hadn't slept together. Lexy smiled and shook her head.

Lily rolled her eyes, turned to look at Zach and called his bluff, "Fine, go ahead."

Zach reached over and touched her glistening silky black hair trickling down her shoulders like a midnight waterfall. Zach started laughing, "It's a joke. I'm not drunk. Do you think I'm a moron?" He turned and winked at Grey. You owe me one if that spanking's amazing."

Lily smoked Zach's arm and he giggled, "Hit me harder. I can take it."

"You think you're pretty funny, don't you?" Lily ribbed.

"I'll be anything you want me to be, beautiful," Zach boldly flirted.

Lily slowly shook her head but was still smiling as they pulled up to the cabin and got out. They carried everything inside. After grabbing their food, Lexy sat down and made herself comfortable on the bed next to Grey.

Frowning as he investigated his styrofoam container, Grey leaned over and sarcastically mumbled in her ear, "Fries gravy and salad…yummy."

Lexy opened her styrofoam container and stared at the unappealing contents. *The first thing she was going to do when they got to a larger city was order herself a steak.* She tuned into the exchange between Frost and Kayn. He'd bought her hot sauce. Lexy stopped devouring her fries as she pointed at the no-name hot sauce gripped in Kayn's hand and whispered, "That was sweet." As she spoke, she'd paused before eating her gravy covered fry, leaving it precariously dangling from her fingers, threatening to drip gravy on the bed. Grey chomped a big bite off the end. Lexy scowled as she swatted him away and scolded, "Eat your own damn fries, food thief." *There was a time when she would have stabbed someone with a fork for stealing a French fry.* He gave her a deliberate soppy gravy lipped kiss on the cheek and she playfully swung at him again. *He was being an annoying pain in the butt on purpose today.*

Grey held his almost empty container up as a peace offering and courteously declared, "You can have one of mine."

Just as Lexy reached for one, he yanked the container away. *He was a stinker.* She rolled her eyes at him, as she got up and wandered across the room to get their drinks after noticing they were still on the counter. Lexy glanced back. *Grey was still grinning at her. God, she adored that goofy fool with everything inside of her.* Lexy grabbed their drinks and was about to peter back to her spot by her shenanigan loving Handler as she identified with the look on Kayn's face, paused and remarked, "It sucks, doesn't it?"

Kayn grinned and countered, "Which thing?"

After smiling in response to Kayn's witty comeback, Lexy clarified, "Wanting something you're not allowed to have." Her eyes travelled to her Handler, scarfing down her fries. She contemplated walking over there and stabbing him in the back of his thieving hand with her plastic fork.

Smiling, Kayn gave her response, "Yes, it definitely does."

Frost took a sip from his straw, finishing his drink with an overemphasized slurp. He rather abruptly changed the subject by pointedly directing his question at Zach, "This new girl, Molly. What's she like? She definitely doesn't look sixteen."

About to eat a fry, Zach put it down and responded, "She does look way younger, doesn't she? I really like her a lot. She's a sweet girl and much tougher than she looks."

Looking in Frost's direction, Kayn disclosed, "She's funny and a bit goofy. I can't even picture her in the

Testing. I can't wait until we take her to the in-between for the first time."

Lexy grinned at Kayn and teased, "I couldn't picture you in the Testing and I have a feeling you're going to miss out on that, she's probably there with the rest of Ankh right now. Listen, do yourself a favour, don't get too attached. They almost never come out of the Testing." She gave her the token, protect your heart speech and turned away. *It still felt like it was her job to guide them, but it wasn't anymore...not really.* It was going to be difficult to follow her own advice this time, with the survival of the three and emergence of the two they'd lost to the Testing so long ago. *This made her heart want to believe it was possible. It was going to sting when the next group didn't make it out of the Testing. Get with the program. She couldn't afford to have a squishy warm and fuzzy heart before a fight the size of the one they were facing tonight.*

Wandering up behind her, Grey whispered, "Don't be so negative." He wrapped his arms around her waist from behind and playfully kissed her neck. *It tickled.* Lexy squirmed out of his embrace and swatted him away. *Her Handler was not being helpful.*

Zach and Kayn left the cabin as Lexy tidied up the room. *Why was she bothering?*

Grey took the empty pop can out of her hand, placed it on the counter and asserted, "Leave the cleaning. We'll have all night to do it. Let's go outside and look around."

Following Grey, Lexy strolled out into the lush green landscape. They strolled to the back of the rustic, quaint cabin in silence. There was a large, perfectly stacked woodpile outback. She grabbed a fireplace sized log off the top and wood bugs scattered. When she was younger, she used to play with these bugs at one of her foster homes. It was one of her earliest memories. She picked up an oval backed bug, and it scampered around on ticklish legs in her palm, she grinned. *It was odd timing for a childhood memory.*

Grey teased, "Having a moment?"

He was watching her intently when she peered up and disclosed, "I used to play with these bugs at a foster home when I was a little girl." She placed her hand close to the top of the woodpile, resting her fingertips flush with it. The grey bug scurried back onto the lumber and vanished.

"I don't think you've ever mentioned that memory," Grey quietly responded.

"I don't remember much about my life before…" Lexy didn't want to finish the sentence. *She avoided thinking about that place.* She closed her eyes as flashes of the dark farm flooded her mind and when she opened them, Grey was gone. *Where in the hell did he go?* She heard a woodpecker and gazed up the tree's intertwining branches towards the steady rat ta tat tatting sound. A tree branch snapped close to the ground in the bushes beside her. She saw his red shirt right away. *It was Grey. You can't hide in the bushes wearing red.*

"Grey, I know you're over there, I can see your shirt," Lexy sweetly sang. "Go change, that red shirt is like wearing a target in these bushes."

He got up and complained, "You're no fun, it will be dark out by the time they show up." He plowed his way through the brush and sighed, "All right, go plot your mass murder. I'm not changing my shirt. I'm wearing red just in case I have to fight tonight. It's a preemptive bloodstain avoidance tactic."

That was a great idea. She should have bought something red.

Her Handler started tossing out ideas for a plan, "We should see if we can feed Kayn more abilities before the fight, amp her right up and then she should be in the back. No, maybe you should. It'll be easier for us to keep an eye on her out front. Zach is going to shit bricks when he sees how many are coming tonight."

Lexy listened and occasionally nodded as she always did. *She usually let her Handler think there was a plan but there never was. Things ran smoother in their relationship if she let him think he was a part of her decision-making process. She operated solely on instinct while in Dragon mode. This time it would be different. She had to hold on to a tiny shred of humanity in order to direct Kayn before the fighting began. She'd give Kayn the back and she'd take the front.*

"I'm going to join the cabin dwellers," Grey remarked.

"I'll be right there," she called after him as he sauntered away. *He wasn't even going to have to leave that cabin. None of them were. There were no visible trail openings behind the cabin. If they came through the bushes, they'd make more than enough noise to give Kayn plenty of warning. Lexy strolled over to the thick brush and saw there was indeed a trail, it was overgrown at the opening. Instinct told her Kayn could handle it. This would just be a faster fight with fewer obstacles. The quicker they advanced upon the cabin, the faster they'd snuff them out. Why was she standing here surveying the area? When the sun set, it wouldn't matter what she had planned. She would be on Dragon fuelled autopilot and so would Kayn.*

Lexy meandered around to the front of the cabin. *They weren't there.* Lexy continued to the shore and saw the group quietly observing Zach and Kayn as they skipped rocks on the clear glassy peaceful surface of the lake. She walked up to stand by Grey. He placed his arm around her, gave her shoulder a squeeze and kissed her head. *This irritated her. It wasn't the time for her Handler to keep her close, it was now that he had to release the reigns on her heart so she could do her job void of emotion.* She hadn't been paying attention to the time, but she could tell by the placement of the sun and the colours in the sky that dusk was almost upon them. The new Dragon and Handler were embracing. *Zach had to let his hold on her go too, so she could become what she needed to be.*

Frost nudged Lexy and whispered, "We need to feed her."

Kayn and Zach's touching Dragon Handler bonding moment was cut short by Lexy's booming voice, "This is not the time for that mushy crap. It's almost time to shut your emotions down. Come over here and take some of my energy. We should feed your Conduit ability by topping up the Healing ability within you. We have a plan and we are running out of daylight." *There, she'd vocalized the plan she planned to ignore so the others would be happy.* The new Dragon and Handler pair released each other and turned to face the Ankh. Lexy held her hands out and she walked over and took them. Kayn's hands gradually warmed until Lexy felt her healing energy travelling a heated trail up her arms and out of her body. *She couldn't allow her to take too much.* Lexy yanked her hands away, purposely severing the connection.

Grey strolled up and announced, "We have a plan here, but first we need to run a test and see how many abilities you can hold at once. Take some of mine. I'm not sure what will happen. My pyrokinesis ability has been stifled by the Third-Tier but it's still there."

Kayn took Grey's hands and after a few moments of connection, she shrieked in agony, as her legs buckled. She landed on her knees on the pebbly shore but managed to keep her grip on him. Grey yanked his hands away and Kayn remained there, gasping on her knees.

Lily tossed a knife at Kayn before she'd attempted to move and as it sailed through the air towards her, Kayn lifted a hand and caught the blade in midair by its handle.

Grinning, Lexy directed the fledgling, "Now, cut your hand."

Kayn dragged the blade across the center of her palm without flinching. The blood didn't even have a chance to pool along the slice before it closed. *That healed instantly. She was impressed. When it came to her own healing ability, how quickly she healed was based on her energy level.*

Frost offered Lexy his energy as a replacement for what she'd given to Kayn. She took his hands and felt the luxuriously euphoric warm sensation as it travelled up her arms into her chest. She hadn't even had the opportunity to thank him when a log on the beach exploded into raging flames. *Well, Kayn had obviously figured out how to use Grey's ability. So, she could absorb, store and access multiple abilities. This was good to know.* Her stomach curdled as the sun descended in the horizon. Lexy knew she had one more thing to do before she left Grey. She walked over, stood beside him, and took his hand as they silently observed the smouldering flames Kayn created with his ability. Lexy used the connection to give him a touch of energy back just in case he needed it later. Grey squeezed and tenderly stroked her hand with his thumb. *He didn't have to say a word. She understood what that meant. He was saying goodbye to this version of her and asking her, without words to come back to him when this fight was over. He'd never needed to fear this for she would always return to him.* Her abdomen twisted with pleasurable pain and she peered up at the others. By the scowls on their faces, they were all feeling the same thing. *The demons…were on their way…*

Chapter 20

Demon Fight Club

Lexy had been standing there staring at the mountain's peak for a while when the final rays from the sun slipped away and the forest was left in shadows. *It was time to explain the ground rules.* Lexy grinned as she began her speech, "First things first." She grabbed an object out of her pocket and dropped it on the ground, directly in front of Kayn. "I'm sure you remember what this is, but just in case you've forgotten, this object is used to block spiritual energy. It will also keep the demons trapped within the confines of the town, so we have a controlled circumstance in which to send each one of those abominations back to hell where they belong."

Grey chuckled, "The first rule of demon fight club is …you must always clean up the evidence after demon fight club."

Frost laughed aloud and then, disputed, "No, the first rule of demon fight club is, you must stay in the cabin while the Dragons fight. Get it right, Greydon." He turned to look at Zach and remarked, "That's your cue. Run back to the cabin, toss our Dragons a few of those Ankh swords and get the hell inside."

Grey made another revision to the list of demon fight club dos and don'ts, "Okay, then, that's the second rule. The third is, "Do not break that line of salt at the front door of the cabin while you're running through it, make sure you jump over it."

Zach leapt over the line of salt, disappeared into the cabin and returned with a couple of demon-slaying daggers. He tossed one to Lexy, she caught it mid-flight, and then, he tossed the other to Kayn, who did the same. Zach yelled, "What happens if they drop them?"

Frost looked directly at Kayn as he disclosed, "Fun fact. The Demons can't even touch those blades, not even with gloves on. With the slightest graze, they will drop and be expelled from those shells. We're all going to go inside now, to find our seats, so we can watch the show. This is where we find out what you two are capable of together. You take out every demon that has the balls to show up." Everyone but the Dragons went back to the cabin. Seconds later, Frost appeared in the doorway and cast more daggers into the dirt. They each picked up spare daggers, dusted them off and creatively hid them.

Lexy motioned for Kayn to follow her around the side of the cabin and they waited in the shadows. *It was time, she felt it like a hollow ache in her bones.*

"What are we doing?" Kayn asked, from behind her.

Lexy glanced back at her fellow Dragon and whispered, "We're going to let them walk their cannibalistic ass's right into our trap. They've probably sent in a few scouts. We'll take these first ones out quickly and easily." Lexy's stomach clenched as she stopped the upward curve of her lips by pressing them firmly together. Suddenly, loud eighties rock blared from within the cabin's walls, and this time, Lexy couldn't stop the grin from forming. Noticing Kayn's scowl, she grinned and explained, "He knows I like to listen to eighties rock while I'm fighting. It's one of our things. Got to love those ass-kicking anthems." Lexy tugged the fingerless glove off her hand and tossed it into the dirt. *There was no need for pretense when dealing with supernatural beings. This was a deathmatch, and there would be no escape for these dark abominations from hell, for she'd been created to be judge and jury of all blasphemous creatures.* They were about to step out of the shadows when a half dozen shells came out of the bushes. *Make that a half dozen scouts.* Lexy paused, glanced back at Kayn and announced, "Allow me to show you how easy this is going to be. Bet you I can take all six without even breaking a sweat. Watch and learn." She strolled out of the shadows with her dagger in hand and ran at the demons before they had a chance to know she was coming. In one swift movement, she slashed one above his collar line. The shell clutched his throat and staggered as blood spurted from his severed artery. A cloud of smoke spewed out of his mouth and dissipated into the ground. Lexy spun in a circle, grazing the arms of the others, and the same thing happened. The fifth assailant ran at her wielding a blade. She kicked him in the chest, he landed on his back with a thud. Lexy didn't finish him off as he lay on the ground stunned, struggling to catch his breath. She allowed him to scramble to his feet. While using fight etiquette, someone stabbed her in the back. *Asshole.* Lexy felt the divine warmth of her life essence soaking into her light-coloured shirt. She reached around and yanked the blade out of her back like a badass. *Well, that was really frigging rude.* The Ankh symbol on her hand lit up the darkness as the heat from her healing ability worked its magic.

In that breath, the game changed. The demons remained froze in place as Lexy lifted her shirt to show them the wound was no longer. The monster Lexy kicked to the ground, fled into the woods as she finished off the fifth with a slash of her blade. Kayn sprinted out of the shadows and gave chase. Lexy followed to make sure Kayn had the situation under control. She pursued the fledgling Dragon, maneuvering uneven terrain with the agility of a mountain lion seconds away from subduing its prey. The shell was quick, but nowhere near as fast as she was while free to be in her supernatural form. Lexy held back as Kayn leapt into the air, knocked her victim down, raised her blade and thrust it into his back. A black cloud of smoke funnelled out of its mouth and disappeared into the forest floor. A foul entity grabbed Kayn by her throat and yarded her off the creature she'd just subdued. In one stealth movement, Kayn flipped it over her shoulder and spun around to see how many were left. Surrounded by fifty, maybe sixty demons adorned in human flesh, clutching a blade in either hand, Kayn provoked, "Bring it on, demon bitches!"

She had this. Snickering at Kayn's combat conduct, Lexy left her counterpart in the mayhem, knowing she was more than capable of covering the back of the cabin and tore through the bushes slaying everyone she came across in a blur of whipping branches. Catching a runner out of the corner of her eye, Lexy sprinted through the woods in pursuit of those attempting to flee. The Dragon ended each demonic vessel she came across in a blur of arterial spray and pitchy shrieking, before they a chance to make it out of the bushes into the open area in front of the cabin.

She'd lost the ability for reason, long before she emerged from the forest covered in the blood of her enemies. The demons who'd unsuccessfully tried to enter the spiritually protected cabin were ready for her. Lexy savaged a brutal path of destruction through the herd of immortal code violations, slashing, stabbing, slicing and dicing until nothing remained of her, but the instinct for the kill. She lost count of how many times their blades sliced into her skin and stabbed her flesh. Her palm kept flashing, and her torso was nothing but a surging fire of healing energy, as it fought to keep her standing by working overtime. A blade sliced into her stomach, another plunged into her back, close enough to her heart to cause discomfort. *If the knife in her back moved an inch, it was over.*

Knowing she was mortally wounded had never stopped her before, but even in the purest Dragon state, she knew if she didn't get it out, she couldn't heal. Taking out assailants with every masterful swipe of her blade, Lexy's vision wavered. They were coming at her in an endless stream, faster than they could be executed. She persevered, brawling with her adversaries, hurling each one aside with superhuman strength. *If she could reach the blade in her back, she might have a chance to finish this.* Lexy unceremoniously yanked a blade out of her stomach, it immediately healed. With an ear-piercing battle cry distraction, Lexy reached for the knife in her back. *Shit, there was no way. She couldn't reach it. Focus…New game, she had to take out as many out as she could before she went down.* Wielding daggers, continuously rotating so they couldn't adjust the knife in her back, the Dragon within persevered as they came at her from every direction in droves. Adrenaline surged through her being as she pivoted again. *She couldn't think. She was in quite the predicament.* Lexy staggered as everything started happening in slow-mo. The hoard paused to witness her demise. *She was finding it difficult to breathe…She couldn't breathe.* From the end of a tunnel, she heard the echo of Grey's voice calling her name, *Lexy…Lexy! Don't make me come out there to pull that out! Lexy!* Even while incoherent from blood loss, her Handler's voice pulled her back from the edge of the abyss and gave a surge of strength created by the sheer will to protect the one thing she truly loved. *She couldn't let him come out.* Reaching for the blade from another angle, she managed to yank it out as the hoard saw she had fight left and surged at her. Lexy spun in a circle, booting cannibalistic creatures in mortal skinsuits away. Each time she lacerated one, a cloud of smoke signified the destruction of their demonic being as they disintegrated into the ground. Holding onto the visual of Grey's smile, she carved up each demon that accosted her. *Protect him. Fight for him.* They were coming out of the bushes faster than they could be destroyed. Lexy remained in the middle of the hoard slicing until one of their blades hit its mark and plunged into her stomach. More annoyed than anything, she recoiled with a surge of fury and launched her assailant into the crowd. She tugged the weapon out of her gut and tossed it aside. *That dirty rotten son of a...* She'd no sooner disposed of that momentary irritation when a blade sunk into her back. She flipped one over her shoulder, twirling at the same time, using the body of one of their own as a weapon, knocking down dozens like a savage game of Dominos. She sputtered up blood and licked it from the corner of her mouth. *Now, she was pissed!* Releasing a primal scream as she swung her knife, Lexy kicked away more, intimidating no one. Sensing the other Dragon in the action, Lexy didn't have to see her to know she had back up. The chaos caused by the additional Dragon gave her sufficient time to heal. Lexy was able to keep her footing as the demonic swarm of cannibalistic beings, closed in. She slashed and fought with everything she had as they dropped to the ground, followed by trails of smoke. With both Dragons fighting, it felt like they were getting somewhere as dark entities fell faster in the swarm. Another surge of demons burst out of the bushes. The next hour was a haze of blood spray and smoke until two Dragons were the only beings left standing.

The cabin door opened and Frost came out talking. She noticed Kayn, in the fetal position on the ground and then, saw Grey. He smiled at her as her vision wavered. *She could die now.* Lexy crumpled to the ground as her world was lost in darkness.

Lexy awoke to the overpowering scent of bleach. It only took her a moment to know she was safe in Grey's arms. He was playing with her hair, it felt nice, she didn't want him to stop, so she didn't open her eyes.

He tenderly touched her nose and whispered, "I know you're awake."

She smiled. *He'd totally caught her.* Lexy opened her eyes and quietly responded, "I love it when you do that to my hair. I just didn't want you to stop."

Stroking her silky crimson locks, Grey probed, "You heard me calling your name, didn't you?"

"Always," she confessed, gazing into his eyes, knowing their devotion to each other would never end.

Emotion flickered in his expression as he explained, "I was going insane. They had to hold me down when you couldn't reach that knife in your back."

"I would have been furious if you'd come out there," Lexy confessed, touching his cheek as she stared into his hypnotizing eyes. Fighting the urge to kiss his lips, she was forced to look away. Lexy sat up and looked at herself. *She was clean, he'd bathed her. Of course, he had. He would always take care of her and she would move heaven and earth to protect him.* Leaning against the headboard, Grey took her hand in his and began to play with her fingers. She closed her eyes as her heart fought to regain its senses. Always the Handler, he raised their interlaced fingers to his lips, Lexy's heart swelled as their emotional tether gave her peace.

Grey suggested, "Do you want to go outside and see the bodies?"

He knew her so well. She totally did. Zach cleared his throat, they looked at him. *Yes, there were other people in the room. Sometimes, in those first moments, after he'd brought her back to the land of sanity, it could be difficult to see anyone else in the room but him.*

Looking concerned, Zach whispered, "Kayn's having a horrible nightmare, she's not waking up. What should I do? I feel like I should be doing something."

She really wanted to see the bodies. Lexy sighed, "I think I know what this is." Lexy sat on Zach and Kayn's bed and felt her forehead. She was physically healed, but Miss Brighton was burning up. *She knew what it was, she'd made this mistake a time or two. She'd fed from a demon's energy, presumably to heal herself during the fight. It was a newbie Healer mistake. Even though her assailants were physically mortal, spiritually they were not. Giving her a jumpstart with her energy might not counteract the dark essence, she'd ingested.* Giving it a go, Lexy laid her hands on Kayn's skin to provide her with a touch of energy and felt her Conduit ability siphoning, she ordered, "That's enough, Kayn! You're taking too much!" Lexy yanked her hands away and stood up, barely able to balance.

Kayn groggily whispered, "What happened? Did I hurt you?"

Sitting on their bed, Lexy questioned, "You absorbed some dark energy last night, didn't you? That can send you on a disturbing trip." *She was dizzy. Kayn had taken way too much from her.*

Noticing her distress, Grey came over, sat beside her on the bed and offered, "Here, take some from me."

Lexy smiled at her Handler as she took his hands to top up the energy, she'd lost healing Kayn's demonic hangover. She got distracted, watching the budding Dragon, Handler relationship. She snapped back to reality, realizing what she was doing to her own. She let go of Grey's hands, and he fell off the bed into a crumpled heap on the floor. "Whoops," Lexy chuckled. "My bad. I gave you shit and then took too much myself. I'll deal with him in a second. Can you chuck him up on the other bed, Frost?"

Frost grinned and sighed, "I've got him." Lily helped by grabbing Grey's legs and they tossed his limp body onto the bed.

After a brief discussion with Kayn about abilities, she healed Grey and apologized her butt off for overfeeding. They wandered outside and she got to see the impressively large piles of bodies from the night before. *She was so proud.* Her Handler's arm was around her like he was concerned she might dive down her rabbit hole. Grey gave her a warm side snuggle. She rested her head on his shoulder, so he understood the Dragon was sleeping as they listened to a speech about how they were going to go about searching the town.

They'd split up to cover more ground. First on her list was the people meat diner with a child's fable name. It was just as messed up as she'd suspected it'd be, with a freezer full of frozen mortal-sicles. As they searched the residences, they found the odd freezer full of tourists but no live ones. They made their way through each home quickly with no signs of living mortals.

Last on Ankh's to-do list was a thorough search of the school. They made their way as a group, down the dimly lit hall, methodically searching each classroom they passed. The walls of the hall were adorned with pictures children had drawn. Kayn reached out to touch one of the pictures, entranced by the simplistic whimsical art. Lexy couldn't allow herself to think about it. *She knew how these situations worked. They'd probably eaten the children first. Their mortal shells wouldn't have been a desirable location for a demon to take up residence.* Against her better judgment, Lexy's eyes drifted to the snapshot of the child who created the picture. *Mary was five years old. She liked the movie Frozen and her favourite food was spaghetti.* Lexy looked away as she teared up. *The little girl in the picture looked like her Charlotte. For many years she'd searched for Charlotte in the smile of every child she'd come across, hoping to see the reincarnated version of her, happy, healthy and well. Eventually, she'd given up and carried on through her afterlife with the notion that it was for the best if she never found her. She could have grandchildren by now and a wonderful life that had nothing to do with the insanity of hers.* Her eyes followed Kayn as she wandered away from the group towards the end of the hall. *If there were bodies to be found here, she'd rather it not be Kayn that found them.* Lexy did her best to ignore the fact that almost all the children had missing front teeth as she tried to catch up, but as she neared the end of the hall, they became even younger. *There must have been a pre-school class here.* The pictures on the wall in front of the last classroom were no more than toddlers. Kayn hesitated before the final room and glanced back at her. Lexy nodded and they tried opening it together. *It was locked.* Something flickered in her soul. *There was living energy on the other side of this door. Someone was alive in there.* Brighton put her ear against the door. *She must be sensing the same thing.* Kayn was smiling as she pulled away. *She'd heard something.* They both shoved on the door, breaking the lock, it swung open. They heard tiny feet scurrying in the dark. Lexy felt around for the switch and flicked on the light. On the other side of the room, three toddlers were cowering in the corner. *There was a yellow aura around the babies.* Lexy's jaw dropped. *What was this? How were they here?* She looked at Kayn and whispered, "Do you know what that aura means?"

Confused, Kayn whispered, "I thought the yellow haze was around the newly claimed?"

"It is," Lexy quietly answered. "The glow usually means they've been Corrected and survived. I'll need to check to see if they've been marked, I think someone is trying to break the rules." Lexy knelt and whispered, "Little ones. We've come to take you home."

The three toddlers hesitantly came out of the corner and shyly moved towards where Lexy was kneeling on the floor.

"I have an idea," Kayn whispered. She slowly stood up so she wouldn't upset the little ones, stuck her head out the door and sweetly called for Frost, waving him over. *What was she up to?*

Frost appeared in the doorway with a fluffy kitten and placed it in Kayn's arms. She knelt with the kitty in her arms, looked at the little boy who'd ventured closest and whispered, "Look who I have here." The child's face exploded into an enormous grin as he ran towards her. She carefully placed the kitten in his arms and whispered, "Is this your kitty?" The toddler nodded and snuggled it. "Matty?" Kayn whispered, "Is that you?"

The child nodded, smiled and squeaked, "Kay."

Shivers trailed the surface of Lexy's skin. *Had Kayn just found the reincarnation of her brother Matt?*

Teary-eyed, Kayn's lips parted in awe as she opened her arms to receive her brother's relocated spirit. Matty placed the kitten on the floor and dove into her arms with the blind trust of a child who'd always known and loved her. She embraced him as tears of insurmountable joy and disbelief trailed down her cheeks. Kayn whispered his name against the nape of his neck, "Matty, it's you, it's really you." With tears flowing from her eyes, Kayn looked up at the group of Ankh gathered at the door and asked, "How is this possible?"

With tears of joy, Lily knelt by Kayn and whispered, "Hi Matty. Do you remember me?" Embracing his sister with his tiny chin resting on her shoulder, Matty met Lily's eyes and nodded. Lily whispered, "I guess you've finally earned your wings." She stood up in tears and walked out of the classroom.

This meant the dynamics of Lily's ill-fated love affair with the mortal she kept finding every twenty years had changed. He'd earned his wings in this last life as the mortal adopted brother of Kayn and Chloe Brighton. He'd died bravely in the end and this sacrifice had been rewarded. If Matt survived his Correction, he would be claimed by a Clan. They would have to make sure Ankh was the Clan that claimed him. Lexy managed to get close enough to each of the children to check for the mark of Abaddon. *There was nothing but these children would all have abilities in the future. They were supposed to be safe until they were of age. After they reached the age of sixteen, they would all be slated for Correction. This was messed up.* Lexy looked at Frost and disclosed, "These toddlers haven't been marked for Abaddon yet. Finding them and holding them captive until they're of age is against the rules."

Kayn held on to the reincarnation of her brother as she spoke calmly so she wouldn't upset the child in her arms, "We have to hide them. There has to be somewhere we can hide them until we can find out what's going on."

"There is," Frost piped in from his spot in the doorway. "I've already called them and they're on their way."

They'd given partially immortal children to the Aries Group before and they'd placed them with good families...Understanding families.

Caught up in Brighton's joyous reunion, Frost came over, crouched by Kayn and greeted the adorable toddler, "Hey, little man, I remember you." The cherub-faced toddler smiled. He got up, squeezed Kayn's shoulder and whispered, "I'll explain everything to you once we're alone. He's going to be alright. They'll hide him and take care of him until he's old enough for his Correction. The Aries Group has hidden a few orphaned Second-Tiers for us in the past."

Lexy's heart warmed as she observed Kayn having the moment she'd always dreamt of having with Charlotte and then she felt the weight of the knowledge that a Correction would be sent for these three adorable toddlers someday. She saw a flash. *Zach took a picture. He wasn't allowed to do that.* Not wanting to interrupt, she squeezed Frost's shoulder, letting him know she was going to deal with the Aries Group. Lexy was halfway down the hall as a group of well-dressed people entered through the main door. *Agent Gingham was there. Good, she knew a couple of these ones.* Grey walked in at the tail end of the pack and waved at her. Lexy briskly shook Agent Gingham's hand and even took a moment to greet Agent Douchetastic.

The Agent she'd befriended by spending the afternoon getting shot at, grinned and queried, "We heard you guys found children alive?"

Lexy held up her hands, signalling for the group to wait, none tried to move past her. *She wished she could give Kayn more time but knew she couldn't.* Lexy began to explain, "There are three toddlers in the room at the end of the hall. They are special toddlers if you know what I mean. One of them is the reincarnation of Kayn's brother. Can we give her a second to say goodbye?"

"Of, course," Agent Gingham replied.

"Kayn's brother, Matt? Are you sure?" Grey questioned.

Nodding, Lexy divulged, "Yes, he recognized her and everything." *Grey missed the big reveal waiting for the Aries group.* As they wandered down the hall together, she tried to keep herself from looking at the walls again for violence towards mortal children had always been her emotional kryptonite.

Agent Douchetastic asked, "Where are the rest of the children?"

Without missing a beat, Lexy far too bluntly replied, "They probably ate them." Her comment was met by deafening silence and all one could hear was the sound of footsteps in the hall and one person's squeaky shoes.

Grey placed his arm around her and whispered in her ear, "Why don't you just let me do the talking next time?"

Yes, she really needed to work on her people skills, but in all fairness, there was no possible way to sugarcoat the horrors that had taken place in this picturesque little town. With solemn, haunted expressions, the mortal agents trudged down the hall, with the weight of the depravity on their hearts.

Agent Gingham ordered one of the others to collect the student records and pictures from the walls so they could keep track of the innocent souls lost in this town.

And this was why humanity was so beautiful. They were frail and easily harmed but they felt so much for each other and for those they'd never even had the opportunity to meet in person. Perhaps, in this way...Mortals were magic too. Lexy remained behind with Grey as the others walked into the room.

They heard an almost decipherable sentence come out of the miniature version of Kayn's brother in an adorable squeaky voice, "Goo bye Kay."

"Wait!" Kayn called to the lady. She paused and looked back at Kayn. "His name is Matt. He likes to be called Matty."

She had to leave. She didn't want to hear anymore. Lexy walked away and Grey rushed to catch up with her. They strolled down the hallway and out of the main doors of the school as Agents collected pictures of the students. Grey placed his arm around her. They stood off to the side, watching as the toddlers were carried out of the school and placed into a vehicle, being spoken to with loving voices. She glanced at Grey. *He was visibly upset.* She whispered in his ear, "This is for the best, we can't keep them." He squeezed her shoulder, knowing her words were more of a band-aid for her heart than a consolation. Kayn's little brother smiled at her through the window and placed his teeny tiny palm against the glass. The rest of the group showed up and stood by them. Nobody attempted to speak until the vehicle containing the children pulled away with little Matty's hand still pressed against the window. *She didn't like to admit it when things affected her like this, so she nudged Grey, prompting him to do the speech.*

Her Handler addressed group, "Lily went back to the cabin with the truck, to collect our things. Members of the Aries group are collecting DNA samples from the bodies in the freezers. There's no need to go back to the cabin. We can leave as soon as she gets back. Markus and the others had to leave the state with the motorhome. I guess they had a run-in with Triad. We'll be hoteling it until we catch up with them." They all sat on the curb to wait. Grey took her hand and whispered, "Just think about how incredible it will feel to have a nice long bath and get all of that blood out from underneath your fingernails. There's only so much a guy can do when you're covered in that much of it."

Lexy smiled as she looked at her nails. *Yes, he hadn't been able to get it all when he washed her up the night before. It was sort of gross.* Kayn sat there with the group and they all watched as the vehicle containing the reincarnation of her brother disappeared. In true Dragon fashion, Kayn blinked away her tears and accepted her Handler's affectionate embrace. It occurred to Lexy in that moment that Handlers were both a lifeline and a band-aid. She smiled at Kayn as their eyes met over Zach's shoulder. Her fellow Dragon's eyes were now peaceful and Lexy knew why. They would see Mathew Brighton again. It was only a matter of time…

Chapter 21

What Happens In Vegas

The six Ankh drove for a full day and night, only stopping to trade-off drivers. When everyone started bickering about everything, their need for a personal day became glaringly obvious. They came to a unanimous decision and stopped for the night in one of Lexy's favourite destinations, Vegas. She adored everything about this place, from the lights to the buzzing, whirling endless noise. It was easy to allow yourself to become lost in a crowd here and it was by far the best place in the country to people watch. They chose a hotel close to the main strip, knowing if they had a decent club and restaurant downstairs, it would simplify things and give them more time to have fun. They could only afford to stop moving for a day and night for they had places to be in the near future and insanity to stop. The plan was to leave by the ten-thirty check out the next day. The boys were plotting a night of bonding and debauchery. So, the girls made plans to pamper themselves in their hotel's luxurious spa. They were going to dress up after, go out for drinks and maybe dinner at a nice restaurant. After getting comfortable in their rooms, Lexy downed a few tiny bottles of vodka from the minibar so she wouldn't feel squeamish while being massaged by a stranger. She bought a new dress in a boutique by the lobby and met up with the others at the spa. The trio of exhausted immortals enjoyed a day of pampering, continuously refilling their champagne glasses. Lexy endured a manicure, pedicure and enjoyed a massage. She felt like a new girl with her sexy updo and slinky dress as they sat in a classy restaurant with more drinks, indulging in the steak she'd been fantasizing about. *Grey would be all over this dinner. What was he doing right now?* The waiter refilled their glasses of wine. Lily took a sip while flirting with their sexy young waiter. Kayn had been well-behaved in the alcohol consumption department that day. Lexy and Lily had not, they were supposed to know better. Lexy's cell buzzed in her purse. She rooted around for it and looked, there was a message from Grey, *'I need to see you.'*

Logic had rarely been her friend while three sheets to the wind. She wanted to see him too, even though spending time with him in this state was a horrible idea. She'd always been far too susceptible to his charming quirks when she was drinking. She texted her response, *'Where are you guys?'* After receiving his answer, Lexy cleared her throat and suggested they go to the club at their hotel. After a short cab ride, they arrived at the club with pounding music attached to their hotel. They had a lot of time to chat while getting their nails done at the spa. Kayn mentioned an irksome comment Frost made. *He'd told her she was in the train wreck stage and truth be told, she was a train wreck, but everyone was after the Testing. Nobody likes it pointed out though. A person is always aware when their life has drastically veered off the tracks. She wasn't sure she'd ever ended up back on the tracks, herself. Hell, Lexy knew if you googled train wreck, you'd probably see a smiling picture of her.*

They were looking damn hot as they strolled right past the lineup into the club. Kayn's hair was piled on top of her head with soft sensual ringlets framing her face. Lily had glistening flowing jet-black hair and curves that went on for days. Lexy's crimson hair was also, in an updo and her short dress left little to the imagination. She was aware of the appreciation on male patron's faces as they followed the trio's movements, it made her feel powerful. The boys of Ankh were in a darkened corner, chatting up a flock of female admirers as they strolled up to the bar to order drinks. Dim red-tinted lighting added hedonistic sensuality to the crowded space. She was trying to keep her hormones in check, but everything in this club screamed, cut loose and succumb to the sexy atmosphere. Everything was a carnal sensory delight from the black velvet barstools to the barely clothed staff. *Where was Greydon? She'd seen Frost and Zach when she walked in but not Grey.* She searched the room for her Handler and in moments, she was able to narrow in on Grey flirting with some random girl as per usual. Lexy smiled, shook her head and looked away. *Why had she come here? What was she trying to do for herself? Coming to him in this state was like dousing herself in vodka and playing with matches.* Logic whispered, *it's not too late, just stay away from him. Protect your heart.*

Nudging her, Kayn warned, "Grey's staring at you."

Lexy turned to look, her heart skipped a beat. Grey was far too drunk to filter appreciation as his eyes followed her long-toned legs up to her slinky barely there, silky dress. Their eyes locked and it was like there was nobody else in the room. She looked away from him as her heart began convincing her to ignore repercussions. *They wouldn't be sharing a room tonight.* Her throat was dry, she took a drink. *She just had to stay away from him. That was all she had to do, but it was always easier said than done.* Staring into her glass, Lexy vocalized her brain's argument, "I promised myself I wasn't going to backslide with him, not anymore."

Kayn nodded and commented, "Understandable." She took another sip of her drink and switched the subject,

"How did movie night go with Orin? I totally forgot to ask you about that."

That night was their little secret. Trying to hide her reaction to Brighton's brilliantly timed question, Lexy couldn't help but smile as she disclosed, "It's Orin. He's trying to move on, but he's still in love with Jenna. We hung out. Nothing happened." Lexy casually sipped her drink and slyly glanced over at Grey. Her cell buzzed. *She knew it was him.* The message read, '*You are by far the sexiest girl in this room.*' She stared at his text, smiling.

Kayn elbowed her. Turning to see what she wanted, Lexy said, "Shit." *Grey was coming and he looked sexy as hell tonight.*

Sliding up beside her at the bar, Grey leaned closer and seductively whispered in her ear, "Looking good, Lex."

Slowly shaking her head, Lexy chuckled, "Here we go again."

"I think we should dance. You've been sitting here long enough," Grey flirted. He got up, strolled behind Lexy, and spun her barstool around to face him. With a roguish grin, he tried to kiss her on the cheek.

Be strong, be strong. Lexy playfully batted him away and sparred, "I'm not into dancing tonight. Go and dance with someone from the ever-expanding harem of hussies over there. Surely, one of them has to be interested in you."

He ran one of her sexy ringlets between his fingers, tempting, "Come on, Lex. You know you want to."

The desire to be with him heated the part of her she was trying to ignore. Lexy crossed her legs tighter and bit her lip. "I don't want to…dance," she sighed.

He kept smiling at her, pouting and giving her puppy dog eyes until she cracked and agreed to dance with him, "Alright." *One dance and then she'd make an excuse and take off.*

Grinning, he tugged her to her feet and towed her out onto the dance floor, comically scolding, "You always end up saying yes, why fight it?"

He was talking about dancing but he'd kind of hit the nail directly on the head there. They started to dance. After two or three songs, Lexy hollered over the music, "Let's go sit for a while." A song they loved came on. *One more song.* He playfully lured her in, and in the next breath, they were naughtily grinding against each other. *She was seriously turned on.* With every gyration of his hips, the resolve to behave slipped further away. *This would be so much better if they were naked.*

He sang naughty lyrics in her ear in hilarious falsetto, "I am, getting so hot, I wanna take my clothes off."

He was just being Grey and she was reading too much into everything. He wasn't really hitting on her. It was just the ambiance of the club and the fact that lately she'd been turned on by a warm breeze on a cool day. By the time the song neared its end, she was having so much fun, she'd forgotten about the reasons why she shouldn't be dancing. They were laughing, having the best time ever as the song slowed with his lips, mere inches from hers. Her heart lost its filter as she kissed him tenderly. There was a shocked expression on his face as their lips parted. *What had she done?* She tried to pull away.

Holding her there, Grey whispered, "Stay," searching her eyes.

She'd never been able to deny him when they were here. She nodded and without hesitation, he kissed her back. There was no mistaking his intentions as he provocatively kissed her in a way that made her loins catch fire with each sexy, taunting dart of his tongue until she was squirming with need. Reality vanished, excuses meant nothing, while lost in the reckless abandon of overactive immortal libidos. As their kiss swollen lips parted, she saw it in his eyes, he was all in. *For tonight. Just for tonight.* It took everything she had to pull away. *She had to stop doing this to herself. She'd started this…It had always been her. She couldn't look into his eyes, if she did, she would be lost in them, and she wouldn't have the strength to walk away.* "I'm sorry, I'm not sure what I was thinking,"

Lexy explained as she backed away. *She had to clear her head.* She took off, forcing her way through the crowd and left him standing on the dance floor. *Escaping him was only an excuse. It was herself she needed an escape from.* She fled the seductive lighting, shoved open the fire escape and stepped out into fresh air. She quickly scaled the steps, knowing he would be right behind her. *He wouldn't allow her to walk away from this, he'd want her to talk about it and she couldn't, not yet.* She disappeared into the flow of the crowd. Standing by the fenced area in front of the fountain as everyone passed, listening to trickling water, she realised how ridiculous she was being.

Grey's voice queried, "Why would you take off and leave me standing there like an idiot? We're adults, Lexy. Doesn't it make more sense to talk it out?"

She turned to look at him and admitted, "You're right, I'm sorry I took off. I needed space between us." They kept up the pretense of watching the water show.

Grinning, he baited, "This isn't just on you. That second kiss was all me."

Oh, the ego. Lexy smiled as she rolled her eyes and teased, "Right, it was all you."

He gave her a light-heartedly playful nudge and chuckled, "You know, that's not what I meant. I meant, I kissed you the second time, even though I agreed to stop myself from doing it. I wasn't expecting the powerful flood of emotion I had when you kissed me. I needed to know, I'm sorry."

"So, what do we do now?" she sighed, continuing to watch the mesmerizing water display. Standing with their arms and shoulders almost touching, their connection had only been enhanced by the exhilarating experience they'd just shared.

"What do you want to do?" Grey reversed her question, with his gaze fixed on the fountain.

Lexy saw no point in further pretense as she gave him the most honest true answer, she had within her, "I want us to love each other without boundaries. I want to wake up in the morning in your arms and know you remember every detail of the night before, but that's not going to happen."

Staring into her eyes, he confessed, "I want to take you up to my room and make love to you all night. I would give anything to do that. Have you tried to talk to Jenna about the clause in the Handler Dragon relationship? Maybe if we speak to her together? We should be allowed to be happy too, shouldn't we?"

Lacing her fingers through his, Lexy squeezed his hand as she gave her response, "Of course I've tried to speak to her about this, but the reason we can't be together is more complicated than that, it was a clear no." *This had backfired. He'd come back to her, even though they hadn't yet consummated the situation. The only difference this time was that he'd hurt too. He would long to be with her too and she loved him too much to allow him to remain in this state.* "Maybe, we should do this. If we sleep together tonight, you'll wake up tomorrow morning and you'll be fine," she whispered, meeting his eyes.

"And you'll grow to resent me for it," he replied as he placed his arm around her.

This was the truth, she'd been there, recently. Resting her head on his shoulder, Lexy countered, "What's the alternative?"

"We get through this together. I'll try to control my jealousy while you move on and you do the same. We just have to love each other enough to let go," Grey responded as he gave her a loving squeeze.

They left the deep end of their conversation at that and decided to enjoy the night together. They spent hours sightseeing, wandering the city that never sleeps hand in hand as they normally would have and on several occasions, the intimacy of the something more they were trying to conceal, slipped through in the form of an intimate touch or a lingering gaze. They ended up at an amusement park acting like teenagers in love as they went on every wild ride and by midnight, they were in the elevator with every intention of going back to separate rooms.

When the other passengers got off at their floor and they were left alone in the elevator, Grey backed her up against the mirrored wall and tempted, "Come back to my room, I hate sleeping without you. There's plenty of things we can do without even taking our clothes off. We'll start behaving ourselves tomorrow."

She had no argument for that logic as the door opened and they dashed down the hall hand in hand towards his room. While Grey was fumbling to slide the card in the door, she kissed his neck, and he dropped the card on the floor. Lexy knelt and passed it to him. On her knees, she mischievously gazed up and motioned like she was about to reach for his zipper. Only teasing, Lexy got up giggling.

Grey thrust open the door, gently shoving her over the threshold, he scolded, "Oh, you're in trouble." Kissing as they maneuvered towards the bed, their hands stayed above their clothes. Nuzzling her neck, he flirtatiously bargained, "How about just our shirts come off... nothing else?"

Lexy was wearing a dress. She'd been in this situation and far too recently to pretend she didn't know exactly what she was doing as she removed it and crawled seductively onto the bed in her lacy bra and G-string panties, knowing he was watching her. She sprawled on the bed, waiting for him as he tossed his shirt and crawled onto the bed to join her. He tenderly kissed each of her ankles. It tickled. She giggled and fought the urge to kick him in the face. *She knew where this was going.* His lips travelled a seductive trail up her calves to the sensitive underside of her knees, then to her soft, supple thighs. Feeling the heat of his breath through her lacy panties, she arched her back and shivered. Clutching the sheets on either side of her, Lexy gasped as he feathered warm sensual kisses through the material, she squirmed beneath him, yearning for more, knowing this game would last all of five seconds before it ceased to be one. *He was going to remove her panties and she was going to forget about everything but the desperate aching need to have him inside of her. This had happened so many times.* She grabbed a handful of his hair and ordered, "Get up here and kiss me."

With a deviously naughty smirk, he trailed kisses up her stomach and gently nipped her lacy, silky bra, concealing her breasts erotically with his teeth, causing her nipples to strain against the material as aching peaks. He continued the seductive quest for intimate knowledge until their eyes met. Obeying her order, his lips parted, their tongues began their torrid steamy dance of submission as she undid his zipper and slid her hand inside. He groaned against her lips but couldn't bring himself to stop her because she knew exactly what he wanted her to do. He gasped as she took him closer to the edge with the perfectly rehearsed sliding of her palm. He hooked his finger around her lacy panties with the intention of returning the favour, but she removed his rock-hard manhood from his jeans, positioned him against her moist warmth and pleaded in his ear, "Please, Grey." There was a loud knock on the door. *No, no, no.*

He leapt out of bed with his wood raised like the mast of a ship and peeked only his head out. Lexy let out an overdramatic sigh of frustration as she heard Jenna's voice coming from the other side of the doorway.

Grey closed the door, leaned against it and said, "Well, I'm going to go have an ice-cold shower. She's waiting out there for you."

Of course, she was. Lexy slipped back into her dress and grabbed her heels in one hand, opting to stroll the carpeted halls barefoot. Greydon was still standing there looking like an anatomically impressive statue of a Greek god. She gave him a quick peck on the lips and teased, "It's nice to know you can't resist me either."

Grinning, he scolded, "Get out of here before I make her stand there and wait, while I drag you into the shower and have my way with you."

She shimmied past her gorgeous naked Grey and slipped out to their Oracle's disapproving glare. Before the lecture began, Lexy sighed, "I know. I know."

Without bothering to say a word, Jenna escorted her back to the elevator, saw her safely inside and their Clan's Oracle disclosed, "Get some sleep, you have to be up in four hours. As the doors closed, Jenna shook her head at her and smiled.

Yes, she'd known exactly what she was doing tonight, but it felt so good to be in Grey's arms. It was familiar and perfect. Her libido had been seriously amped up lately and it was becoming a bit of an issue. In the elevator, she set the alarm on her phone for five am. The doors opened. Frustrated, she padded down the hall with heels in her hands, went into her room and got ready for bed, noting she was still drunk as she teetered over while trying to remove her underwear. Just as she slipped under the covers and closed her eyes, Kayn arrived.

She heard her fiddling around and then, Kayn screamed into her pillow.

Without lifting her head off her pillow, Lexy chuckled, "Jenna caught you guys too, didn't she?"

Kayn gave her a muffled reply, with her face buried in her pillow, "Yes, she did. She also caught me trying to sneak up to his room after she told us not to."

Lexy started to giggle. Kayn lifted her face up from the pillow and tossed it at her. She started to howl.

"Glad you think this is so funny," Kayn hissed.

Getting cozy, Lexy sparred, "Tomorrow morning when you wake up, this whole fiasco will be nothing more than a laughable memory. Jenna expects you three newbies to throw a little bit of rebellion into the mix. It's totally normal for someone your age."

She didn't have an excuse for her behaviour this evening.

Everything was quiet for a minute and she was just beginning to relax when Kayn blurted out, "Can you turn the viewing everybody's aura part of being a Healer off?"

Rolling to face her, Lexy answered, "No, but it becomes normal after a while. You can turn it down. It's strongest when your body's been freshly healed. You'll notice it beginning to dim over the next couple of days if you haven't used your healing ability for anything. We'd better get some sleep the alarm is set for five am. We need to be back on the road in four hours."

Kayn responded, "Night, Lex."

Closing her eyes again, Lexy allowed her mind to shut down and slipped into a beautiful dream. It was a highlight reel of her forty years with Grey. She awoke to the song on her alarm with a smile on her face, but when Lexy tried to stand, she found her legs wobbly and comically unreliable. *It took her a moment for her deviances to filter through the fog of her hangover. Yes, she'd been naughty last night. What happened in Vegas might have stayed in Vegas if Jenna had given them twenty minutes before knocking on that door.* While getting ready, she read the long, detailed text on her cell, explaining the next job. She was going to need to be awake for this. She drank a crazy amount of water from a covered plastic cup by the sink and stared at her frazzled reflection. *She felt rough and it was time to share the wealth.* Grinning, she raced over and leapt on Kayn's bed, "Wake up! Wake up! There's no time to waste, I'll explain on the way to the truck."

Kayn stretched and launched herself into an upright position. She yawned and snatched her backpack off the chair as she sauntered by on her way to the bathroom. Lounging on the lumpy, uncomfortable bed, Lexy recalled the conversation she had with Kayn before they went to sleep and grinned. *At least today was going to be equally awkward for everyone.* The two Dragons of Ankh grabbed their bags and ambled down the emerald toned carpeted hall to the elevator in their flip-flops, opting for a more logical choice of footwear. Lexy pressed the button and started explaining the text, "Astrid, Melody and Haley are hiding with Molly in a small town in the desert. It's only a couple of hours', but we'll have to take backroads for at least three more, to make sure we're not being followed. Apparently, the drive has amazing scenery. Jenna, Markus and Orin are taking the boy. Jenna's premonition said we need to split them up if we're going to stand a chance of keeping them both. I guess Zach's already gone to get the truck." The elevator opened, revealing Frost, Grey and Lily also on their way down to the lobby. They stepped into the elevator.

Frost looked at Kayn and teased, "Going down?"

Kayn gave no reaction to the naughty meaning behind his words as she responded with a straight face, "Yes, we're obviously both going down." Everyone's cheeks burst into a smile and immature giggling.

Lexy elbowed her and ribbed, "Speak for yourself." Kayn gave in and started to laugh. Lily asked for their key cards and placed them on the empty front desk as they left. They all stood outside, haggard and worn after a night of partying, waiting for Zach to show up with the truck. Grey took her hand and they smiled through the hangover fog as they saw their truck coming. Zach pulled over and they all quickly got in.

Lexy strolled around to the driver's side and offered, "I'll drive first if you want more sleep, Zach." He nodded and moved into the back.

Chapter 22

Duct-tape Tuxedo

Lexy fiddled around, trying to find a decent station. She was just about to pull away when someone knocked on the window. She took in the shifty jittery movements of the man standing beside the truck and rolled her eyes. *Really? Was this dipshit really going to attempt a carjacking? She was too hungover for this shit.* Lexy sighed, rolled down the window a bit and sweetly asked, "Is there a problem, sir?"

The shady looking man answered, "Your back tires are almost flat and you have a broken taillight. I thought I'd warn you before you drove too far and bent the rim."

Trying to keep a straight face, Lexy replied, "Oh, thank you for telling me. I'll be right out, sweetie." She rolled up the window.

Zach leaned over the front seat and whispered in her ear, "The tires are fine."

No Shit, Sherlock! She glanced back at Zach with an innocent smile and said, "Oh, I'm sure they are."

Attempting to be the voice of reason, Frost pointed out, "There are cameras all over the place. You're going to have to handle this tool carefully."

This guy was too cranked up to feel any pain. Lexy stretched a few times, yawned and announced, "Lock it as soon as I get out, I'll only be a second." She opened the door and stepped out, ready for her Oscar-worthy performance as a naive southern belle in the big city. Grey grinned and slowly shook his head. Lexy winked at her Handler as she heard the lock click behind her.

"That poor unknowing dumbass," Grey sighed.

Lexy strolled around to the back of the truck, looked at the tires and stated, "The tires are fine. Are you really sure you want to do this?"

Realising she was onto him, the stranger yanked a gun out of his pocket and scathed, "That's right bitch, the truck's fine. So, fine, it's screaming my name. Tell those shits to get out. I'd hate to wreck your beautiful smile by forcing you to eat a bullet."

Casually checking to see where the cameras might be positioned, Lexy provoked, "Oh, would you like the keys? They're in my pocket. Tell you what, if you can take the keys from me, you can just have the truck." She allowed him to press the gun into her shoulder and put an arm around her neck as he searched through her pockets. She started giggling.

"Do you want me to shoot you?" Her assailant hissed. "I told you to tell those assholes to get the hell out of the truck! What kind of sadistic friends do you have? They're all smiling, I'm going to kill you." He shoved her towards the driver's side door.

"No, you're not. They know I'm allowing you to point your little gun at me, and they also know, I'm going to kick your ass as soon as I grow tired of playing along," she taunted. Lexy allowed him to toss her up against the hood of the truck as she laughed harder. *She was going to pee herself if this skinny, fragile little man didn't stop his cranked-up testosterone show.*

Grey rolled down the window and suggested, "Hey, Honey. While you're playing with this moron, don't let him accidentally shoot the engine, that would be inconvenient. We have places to be. Can you wrap this up?"

She winked at her Handler and sighed, "Alright, game over my friend. I'll give you one more opportunity to walk away." She took a step towards him. A shot rang out. *That dick!* Lexy barely flinched as the blood seeped through her shirt. *A shoulder shot wasn't even going to wreck her morning.* Moving her shirt aside to show him the wound as it closed and spit the bullet out, Lexy exclaimed, "Now, that wasn't very nice."

"What are you?" He stammered as he dropped the gun on the cement and ran away.

Contemplating the merits of getting into the truck and driving away, Lexy looked down at the bloodstain on her new shirt. *She wasn't going to be able to wash this. It was now, nothing more than a rag and she liked this shirt. On principle alone, she needed to kick this tweaker's ass.* She looked at Grey and hissed, "He wrecked my new shirt." Lexy kicked off her flipflops and sprinted away from the truck barefoot after the man who shot her.

Grey yelped, "Oh, Shit!

Lexy jogged after the man. *She couldn't grab him until after he was off the main strip, this was Vegas, there would be cameras everywhere. Frost was probably already on the phone with the Aries Group covering up her shooting and healing. It happened right in front of the hotel. Whoops.* Predictably, her assailant swerved into a shadowed alley. The second they were out of view, she nabbed him by his shirt as he struggled in a ridiculous way. Lexy looked around to see what she had to work with. Fortunately, there were rolls of duct tape and rope lying beside the dumpster. *What were the chances of that? Guess this was her lucky day.* Glaring at the mortal as he continued his futile struggle, Lexy's voiced dripped with sarcasm as she debated, "Now, what am I going to do with you? You wrecked my shirt." *His struggling and screaming was beginning to annoy her. It was more what he was screaming than the pitch.*

He kept shrieking, "Aliens!"

She'd always found that assumption slightly offensive. She tore his shirt off, stuffed it into his mouth to shut him up and duct-taped it in place so he wouldn't be able to spit it out. Grinning, Lexy looked at the roll of duct-tape and decided to go just with it. By the time Grey showed up, she had her assailant muzzled, strung up naked and tethered to a fire escape with full body duct-tape. She was applying the final touch of duct tape up his ass crack and couldn't stop giggling.

Her Handler's frustrated voice commented, "What in the hell, Lex?"

"I'm almost done," she assured as she duct-taped his gun sideways to his forehead. *It was missing something. If only she had a jiffy marker to draw a bow tie on his neck. They were in Vegas after all. Oh well. No, duct tape tuxedo for the sketchy mortal. Next time.* Satisfied with the diabolical genius of her work, Lexy hopped down from her perch to the addition of Kayn and Zach's astonished expressions. Grey was just standing there shaking his head, pretending he didn't think her creation was awesome, but she knew him better than that. Smiling proudly at her incredibly twisted work of art, Lexy announced, "I'm willing to bet this wasn't the first time you've used that weapon on someone. Don't worry, the police will be here soon to get you down. If you haven't used that gun for any other crimes, you'll be free to go." The man frantically squirmed and wriggled in his duct tape suit. She grinned, "That's what I thought. Gee, I sure hope it's not excruciatingly painful when they remove the duct tape from your butt crack. You know, people pay big bucks for the Brazilian you're about to get for free. No, need to thank me. Have a lovely morning." Lexy wandered away with a skip in her step.

The others pulled up in the truck and got out in awe of Lexy's duct-tape creation. Looking up at the wriggling scumbag, Frost questioned, "Why does the kid look so mortified."

Grinning from ear to ear, Kayn replied, "He's naked under that duct tape. He's also wearing a duct tape G-string. Think about it for a second. Let it sink in."

Lily started to giggle and soon, everyone was howling as the man continued valiantly trying to free himself.

Lexy got into the truck, picked up her cell, called 911 and creatively reported her assailant in a way certain to make sure he had the most uncomfortable day possible. The light went off to signal the end of her call.

Grey opened the door and hollered, "Let's go. This guy has a date with a body cavity search."

The man let out more muffled screams as he flailed. They all climbed into the truck and sped away as Grey told the group about her phone call, "She told the police he's a drug smuggler who just arrived on a flight. His car broke down, he tried to carjack us and we caught him." They'd been driving for many hours before the group stopped laughing every time somebody brought up duct tape guy.

Frost finally turned off the highway and began to drive down the backroads. He glanced in the rearview mirror, and explained, "We need to drive the rest of the way on the backroads. We're almost there. I need to see if we're being followed. On the highway, it's difficult to know for sure."

Grey piped in, "Hey, when are we stopping for brunch? My stomach's been singing for over an hour."

"There's no time to stop for long, but you can heat up something at the next convenience store we find. It'll be a good opportunity to grab drinks and snacks to have in our rooms for later," Frost answered.

It took them a whole hour to find a convenience store on the road less travelled. They raced inside, absolutely famished by then. Grey cornered her at the microwave when they had a second without witnesses and whispered, "Let's do something alone tonight."

"Like last night?" she teased as the microwave dinged telling her that her barely edible ham and cheese melt was done.

Grinning, Grey hip-checked her and countered, "I'm thinking more along the lines of laying in the desert and looking at the stars."

She smiled at him, knowing anything they did would be fun. They always had fun together, it went without saying that she would go anywhere he went. They piled back into the truck and drove for the remainder of the afternoon until they reached a familiar hotel. *She was pretty sure they'd stayed here before, but it looked a little different. Maybe, it had been painted? Perhaps, there was a new owner?* Grey passed her bag to her and remarked, "I'll catch up with you, make sure our room has a view."

They were in the desert, there was no view…not really. There would be no Jenna to interrupt them tonight. They were on their own. The thought excited her, but if they didn't go through with it, they'd be able to stay in love and this feeling would continue. For the first time, they were equally in love, well into the next day. Every fibre of her being wished this could be real. Lexy strolled over to the outdoor pool and grinned as she recognized Melody, Haley, Astrid and Molly. *They were here.* The group laughed and embraced. *The three newbies managed to keep the girl.*

She wasn't feeling a large group of people, she felt like a bubble bath and a nap. Lexy left the Ankh canoodling at the pool. As she snuck away, she heard the calamity created by one of Grey's cannonballs and smiled. *She adored that lovable goof ball. She'd leave him to his shenanigans. He'd notice her absence once he stopped messing around.* Lexy made her way to their room and as she entered, she knit her brow. *This was a strange room. Ironically, every surface had been decorated with black jiffy marker. There hadn't been a jiffy marker anywhere when she'd needed one for her duct tape tuxedo idea after the attempted carjacking in Vegas.* She took in the art on the walls. *There were poems and signatures…everywhere. It was a little weird and that meant a lot coming from her.* She slipped off her flip-flops and wandered across the funky plush carpet. At first glance, the bathroom appeared normal. Lexy started to fill the tub. *She didn't have bubble bath. She'd have to get creative.* Lexy dumped tiny bottles of body wash into the tub and watched as white foamy bubbles formed on the surface of the water. *That would work.* Lexy noticed a marker attached to the wall by the sink and found it strange that nobody had graffitied the bathroom walls. She took the felt pen out of its holder, opened it and grinned…*it was invisible ink. What an amazing idea.* There was probably tons of graffiti, she just couldn't see it with the lights on. Lexy strolled over, turned off the lights and smiled at the masterpieces that could only be viewed in the dark. *It was kind of incredible.* With the invisible marker, she drew a heart and wrote, Lexy loves Grey in it and then tried to wipe it off. *Oh, lovely, it was invisible, permanent marker. Of course, it was.* She turned on the light and noticed the water was close to the rim. *She'd gapped out. Whoops.* Lexy turned off the water, stripped her clothes off and got into the luxurious, comically tiny tub of bubbles and closed her eyes. She'd just started to relax, when Grey knocked on the door, and complained, "You locked the door, Lex."

Picturing his pouting face, she smiled and responded, "I just got in the tub, give me a minute."

She heard the lock moving and knew what he was doing. Making sure the bubbles were covering her, Lexy scolded, "Greydon! Quit picking the lock with that wire hanger!"

The door opened and her naughty privacy ignoring Handler came in with an enormous grin on his face. Grey strolled over, knelt by the tub and seductively baited, "Don't you need me to wash your back?"

A breast peeked out from beneath the layer of bubbles. As Lexy shifted bubbles to conceal herself, she giggled, "Grey, we don't have enough time. We have to order pizza and…" Ignoring her pleas, he got into the tub with his swim shorts on. She shimmied forward to give him room, as he sat behind her, wrapped his arms around her waist and mischievously tugged her against him.

Grabbing the soap, he deviously taunted, "Don't worry about the time. I've already ordered the pizzas, we have at least half an hour, I'll start with your front."

As his soap-sudsy hands slipped over the peaks of her breasts, she arched her back and blissfully closed her eyes, succumbing to his pleasurable touch. *What a perfect world it would be if they could always be like this. But this would end, as it always had, and she would be the only one with these beautiful memories. Why was she doing this to herself? Her heart would be shattered and left in ruins if she didn't take a step back.*

Grey whispered, "The bathroom door is locked. I'll let you get out of the tub in five minutes, if anyone shows up before then, they can bloody well wait. Five minutes, that's all I'll need to satisfy you." He boldly slid his sudsy hands between her thighs.

Lexy gasped, laughed and tried blocking his naughty soapy exploration by grabbing his wrists. It didn't deter him. His instinctual stroking created undeniably pleasurable friction, making her quiver and ache for more, as the wave of intense carnal gratification built within her. She relaxed her hold on his wrists. *They didn't have time. They might hear them.* Nearing climax, she ceased to care and succumbed to his decadent game. His rapid expert rubbing created a molten eruption of gratuitous pleasure. Lexy whimpered, moaning as she reached her climax and melted against him.

When her head stopped ringing and her limbs finished humming, she sighed and whispered, "What time is it?"

Grey chuckled as he quietly responded, "Don't worry, we have plenty of time.

Lexy smiled as she soaped up her hands and returned the favour. *Perhaps, it was possible to keep their relationship going if they didn't fully consummate their love? Maybe, this was the way around it and his memory wouldn't be wiped if they strategically bent the rules? It was worth a try. What could it hurt at this point?*

They got out of the tub and towel-dried each other off, stopping periodically to make-out. *It was perfect…almost.* They were dressed and ready for company to arrive when the pizza delivery guy showed up. They paid and before they'd closed the door, the rest of Ankh arrived with six-packs and witty banter. They behaved as they always did, without allowing anyone to know that anything had changed between them. The group devoured pizza and drank together until the party broke up, and everyone went back to their rooms. Grey convinced her to go for a walk. They took off hand in hand as the sun began its inevitable descent, marking the end of another day. They wandered to the back of the hotel, while strolling through the sandy lot, they noticed a vehicle parked by itself with a sign on the dusty window that read, 'Free, if you can start it.'

Greydon glanced at her and announced, "Drive it is." He opened the door and the keys were conveniently in the ignition. He popped the hood and declared. "She's from the early nineties. Do you mind if I tinker with this and see if I can get her to run?"

In another life, Grey could have been a mechanic. He loved tinkering with old vehicles and he was good at it. Just as Lexy was beginning to lose patience in his extracurricular activity coming to fruition, the engine purred. They got in and cruised away in a cloud of dust. *The goal was to find a place to park to watch the crimson fire sunset.* In the desert, day's last light lit up the grains with vibrant colours before vanishing into the sand. *Grey found the perfect spot, as always.* They got out, slipped off their sandals and sat on the hood of the car, witnessing the vibrant crimson sky growing darker.

The orb vanished in the horizon with a flash of red glow on the sand and the desert was swallowed by a veil of darkness. *A sunset like the stunningly gorgeous one they'd just witnessed had always been the closest thing on earth to watching the time shift in the clean slated desert of the in-between.* She missed the in-between. *It felt like it had been a long time since they'd been there, even though it hadn't. They'd been insanely busy and that always seemed to make the hourglass of time in the afterlife flow faster. Weeks would whiz by feeling like days. She couldn't even imagine what this afterlife would be like for the older ones.* Looking at Grey, Lexy exclaimed, "Could you imagine what life would have been like a thousand years ago?"

"Where did that thought even come from?" Grey chuckled as he slid off the beater and held out his hand.

Lexy took it and he gently tugged her into his loving embrace. The warm desert sand felt wonderful underfoot, yet not nearly as glorious as it did in the in-between. She rested her head on his shoulder and replied, "It was just a random thought."

He swayed her back and forth as he ribbed, "Those are the best ones."

He always wanted to dance, and she could never deny him anything. She wrapped her arms around his neck, and for a moment, everything was right in her world. Lexy suggested, "Let's just stay out here until morning."

"That was the plan, wasn't it?" Grey whispered as he nuzzled her neck.

Recalling their conversation, she teased, "It's a good thing your memory works." *Poor choice of words. His memory didn't work. It had been tampered with repeatedly, the most beautiful events were wiped.* Looking up at the glittering ceiling of wish worthy stars saddened her. It wouldn't matter how many wishes she made their tryst would end. *What was she doing to herself? She'd been trying to get over him.*

He pulled away to look into her eyes as he spoke, "I don't think it's possible for me to love anyone else more than I love you. Maybe, that's why my feelings for you can't be permanently erased?" He opened the door to the backseat.

Grinning, she grabbed Grey by his T-shirt and towed him in with her. He chuckled as his lips met hers in the hilariously cramped backseat. They squirmed and he sat up. She straddled his lap with her head cocked because there wasn't enough room to sit upright.

"Making out in this car isn't going to be easy," he provoked, clutching her rear.

She shimmied off his lap and got out of the car as she tempted, "Maybe, there's a blanket in the trunk? We can sleep under the stars."

"Now, you're thinking," Greydon answered, slipping out after her.

He wandered to the back as she reached in the driver's side and popped the trunk. She slammed the door and wandered back there. Grey was searching through the impressively creepy contents using the flashlight on his cell. The trunk was suspiciously lined with plastic. There was a blanket, a bag of salt and a shovel. *To each their own?* Lexy shrugged, grabbed a ratty dusty blanket, shook it out and commented, "This will do." She spread the blanket in the sand and they sprawled side by side, gazing at the twinkling stars in the night sky. *This had always been one of her favourite things to do with him.* She glanced at Grey and smiled. *She'd had a shortage of favourite things before she met him that day in the woods. As her mind travelled back to their fated meeting, she wondered if her heart always recognized him as someone who would be of importance to her, even when her only concern was her next meal.* Her phone buzzed. *It was late, far too late for a random communication that wasn't about something serious.* Lexy sat up, dug her cell out of her pocket and checked the message. It read, 'Where are you?' *Who would be texting her at this hour?* She didn't have everyone's contact info in this phone.

Maybe it was Orin? She texted back, I'm with Grey. *If it was Orin that would silence his end of the conversation.*

Grey questioned, "What's up?"

"Nothing important," Lexy replied. She placed the cell on the blanket and scooted closer. Snuggling against his chest, she whispered, "This is nice." She slid her hand beneath his shirt and sensually traced his defined abs with her finger. She slid her hand down and was pleased to find he was already straining against his jeans.

Stopping her naughty exploration by grabbing her hand, he mischievously threatened, "If you keep touching me there, I'm going to snap and take you right here."

"Maybe we should do it?" Lexy deviously provoked.

Grey mimicked her last sentence, "Maybe we should do it, funny." He chuckled as he playfully tickled her sides.

Giggling, she squirmed away, swatting at him, but he wouldn't stop. She reached past the edge of the blanket, grabbed a handful of sand and tossed it at him. *Whoops. She hadn't meant to toss it into his face, but she wasn't sorry she did it.*

He blinked the sand out of his eyes, glared at her and menaced, "You need a good spanking."

"You can try but we both know in the end it will be me spanking you," she mischievously sparred.

With an enormous grin, he jousted, "God, I hope so." Raising his brow, he reached for the button on his jeans.

Clicking into his naughty interpretation, Lexy laughed and swatted his arm. *It wouldn't matter if they were both aware of the situation or if it was only her that carried the burden of loving him alone. Their Clan's Guardian could stifle their love temporarily, but he would always return to her.* Smiling, she pulled him to her and their lips met. Succumbing to the intensity of their passionate embrace, his tongue naughtily provoked hers, as his free hand delved between her legs, stroking her jeans possessively until she softly mewed and quivered with pleasure. Grey grinned as their lips parted. Proud of the effect he was having on her, he trailed heated sensual kisses on her neck and nipped at her throat. As his hands slipped under her shirt, her breath caught in her chest.

He naughtily commanded, "I'm going to need you to take your shirt and bra off."

She usually didn't follow orders, but it was in her best interest to follow this one. Biting her lip in anticipation, Lexy slipped off her shirt, tossed it aside and reached back to undo the trio of clasps on her bra. She slid it off one arm and chucked it into the sand. Grey intently watched every move. Once her breasts were free of restraints, he didn't waste time, cupping them and skillfully massaging each aching peak between his fingers, until she closed her eyes and melted into the blanket beneath her. He took one in his mouth while playing with the other. They were painfully sensitive and throbbing by the time he moved down to her stomach.

Pausing, he groaned, "Watching you squirm around on the blanket like this might be the hottest thing I've ever seen."

He kept her jeans on as he kissed her hip. She felt the heat of his breath through the material of her jeans and arched her back with pleasure as he ran his tongue over the rough material between her legs. *She was about to lose her mind.*

"Let me take your jeans off," Grey tempted.

They were playing with fire, but she wanted it so badly ration was an afterthought. "Only if yours come off too," she bartered.

Conflicted, he paused but got over it. Straddling her grinning, he removed his shirt. He was rigid between her legs as she seductively travelled his tanned, defined chest with her fingertips.

Gazing down as she boldly undid his jeans, his raspy voice cautioned, "This could get out of hand."

Certain it would, she'd ceased to care about what-ifs and tomorrows. He struggled out of his pants as she undid her jeans and he helped her tug them off. With frenzied passion, their lips met as the X-rated portion of their seductive dance beneath the stars began. They brought each other to the heights of ecstasy, again and again. After spending the night satisfying each other, while somehow managing to stop short of consummating their love, utterly exhausted, they fell asleep in each other's arms.

When Lexy awoke, her head was resting on Grey's lap, and he was playing with her hair. She smiled and looked up at him. Her heart clenched, for a split second as the fear he wouldn't remember the night they'd shared brought her back to a place she'd been far too many times before.

Her Handler's eyes crinkled in the corners as he gazed into hers and affectionately affirmed, "I love you...Promise me you'll always know that even if someday I don't know it myself."

Oh, thank God. She took a deep breath and gave him her truth, "I'll never love anyone like I love you, I can promise you that...but..."

Smiling at her, Grey prodded, "But?"

Lexy maneuvered off his lap and lounged on the blanket. Without looking at him, she released the words teetering precariously on the tip of her tongue, "How long are we going to keep pretending this part of our relationship can last?"

"Way to be a party pooper, Lex," Grey taunted, as he stretched out beside her and let out an exasperated sigh.

This was going to hurt like hell, and the longer they played this game, the more devastating it would be for her when it happened. She'd ripped the figurative band-aid off that difficult conversation because they had to have it. They couldn't avoid this topic forever. They were no longer touching and her heart ached. *All it had taken was the slightest glimpse of want in his eyes and as always, she'd been incapable of walking away. This time they'd both known better, but even that, hadn't stopped their inevitable reunion as more.* Their fingertips were almost touching, as he took her hand, she felt whole again.

Meeting her eyes, Grey probed, "What we're doing is the wrong thing for you, isn't it?"

"For a minute, I was afraid you weren't going to remember last night, I'm not afraid of many things. You know me but… what I'm most afraid of is believing in us, being all in with you and having the rug pulled out from under me," she confessed, gazing into his eyes.

"You know I would never intentionally hurt you," Grey responded, caressing her fingertips with his.

"That's the problem. I've always known but it's never made a difference. There's only one way this goes down, and even though it kills me to say this, I think you had it right when you said we have to work our way past the love we feel for each other," Lexy quietly disclosed, tightening her grip on his hand.

"I know what I promised Frost, but I don't think I'm capable of doing it. Lex, I can't let you go," he admitted, looking at the heavens, avoiding her eyes.

She knew what she had to do. Gazing at the stars, she whispered, "You don't have to." *She was the one that had to let him go.* Her stomach cramped, and just like that, the subject changed, Lexy scowled and cursed, "Crap."

He questioned, "What?"

It happened again. The pain was intense enough to curl her toes. She launched herself up and scrambled to pick up the clothing she'd haphazardly tossed aside. Grey took her lead as he put on his clothing.

In the driver's seat, fully dressed when Grey looked up, Lexy ordered, "Get in!" Leaving the blanket by the side of the road, as they peeled away from their temporary solitude, they raced back to the motel. *Stupid, stupid, stupid!* There was another car kicking up dust travelling on the other side of the road towards them. *Now, who would be driving down this road away from the motel before dawn? It was one of the other Clans, she could feel it in her bones.* Even with the glare of their headlights, Lexy was able to focus in on the occupants of the approaching car. *There was a large thug of a man, she didn't recognize and Tiberius. Son of a bitch, she knew what this was.* "They've got Molly, put on your seatbelt."

Grey only had time to say, "Oh, Shit!" As he braced himself for impact.

Lexy's seatbelt was already on, she smiled at Tiberius as their eyes met, pushed the pedal to the floor and drove their beater at full speed into Triad. Her body lurched forward as she violently smoked her face on the steering wheel. There was the sickening sound of crushing metal and shattering glass as occupants of the other vehicle soared through the windshield.

When her head stopped ringing, Lexy glanced over at Grey. *He'd slammed his head into the dash, but he'd live, if not, she'd fix him when she'd taken back their girl.* She casually undid her seatbelt, wiped the blood off her nose on her wrist and tried to open the door. *The frame was compromised. Lovely. What did she expect?* She thought of Molly and her actively healing body fed her a surge of welcome adrenaline. She kicked the door open, it came off the hinges and landed on the ground. Her face throbbed with pain as she strolled over and gave Tiberius' body a soft boot with her foot. She hadn't needed to do that because his lifeless open eyes made his predicament more than obvious. *Well, he was dead.* She noticed the other Triad struggling to crawl away. *Well, that was just silly. Where in the hell did this asshole think he was going?* The Dragon of Ankh casually strolled over to mess with his head. He'd managed to wriggle off the dusty cement into the sand by the side of the road. *It was rather entertaining. It looked like he was trying to dig himself a hole. Brilliant idea!* He started choking and sputtering out blood. Knowing he was almost dead, she opted to let him start digging his own grave as she went to look for Molly. The rest of the Triad would know one of their own had died. Their brands of Clan all worked the same way. *This was a good thing because they were going to need a new vehicle, she'd totalled this one.* Lexy peeked into the empty backseat. *No Molly.* As she wandered over to pop the trunk, a thought crossed her mind, *why hadn't their symbols gone off? How had they taken the girl without wounding any of the Ankh?* She glanced into the trunk. There was a bound, gagged very much alive, Molly. *Hmmm, maybe they'd drugged everyone in their sleep? That was an unsportsmanlike thing for them to do.* She recalled them drugging a restaurant full of people and smiled. *That's exactly what they'd done.*

Her comically disorientated Handler staggered out of the passenger side of their vehicle and announced, "Just in case you were the slightest bit concerned, I'm okay."

Lexy grinned at her Handler and continued to work out a plan in her head. *There was a shovel in the trunk of the ancient beater they'd taken for a joyride. The thought of her sexy archrival Tiberius coming too six feet under in the desert made her little black heart jump for joy.* Deviously grinning, Lexy hollered, "Grab that shovel and dig a deep hole. Let's severely inconvenience our Triad friends. I'll take care of the next group that comes for them, we'll need a new ride." Grey shrugged and disappeared. Lexy ungagged the new girl, untied her hands and looked at her palm. *Molly was out cold, but still Ankh. Obviously, nobody had time to change her before they hightailed it away from the hotel.* She dragged Tiberius' body to the side of the road. After removing Molly from the truck, she heard another vehicle approaching. *Awe, the Triad rescue squad was coming, sucks to be them.* Lexy yelled into the darkness at her Handler, "Dig a really big hole, I'll be bringing you more bodies!" She darted to the rear of their demolished vehicle, punched out the taillights and ducked. *The element of surprise was always important, especially when you're unarmed. She was healing remarkably fast today.* She wiped the excess blood from her knuckles on her shirt and smiled, knowing if she took a carload of his men out without a weapon, it would make Tiberius' day. They pulled over, two men rushed towards the wreckage. *Were they travelling two by two? That was smart.*

She hid in the shadows. As one of his men came to check the trunk, she swiftly choked him out. Lexy stealthily crept around the vehicle under cover of darkness and snapped the other Triad's neck. *On second thought, maybe travelling in pairs wasn't the smartest move. Taking their vehicle had been like taking candy from a baby. She didn't want them to heal before Tiberius. Broken bones ought to do it.* She jumped on the Triad's arms, snapping bones and did the same to each of their legs. *Any extra work for Triad's Healers translated to more time before they'd be followed. If there were more Triad close by, they'd felt her subdue two more of their men. They may already be on their way. They'd better bury these four and get out of here.* She dragged the other corpses over to the side of the road as dawn broke and a warm glow lit up her surroundings. *Interesting, the other two bodies were already gone.* Lexy grinned as she called out to Grey, knowing how super motivated he'd be to bury Tiberius in the desert. She found him standing in front of his latest masterpiece. *Now, the act of revenge was more her style, but Grey despised Tiberius with every breath of his being, even more so, since he'd found out she'd been messing around with him on the down-low.* She peered into the hole and grinned. *The first two bodies were already at the bottom naked. Oh, this was magnificent.* Lexy didn't feel the slightest twinge of guilt as she stared at Tiberius' nude form. *She was, however, impressed, he'd obviously been excited to see her. That naughty twisted boy.* She picked up a handful of sand and tossed it on him. *He'd understand it was all in good fun. His spirit was more than dark enough to appreciate creativity.*

They stripped the others down and tossed them into the hole. Taking turns with the shovel, they buried the four Triad a good six feet under. Grey shifted the sand around with his foot so you couldn't even tell the ground had been disturbed. *They'd come to naked and buried alive in the desert. Oh, if only she could be around to see the pissed off expressions on their faces as they dug themselves out.* Molly appeared looking no worse for wear just as they were walking away with their arms loaded with the Triad's clothes. *That would be the best part. They'd dig themselves out and have to wander through the desert naked.* Smiling innocently at the newbie, Lexy announced, "Good, you're up. We should get back to the motel and find the others."

As Molly followed, she gave them the information she could recall, "They're not at the motel. I heard them talking about frying Ankh in a storage container. The kind of hot one chucked me into the trunk and made a crude comment about how easy I'd be to toss around in bed, then he sprayed something in my face. I don't remember anything after that."

Lexy grinned, knowing it was Tiberius, Molly was talking about. *She'd never even had the misfortune of meeting any of the other Clans. This was her first trip to the rodeo.*

Grey smiled and complained, "My face still smarts, I'm driving this time."

Lexy didn't argue. *She'd had her fun.*

"So, we're looking for a storage container in the desert. How hard can that be to find?" Grey remarked as they pulled away from the crash site.

They drove past the motel and carried on further down the only visible road until they saw a barely noticeable dune buggy trail. *Bingo!* She didn't even need to say anything, Grey veered off the main road and carried on down a side road that led off into a hilly area of desert. Using nothing but instinct, they travelled into the barren land. As the temperature rose, they discovered the inconvenient lack of air conditioning. They saw the cloud of dust from another vehicle's tires and headed in that direction.

Chapter 23

I Crashed Into You

They drove towards the cloud of rising dust. *It was much further away than they'd initially thought.* By the time they had an actual visual on the storage container, their captive Clan had escaped. Lexy grinned. *If this had been Tiberius' plan, it was rather impressive.*

Molly announced, "There are cases of water on the floor in the backseat. Do you want one?"

Lexy glanced back and answered, "Oh, that's amazing, I'm so thirsty. I'd love one." The others sprinted to their vehicle, ecstatic because Ankh still had Molly.

Frost leaned in the window and chuckled, "I have to know how this happened."

Grey's explanation sounded way better than the truth. He had her back as always. The real story sounded far too reckless to be repeated.

Lily, of course, looked gorgeous, as always, even though she was sweaty and covered in sand. She raked her fingers through her damp midnight hair as she opened the door and asked, "Where did you find this car? How does it still run?"

Grey passed Lily a bottle of water and disclosed, "Let's just say our options were limited. We should get out of here. They'll be back soon, and I'm sure they'll be seriously pissed."

Oh, that was the understatement of the year.

As Frost got into the backseat of the sketchy vehicle they'd commandeered from Triad, Lexy glanced back at him and prodded, "How in the hell did they capture all of you?" She passed Frost a bottle of water.

Frost shrugged, twisted off the lid and replied, "I came to, sweating to death, chained to the wall in the back of that sweltering storage container, I have no bloody idea how it happened." He chugged the entire bottle of water and began passing bottles of water to everyone else.

"We all woke up there, except for Kayn." Mel piped in, as she passed a bottle of water to Kayn.

Kayn downed her bottle and started to explain, "I went to sleep early. When I woke up, my hands were chained. Kevin was in my room. He used that spray chloroform stuff on me. I came to in the backseat of his car. Stephanie said he left me ungagged because he wanted to talk to me. I overheard Stephanie saying they hadn't found Grey or Lexy. So, I bit a chunk out of my shoulder to signal you guys. Then they brought me to that stiflingly hot storage container and chained me to the wall, with everyone else."

That's weird, their symbols hadn't been triggered.

Frost spurned the tale on by saying, "Oh, don't stop now, you're leaving out the best part of the story."

Kayn met Frost's penetrating gaze, glared and not so innocently egged him on, "What part is that?"

Frost smirked and teased, "Kevin kissed her before he left."

Grey chuckled, "While you were chained to the wall in front of everyone…Kinky."

There were important pieces missing from this story. Lexy asked the obvious question, "How'd they chain you to the wall?"

"I'll be right back," Kayn announced and ran back to the storage container. She reappeared, holding the chains they used to restrain the entire group.

Lexy grinned as she saw what Kayn was holding. *These were used to restrain immortals. They'd been used on her before.* Lexy took them off her and commented, "I see what they used. These are foolproof, how did you get out?"

With newfound confidence, Kayn explained, "I got them to touch each other, drained their energy and used it to overpower the spelled chains. I ripped the lock off the storage container and opened the door, then we ripped their chains off the walls and removed their cuffs."

Mel piped in, "And then, we pulled them all outside into the sand."

Molly was seated between Lexy and Grey in the front seat. Lexy glanced over and smiled at Grey, silently thanking him for not telling the others how recklessly she'd behaved earlier. He winked at her as everyone else piled into the back of the car. *It was already bloody sweltering outside.* They were packed like sardines in the back and desperately needed that current of air from the open windows. Grey started the car and peeled away. As wind flowed through, Lexy grinned, wondering if Tiberius had come to yet. *She was looking forward to bumping into him again just so she could witness first-hand the fury of his reaction to being buried in the buff.* She glanced into the back as Kayn and Frost were arguing about that kiss from Kevin. *She'd stay right out of this one it sounded far too much like the fights she'd been having with Grey over Tiberius.* She was trying to tune them out, and she'd almost done it when Grey started giggling. *Her Handler was finding the whole situation rather entertaining.*

Looking back, Grey teased, "I'm a little disappointed you're not wearing superhero underwear today."

What was he talking about now? Lexy peered back at Kayn. *She'd been kidnapped wearing a tank top and underwear.* Lexy grinned, she'd learned that lesson long ago, but inevitably, she still ended up naked on occasion. *She'd been lucky. It was more than that. Her internal warning system was much stronger than most of the others. She was usually given plenty of warning if she chose to listen to it.* The tires rattled over the road with a thin layer of sand and pebbles. When they picked up speed, it sounded like someone was shaking a rattle full of sand.

Kayn tapped Molly on the shoulder and said, "I'm glad you're still with us."

Glancing back at Kayn smiling, Molly answered, "I'm glad I'm still with you guys too."

Mel reached forward, squeezed Molly's shoulder and added, "That was a close one."

Flipping perspiration damp ebony hair over her shoulder, Lily remarked, "Too close. She's only sixteen. We have to keep her until she's eighteen. I talked to my father; their group might have to stay close to us for a while, they have another teenage boy named Dean. So, we already have three, this never happens. They're going to pass them off to us and shadow us as our back up."

Lexy smiled at Molly but didn't say anything. *She was glad they hadn't lost this one, but they may at some point. They couldn't spend two years running when they had other jobs to do like training the next batch of newbies. At a certain point, it would be all about forming a bond between the new Ankh, so they'd have a fighting chance to survive the Testing. The odds of keeping her until her eighteenth birthday weren't high, if she was taken by another Clan to close to the Testing, it would throw everyone else off.*

Lexy was brought out of her thoughts, back to the conversation the others were having as Kayn asked, "How old is Dean?"

When Lily turned, her raven mane whipped wildly in the wind from the open windows as she responded, "He's almost eighteen, and by almost, I mean his birthday is either today or tomorrow."

This Dean kid was almost officially Ankh. She'd give liking him more thought when he was. Lexy glanced at the tiny doll-like features of the girl sitting next to her and wished she was the one that was theirs. She appeared to be much younger than the rest. Molly was sixteen but looked thirteen at best. The scenery changed and suddenly the monotony of the desert became scenic canyons of clay. *This also reminded her of the in-between. It wasn't that long ago that she'd been training Kayn, Zach and Melody to stand back up after plummeting off a cliff like this one. The trio had come a long way since then and she was proud to say, they'd exceeded her expectations.*

Zach tapped Greydon on the shoulder and mimicked a small child on a family vacation as he whined, "Are we there yet?" Grey swung his arm in the back, Zach ducked out of the way, laughing.

"I will pull this car over, maim you and leave you incapacitated by the side of the road as an afternoon snack for the buzzards," Grey threatened.

They all laughed as Lexy's stomach cramped. *She could be hungry. They'd skipped breakfast.* Interested in the drama unfolding in the back, Grey kept glancing in the rearview mirror. *Eyes on the road, Greydon.* Lexy's stomach twisted into a tight knot once again, she glanced out the window. *They were on a winding canyon road with treacherously sharp corners, but they appeared to be all good. Her Handler's thoughts were indeed sidetracked, but he appeared to be concentrating on the road. Was it hunger or a warning?* Lexy made sure she had her seatbelt on just in case and could tell everyone in the front had theirs on, but the backseat would be a shitshow if they crashed, they were sitting on each other's laps. *She shrugged it off. They were immortal, nothing was as big a deal when you knew death wasn't a permanent state.* As they hit another straight stretch, Lexy decided it must have been hunger pains, everything appeared to be fine. She closed her eyes for a minute and just listened to the humming rattling of the tires but there would be no possible way to take a nap with the stimulation of the drama unfolding between Frost and Kayn in the backseat. She smirked and glanced over at Grey, as the wind moved through his hair. He winked at her, grinned and then peered into the rearview mirror. *They were a distraction. They'd been either arguing or flirting since they got into the car.* Lexy was just about to say something, when Frost whispered, "Don't be mad. I was just jealous, that's all."

Kayn whispered back, "Forget about it. I was shocked to see him. I was frustrated and angry, I'm sorry I took it out on you."

Grey turned around and teased, "Awe, is everybody friends now?"

Lexy stomach cramped and she doubled over. When she looked up, Trinity was driving directly at them at full speed. *Crap!* The driver Glory had a shit-eating grin. *Karma was such a bitch.* Bracing herself with an excited grin Lexy laughed as the carload of Trinity smoked them dead on with a loud crash; their car lurched, spun and flew into a barrier. *Yup, they were going over the frigging cliff.* It was far too late to yell, seatbelts as the second crunch tossed the vehicle over the side of the cliff.

Molly cried out, "We're going to die!"

Everyone in the car grinned. *The newbie didn't get it yet. Death wasn't permanent, but yes, this was going to suck.* The first impact with the cliff tore the back passenger side off. Kayn grabbed for Molly's arm and squeezed it for a split second before being launched out, as the vehicle flipped and smashed again. Lexy braced herself on the dash, riding the ride until the bitter end like a champ. There would be a few hard impacts before the big one at the bottom. On the second hit, both of her arms snapped and glass flew everywhere. As the car plummeted towards the bottom of the ravine, there was one thing repeating in her mind, *Please, let there be no fire.* Her neck snapped on impact and then, there was nothing…

Lexy heard whispering voices coming from a distance, followed by the humming of an engine, but she couldn't open her eyes. She passed out again, when she awoke, her head was hot and pounding. She opened her eyes, they felt like they were on fire, her vision was blurry, everything was spinning, as her brain fought to restore her equilibrium. Lexy managed to shift her heated torso to look at the backseat. She was instantly relieved to see how many bodies remained inside the car's compacted interior. *The frames of older vehicles held up better than most of the newer models. She'd been in a rather humorous amount of car crashes in her time for this was the number one way the Clans took each other out. It was a simple, effective way to render a large group of Clan utterly useless so you could capture a recruit. Hell, she'd done it last night to Tiberius. Karma could always be counted on to serve you exactly what you deserved.* She tried moving her fingers and her ears began to ring. *Well, there was a bright side, at least Trinity hadn't buried them six feet under in the desert.* Lexy struggled to move her limbs, nothing would budge. She grinned, *perfect, her arms were rigour-mortise stiff. Had she died? Sometimes, she couldn't tell.* Lexy knew the drill, if she waited until her ears stopped ringing, she'd have better luck operating her limbs. Once she was able to focus the pitch dulled to a hum. *Everyone was in the car except for Molly, Melody and Kayn. Shit happens, they must have been tossed out.* Her mind brought her back to the voices she'd heard while coming to and the rumble of an engine. *Molly had been taken.* She stretched, cracked her neck and cleared her throat. When critically wounded, her healing ability rebooted things by order of operation. Usually, her head, neck and torso were repaired long before she could move her limbs. *Man, Trinity was organized, they must have had a car waiting at the bottom of this ravine.* As heat travelled down her arms, she knew she'd be healed in moments. Lexy wiggled her fingers and knew, she was good to go. She undid her seatbelt, reached over and gave Grey a poke, his body slumped to one side with his eyes wide open. *Well, he was dead. Both of his legs were crushed under the compacted dash. Lovely.* Lexy got out of the car. *She was going to need back up from Mel on this one. The vehicle was impressively demolished.*

Conveniently, Mel's body was lying beside the wreckage. She opened her eyes, cleared her throat and comically said, "Well, that sucked."

Grinning, Lexy spared, "You get used to it." Looking down at the other Healer, she disclosed, "Grey's dead and crushed under the dash, I'm going to go get him out. When you're ready, start healing the others." Lexy wandered to the driver's side, gripped the structurally compromised door, yanked it off and tossed it. Grey's legs were disgustingly morbid shreds of meat under twisted metal. *Shit, that had to hurt. With any luck, he died before it happened.* She braced herself with one arm on the seat, the other on the dash and easily freed his legs. As Lexy placed her hands against his chest, she noticed Mel struggling to get up. *There was a lot of healing to do, they could use Kayn. This was a big job. Kayn was thrown out right away, she was probably up the ravine somewhere. First things first.* Lexy strolled over and helped Melody up.

A man's voice yelled from the top of the ravine, "Do you need me to call for help?"

When they looked up to where the voice came from, they saw Kayn precariously perched halfway up the ravine on a ledge. *How were they going to explain this one away? Shit, they might have to kill a 'Good Samaritan.'*

"It's okay, we're filming a crash for an independent film, everyone's fine!" Kayn shouted back.

Oh, Brighton was good. "It's just dummies in the car, they're fixable," Lexy sarcastically hollered up.

The flustered man yelled back, "That scared the crap out of me, it sure looked real!"

She'd referred to everyone in the car as just dummies. That was funny.

"Thank you for coming to help!" Kayn hollered and waved.

They had no movie equipment, not a damn thing. What did he think they were filming a movie with, their minds? The Good Samaritan didn't even question it, he just waved and went on his merry way. They waited until they heard the echo of his tires before attempting to speak. Lexy bellowed up the hill, "Molly's gone!"

Kayn yelled back, "Dead?"

Lexy shouted, "She's gone! They took her!"

Mel was upset. This was a first for the new Ankh. Lexy looked at her and assured, "She'll be alright, she's with Trinity, we have lots of time to get her back."

They climbed into the wreckage and started healing the others. *They were all alive except Grey. She wasn't at all worried, he was enjoying a well-deserved vacation in the in-between. He was probably sitting in a meadow twiddling his thumbs or sipping one of those icy drinks, lying on the beach, waiting patiently for her to wake up and get her shit together, so she could heal him.* Healing someone from death took four times the energy of a normal job, so they healed him last. She heard Kayn's landing. *She'd jumped and stopped herself before hitting bottom.* Lexy smiled, because there was no way Kayn could have known she could do that in the real world, she'd taken a chance. In a couple of minutes, they were all healed, awake and hanging out in the sweltering sun's rays at the bottom of a ravine in the desert, without transportation, or Molly.

Curious, Kayn asked, "Was that Triad?"

Lily shook her head and replied, "No, that was Trinity. Glory was driving, she's hard to miss."

Lexy looked up at the ridge they'd have to scale. *It was possible. All she needed was a vague possibility to make it the plan.*

Lily held up her cell and laughed, "I was all excited for about five seconds because I still had my phone, but then I remembered Triad took our batteries."

Grey snatched it out of her hand, took off the back and laughed, "That's so evil. I guess we should be thankful they left you guys phones. We need to go. Let's get out of here before another 'Good Samaritan' shows up to help."

Lexy smiled in her heart and with her eyes without showing it on her lips. *Good Samaritan. They used so many of the same expressions.*

Frost was leaning against the trashed beater, aimlessly picking away at the rust and peeling paint. He chuckled, "Go where? We're at the bottom of a ravine in the stifling heat. There's nowhere to go, but up. We'll have to scale the side. I don't know about you, but I'm sure not in any hurry to climb up there in this sweltering heat."

Lily picked up a pebble and pitched it at the side of the demolished car. It tinged off the metal an inch from Frost's leg. He scowled at her and stood up. She sighed, "You're such a baby sometimes." She took out an earring, stuck the sharp end into her palm and remarked, "Quit being a whiner and climb. We're supposed to meet up with the others, better to scale the side now, than when you're dehydrated."

Now, Lexy couldn't help it, she was smiling until her cheeks hurt. *They'd just gone over a cliff. If that hadn't signalled Markus and the others, an earring stuck into the palm of Lily's hand wasn't going to do a damn thing.* A thought popped into her mind, *what if those supernatural proof chains also blocked their distress calls? That would explain it all. That was probably why they hadn't known the others were in trouble.* Lexy wandered around to see if they were anywhere obvious. *Kayn had them last.* She peered into the back of the heap and there they were, in the storage netting on the back of the driver's seat. Lexy pitched them as far away as she could, they landed a distance from the group. *Maybe their marks worked like a missed text?* Lexy strolled over to the side of the ravine and looked up. There were little ridges in the stone that went almost all the way to the top. *This climb was going to blow.* She touched the stone, stared at the feat before her and said, "I can climb it."

Kayn nodded at her and wandered to the annihilated car. Lexy followed her, knowing she must have also seen the one area they wouldn't be able to scale without creating their own steps. They grabbed raised metal on what was left of the trunk and yarded it open, revealing its contents. Amazingly enough, there was a roadside assistance kit with a tire iron. *That might be useful.* Kayn looked in what appeared to be a toolbox. *Perfect!* Inside, there were many sizes of screwdrivers, wrenches and even large thick metal nails. Lexy tucked various objects into her jeans. Zach was searching the car. In the netting on the passenger side, he found a hammer and passed it to Lexy. *Where was Grey?* Lexy peered up from what she was doing and saw her tender-hearted Handler trying to make Mel feel better about losing Molly.

Kayn glanced at her and declared, "I've got more than enough energy to drive those spikes into the side of that ravine."

She could see Kayn's raised veins and agitated state. She couldn't be the one in charge of anything, not until she got her ability related urges under control. Fun fact about predators; they could always sense their own and Kayn's, 'I'd like to absorb all your abilities' bell was ringing loud and clear. Lexy smiled and responded, "That's why I'm going first. If your ability operates like mine, the more you burn off, the more you'll need."

Lexy climbed until she couldn't find anywhere to grip and hammered the first steps into the side of the ravine, with Kayn, right behind her. She heard a commotion but had to remain pressed against the side or she'd fall. She couldn't look. *It sounded like Kayn slipped.* Lexy called out, "Are you alright?"

"I'm fine," Kayn answered. "These nails are slick. They'll be too hot to hold onto soon. The others will need to wrap their hands in material to climb it."

A wave of dizziness washed over her, Lexy remained motionless as it passed. Growing short of breath, she hollered back, "Good idea! We're almost there. I don't need to drive in more metal spikes. It'll be easier now." *You are almost at the top. Show them they can do it.* Lexy gripped the ledge and hauled the dead weight of her tired body to safety. She was slick with perspiration and seriously dizzy. *She needed energy and badly.* Kayn had a hold of the ledge. She slipped and Lexy dove for her, caught her wrist and yanked her up over the edge. They were sprawled flat on their backs, trying to catch their breath as Kayn started to giggle. Lexy closed her eyes and exhaled. *It was difficult to convince herself to move a muscle, but she had to warn the others.* Lexy leaned over the edge and called out, "You'll need to wrap your hands in material, the spikes are hot and slippery." Cracking her stiff neck, Lexy struggled to her feet with legs as wobbly as a newborn fawn's. *This wasn't good.* She looked at Kayn. *Her eyes were squeezed shut and her veins were visible. She'd been there before.* Preempting an ability related meltdown, Lexy held out her hand, knowing she'd heal fastest if Kayn accidentally killed her. *Her friend's Conduit ability was too volatile to mess around.* Lexy whispered, "Quickly, before the others make it to the top. Don't take too much we might have a full day's hike through a stifling desert ahead of us." Kayn looked up, grinned and took her hand. Their joined hands heated, followed by a sensation of energy being drained. Lexy snatched her hand away, knowing she could only afford to give her a small energy bump.

Scrambling to her feet, Kayn looked at Lexy and said, "Thank you, I needed that." She peered over the ledge.

Lexy wiped the sweat off her brow, grinned and replied, "I know what it's like."

They helped the others in those final moments as they reached the summit of their climb. Once they were all at the top, they were standing as a group in the broiling heat once again, staring out at the seemingly endless terrain of nothing. *There was not a vehicle in sight on the lengthy span of desert road and no water supply in their near future either. She was so thirsty. Her brain was screaming for hydration. She had to force her mind to focus on something else. Logically, it had only been a couple of hours since her last bottle of water, but the blistering heat and the physical activity made it feel like she'd been without water for days. It was an uneasy feeling to be without one of her body's basic needs. It took her back to a dark place within her mind, a place where starvation and depravity clouded her judgement.* In these moments, she always searched for Grey, for it was his job to be her tether to all that was good and right in the world. They were walking as she noticed Kayn licking her lips and swallowing to wet her throat. The fledgling was repeatedly licking her lips. *She'd end up with harshly chapped lips if she didn't stop. You never lick your lips while you're walking in the desert. It was a thing.* Lexy nudged Grey, prompting him to stop her.

Gently grabbing Kayn's arm, Grey cautioned, "Don't lick your lips it'll only make it worse."

They chose the direction they were driving when forced over the cliff and began wandering down the deserted disgustingly sweltering stretch of desert road. From this vantage point, Kayn's attire was hilarious. Her damp wild mane had broken free of its restraints and she was wandering through the desert barefoot, in her underwear and a tank top. Kayn tried to walk on the cement and then leapt back into the sand. *They were probably both equally hot.* Lexy thought about offering Brighton the sandals she was wearing but stopped herself as she noticed all the Ankh taken from their beds were barefoot. A wave of nausea washed over Lexy. *What now?* She staggered, almost losing her footing.

Grey put his arm around her and whispered, "You gave Kayn your energy, didn't you?"

"Guilty," Lexy disclosed. "I thought it would be better if it was me." He pulled her close and gave her a protective smooch on the forehead. A light breeze moved across her skin and the moment became beautiful. *It felt like they were wandering through heaven together instead of trudging through the broiling desert on a journey to nowhere.*

Hours passed by uneventfully, they were now holding hands instead of hugging. The scorching heat of the afternoon sun made being in close confines with anyone, torturously hot and not in a sexy way. The only reprieve from the hellish heat was a light breeze that occasionally tossed up the sand. It was both a good and bad thing because it blew sand into her eyes and left a thin layer stuck to the perspiration on her forehead. On the bright side, it kept the sweat from running and she didn't need to wipe her forehead as often. Lexy's legs were working on autopilot and her throat was painfully dry. *It hurt to swallow.* Lexy heard a noise and looked up at the sky. There was a buzzard, circling the group. Lexy grinned, knowing she could be hallucinating and there might be nothing there at all. Kayn had been shaky for a while, she was obviously having problems when she panicked and hit the sand like there was an airstrike.

Zach knelt beside her in the sand and taunted, "Seeing things already? We could be walking for many more hours, even days." He took her hand in his and whispered, "Take some energy from me. I'll be okay for a while. We'll make finding shelter and water our priority."

She looked at her Handler and whispered, "I can't, I don't want to hurt you. You can't heal as quickly as some of the others."

"It's my duty as your Handler," Zach replied as he held out his hand to help her up.

Lexy smiled as she thought about how far Zach had come in accepting his new role as Kayn's Handler. Her Handler had left her side and ran up ahead to catch up with Frost. She was just casually strolling through the desert next to Lily, who could look sexy anywhere. Right now, she looked like a seductively curvaceous exotic model from a cologne commercial. Frost and Grey were so far ahead they looked like specks, searching for a shady place to wait for the arrival of the others. *If they even knew they were in trouble.* Lexy felt her pocket. *She still had her cell, but the juice had run out shortly after that mysterious text last night. Her charger was back at the hotel room with the rest of her belongings.* Kayn staggered ahead of her.

Zach grabbed her by the shoulders, stopping her from falling. Holding her against him, he urged, "Do it. You have to."

They couldn't do that. They'd end up having to carry Zach. Knowing Grey was too far ahead to catch her and scold her, Lexy offered, "Not you, Zach. We'll start rotating between Mel and me."

Appearing to be fine, Mel held out her hands to Kayn and asserted, "Me first. You probably can't stop cold turkey after the amount of energy you took this morning."

Kayn took Mel's hands, Lexy looked away. *It was a creepy feeling when someone siphoned your energy.*

"That's enough, Kayn. I still have to be able to walk," Mel cautioned.

Kayn abruptly let go of her friend's hands, surprisingly coherent enough after her feed to follow orders, she said, "Thank you. I needed that."

Mel grinned at her and replied, "No problem, Hun."

Their attention was drawn to the road ahead as Grey let out a hoot and sprinted back down the road towards them. He stopped, spun around and pointed to the horizon. *I'll be damned. There was a building in the distance.* Frost took off ahead to get a closer look. *At least now there was a possible end to their stroll through this sweltering hell on earth.* Everyone's spirits perked up as they began to joke around, guessing what the building might be. Lexy's stomach turned and she grimaced. *Here we go again.* They walked for another hour before it was obvious it was a motel. They picked up their pace. As they came closer, they saw the massive industrial fence surrounding it. Lexy's stomach clenched again and she sighed. *What fresh hell was this?* There were a few cars parked out front, they were older models with a thick layer of dust. *This place had been abandoned for quite some time.* The hotel's large stained double doors swung open with a high-pitched squeal, startling everyone. Frost was standing there, grinning.

Lexy glared at their Clan's pretend leader. *Well, spit it out already.*

Frost announced, "I have good news and bad news. Which do you want first?"

Zach rolled his eyes and sighed, "Always the good news first. Let's just make that the new rule. We all have the same queasy sensation. I'm pretty sure we can all hazard a guess at what the bad news is."

Frost grinned and started his announcement, "Well, there's food in the freezer, the kitchen is stocked, the water is turned on, and nobody lives here, but I think I know why this place was closed. Saying it's haunted, would be an understatement. I know you're all exhausted, but we're going to have to clean house before we can relax. I found a couple of creatively deceased workers. They were probably killed by the entities that are stuck in here. I also found police tape from a crime scene. So, I'm running under the assumption that the workers were in here cleaning up after something that happened. The main entry is thick with dark matter. Do you three remember the dark entity that was in that house before your Testing? Well, there's at least a dozen of those demonic entities in there. I know it's probably been a while since Astrid and Haley have had to deal with these things, but you never forget dealing with these assholes. We are going to have to work first so we can play later, and by work, I mean take a scenic stroll through hell."

And that was where she stopped paying attention. She knew the drill. Grey started walking towards one of the dust-covered vehicles. Lexy sprinted past, picked up a boulder and effortlessly heaved it at the window, smashing it.

Grey sparred, "See, this is why we never have nice things. The bloody door is unlocked." He opened it.

Lexy shrugged and climbed into the back. *Water bottles.* She grabbed the case and passed each of them a bottle.

Scrunching up his face, Grey commented, "If bottled water has been in the heat for too long, it's supposed to be like poison."

Lexy wiped the layer of scum off the lid, passed one to Grey and chuckled, "Suck it up Buttercup. It's liquid, and if I have to kill myself in five minutes, I'm going to need to drink this nasty stuff first."

"One more thing," Frost announced. "I found the workers in the freezer. I opened the door with no problem, it was just locked. I bet they hid in there from whatever evil shit came after them and were locked inside. They're dead and frozen solid. So, they don't smell. That's always nice, especially if we could be stuck here for a few days waiting for the rest of Ankh to show up. After we're done here, we'll drag them out of the freezer and burn the place. It would be fair to assume nobody's come looking for these guys."

Lily shimmied past Frost at the door to sneak a peek inside. She came back out with a solemn expression and didn't say a word.

Excellent, this was going to be fun.

Grey chimed in, "A situation messed up enough to render Lily speechless. This, I've got to see." He stepped inside and darted back out a second later. "How in the hell did that happen?" He laid his hand on the side of the building and disclosed, "Obviously, we'll need a plan of some kind. There's no way our usual routine will work for that many."

Kayn tried to slip past Frost to get a look at what they were talking about. He blocked her and stated, "You've been in a volatile state ever since you siphoned all of that energy this morning, you should stay out of this one." Frost walked over to the side of the building, grabbed a few bags of salt, tossed one to Grey and announced, "I found these in the kitchen. They didn't attempt to stop me from entering or exiting the building. We can create a circle in the doorway and see if we can disperse them old school demon style. It won't kill this kind of entity, but it might scatter them. It'll be easier to take them out one at a time." Frost walked into the building and poured the circle of salt. He stood in the center of it as Lily held the door open and called the rest of them into the building. They all walked inside and dove into the spiritual safety of the circle. Ignoring Frost's wishes, Kayn also entered the building. He hadn't noticed her standing there yet.

Kayn whispered, "Shit, how is this even possible?"

Frost glared at her, but obviously decided she might as well stay because he didn't order her to leave. The entire ceiling was a snaking web of black intertwined spindly spider legs of energy. They writhed, moving through each other like entangled limbs reaching out, beckoning them closer, willing the group to become a part of their darkly twisted dance of vile entities. The Ankh joined hands.

As Mel reached for Kayn's hand, she stepped away and exclaimed, "Look at me. I'm going to take your energy the second you touch me."

Kayn's veins were raised and visible. *She had an idea.* Lexy dropped her hand from the others and questioned, "This morning when you took the energy from everyone else in order to break those chains created to immobilize an immortal, how did you know what to do?"

"It felt like logic," Kayn replied. "I knew I could channel someone else's energy and make myself stronger from the Testing."

Mel's eyes lit up as she shared their Testing war stories, "Oh, you should have seen her in the Testing. She created this ball of energy, tossed it at that Kevin's girlfriend and blew her into a million pieces."

Fascinated, Frost nodded and asked, "Do you think you can do that again? Lexy and Melody can save their energy to disperse them after you've scattered them."

Kayn nodded and explained, "I'll still need to use energy from you guys. I was feeding from the walls of the Testing. I have no idea how many of you it would take. When we destroyed these things the last time, you had to allow it to feed on one Healer and then send a jolt of energy through the other. What if we tried the same thing with one of the Healers and then I sent the jolt of energy? I can send more. Maybe, even enough to take them out two or three at a time. Lexy can come in after and heal us. Then, we'll go deal with the rest."

Kayn's Handler was extremely agitated. That was a first. Their connection was becoming stronger.

Meeting Kayn's eyes, Zach firmly stated, "Absolutely not! You don't know how to control this. Frost was right when he suggested you sit this one out. Go and wait outside, Kayn. We'll join up and send a jolt of energy to separate the cluster on the ceiling. We can take them out one at a time after that if we have to." Kayn scowled at him.

Grey squeezed Zach's shoulder and asserted, "He's her Handler. If Zach feels like this might be too much for her, then it probably is. It's not worth the risk. We'll stick with the original plan. We can bring her in once we've exhausted the other possibilities."

"Fine, I'll wait outside," Kayn decreed and walked out.

She left way too easily. Once Kayn left the building, Lexy looked at Mel and said, "Which role do you want?"

Smiling, Mel ribbed, "Hmmm, do I want to hang from the ceiling like a warped demonic marionette while demons feed on me or do I want to be an energy bomb today? Either way, I die. You decide."

She liked this girl. Impressed, Lexy probed, "How much fighting do you want to do? The bomb usually gets up faster."

"It's decided, I'll be the marionette," Mel volunteered. "You're a better fighter. The practical decision is obvious."

Unfortunately, there were some jobs only a Healer could do, and this was one of them. Lexy was fine with any job, her pain tolerance was higher than most and being fed from by a writhing hoard of dark entities hurt like hell.

Without hesitation, Mel stepped out of the circle of salt and raised her arms into the air, beckoning the demons to feed on her. They were moving slowly. She sang, "It's dinner time, you dirty soul-sucking bastards." They accepted her invitation as she was lifted into the air suspended by writhing wriggling spider web-like entities.

Feeling like her Handler wasn't safe, Lexy spun around. Grey was ready to offer her his energy. She grabbed his arms and looked deeply into his eyes as her hands heated to where she would usually stop. She kept going until he crumpled to the floor. Zach offered himself up next and once he dropped, Lexy leapt into the air and grabbed Mel's legs, yanking her down about a foot as she dangled. Lexy shrieked as she forced the healing energy she'd taken into Mel. The inhabitants of the ceiling exploded, in a blinding black mist. Lexy dropped to the stairs with an ungraceful thud. As she lost consciousness, she felt what was left of her demonic foes snowing down from above.

With a rather epic dark energy induced hangover, Lexy stirred. *That was unpleasant.* Sensing she wasn't alone, she glanced up to survey the damage. Mel's body was right beside her. Kayn was standing on the stairs, touching her fingertips together and separating them. A pastel yellow haze formed between her hands as Brighton manipulated it into an enormous glowing orb of what looked like pure energy. *This was trippy as hell.* Undeniably intrigued, Lexy sat up and probed, "What do you have there?" Kayn creepily grinned, emotionally vacant. *Well, shitty. She was in Conduit mode and Dragon mode. Where was Zach?* Kayn continued to mould the hypnotizing orb of energy between her fingertips as Lexy decided to let her get down with her Conduit Dragon bad-self and see what she was capable of when nobody was there to pull her reigns. Lexy provoked, "Show me what you can do with that light before our wardens wake up." Kayn scaled the stairs. Not wanting to miss the action after hearing about what she did to Stephanie, Lexy pursued her, pausing at the beginning of a hall with horror movie-worthy red doors appearing to go on forever. The ceiling was thick with writhing madness. Erring on the side of caution, Lexy opened a red door, stepped behind it and peeked out so she'd be out of the blast zone. Kayn pitched the energy into the center of the wicked things and they disintegrated. All that remained of the entities was a pile of dust on the burgundy carpet, where each had been. Kayn peacefully strolled down the hall towards her.

Lexy stepped out and chuckled, "That was amazing!"

Standing on the stairs as they came back down, Mel enquired, "Do you happen to know where the others are?"

Of course, they didn't. They'd been doing things only a Dragon could appreciate. The trio searched the hotel, ironically finding the others nearly drained of life in the freezer below a whirling mass of shadowy things. Lexy grabbed Mel's arm and towed her out of the freezer, saying, "Trust me, Kayn's got this."

The dark mass whirled above Kayn as she raised her hands to the twisted abominations and enquired, "Are you guys hungry?" The demonic infestations began drinking from her essence, levitating her body as they devoured her spirit. Lexy and Melody dragged the bodies of their friends out of the freezer while Kayn kept the darkness occupied. She allowed it to feed on her. After she dropped to the cement floor with a thud, she touched her fingertips together and began moulding a new yellow orb of energy.

Melody saw what she was doing and panicked, "Crap," closing the freezer door.

Kayn tossed the orb into the mass of dark things and stepped out of the way as they turned to ash and became nothing but piles of dust on the floor. Her grasp on reality instantly returned and she comically knocked on the freezer door.

Lexy opened it and asked, "Are we back to normal now?"

Kayn laughed as she replied, "Yes we are," and strolled out to a freshly healed group of curious eyes.

Chapter 24

Over Again

They raided the vending machines because it was the only option and wandered upstairs to find a room. They were all exhausted after being kidnapped and strung up in a storage container in the swelteringly desert. Lexy was tired for so many reasons. The initial healing job prior to scaling a ravine and wandering aimlessly through the desert energy-deprived had done her in. She'd powered through feeding Kayn and battling demons, using stubbornness as fuel. Now, she was looking forward to a good night's sleep. After they'd chosen their room, Lexy kicked off her flip-flops, looked at Grey and flirtatiously said, "Want to have a shower?"

He blankly shrugged and answered, "Sounds like a plan." She got up to follow him. When she turned the knob, he'd locked the bathroom door. *That was weird. Maybe, he was just too exhausted to even contemplate it?* Lexy stretched out on the bed and closed her eyes. Planning to rest for only a second, she fell into a deep comatose slumber.

She opened her eyes in the darkened room and heard Grey's rhythmic, soothing breathing. *She'd fallen asleep without bathing. Usually, Grey would have at least given her a sponge bath, but last night, he hadn't. He must have been absolutely wiped.* She swung her legs over the edge of the bed and padded barefoot across the carpet to the bathroom where she decided a middle of the night shower was better than not having one at all. After a lengthy shower, she realised she had no clean clothes. Lexy put her sandy clothes back on and snuck back into bed so she wouldn't wake her dead to the world Handler. After about twenty minutes of trying to rest, she sat up and watched Grey sleeping for a while. Smiling, she gently shifted his long blonde bangs off his face.

Grinning, he opened his eyes and whispered, "Are you watching me?"

"I got up to have a shower, and now, I can't sleep," she admitted. Stroking his hair, she whispered, "Go back to sleep, don't worry about me."

Grey stretched, yawned and asked, "What time is it?"

She yawned her reply and slapped him as he chuckled. *She knew what she needed.* Moving closer, Lexy provocatively seduced, "Maybe I just need this." She kissed Grey's lips when their lips parted, he had a puzzled expression.

Knitting his brow, Grey uncomfortably questioned the intimacy of her gesture, "What was that for?"

Oh, no. He was gone. She was going to be sick. Even though she'd known this moment was inevitable, it felt like her heart had just been smoked by a big rig. She turned away from him, swung her legs over the edge of the bed, swallowed the hurt and sat there trying to control her reaction.

He touched her back and said, "Hey, Lex, I didn't mean to hurt your feelings. I mean…I just don't think of you that way."

She blinked away the tears forming against her will and told herself to shut it down. *It's over. You knew this was coming. Suck it up, Lexy.* Without looking at him, she calmly stated, "It was nothing." *But it wasn't.* Laughing it off, she sparred, "Come on, as if I'd be interested in you, Greydon. Get over yourself."

He seemed relieved as he laughed, "I knew you were joking."

Lexy rose, glanced back at him, playfully stuck out her tongue and briskly retreated into the bathroom. She locked the door and sat on the edge of the tub. *It happened.* Covering her eyes with her hands, she silently wept. *She'd allowed the loss of their intimacy to gut her once again. When had this happened?* It sunk in. *He'd died in the car crash. If Azariah saw him while he was in the in-between, she would have asked him to make a choice. He'd probably thought he was helping her, by making the decision, his alone. She knew how they worked. It was all about the selfless choices and greater good.* She heard the rapping of his knuckles on the door, followed by, "Hey, Lex. Are you okay? Listen, I know you have needs. You know Orin and Zach are available, I just don't think it should be me."

Oh, was he frigging serious? Now, she was livid. She gave him a viciously cold response, "No thanks, I'm saving myself for Tiberius." Her spiteful comeback was met by dead silence on his end, she knew the verbal dagger she'd tossed hit its intended mark. Lexy cringed as Grey dramatically slammed the motel room door. She wandered out of the bathroom and sat on the bed. *They'd both handled that situation poorly. She knew she needed to go and find him. She'd just apologize and get over it. He hadn't done anything wrong. She was the asshole in this scenario.* Lexy left the room fully intending on kissing his ass, but as she stepped out into the hallway, she saw him duck into Mel's room. As she started walking down the hall, she paused in front of the fire alarm and thought of pulling it. *What would that accomplish? He couldn't remember he loved her and Melody was innocent.* Emotionally defeated, Lexy descended the stairs and wandered over to the vending machine at the end of the hall. *It had been strategically picked over. Everything she wanted was already gone.* She sighed... *Wasn't the afterlife frigging hilarious, it was even screwing up her choice of potato chips.* She waved her hand in front of what she was willing to settle for and it dropped into the metal bin below. Lexy sat on the floor in the hallway and tore open the package of plain bland chips. About to put the first chip in her mouth, she felt someone watching her and looked up, it was Grey.

He asked, "Can I sit here with you?"

Confused, she nodded her silent consent, and he got his own bag of less than satisfying chips out of the vending machine and sat beside her.

Grey grinned as he sheepishly began to speak, "I'll be the one to start then. I'm sorry, I panicked when you kissed me. Maybe, it's because it's not supposed to happen? I just need you to know that it wasn't that I didn't like it. If that's what you want, I'm in."

Oh, Lordy. She was going to bang her head against the wall until she knocked herself out. She couldn't keep doing this with him. Lexy didn't know what to say but knew, she needed to change the subject, so she blurted out, "I slept with Orin."

Intrigued by her risqué confession, her Handler scolded, "You're a naughty little fibber, you acted like nothing happened between the two of you."

She shoved him and whispered, "You say nothing to anyone. It's private, I don't even know if I want it to be anything."

He motioned like he was zipping his lips, tossed away the imaginary key, smiled and promised, "I won't say a word. This is a good thing. Oh, I get it, the Tiberius comment was a joke. Well, I feel like an idiot now, for making that kiss a bigger deal than it was supposed to be. See, that's why you have to tell me these things, I just made a total ass of myself."

What had she just done? She felt a little bit guilty. She'd just launched herself into a relationship with Orin in Grey's head. She should admit to it all and confess everything right now because, in her experience, little white lies always got out of hand rather quickly. Instead of a confession, Lexy opted to just change the subject as she questioned, "So, it didn't work out with, Mel?"

"We had an argument. I knew I wasn't going to get any sleep until we hashed it out. Plus, I think she might be into someone else," he explained as they started to make their way back to their room. Once there, they both lay their heads on their pillows. Greydon was off to sleep in no time at all, unaware of the excruciatingly painful vacancy the loss of their intimacy caused in her heart. She ached for his touch. *This time, she had to fill that vacancy and take advantage of the distance they had when his memory was freshly erased. It was time to start the healing process...again.*

Markus and the others showed up in the morning but didn't stay long. They left them a few running vehicles and ditched the new kid with them because they were rushed to leave for a Correction up north. *Dean was officially Ankh, and Lexy honestly wasn't sure how she felt about that. Perhaps, it was because she still wanted him to be Molly.* On a positive note, the new guy helped them dispose of the bodies and burn the once demon-infested hotel to the ground like an old pro. *He'd been with Trinity for a while. He'd obviously been trained well.* After they were finished, they piled into the vehicles and travelled back to the hotel the others were kidnapped from to retrieve their belongings. Once they had what they needed, they separated into their usual driving shifts, and the group began their own journey up north in the RV and truck.

The first days after Grey forgot his love for her had always been nothing less than torture. Her heart was still all in and he was on the prowl with no filter to lighten his repetitive blows to her ego. When his flirtatious behaviour was more than she could take, she always knew that she held the trump card and that winning hand's name, was Tiberius. If ever she wanted him to feel just a touch of the agony, she was going through, she'd toss out his name in conversation. Aware of what she was going through, Frost would run interference with Grey, knowing how much she was hurting because he'd had a similar experience. Kayn and Lily also knew everything, but Mel, Haley and Astrid did not. The never-ending tedium of spinning tires and blindingly boring highway hadn't helped the friction with Grey. They'd been doing nothing but arguing and had hit the point where there was no purpose in even attempting a conversation. By the time they travelled over the border and into British Columbia, everyone was mind-blowingly exhausted. They set up the campsite and only had a day to rest before the two groups were planning to split up again, leaving the newbies to sink or swim. Frost and Kayn's relationship had been moving along in leaps and bounds. They were leaving the group to spend the night together. Watching Frost with Kayn gave her hope that someday she'd be able to find a way to move past her love for Grey. *Lily approved of the union and that somehow made everything seem right.* Lexy glanced over at her Handler and her eyes softened. Grey took her look as a flag of surrender, he wandered over to stand beside her and passed her a cold beer. They watched Frost and Kayn drive away and as they disappeared, Grey whispered in her ear, "Well, this virgin sacrifice feels way less shady than the last."

Lexy had to hold her hand over her lips and press them together to stop herself from spraying a mouthful of beer all over the Ankh sitting in front of her at the picnic table. She gave her Handler a playful shove and all was forgiven. They spent the night together playing board games, roasting wieners and marshmallows over the firepit, fixing their reality stunted bond.

By the time they left the newbies the next day, all was settled, and their harmonious friendship had returned. They had to take Dean because the five needed to find their way. Lily had this adorable friendship going on with the dark-featured, chocolate-eyed charmer who was quite obviously into dudes. Once she figured out that part of his persona, Lexy allowed herself to attach to him. When she found out they were headed into the city to meet up with Markus' crew, she knew she had to find Orin and let him know she told Grey about their one-night stand. She sincerely hoped Grey's knowledge of the booty call wasn't going to make things awkward but couldn't be certain he wouldn't blurt it out if too many drinks were involved.

They pulled into the parking lot of the five-star hotel where they were staying on Lucien's dime. A few members of their Clan were meeting up with Lucien and his entourage this evening at his club. The rest were free to hang out and enjoy his hospitality. Lily was excited, the hedonistically attractive Lucien had always been one of her favourite distractions. Whenever they met up with the King of the Lampir in the past, Lily was his for the remainder of the evening, or he was hers. *She wasn't sure how that worked.* There was always a plan in place. Tonight, it was Lily's duty to find out how involved Lucien was in the Lampir plague. They were along for the ride.

They'd initially thought it was one town and one rogue Lampir, but in the following weeks, Markus and his crew dealt with three Lampir hybrid infestations, each with a different immortal species in the mix. It was beginning to look like someone higher up in the Lampir community had a flexible interpretation of the immortal code.

The mirrored lobby of this hotel had always appealed to her, not to look at herself but for people-watching purposes. Their bags were brought up to their rooms and they were all sent to the hotel's spa where they soaked in the mineral pool. After a while, they were each ushered off to a stylist. Lexy's hair was rewashed, conditioned and styled like she was an actress preparing for a fancy Hollywood event. With seductive waves in her crimson hair, Lexy was presented with her outfit for the evening and helped into it. She looked in the full-length mirror. *Tonight, she was the lady in red.* The red knee-length slip like dress hung from her curves in a glorious way with a sexy slit that stopped at her thigh. The champagne was flowing and the tapas they brought around on a tray occasionally took the edge off her appetite. When she saw Grey, she couldn't stop the grin from forming on her face. *They'd convinced him to cut and style his hair. There was still length to it, he hadn't allowed anyone to get too carried away. They'd dressed him up too.*

Grey's jaw dropped as Lexy strolled towards him. He took her arm, smiled as he leaned in and whispered in her ear, "You look stunningly beautiful tonight, Lex. That dress could stop traffic."

Lexy caught him staring at her cleavage and then blew it off as wishful thinking. *It was far too early in the mind wipe for those feelings to be returning.* She looked into her Handler's eyes and baited, "You're looking mighty hot tonight too, Greydon." Lexy was feeling glamourous as she strolled into the club on Grey's arm. She'd been to this club many times before and this was why she'd been so surprised by that hive of inbred Lampir. *They were usually refined eloquent speakers that could easily pass for mortal. This was how they'd blended into society for thousands of years.*

Giving her arm a gentle squeeze, Grey whispered, "You know that G-string you have on makes you look like you're going commando."

She followed his line of sight to the mirrored floor. There was a clear view, up her red silk dress. *Like she gave a shit.* Lexy scanned the room for the rest of Ankh, spotting Markus, Lily, Frost and Jenna right away. They all looked amazing tonight sitting at a mirrored topped table with their eccentric undeniably sexy dark-featured host. *The job was to let Lily work her Succubus magic so they could find out if Lucien knew anything about the sudden influx of hybrid hives. She'd be seriously disappointed in him if he had anything to do with it but she was pretty sure he didn't. Lucien was all about honour and integrity.* Lexy turned back to look at Lucien. *As always, he only had eyes for Lily. She'd always seen him as a classy guy, but with the addition of the voyeuristic flooring in his club, she knew there must be more to him than meets the eye. If anyone could get the truth out of him, Lily could.*

They were led to a section of tables closer to the dance floor, where others were sitting staring at menus preparing to order. *Most of the people in the room were mortal. She could tell who the Lampir were by their unique aura. Lucien trusted their Clan, there were only a half dozen Lampir in the room.* She knew where Orin was sitting because she could see his light blonde hair over the top of his menu. *Why wasn't he at the head table?* Arrianna, the third in their trio's golden locks were styled in perfect waves down her back, and she was smiling at them as they took their seats. Dean, the new guy, was looking dapper in a grey suit with a lavender tie. He animatedly waved, but Orin didn't look up. *Was Orin intentionally ignoring her or was he just upset that he had to sit at the kiddie table with them? Had Grey said something to him already? She'd never had to deal with this situation before. She had no idea what she was supposed to do?* Lexy opened her menu, crossed her legs in a ladylike manner and decided, two could play at this game. *She'd just hide behind her menu and pretend she could understand it.* They brought a tray of martinis and placed one in front of each Ankh, compliments of Lucien. Lexy glanced over at the head Lampir's table, Lucien smiled at her and raised his glass in salute. The volume of the music was turned up and the lights were dimmed. She heard Grey's chair shift, and her Handler was off to the womanizer races.

Dean gave her menu a poke. She lowered it as he asked, "How come we can see their reflections in the ceiling?"

Of course, they had a reflection. That tell-tale sign of Hollywood's favourite immortal beings was complete and total bullshit. Orin giggled behind his menu. *Had he heard her inner commentary?*

Grinning, Arrianna quietly explained the ins and outs of the Lampir, "Most of the things you've heard about are false. They eat garlic, have reflections, and their skin is only pale if they haven't been regularly feeding. They aren't cape-wearing soulless abominations as literature and movies would have you believe. They have a society with rules and regulations that they have to follow just like we do."

Dean nodded to show he understood and then, he whispered, "Is Lampir short for Vampire?"

Arrianna cautioned in a whisper, "They consider that word as an insult, so you might want to take that term right out of your vocabulary."

Dean, the newest Ankh leaned in and asked another question, "Do they still drink blood and can they turn people into Lampir if they drink their blood?"

Smiling, Arrianna disclosed, "Yes, they do, but most often, a new Lampir is created by a broken condom followed by a random accidental death. If the feeding is voluntary and there are not many accidents, we tend to leave their community alone."

Someone was playing footsies with her. A waiter showed up, placed a mixed tray of appetizers in the center of the table, nodded and walked away. Lexy tried to keep her game face on as someone's foot intimately touched her leg. *It had to be Orin.* Lexy peered over her menu, locked eyes with him and mouthed one word, "Hi."

Orin grinned as he mouthed, "Hi," back and placed his menu on the glass topped table.

Lexy probed, "Have you decided what you want yet?"

Orin mischievously baited, "From the drink menu?"

Oh, it was a drink menu that made sense. She selected a bacon-wrapped scallop as she caught the flirtatious double meaning. Casually, so the others wouldn't catch on to their secret flirtation, Lexy innocently picked up her menu again, looked at it and repeated, "Do you know what you want?"

Seductively caressing her leg, Orin taunted, "I'm not sure, I haven't decided yet."

Well, that was a loaded statement. There were witnesses, and she also wasn't sure what she wanted. Hiding behind her menu, so he wouldn't see her reacting to his naughty game of footsies, she giggled.

He grabbed a pastry from the tray of appetizers as he chuckled, "You have no idea what that menu says."

She lowered the menu and laughed. *She'd been busted.* "Not a damn clue," Lexy confessed as she placed the menu back on the table. Everyone else left the table, they were out on the dance floor. *She hadn't heard them leave.*

Orin flirtatiously questioned, "What exactly have you told Grey?"

She knew he wouldn't be able to keep his mouth shut. Lexy shook her head and felt the heat of embarrassment in her cheeks as she prepared for her awkward confession, "Do you want the truth?"

"Why dance around it, I think we're both far past the point of needing to be coddled," Orin dared as he took a sip of his martini. He looked surprised. With a random change of subject, he stated, "These are delicious. It tastes like a caramel apple."

The tension dissipated as she took an experimental sip of hers. *It was heavenly.* She met the penetrating gaze of his ice-blue hazel flecked eyes and started at the beginning, "So, I fell back into that situation with Grey again. We tried to cheat the spell by not consummating our relationship, and it worked for a while. We went off a cliff when Trinity took Molly and Grey died. I think his memory was wiped then, but I didn't notice until that night when I kissed him and he freaked out. Long story short, after a huge argument, I confessed to sleeping with you to change the subject. He took it so well I just decided to let him think I might be interested in you."

Orin couldn't stop grinning.

"I was just trying to shut him up. I'm not expecting anything from you," Lexy assured as she sipped her tasty martini.

Intrigued by her honesty, Orin clarified, "So, you want to pretend we're into each other and see if that deters your Handler from having feelings for you?"

She honestly hadn't thought that far ahead.

He flirtatiously provoked, "Do I at least get a steady booty call out of the arrangement?"

Lexy wasn't sure what she should say. *Maybe?*

"I was joking," Orin laughed as he snagged two more martinis' off the waiter's tray as he passed the table and handed one to her. He teased, "I don't see any reason why we can't spend time together for the greater good. I've been whoring around lately, and frankly, even I'm feeling like it's getting ridiculous."

Oh, good. He wasn't waiting around for her. That made her feel like a little less of an asshole.

They sat together laughing, joking around and drinking for hours. She was just a girl sitting at a table with a cute guy having a conversation about life. *There were no expectations and it felt good. It felt normal. Was she ready to live life as a normal girl unencumbered by the chains that had always bound her?* She'd been enjoying their conversation and she hadn't looked for Grey in hours, but as he crossed her mind, she did and saw him in an intimate conversation with a beautiful brunette. It stung less having Orin as a distraction.

Orin placed his drink on the table, stood up, held out his hand and announced, "Alright, my stunningly gorgeous break-up buddy. I'm in if you're in."

Lexy laughed and the weight lifted off her heart as she put down her drink and took his hand. It felt surprisingly wonderful as he tugged her into his embrace and they started moving together on the dance floor. *Different, but still good.* She rested her head on his shoulder, closed her eyes and smiled nervously. *It felt exciting and new. She didn't know how this would end, or even if it would really begin, but for the first time, the ending of the story wasn't already written, and she could choose her own adventure.*

He whispered in her ear, "Let's get out of here."

There was change in the air. It wasn't like the feeling that she had when a storm was brewing, it was more like how she felt in the moments before the dawn of a new day...

The Beginning

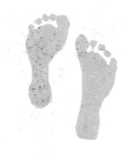

Biography

Kim Cormack is the always comedic author of the darkly twisted epic paranormal romance series, "The Children of Ankh." She worked for over 16 years as an Early Childhood educator in preschool, daycare. She's lived most of her life on Vancouver Island in beautiful British Columbia, Canada. She currently lives in the gorgeous little town of Port Alberni. She's a single mom with two awesome kids, Cameron and Jenna. She spends most of her time parenting, creating hi-jinks, or disappearing into her own mind, journeying through other realms and winning battles. When you read one of her books... May you laugh, cry and step out of your box for a moment and realise that no matter what the circumstance...Magic is everywhere.

Happy Reading

Warning

The information contained within this book is not intended for mere mortals. Reading this book may inadvertently trigger your Correction. If you show great bravery during your demise, you may be given a second chance at life by one of the three Guardians of the in-between. For your soul's protection, you must join one of three Clans of immortals on earth. You are totally still reading this, aren't you? You've got this. Welcome to the Children Of Ankh Series Universe. This is not a fairy tale. This is a nightmare. Let's do this.

She slept a dreamless sleep free of Dragons for she had slain them once again.

The next book in Lexy's series is. Deplorable Me.

Made in the USA
Middletown, DE
09 October 2021